Look for these titles by
Sherwood Smith

Now Available:

Sasharia en Garde! Series
Once a Princess (Book 1)
Twice a Prince (Book 2)

The Trouble With Kings

The Trouble With Kings

Sherwood Smith

A Samhain Publishing, Ltd. publication.

Samhain Publishing, Ltd.
577 Mulberry Street, Suite 1520
Macon, GA 31201
www.samhainpublishing.com

The Trouble With Kings
Copyright © 2008 by Sherwood Smith
Print ISBN: 978-1-60504-025-7
Digital ISBN: 1-59998-448-2

Editing by Anne Scott
Cover by Anne Cain

First Samhain Publishing, Ltd. electronic publication: February 2008
First Samhain Publishing, Ltd. print publication: December 2008

Dedication

With grateful thanks to Beth Bernobich, Marjorie Ferguson, and the gang at Athanarel on LiveJournal.

Chapter One

I woke up.

By the time I'd drawn one breath I realized that if I'd had anything else to do, I ought to have done it. My head ached before I even tried moving it. I decided not to try. Some experiments just aren't worth the effort.

So I closed my eyes and drifted, hoping for a dream to slip into. Then the squeak of a door and footsteps banished the possibility of sleep.

I turned my head—yes, it did hurt worse to move—and almost panicked at the fact that I couldn't see anything until I remembered that my eyes were still closed.

Oh.

That's how bad the headache was.

Eyelids up, then. An old woman looked down at me, her hair hidden under a kerchief, her countenance anxious. When our eyes met, relief eased her brow.

"Ah. So glad you have rejoined the living, child. Don't worry none. My husband's gone away straight to them't should know, and you'll be taken care of proper."

I tried to talk, but it came out a groan. So I tried again, making an effort not to move my head.

"Thank you..." Ho! It worked! Though only at a whisper. I added, "Don't know who 'them' is...but if you think 'they' should know...I won't argue." It took some time to get that out, and though I was trying to be reasonable, the poor woman was looking more anxious by the moment. "Uh, what happened?" I finished.

"You do not remember?"

"No." Could be this headache... *Where am I?* I thought—or tried to think—but the process was like trying to chase fireflies in a fog, only it hurt. "Uh." I made another discovery. "I know it's going to sound somewhat scattered, but I can't seem to place who I am, either."

"Those knots on your head would account for it," she said in a soft, soothing voice. "I've heard o' that. Don't worry none. Your memory will return."

"Must have been some tiff." I struggled for humor.

"He found you face down on the south road, my husband did. You fell off a horse, hit your head against a stone."

I winced, trying again to remember, but the hammer inside my skull increased its frenetic banging. She straightened up. "Enough chatter. What you need is sleep."

My eyelids, by then, weighed about as much as a brace of draught horses, and I gladly complied.

When I woke again, it was to noise. Lots of noise. Boot heels, clanking, and the old woman's voice. "She's in here. I beg you, your highness, not to make too much noise. She's fearsome done."

(I'm a she. Good. I'd just as soon be, I decided.)

"I've bade her sleep." On that, the door creaked open again. "'Twas so good of your highness to come yourself. We hardly expected such an honor."

A man walked in, flanked by liveried men in violet, blue and gold. He was tall—his head nearly brushed the low plank ceiling. Red, wind-tousled hair lay on his shoulders, and hazel-green eyes looked down on me from a bony face. He threw back a fold of a green cloak, put his head to one side, and smiled at me.

"And so we are reunited," he said.

"Glad someone seems to know me." He bent to hear me, frowning slightly. "I wish I could say the same, but..." I ran out of breath again.

"She's lost her memory," the old woman said.

The man glanced her way. A diamond glimmered in one of his ears. A singularly beautiful gem. Was it familiar? How did I know it was a diamond?

That many thoughts made me dizzy, and the hammer

plonked my skull again. "Uhn," I commented.

The man gave me a quizzical look and turned around. The breeze from his long cloak sent cool, horse-scented air over my face. Horse. How did I know that?

"You will be suitably rewarded," the young man said to the woman.

He gestured to one of the silent liveried men, who were about his same age—late twenties, say—both big, well armed. One handed the woman a clinking pouch.

The fine woolen cloak moved, the lining gleamed blue as a long hand gestured toward me. The second liveried man stepped close, a tall blond fellow. He paused, looking perplexed, then bent and slid one arm beneath my shoulders, the other under my knees, and lifted me up.

Aches tweaked all over me, and I tried not to groan, because I could see that he was trying to be careful.

"P'raps she ought not to be moved yet," the old woman said anxiously. "We can tend her."

"Ah, but this is your room and she has displaced you, has she not?" the red-haired man responded. And, smiling, "You may be sure she will receive the best of care at the castle."

"Perhaps a wagon?" The old woman's voice was uncertain.

"But I would worry. Poor little Cousin Flian." The man smiled on everyone. "I'll feel better to have her safely home." He stepped near enough so that I could smell the scent in his hair, a subtle perfume that muted the aroma of horse and sweat and mail-coat that was under my nose now. "Kardier here will ride gently."

The woman clucked to herself and trailed after, offering suggestions and comments as, *clomp, clomp,* our procession passed through the small confines of the wooden cottage and out into the sunshine. I closed my eyes against the glare.

The man's breath was warm on my cheek as he set me across a horse's withers then mounted behind me.

The prince tucked my left arm across my middle and patted it. "It will be best. Thank you again."

His smiling voice had altered from assurance to command. The woman's twittering protests stopped. Weapons clanked, well-shod hooves clopped. A quick glimpse: quite an armed company. All for me? And how, and why, was all this panoply so familiar?

The man carrying me shifted his grip, picked up his reins, the horse moved forward, and I knew I was not going to enjoy this journey at all.

A shadow on my face made it possible to open my eyes. The red-haired prince rode next to us. "We searched most assiduously for you, Flian," he said. "I promise you will receive the most attentive care at my castle."

"Good," I muttered, wincing at the increasing gait. "I'm going to need it."

The walk became a trot, and stars splattered across my eyelids; they whirled larger and larger and engulfed me. I sank with gratitude into insensibility.

My next awakening inspired from me a bit more enthusiasm once I'd registered a few facts.

First, no horses. Second, I lay in a soft, clean bed. A quilt of silk and down covered me.

My bed was in a large chamber with white-plastered walls and blue leaf and flower patterns painted below the ceiling.

Need made me automatically whisper the Waste Spell—which I was glad I remembered, even if I couldn't remember where I was born.

A sweet voice murmured, "Please, would you take some broth?"

"Gladly," I croaked. "So hungry I can't even remember my last meal." I was going to add, *Ha, ha, natural wit can be counted out of whatever talents I might possess*, but it took too much effort to speak.

A stout, middle-aged woman sat near the bed, wearing livery that called the guards to mind. So some memories were staying, then. I remembered the old woman, the cottage, the blond-haired young fellow—what, Kardier? Yes, Kardier. Who had carried me so carefully out, as if I'd been a basket of eggs.

And I remembered the red-haired prince who commanded them all.

As these thoughts limped their way through my mind, the woman lifted my head from the pillow, and a very savory-smelling cup was pressed against my lower lip. I sipped, felt warmth work its way down inside me.

Another cup, this one with the pleasantly astringent smell

of listerblossom steep, and then I lay back down.

Slept.

Woke up feeling much less nasty.

Enough so that I could look about the room, note the bank of windows, one of which was open to let in a cool, pine-scented breeze. And over there against the far wall, a wood-framed mirror.

A mirror.

Intense desire made me struggle up, fighting against dizziness.

The dizziness won. I flopped back, and my nightcap came askew. So I reached up, pulled that off, and with it unrolled a long length of waving blond hair. Dirty, twig-decorated blond hair, I realized, as I looked at the tangle lying across my lap.

I was engaged in working my fingers slowly through the knots when the door opened and the woman came back in. She smiled. "Ah, you are awake, and if I may be permitted, you do look more awake."

"I feel it. In fact, I think I might even be hungry."

She moved from window to window, opening out the casements and letting more air in. It smelled wonderful.

"His highness wishes to visit you as soon as might be," she said.

"Why not now? I have so many questions."

She straightened the quilt and fluffed more pillows to put behind me to help me sit up, as I chattered on.

"Like who am I? Do I live here? What happened to me? I hate to be talking about myself so much. But it's not like I'll be hearing things I already know."

She smiled. "I can't answer that, my lady. You met with an accident, is all I know for certain. The rest his highness can better relate."

"Well, then, tell me about myself. Am I ugly?"

She laughed, a soft sound. "No. No one is really ugly, unless ugly inside, and it shapes the outward form. You are a young lady of medium height, I should say, and on the thin side, but good food will take care of that. You have gray eyes and blond hair, and you are covered with too many bruises and scrapes to count."

I touched my face as she spoke, discovered what had to be

a black eye and swelling behind my ear. The headache was a dull reminder of my earlier awakenings. "May I comb my hair and put on a wrap first?" I added, looking down at the nightdress. "Unless that fellow you mentioned is...my brother?"

For a moment, when I thought the word "brother", an image flickered through my thoughts, too fast to catch. Trying to recapture it made the headache pang in warning.

"Bide easy," the woman said. "One thing at a time."

She brushed out my hair and brought me a silken shawl of a fine shade of violet. Presently that red-haired fellow entered the room. He was dressed in a long dark blue tunic with gold embroidery that made a fire of his hair. He did not wear a blackweave sword belt, instead a belt of golden links. More gold on his hands.

"Good morning, Flian." He studied me while I looked him over. "Feeling better?"

"Well as can be expected. Will you answer some questions? It hurts to think, but I want to know where I am, and who you are, and who *I* am, to begin with."

"Don't press for it, you'll only feel worse." He glanced at the woman, who moved swiftly to fetch him a chair. She set it, and he sat down, and smiled at me. "I am Garian Herlester of Drath. You are Flian Elandersi, my cousin. You were on your way to visit me before your marriage. You rode in an open carriage, and you encouraged your driver to go too fast. The carriage overturned and your driver was killed."

"Oh." I winced. "I caused a death? No wonder I don't want to remember." Distress made my head pang again, more insistently.

"Don't be. He was drunk." Garian waved a ringed hand. "Or he wouldn't have driven so badly, for my roads, by and large, are quite good. The animals escaped injury, but your carriage was a ruin."

I sighed. "The old woman told me none of that, only that they found me face down in the road. And—did she not say I'd fallen from a horse?"

"Well, they didn't want to mention the driver, no doubt, and as for the horses, they'd worked loose and we recovered them farther down the mountain."

"Ah. Does my family know what has happened? And who are they?"

14

"You have a father and a brother. They know. They wish you to stay here. You have never gotten on well with your father. He is old and autocratic, and favors your brother, who incidentally opposes your marriage because you are betrothed to a king. This will place you in a position of power. So you came here. We have always been friends." He smiled, his hazel eyes unblinking as he watched me assess his news.

"It doesn't sound dull, does it?" I ran my hands over the shawl's fringe, not sure what to think—or to feel. "My intended, does he know?"

"Rode straight here, soon as my messengers reached him."

"So when can we meet? Er, that is, see one another? Again?"

Garian hesitated, then stood. Without warning he bent and picked me up, quilt and shawl and all. He said over his shoulder to the open-mouthed woman, "Find King Jason, will you, Netta? We'll meet him in my library."

"But—your highness—"

"Now, Netta." Garian sounded impatient.

The woman fled.

"I appreciate your wanting to help me sort it all out at once. It can't wait? I feel like a fool being barefooted, and in a nightdress."

Garian smiled down at me. He smelled of wine—recently drunk, too. "But he'll be seeing you in that soon enough, won't he? And truth to tell he's been up here and seen you sleeping, so why not awake?"

"Then one last request, please? Step near yon glass. Maybe my reflection will jar loose this wall between me and my past."

He laughed a little. "Believe me, you'd regret it just now."

I groaned. "And this king is going to be glad to see this black eye?" I fingered my sore cheekbone.

"Remember, you two are quite passionate about one another." Garian passed out of the room and down a curving stone stairway. Past arched windows, old hangings, fine furnishings.

A sense of the ridiculous chased away the anxious worries that I couldn't place. Outside two carved doors, Garian stopped. "We're here."

One of the doors opened.

I turned my eyes toward my beloved.
And stared, aghast.

Chapter Two

The two were about the same height, but Garian was built rangy and the other was as lean as a wolf. The similar height was all they shared.

Whereas Garian possessed all the smiling grace of a courtier, King Jason was as expressive as a stone. A stone in the dead of winter, to give an idea of how much warmth there was in his countenance. His hair was black as a moonless night, combed straight back from his brow and tied with a plain black ribbon. His eyes were a light blue under long black brows, a long mouth set in a face made square by sharp cheekbones and jaw line. His only affectation was a thin moustache following the curve of his upper lip, angling down on either side just far enough to emphasize those sharp bones. It made his age difficult to guess, and its effect was rather sinister.

He wore a long, black, heavy linen tunic-shirt with plain laces, trousers and boots—riding clothes. Something silver, a chain, glinted beneath the slack laces of his shirt. I wondered if I had given it to him.

He withstood my scrutiny for the space of three or four long breaths, then glanced Garian's way, then spoke. "Good morning, Flian. I'm glad you're feeling better."

His voice was soft, with little expression, and the sentence seemed awkward—as if that much effusion did not come naturally.

I was in love with that?

I tried to hide my utter dismay.

Puffing slightly, Garian set me into a large carved chair.

I struggled for politeness, even if I couldn't fake delight. "I am glad to meet you, Jason. I guess you'll have to be pretty fond of me if you can stand the way I look now."

Garian laughed, but Jason didn't. He stood there, gazing down at me with that stone-cold expression I was soon to discover was habitual. Then he smiled. Very faintly. Not the big, edgy grin that Garian kept giving me. Jason shouldn't have bothered. His smile was even more sinister than his stone face.

He stepped closer, reached down, and lightly flicked my good cheek with a finger. "You asked for it," he said.

"You have always traveled much too fast," Garian put in. "I fear one of the many instances of thoughtlessness that has given extra concern to those who know you best. But spoiled young ladies do like to have their way."

"I apologize for the extra concern," I said, thinking: *asked for what?*

Jason said, "Meanwhile, in your turn you'll have to get used to my face." His tone was wry.

Garian spoke quickly. "We think you'll be better off having the wedding here, so that you can go home with Jason and recover. That way you won't be required to suffer the recriminations of your family while you're still weak."

"Here? Isn't that too much of a hurry?"

Garian's eyes narrowed.

"I mean, shouldn't I be able to recognize the guests at my own wedding?"

Garian smiled. It was that impatient smile; the feeling it sent through me was not reassurance, but warning. "And here I thought you would be pleased with my efforts on your behalf. All the plans have been set in motion."

I closed my eyes. It still hurt to think. "Well, if you've gone to that much trouble."

"Maybe by the time the guests arrive and the gown can be made, you'll have your memory again." Garian spread his hands.

"I didn't have a gown made?"

"Everything ruined." Garian shook his head sadly. "Rain, too. Mud. Torn to shreds. Before you were found."

"What sort of a gown do you wish?" Jason asked.

"I-I don't know."

"We'll sort it all out later." Garian waggled his fingers, rings glittering.

I started to rise, then spotted a fine, inlaid twelve-string lute lying on a side table. Two steps, three, took me to it. I reached, stroked the wood gently. My right hand moved over the frets, pressing, pressing, and my left strummed softly. Sound, rich, shimmering sound delighted me, and I closed my eyes, reaching—

My head hurt, my hand faltered, and a false note shocked me. I clutched the lute against me. Tears burned my eyes.

I turned around, and dizziness made the room gently revolve.

Jason disengaged the lute from my fingers and laid it aside. "Come. I will take you back. You had better resume your rest."

"All right. Why can't I remember?" I whispered.

Jason did not answer. He carried me back upstairs. I tried to feel whatever I was supposed to feel, but all I was aware of was headache. Jason didn't speak as he set me on the bed, near which Netta waited, her face anxious.

She covered me, and I didn't hear Jason go out.

When I woke, I was alone. The dizziness was gone; the blue curtains stayed still. The windows had been closed against rain. Near the bed someone had placed a side table on which rested a water pitcher, glass and an apple. Above hung a bell cord.

Netta brought me a tray, and stayed to watch me eat. Then she lit some candles and left.

I sat in bed with a glass of water in my hands, watching the candle light on it, not really thinking—until I realized I was seeing a face in the water.

Water splashed onto my quilt as I jerked the glass up. I held it close to my eyes and shook it, but all I saw was the golden gleam that liquid and light make together.

The headache crashed on me. Did I cry out? I dropped the glass and flopped back onto the pillows. Netta reappeared, and I heard her gasp. "My lady?"

"Saw a face. In the glass," I muttered, my eyes closed.

"I-I'll get another quilt." Her voice shook.

I lay where I was, not even feeling cold or wet. When the door opened, Netta entered, with Garian behind her.

Garian came close, still dressed, the candle glow outlining him. "You experienced some sort of vision, I am to understand.

Whose face?"

"I don't know. I think—" I rubbed my eyes, trying to remember. "Jason's?"

He took my shoulders. "Jason," he repeated.

I plucked ineffectively at his fingers. "I don't know. Ow. That hurts."

"Your pardon." He loosened his grasp. "I don't want to find out that any evil mage hired by your father is trying to get at your mind."

"Evil? Mage?" I shuddered. "Oh, I hope not."

Garian straightened up. "Sleep." To Netta, "Bring water when she needs it, then take it away again."

He left, I lay back down, and slid into dreams—but not for long.

When I woke this time, it was from a cold breeze. One of the windows stood open. And outlined in front of it, a silhouette.

I opened my mouth to scream as the figure dashed across the room. Before I got out much more than a squeak, a hand clapped over my mouth.

"Don't squawk, Flian. It's only me." It sounded like a young man.

"Who's that?" I tried to say, but it came out sounding like "Grmph?"

The hand lifted, a tentative movement, and a male voice said, "I know I'm not much of a bargain in your eyes, but you have to realize by now that I'm preferable to them."

"Well, who are you?"

I heard him draw in his breath. "You don't recognize me? I'm Jaim."

"Jaim who? I ought to add that I managed to misplace my memory—"

He stilled, profile outlined against the glass, then slid out the window and was gone.

My door slammed open. One of the liveried men entered, his sword drawn, and behind him Netta, a lamp swinging in her hand.

"My lady?" Netta gasped. "Did you cry out?"

"He went out the window." I pointed.

The guard ran out, bent over the balcony rail, and peered

in all directions. Then he ran back in and through the door, boots and weapons clattering, a contrast to Jaim's silent step.

Garian and Jason appeared, fully dressed, each carrying a weapon. Netta hadn't been idle; the room was lit by then, and I had my nightcap off and shawl on.

"Seems to be a night for excitement," Garian commented, grinning. "Someone was here?"

I shrugged. "Seems odd to me too. He said his name was Jaim."

"Damnation." Garian sent a look at Jason, who did not react.

Several more armed men appeared at the door, and Garian gave out commands for a search.

When they were gone, Jason said, "It has to be Jaim. No one else could get past your guard. I trained him myself." That last with a sort of wry smile.

Garian opened his mouth, then glanced my way. They both did.

Garian forced a hearty smile. "Go back to sleep. The, ah, thief will be apprehended. Not to worry."

"What did he want in here?" I asked. "Jewels?"

Jason turned away, but not before I saw that he was on the verge of laughter.

"What did Jaim say to you?" Garian asked.

"Nothing that made any sense."

Jason's stone face was back. "He's an enemy of mine. No one for you to concern yourself with. Good night."

They left, and soon after I heard footsteps outside the door—a posted guard. Poor soul, I thought as Netta fussed about me. What a boring job.

She offered to stay with me. I apologized for waking her and assured her that whatever guarding I needed could best be done by the fellow outside the door, and I lay back down.

This time I made it all the way to morning without incident.

After breakfast, Netta brought me a pale green silken underdress and fine, dark green cotton-wool gown that laced over it. In the corner was a cleaning frame; I did not feel like insisting on a bath, so I stepped through, and the magic sparked over me, leaving me fresh and clean.

As I dressed and she combed out my hair, we chattered about little things: birdsong, the season. She told me about her daughter, who was a hairdresser.

Once I was dressed I walked to the window, which opened onto a balcony. I stepped out into summery air, which was filled with the delicious scent of flowers and trees after a rain. My headache had receded to a distant throb, only nasty if I moved or turned quickly.

Below the balcony lay a garden, which sloped away down a steep hill to a stone wall with sentries walking along it. Adjacent to me were the corners and towers of a fairly large castle. The rest of the mountain the castle was built on was hidden in forest and morning shadows. Above the castle, snowy peaks etched jagged tooth-shapes against the blue sky.

Remembering my unknown visitor, I tried to figure his route: up a smooth, white-boled tree to the adjacent balcony, over the vine-covered wall to mine. Not an easy journey at night, in the rain.

He must have had some fairly urgent purpose. And what was that about preferences?

I remembered the mirror, then discovered that it had been taken out. I really must look terrible!

I opened the door, found myself face to face with a huge man of determined mien.

"Can you show me to the dining room?" I asked.

"Prince's orders are, you can't negotiate the stairs."

"Oh, I can walk, I feel perfectly fine—except for this great bruise on my head. And I do really want to leave this room."

"I can carry you, my lady," the man offered, his gaze lowered.

"Well, I have no objection if you don't."

And so the man picked me up and carried me down two flights of curving stone stairs, directly to a dining room. This room was long and narrow, made of stone, with a high ceiling. Halfway up the walls banners hung, new and old, a variety of colors and designs, none of which looked familiar to me. The table was long, with a short table set perpendicular on a dais at the fireplace end. The room was cold, the fireplace bare. Despite the wall of tall diamond-paned windows that looked over a terrace, it was not a very inviting chamber; I couldn't say why, since there was nothing ugly about it. But I misliked the atmosphere.

The guard set me gently on my feet, and I heard Garian's voice. "Good morning, Flian. How do you feel? Essaying the rest of the house?"

"I'm bored," I admitted. "As for how I feel, I am fine—except for a pang here, if I move too quickly, but a slow walk takes care of that." I touched the side of my head. "I wish you'd return the mirror. I can't imagine that the sight of a black eye and a few bruises and scrapes will kill me—but it might jar my memory back."

"That's exactly why we won't." He took my elbow and escorted me out again. "I consulted a healer. He said you might try so hard it will make your head feel worse, and your recovery will be twice as long." He smiled. "I feel obliged to tell you that you're somewhat, ah, stubborn, often preferring immediate gratification over sense."

I grimaced, resenting his words. I had to remind myself that he was my favorite cousin, and so we must have been honest with one another.

"We usually eat in here." He led me along another stone-floored corridor. "Less drafty than that blasted room, which I only use for formal occasions."

We entered the library I'd seen the day before. I looked around—but the lute was gone.

Jason sat in one of the chairs, dressed much as he'd been the day before. He greeted me, I greeted him, and the conversation foundered there until servants came in bearing covered trays.

Garian dismissed the servants. He prepared my plate first and served me himself, saying easily, "I'd propose a topic for conversation, but I suspect you won't have much to contribute about the latest fashions or plays."

I gave a laugh at the joke, then sighed. "I apologize for being so boring. I bore myself, lying up in that room and not knowing what I ought to be doing."

"Resting." Jason's voice was flat.

"He's right." Garian made an elaborate gesture to Jason to help himself.

Jason looked over at the three trays of fresh food, some of it steaming invitingly, but all he took was a roll. He stood on the other side of the fireplace, tossing the bread up and down on his palm as he watched me eat. Garian shrugged, loaded a plate and sat in the chair opposite mine.

For a time there was no sound but that of cutlery on porcelain and the snapping of the fire. I'd happily worked my way through braised chicken, rice-and-cabbage and a tart before Jason appeared to remember his bread, which he ate.

Garian finished first, got up and went somewhere behind me. As I set my plate onto a side table, I felt warmth spread through me again, and the headache dissipated. I felt great. Maybe I could take a walk. Fresh air, I was certain, would thoroughly restore me.

Then Garian appeared at my side with a small gilt-edged goblet. "Here. A sip of spiced wine."

"In the morning?" I made a face. Though I didn't remember who I was or what my life had been like, this suggestion did not seem even remotely part of my habits.

"Healer said it would be good for you. Get rid of the headache. Help you to sleep better."

"All right."

He pressed the cup into my hands, and I raised it to my lips. Over its rim I saw Jason's pale blue eyes watching, their expression impossible to interpret.

The wine, despite the cinnamon and other fine spices, had a bitter edge. I shuddered, then drank it all off in a quick gulp.

"There." I shivered again.

Garian put his hands on his hips. "A comment on the quality of our Drath wine?"

"Pardon." I got to my feet and curtseyed. "I really wasn't ready for wine in the morning."

"Never mind. I was teasing." He held out his arm. "Shall I walk you back upstairs?"

I rose. My head felt odd—light, almost. "I think—I fear I'd better."

It was a long journey, but Garian talked the entire time. Inconsequential chat, mostly, at least I found it increasingly difficult to focus on his words, which were about horses, and a ride, and the menu for dinner on the wedding day, and he really believed the dressmaker would have something for my inspection that evening.

When we reached my room, I made for the nearest chair,

which was set by the open balcony window. Garian bent, kissed my fingers with light, easy grace and departed.

I don't think I was aware of him going. I meant to look out at the whispering trees, but sank into sleep.

Chapter Three

Netta woke me. My neck ached, and my mouth was horribly dry.

"Oh, my lady, are you well?"

"I—" I swallowed, determined to say I was well, and what's more, to *be* well. I had no idea what sort of person I'd been before, but right now I was very tired of being an invalid. "Yes. I am."

Netta smiled. "The gown is here. His highness sent me to seek your approval. He said any adjustments can be made by morning."

"That's all-night work." I rose, no longer bothering to wonder how I knew that. "If you see the seamstresses, please convey my appreciation."

Netta bowed. "I shall." She gave me a troubled glance.

My head swam nastily, then righted. "May I have water, please?"

Netta went out again. Once I'd drunk a full glass of water I felt measurably better. Soon I stood in the middle of the floor while she she fitted me into a very fine gown of cream lace and green ribbons over a green silk underdress. Netta frowned, twitching the folds and clucking to herself about the laces, while I admired the pearls sewn along the edges of the long sleeves and the hem.

At last she stood back. "What shall I say, my lady?"

"That I approve. But I wish they'd permit me a mirror. Heyo, the black eye must be a fetching green by now—matching the gown."

My attempt at humor only made her cluck louder as she helped me out of the wedding dress. When it was laid aside, she brought the nightgown. So it was to be another long evening alone, then? I pulled it on, and moments later a quiet maid brought in a tray on which there was, besides the handsome gilt porcelain dishes, another glass of wine. Netta sat down with me as I ate, and when I was finished, she looked at me with faint worry. "His highness insists that you drink the wine, my lady. I'm to stay and see it done."

I made a face. "Either I don't care for this grape, or else the healer gave him some sort of draught to put in. Latter, most likely." I sipped the bitter drink. "Eugh!"

But I finished it, then climbed into bed, wondering what I ought to do, as Netta took away the tray. I considered asking Netta to bring me something to read, but dozed off listening to the sound of the trees rustling outside the balcony.

I woke with the usual dry mouth and lassitude. The windows were dark. Rain was on the way, but someone had lit a fire.

With an inward jolt, I remembered that this was to be my wedding day.

To the library I was taken, where I found Garian waiting. He greeted me with a broad smile, his hazel eyes very green against the splendid emerald velvet tunic he wore, all embroidered over in gold.

"The guests are beginning to arrive." He made a grand gesture toward the windows. "Jason's doing the honors as bridegroom. Since you have ventured forth, let's have this last meal together, you and I, if you've no objection, Cousin?"

"None," I said.

He sauntered to the bell-cord and pulled it. On his hand a great square emerald glittered in the light of the fire. "Are you delighted with the prospect of your wedding?"

"To speak truly, I don't feel anything at all. I know that's scarcely fair to Jason. I do wish we could wait."

"Alas." Garian made an airy gesture and smiled. "There is the little matter of politics. Great matter."

"Politics?" I repeated. "Oh. Well, he's a king, that I remember. King of—"

"Ralanor Veleth." Garian's eyes were narrowed in mirth. "You don't remember?"

"Ralanor Veleth." I shook my head slightly. "Means nothing."

"It will all come back soon. I promise that much."

A tap at the door.

"Enter."

And in came a steward carrying a meal on trays.

The food was excellent and did much to revive me. But as before, Garian gave me spiced wine, and stood before me until I had drunk it all. Afterward he summoned another servant. "Send Alem down."

The guard appeared as I began feeling that weird floaty sensation and he offered his arm.

"See you this evening, Flian," Garian said, now grinning. "I fear I have to resume my duties as host."

He watched the guard escort me out. The man matched his pace to mine. We proceeded slowly up the stairs. On the first landing, I was vaguely aware of footfalls, and a dark shadow appeared on the edge of my vision.

I looked up to see Jason standing on the lowest step of the next stairway.

"Flian."

The voice was quiet enough to take a moment to register. I thought I had imagined it, paused, and nearly lost my balance. Waves blurred my vision, as though I were swimming underwater, sinking down farther by the moment. I staggered.

"I came," he said, "for a last interview. Are you ready to go forward with the plans?"

My mind sank deeper into the shadowy depths of my underwater hideaway. "As you wish..." Like a silver eel, a stray thought appeared, one I'd worked at all the day before, and I grasped it, endeavoring to express it before it vanished again. "I don't—I wish we needn't be in haste. But our troth. It means you once had my trust. I must trust you again. Must I not? Isn't that part of the vows?"

I tipped my head back to look into his face. There was no reaction to be seen at all.

"I don't make sense, do I?" I swayed. A fierce yawn took me.

Jason stepped aside and gestured to the guard.

He picked me up and bore me the rest of the way upstairs.

I think I was asleep before we reached my room.

When I woke, I felt worse than I had that first day in the cottage when I came to with my memory gone. Night had fallen, but two branches of candles had been lit, as well as the fire.

Netta had fresh listerblossom leaf, which she gave me in such a furtive way that I was confused. It wasn't until after I'd drunk it all down and she poured water into the cup that I wondered if she'd sneaked it to me, and why. Perhaps she did not have the faith in Prince Garian's healer that he had.

I certainly felt better as I stepped through the cleaning frame and into the linen underdress. Netta lifted the heavy overgown, I put head and hands through, and she let the ribbon-edged hem fall to my feet.

The lovely fabric foamed around my feet as I sat. She wove flowers and green gems into my hair. My throat felt dry and nasty, my body heavy. This was my wedding day, but I had no emotion whatever.

Presently a tap at the door caused Netta to scurry in fright to open it. Garian entered, the candlelight shimmering over the gold brocade and embroidery on his long tunic. Gems sparkled with starbright color in his hair, at his ear, and on his hands. Round his brow he wore a golden circlet.

"Are you ready, Flian?"

"Yes. You look quite fine. Netta, first may I have a drink of water?"

Garian waited while Netta brought me water in a crystal wine goblet. I raised it, looking into its depths. The swirling reflections of the fire coalesced into two eyes, and I almost dropped the goblet.

"Seeing again?"

Garian was right next to me; I could feel his breath stirring my hair, and his fingers gripped my wrist.

"A face. Jason's, I guess." I shrugged.

Garian let me go and I drank the water, which eased the dryness of my throat. Garian took the goblet from my fingers and set it with a crystalline *ching* on the table.

"Let us depart." He took my arm and led me from the room.

"I wish I could see myself once." I frowned down at my hair swinging against my skirts.

From the gloom on the stairway came a quiet voice. "Why

not let her?"

"It's too late to do any harm." Garian chuckled.

An arched door stood open off the first landing. Garian led me inside, Jason's quiet tread behind us. The room was lit by several branches of candles. Jason was dressed for the first time in something besides riding clothes. Over a tabard-woven, loose-sleeved linen shirt, he wore a long, dark green velvet tunic belted with blackweave, undecorated by any trim or finery, his black hair as always tied back. Except for the wedding green, he looked less a bridegroom than did Garian.

Then Garian gestured, and I faced the mirror.

Vertigo—memory—made me dizzy. I peered into the wan face of an ordinary young lady with rather bland coloring—skin and hair more or less the shade of honey, and eyes too pale to be considered blue. The gown was beautifully made, but I scarcely gave it a glance, for I was more interested in myself. The bruises were visible, dark smudges that made my features difficult to descry, but I did not faint or quail away. I felt no reaction at all besides a faint curiosity, even when I gazed straight into my eyes. They were the eyes of a stranger.

A tall shadow moved to my side. Jason stood next to me; the top of my head came to his shoulder. His smile at my reflection was brief. "Come along," he said.

"The guests are waiting," Garian added.

I glanced up into Jason's face. "For a moment I almost had it."

"I know. I saw." He slid his hand under my arm.

I whispered, feeling acutely self-conscious, "I wish it had come. I am sorry I cannot pretend a happiness I ought to feel."

"No matter." The answer was quiet, and without any emotion.

Garian stepped up on my other side and took my other arm.

Together the three of us walked downstairs to the dining hall. The panes in the windows were old-fashioned diamonds, which glistened with fire-reflections from the candle-sconces along the walls. Above the candles, the banners glowed with muted color. Around the perimeter of the room about thirty well-dressed strangers waited, their jewels winking and gleaming.

Most of the people smiled. One tall, black-bearded man

laughed, then turned away quickly and coughed.

Jason led me to the high table.

"...all right?" A matronly lady was before me, giving me a questioning look.

The man who had laughed said in a hearty voice, "As right as she'll ever be."

Garian responded in a similar hearty voice. "We explained about the carriage accident, Lady Ordomar. Flian is otherwise quite well, are you not?"

"Of course." I willed it to be so.

The three of us took our places behind the chairs at the high table, and Garian lifted a goblet high. He spoke our names, the guests echoed, and they all drank to Jason and me. We would share wine after the ceremony—

How did I know that?

I closed my eyes, dizzy.

Crash! Glass shards from the windows flew everywhere, glittering as bright as the guests' gems as they recoiled, screamed, shouted, cursed.

Silent black-clad figures leaped in, one of them on horseback, glass crunching and tinkling under the animal's hooves. They spread round the perimeter of the room, their faces obscured, some holding bows, others swords; the two men-at-arms converged on the mounted figure, whose sword arced and hummed. In five strokes he wounded both men. They dropped to the floor, groaning.

Garian was hemmed by two of the intruders, so he could not reach the bell-pull. The horse skidded on the glassy slate flooring, and pranced toward the high table.

A hand tightened on my arm. I felt curiously distant, as if this all happened on a stage, and I watched from far away.

Jason gripped a long dagger in one hand. But before he could raise it, a sword slashed down from behind and stopped at his neck. "I wouldn't if I was you," growled a man in Garian's livery. "And I might add I'm glad I ain't."

At that moment the dancing black horse reached the high table. It tossed its head, eyes wide. The black-clad figures collected weapons from the guests.

"Stand, Flian," commanded the horseman.

Garian's face was white with rage, but a gauntleted hand

held a sword at his neck as well, held by a sturdy man dressed in Garian's own livery. Garian's eyes flicked back and forth, back and forth, sweat beading his brow.

Jason stood very still, his attention entirely on the rider of that horse.

The animal stepped closer. Round dark eyes reflected the candles behind me as I got to my feet. An arm slid round my waist and I was lifted into the air.

A grunt, and I sat astride the horse's withers. A hard arm held me against a slim body whose heart beat a steady tattoo. I smelled horse and human sweat, a sharp scent over the wine and perfumes of Garian's hall.

"Do you desire the consequences, Jaim?" Jason asked wryly.

"No." The man holding me laughed. "But the thought of putting a hitch in your gallop will warm me those cold nights on the run."

I felt the rider nod.

The second man in Garian's livery reversed his blade and brought the hilt down across the back of Jason's head. Jason dropped soundlessly to the floor. The second man served Garian the same way—shouts, screams—and next to my ear, the rider clucked. An edge of cloak was flung over my head, so I no longer saw the shocked faces of the guests or the shard-framed window. The horse gave a powerful leap, landed, trotted, and then gathered speed.

Chapter Four

After a time the horse slowed, and stopped.

The cloak was pulled from my head and cool, sweet air ruffled across my face. A number of mounted people waited under a great spreading oak.

"Cover 'em." My rider hooked a thumb over his shoulder. "The rest of us ride."

I twisted around. In the weak moonlight, Jaim looked a lot like Jason, only without the mustache.

"So you're Jaim."

"Yes. We have a long ride. Will you cooperate?"

I said with as much dignity as I could muster, "I have neither the strength nor the inclination to scuffle." Added more normally, "Where are we going?"

"Away from here."

He raised a hand. The horses began their gallop.

He was right. It was a long ride. The gallop eventually slowed to a trot and then to a walk. Jaim began turning this way and that.

A sigh went through him when someone rode out from a shaded gully, leading a string of horses. In silence the riders all exchanged mounts, and once again we galloped.

I did not stay awake for the entire night, but drifted in and out of a kind of strange sleep, my dreams disturbed by the rhythm of the horse's hooves on the road, by the heartbeat beneath my ear, by the memory of those swords reflecting the firelight in blood-red glow. Down and up mountain roads, across bridges that spanned thundering falls, and at last into a narrow tree-protected valley, and thence into an old cave.

At once people crowded around, everyone talking.

Jaim lifted his voice. "How about letting us dismount?"

The press of people eased.

Jaim climbed down, then pulled me after and set me on my feet. "She's had a rough month. First let me get her settled."

"If you're going to talk about me," I said, "I want to hear it as well."

"Anon." Jaim led the way through a narrow crevice into an oddly shaped room lit by candles. It was bisected down below by a dark, rushing stream. At the other end was a kind of shelf, with a pile of woven yeath-fur rugs and pillows. "You can sleep here."

I dropped onto the inviting rugs. "I don't understand anything."

"I'll explain come morning. And there's plenty to explain. You have to be awake to hear it all." He pointed a finger at me. "That means you need to sleep off whatever potions Garian's been slipping you."

"Healer's draughts, he said. In the wine. So that's why I kept getting sicker!"

Jaim snorted. "Sounds like Garian's usual trickery, all right. Never mind. It's over. Sleep!" He left, taking out the light.

I tried to unlace the wedding gown, but it was too much work. So I just stretched out, pulled the soft rug over me, and slept.

I woke when lamplight flickered over my eyelids.

Jaim walked in carrying a lamp. He leaned against the wall, which glinted in layers slanting upward at an angle. "Do you feel any better?"

"A lot better. But ravenous."

"Food is being prepared. For now, I really want to hear what happened to you."

"You don't know?" I asked.

"Not the way you understand it." His jaw tightened—fighting a yawn.

I paused, looking at him more closely. Bony face—no mustache—long black hair tied back. His shirt was unlaced, rolled to the elbows, his posture the tight stance of someone who needs to sit—has needed to sit for time past counting.

"You're tired," I observed.

He nodded. "Very." Blinked down at the rugs and made a curious grimace. "Since you noticed, mind if I avail myself?"

Surprised, I shrugged. "There's room for five here, in truth. Go ahead."

He disengaged from the wall, set the lamp down and stretched out on the blankets just beyond arm's reach, his nose pointed toward the ceiling and his eyes closing. "Ah."

"Why do you look like Jason?"

"I'm his brother."

"He never mentioned that," I said. "The brief references were more that of an enemy. That's one confusion. The entanglement of relatives who dislike one another is another. Then there's my own dilemma, such as: will I like myself when I regain my memory? From what Garian hinted, I might not be so pleasant a person, and I can't for the life of me see why I betrothed myself to Jason..." I rambled on, mixing questions with observations until I realized I wasn't getting any answers.

Jaim was breathing the slow, steady breathing of one who is dead to the world.

I laughed, cast my rug over him, and got up. I'd find that food myself.

I made my way to the other end of the cave, where I was met by a tall blond man dressed in rough forest clothing and mocs. He bowed, which surprised me.

"Good, what, morning? Evening?"

"Good evening, Princess."

Princess? That explained the bow. Interesting that Garian hadn't told me and Netta had called me just "lady".

"Where may I get something to eat?"

"Come this way, please, your highness."

He led me up a narrow rocky corridor lit at intervals by torches. A sharp angle opened into a huge cavern that had a waterfall at one end, as well as a stream. A group of people turned and one came toward me, a young lady somewhat shorter than I, with a vivid face and lovely figure. She had long, curling black hair and expressive dark blue eyes. She was dressed plainly in a woolen skirt and bodice. Her linen blouse had full sleeves and a low neckline that made the best of her figure.

"Welcome, Flian." She put out her hand. "I'm Jewel. Jaim tells me you've lost your memory, but we haven't met in any case."

"It's nice to meet you, Jewel." I peered past her, sniffing the air. "Oatcakes! I am famished."

"You look it," she said with brisk sympathy. "Far too skinny, if you don't mind my adding. Felic, would you fix a plate? Where's Jaim? He said he was going to interview you."

"He fell asleep."

"Good! I put the sleepweed he stole into his wine. After all, if it can work for our big brother, it can work for me—not that it took much. He's been on his feet for too many days." She cast me a laughing glance. "I hope I won't have to take care of him any more."

Food appeared then, plain but well-cooked oatcakes and baked potato with vegetables stuffed inside. We sat on hay-stuffed pillows a ways from the others, who appeared to be young men and women of our own age. Most of them; some were older.

For a time Jewel watched me eat. I gathered the impression that she was endeavoring to be patient—and that patience did not come easily. When I was done, she pounced. "What happened? What lies did they tell you?"

"Lies?" I told her my story from the time I woke up in the cottage. I'd thought it innocuous—I could not really believed that astonishing business in the dining hall had happened to *me*—until I ended with, "So I guess what I really wish to know is, why did Jaim abduct me?"

Her cheeks bloomed crimson, her eyes widened. I almost dropped my fork as she declared, "Oh! I can't bear it! Lies indeed, worse than I thought!"

I sat back. "I assure you I haven't purposefully lied—"

"You were not abducted. You were *rescued*." She jumped to her feet and began to pace, waving her arms. "Absolute, ridiculous, rotten, miserable lies! No wonder you went along with everything. Jaim was afraid Garian had broken your spirit, forced you in some nefarious way to fall into their horrid plans. Oh, Garian'd love that, he would. Only we didn't think he'd dare, because too many people would know, but how else to explain that marriage? When the couriers went out to the local nobles two days ago, Jaim knew he would have to act fast, or it would be too late—"

"I'm lost," I said.

Jewel stopped, snorted, looked back at Jaim's people, some of whom were staring at us.

She put her fists on her hips. "Oh, I ought not to get so mad, I know it, because I exaggerate terribly. But it's not good to bottle your feelings inside, like *they* do. Jaim does. Jason *has* no feelings, unless you count cruelty, nastiness and evil! Do people really *feel* evil?" She sidetracked herself, looking perplexed. "Well, if anybody does, Jason is the one. If he'd managed to marry you, once he'd gotten his claws on your holdings—" She drew her finger across her neck and made a squelching noise.

I shivered.

"Huh! So, Jaim really did rescue you. He saved your life! Say, you're finished, and the dishes barrel is here. We haven't many luxuries, but we do have a kitchen cleaning bucket. And a cleaning frame. Or, would you prefer a nice bath?"

"Oh, would I ever!"

We put our dishes in the water-filled barrel; someone had managed to get a cleaning frame on it, because I saw the sparkle of magic.

She led me down a narrow passage. I smelled running water, and even steam. She stopped at one point and called, "Anyone here?"

"Yes!" Several male voices echoed back.

She sighed. "We'll have a turn later. Let's go to where I sleep, since Jaim's asleep in his place."

"I was using his bed?"

"Well, it was the only empty one, because he knew he'd be staying up, the idiot." She snorted, plunging up another narrow tunnel. Along the way I saw various cracks and crevices leading in different directions. Some had tapestries hung over them, and some didn't.

Jewel had laid claim to a small water-hollowed cave with one thin connection of rock left. Stalagmites and stalactites stippled the rest of the cave, except for a smooth area in the far corner on which she had scattered brightly colored quilts and lengths of fabric, including silk and velvet. She also had a small glowglobe, evidence of Jaim's regard for his sister, for he hadn't one in his own chamber.

She flung herself down on this magpie bed, and I stretched out next to her. "There's one thing I can safely tell you, and that's my story," she announced. "You'll understand more about us, don't you think?"

"Certainly," I said, though I wondered why I needed to understand her family.

"Jaim can tell you his part," she added. "You already know that the three of us are siblings. Our mother died a few years ago. Drink. Father was assassinated when I was little. They used to fight a lot, that previous generation. Of them, only your father is left—and he tried to use diplomacy or trade rather than fight, which got him sneered at in the past, but he's still alive. *And* rich." She gave me a wry sort of grimace. "We're not, you see. Ralanor Veleth is twice the size of Lygiera, your kingdom. Larger than twice, probably, but it's rocky and soil-poor, and we've had a long history of fighting to get access to better land. We've expanded to the eastern mountains and—"

She tossed her curls back. "This is harder than I thought! Jason took over from our mother when he was, oh, twenty-two or so. That was because he could best all the warriors, and he thought he could rule. He forced Jaim to be as good. Jason wants to keep the army large against others coming against us, or against Norsunder, but actually we think he's intending to go over and take Lygiera and maybe even Dantherei. It would certainly solve our treasury problems! Jaim says we can't, that all the fighting has to stop, that we solve our own problems without being grabby with other people's land and treasury."

"Where do you fit in?" I asked.

She made a face. "Jason told me early on I'd marry whoever he told me to, for alliance purposes."

"That doesn't sound like war."

"Probably to get more warriors for his plans."

"Ah."

"So that horrible Garian arrived in Lathandra to court me. See, Drath's small, up here in the border mountains, but because of the gem mines and the wine it's rich. He pays lip service to your father and to Dantherei and the rest of the kingdoms, but we think he's allying with Jason in order to get some more land that isn't mountain. We—that is, Jason—

provides the army, and Garian the money to equip it."

"Do I know all these people and problems?" I asked.

Jewel grinned. "I don't know."

I laughed. "It does sound odd, doesn't it?"

"Yes! But you do know you don't like Garian. Neither do I. He's arrogant and sarcastic, and mean. He was just pretending to court me. I could tell he thought I was too stupid to see how all his compliments cut two ways. I was as nasty to Garian as I could possibly be, so he would go away. But he wouldn't go away, and then one night he was bored and drinking and he set one of Jason's dogs on the castle cat, who was feeding her litter, and I, um, tried to knife him. Jason got angry and locked me in my room, saying I could either learn to behave or sit there and starve. Me! It was not *I* who set the dogs to harry the cat! Well, Jaim tried to defend me—oh, I don't even want to talk about it. It was horrible. Jason locked us up, but Jaim's got loyal liegemen same as Jason, and Daraen came with some of his men and got us out, and so here we are, in an old hideout for thieves."

I shuddered. "That sounds terrible. Garian likes cruelty? He laughed so much. Though when I think back, I really believe he was laughing at me."

"Of course he was." She wrinkled her nose. "Back to us. Malcontents—people who won't stick Garian's rule—or Jason's—find their way here. The real criminals Jaim sends away again. The rest, well, some of them are, um, somewhat rough, but if anyone gives you trouble, tell Jaim and he'll straighten them out."

"So you live by stealing?"

"Yes—from Garian. And from Jason's strongholds. Good practice, Jaim says, though it's risky. And there've been times when he's gone into Lygiera to forage, but I'll leave him to tell you why and how."

"Sounds complicated." I fought a sudden yawn, and when I saw her brows curve up in reaction, I said, "I am not bored. I am tired from the residue of the sleep-herbs Garian forced on me."

"Well, truth to tell I'm also tired," she admitted. "Staying up all night waiting on word. I wish I'd had the patience when Jaim tried to train me, but I hadn't. All I wanted—still do—was to dance, and have parties, and a lovely life—and that sure was not possible in Ralanor Veleth." She made a dismissive gesture. "Anyway, if you like you can sleep here with me."

I thanked her gratefully. We buried ourselves in her collection of fabrics and I slid into sleep despite the soft glow of the globe.

Memories, imagination, and what Jewel had told me, all formed into a terrible dream from which I was glad to awaken. I lay quietly enjoying the silence and the faint echo of rushing water, until Jewel's eyes opened.

"Come! Let's see if the baths are free."

This time the cavern was empty. At one end a cold waterfall mixed with hot water from underground, making a wonderful bath that swirled around one. The last of my aches drained away as the rushing water massaged my body. I was reluctant to leave when she suggested we dress and go in search of breakfast.

I had to wear my wedding gown again, but a step through their cleaning frame snapped away all the dirt and grime, so at least it was clean.

At the far end of the dining cavern were the cookfires; the great rocks above were stained with smoke, but there seemed to be some kind of flue functioning among the shadowy cracks overhead, for the chamber was not smoky. Two women and a man with gray hair appeared to be in charge of the food; behind their area were sacks and barrels of supplies.

On our approach, one of the women handed us each a plain ceramic plate loaded with eggs and fried potato cakes.

Jewel led the way to a seat apart from the other people. We sat on benches and ate, with our wet hair hanging down our backs and dripping onto the stone floor. A couple of young women glanced my way, expressing curiosity. One grinned and half-lifted a hand. She was tall, strong looking, with curly brown hair and a wicked knife at her belt. I liked her grin at once and waved back.

Jewel said in a casual voice, "That's just Vrozta, a weaver's daughter. She—" Jewel changed her mind, said nothing more.

Jaim walked in shortly after, his black hair wet and slicked back, his clothes fresh.

Jewel leaped up. "Jaim," she cried happily. "Sleep well?"

"Quite." He gave her a mock frown. "Someone slip dreamweed into my wine? Because I behaved rudely to our guest."

She chortled. "Fell asleep! Right when she was talking. But you needed the rest."

"Obviously, or I'd have noticed the taste."

It was clear they were fond of one another. She laughed, then touched his wrist. "Seemed a handy trick—Garian is good for something, who would have known? Guess what. She saw your face in a glass that night you first came to her room in Garian's lair."

Jaim looked my way. "And you didn't recognize me?"

I shrugged, smiling. "Your face looked, oh, so serious. I thought it was Jason at first, only without his fuzz." I traced a mustache along my upper lip.

"Oh, you *must* hear the rest," Jewel put in. "Garian told her all these lies about how she was so in love with Jason. It quite turned my stomach!"

"I'm as glad to find out it's a lie, if it indeed is. Because I took one look at him and my heart went thud into my slippers."

Jewel snickered.

Jaim ran a hand through his wet hair. "It's funny in retrospect, but we're going to have to think of some sort of plan to keep them from getting you back. I didn't think you'd last out that month."

"Month," I repeated. "You said that before. I only have memory of a very few days."

"A month." He slicked his hair back again, plainly hesitating.

I said, "If Garian lied about my family as well, and I do get along with them, I'd as soon go home."

"We can talk later. Is that all right with you?" Jaim gestured toward the food. "Right now I can't think about anything but my empty gut."

"Fair enough."

"Let me show you around," Jewel offered. "You can even meet some of our terrible ruffians."

Jaim got a plate, and Jewel led me away before any actual introductions could be performed. Before we left the dining area, Jaim sat down next to the strong-looking woman who'd given me the friendly wave, and kissed her.

Jewel showed me the trails up to the surface. We came out overlooking a long, narrow valley thickly forested. Heavy clouds were coming in, bringing the prospect of rain. When we returned to their cavern hideout, she showed me their weapons stores, where several people were busy repairing tack, sharpening steel and doing related tasks.

There was also a room for training. We heard the clang and clatter of weapons before we came upon them. Jewel was quite proud of the gang's exploits, and even more proud of her brother.

Finally there were the oddments—old, worn-out clothes, fabric, broken tools, horse tack that needed mending, and in the corner a lute. I walked straight to it, but discovered it was missing its strings. Disappointment hit hard, though I did not know why. When I turned around, it was to find Jewel watching me, puzzlement plain in her face.

"There's more to see, if you like." She pointed behind her.

"Lead on."

During that tour, I learned not only a wealth of detail about how Jaim's outlaw band existed, but about Jewel's own romantic hopes. For she was very romantic and not the least subtle. At least a dozen hints were dropped about her hopes that I would like the outlaw band so much that I would stay and fall in love with Jaim.

And make his fortune—but to be fair that was not her entire motivation. That they all saw me as a wealthy piece in several international games was soon apparent, but Jewel really wanted her brother to marry a princess, in as romantic a way as possible, and in turn I could provide Jewel with what she desired most: a life at court and her own chance at romance.

As we passed by the gang members, they exchanged greetings. She was clearly fond of them all, but her own goals were so dazzling that she did not see the admiration she inspired in certain of the young men. Nor did she seem to notice that Jaim was affectionate to the merry-eyed, knife-carrying Vrozta, and flirted outrageously with more of the young women of the band.

By nightfall I had observed all these things, though I kept my thoughts to myself. I had yet to find out my own story; I resolved I would make no decisions until I knew it.

If, that is, I was to be permitted to make my own decisions.

For Jewel did not see Jaim's actions as an abduction. My own definition waited on the results.

How long would it be before I recovered my memory?

I expected some dramatic resolution.

I was wrong.

The entire band had gathered to sup. Jewel was entertaining Jaim and several other young people with an absurd plot to sneak into Drath as traveling players and right in the middle of a popular blood-and-guts historical play turn on the watchers and rob Garian of everything he owned, all while quoting the best lines. I enjoyed watching them as much as I enjoyed the repartee. The light from the torches glimmered and sparked with reflected fire through my water glass.

And I saw another face.

A male face, supercilious, with a refined nose lifted into the air. Long upper lip, gorgeous blue eyes with lashes that Jewel would envy, and wispy red hair—

"S-spaquel!" I gasped, and laughed.

My mind jolted. Had the cavern quaked? No. That was me, fighting vertigo and an unpleasant wash of nausea.

My memory was back.

Chapter Five

I must have made a noise because everyone went silent.

I met Jaim's watchful gaze. "Ignaz Spaquel, now Duke of Osterog," I said, numb. "My father's prime adviser. Prime sycophant. I saw him—I know him. I—"

Memories cascaded then, so fast I could not control them, and so I set the glass down, mumbled, "Please. Pardon." And I fled, thumping into rocky outcroppings, stumbling up toward the surface until I reached that opening overlooking the valley.

There I stopped, panting, and wept. Hard, hiccoughing tears burned my eyes and my heart, for discovery, for loss, for regret and, to write the truth, shame. I turned away from the spectacular view and buried my face in my arms and sobbed until I was exhausted.

Finally I raised my aching face to look at the purpling sky. I had to get home and warn Papa about what I knew.

"Flian?"

It was Jaim.

I turned around. "What."

"Your memory has returned, I take it."

I snuffled. "I want to go home."

He leaned against a pine branch, unsheathed his belt knife and began flicking at the bark. "I didn't tell you about us, because I wanted you to accept—"

"I already know your sad story from Jewel. I'm sorry you Szinzars have your problems, but they have nothing to do with me. I am not a part of your games. I did not want to be one in your brother's. I want to go *home*."

"Listen—if you stay—"

"So you can ransom me against my father? Is that it?"

He waved the knife in the air. I don't think he was even aware that he held it. "No, that's not what I meant."

But I was far too upset to listen. I pointed at the knife and snapped, "At what, threat of death? I had enough of *that* from Garian. And, if you'll remember a certain occasion—"

He jabbed the knife toward me. "I never threatened you with death!"

"Jaim!" Jewel rushed out, exclaiming.

Jaim blinked. Looked at the knife in disbelief. Jammed it into its sheath, glancing skyward with expressive exasperation. "You *know* I didn't. Even your brother knew—"

"Knew what?" Jewel looked from one of us to the other. "You've met before? Jaim, you said you had to talk to her— what? What? *What?*"

"You're trying to say you suborned Maxl?" I crossed my arms. "Then I say you are a liar."

Jaim flushed. "I never spoke to him, except once. And it— never mind that. But he saw my letter, and he knew. I'm sure he did, because your city guard did not have orders to shoot to kill if they did manage to lay me by the heels."

Jewel stamped, put her hands up to her ears and growled. "I. Will. Go. *Crazy.* If. You. Do. Not. Tell. Me—"

I said, "Your dear, pitiful brother Jaim tried to abduct me from my own home."

Jewel blinked, and then sighed. "He did?"

"Jewel!" I couldn't help a laugh, angry as I was. "It was *not romantic.* He only wanted money, and I know it would have killed Papa—"

"But he wasn't to know," Jaim said. "Maxl would have seen to it I'd get the money, and incidentally, he'd be able to get round that blasted Spaquel on the guard issue—"

I drew in a breath, thinking rapidly. My brother Maxl was in charge of the city militia, a job made more difficult by the fact that Spaquel thought they used too much revenue and ought to be cut. Had Maxl actually told Jaim his plan for how they ought to be increased against threatened trouble?

"Argh!" Jewel covered her face with hands. "I don't understand!"

"Yes, but you do." Jaim studied me with narrowed eyes.

"You *do* understand. Maxl is being outfaced by that slimy toad who is dealing with his dear cousin Garian behind the king's back, and undercutting Maxl's efforts at putting together a defense. And Maxl hasn't done badly, either. The city guard needs training—"

"From whom?" I asked. "You?"

"I know how." He shrugged. The knife was out again, carving at the tree branch.

"Yes, and then what? Take over from within? No, you are not getting me to stay here and try your stupid ransom idea again. Nor will I try to get my brother to hire you as some sort of commander. And if you dare try to make me—"

"Yes." His voice went low and flat, reminding me unsettlingly of Jason. "I'm going to act the Great Villain and ransom you against your family so that I can pay for taking over from my heroic, angelic brother. What would you do, Flian, if I did? Scream? Cry? Fling yourself from yon cliff? Go ahead, entertain us."

He eyed the tree branch whose bark he'd been shredding, then he pushed himself away and again resheathed his knife.

Jewel tried to catch at his hands. "Jaim. Your temper is almost as bad as mine. Can't we try to reason—"

"Go away," I cried. "Both of you."

Three long, angry steps and Jaim was gone. Jewel groaned and reached to stroke my hair. "Admit it. You don't want me to go."

"I'm tired," I quavered. "I want to go home. I hate your brothers. It would kill Papa if he knew about anything that's happened. I have to get home, it's the one thought that kept me going through Garian's torture sessions—"

"Torture?" She put her hands to her mouth.

"Well, he slapped me a lot. He *enjoyed*, it, too. You were right when you said he's mean. Garian adores being a bully, especially if you try to fight back. And I tried. A mistake. The black eye was the result." I pointed.

"I thought you fell off a horse while escaping. That's what Jaim said."

"I did. The rest of the bruises—including the big one behind my ear—are all from the fall from the horse, but not that." I fingered my eye, giving in thoroughly to self-pity. "He knocked me down after I got off a ripping good insult about his methods of courtship. Hah," I added, remembering.

"Tell me *everything*," Jewel breathed.

I snuffled. "Oh, there isn't much to tell that isn't dreary. Truth is, they *all* see me as a kind of stuffed doll worth a lot of money. Garian's sarcasm—"

"Oh, I remember." Jewel looked grim. "I had my own time with him, as you recall."

"He described, in detail, how weak, spoiled, stupid and foolish I was, always in front of Jason. In truth, I sometimes wonder—no. I'm already getting tangled up." I drew a deep breath. "All right. The beginning. Garian came to Carnison for New Year's Week. The only bit of truth is that he really is related to us, through my mother, though we're cousins of cousins. He was supposedly courting me. He has wonderful manners when he has to, and Papa really liked him. It was disgusting how Garian used the old-fashioned style of bowing and all those old-fashioned compliments. He does it with style, but..." I paused, reaching for words. I'd never spoken about such things except to my brother and half-expected Jewel to go right on talking, but to my surprise, she waited.

"But what?" she prompted.

"I-I find it hard to express. Even when he's not being obvious with those nasty two-edged compliments there's a difference between his tone and his manner that makes me feel, oh, that the ground is uneven. He's not the only one. There are some in court who also learned that skill. *Is* it a skill?"

"If using weapons is a skill." Jewel waved a finger in the air. "Because it's a weapon. You just don't see the cuts. But you feel them."

"Yes, you're right. One of the reasons I avoid court. When some people use it on me, I don't know whether to react to the manner or to the words, and I end up standing there like a fence post."

"So what about the marriage?"

"He made formal application to Papa for a marriage alliance, and Papa was trying to talk me into agreeing to a betrothal, and if not that, to accept Garian's invitation to visit him in Drath."

"Grrrr."

"Well, around that time Jaim showed up. Not honestly— and now I know why."

"Ah." Jewel clasped her hands. "I knew he was gone, but not where. Why didn't he tell me? Well, go on."

"All I know is he sneaked around spying us out, and he and Maxl did meet, because Maxl told me about it. Well, one night, I was eating supper out on my own terrace before getting ready for a ball, for court was yet in residence. And your obnoxious brother steps over my balcony as if it weren't three stories up."

Jewel choked on laughter. "I can sooo see it."

"He didn't stroll, he *sauntered.* Oh, he was enjoying himself, the rotter. At the time I thought he might be some fatuous swain I hadn't noticed in court, another one after my wealth."

"How do you know he was just after your wealth?" Jewel asked, defending her brother. "He could have, well—"

"Oh, Jewel. We'd never met, so how could he possibly be in love with me? I'm not beautiful, or clever, or famed for any accomplishments except maybe dancing, because no one ever hears me play my music, because princesses aren't supposed to entertain, only be entertained—and dancing anyone can do. I've been courted since I turned sixteen, and they *all* talk about themselves, or rather their holdings and what they can do *if.* All they want from me is my inheritance."

She said under her breath, "At least you get courted."

"No. My wealth gets courted."

"I wish I had the problem of too much money." She rolled her eyes, and then shook her head. "Never mind! Too many days wearing castoffs that we pick off clotheslines on raids. Go on."

"Well, he took my arm and told me we were going for a ride—and if I screamed he'd be forced to use his dagger. He had a fold of his cloak over one arm to hide this weapon. So we went downstairs, and he knew all the byways of our castle—and we didn't see a soul who could help me. The two guards were snoring. How he'd gotten them to drink his dreamweed-laced ale, I don't know."

Jewel snickered.

"It's not funny! We got to the bottom floor and saw people, but he squeezed my arm, and so I said nothing, for I didn't want to get anyone killed, and they said nothing, only bowed, and next thing I knew I was bundled into one of the city coaches. They are anonymous. Some of them are also old. And rickety.

And he'd managed to pick one of the very oldest, into which someone had spilled pickling juice, and it stank."

Jewel valiantly tried to suppress a snort of laughter.

"So then I realized—too late—that his blasted threats didn't make any sense, and so I said—No. I snarled, 'What kind of a stupid threat is that, to kill me? What use would I be to you dead?' And he said, throwing back the cloak, 'Well, it worked, didn't it? Even though I don't actually happen to have a knife.' And sure enough he was empty handed."

By now Jewel was rocking with silent mirth.

"He said he broke it, but I suspect he lost it in the fishpond below my balcony when he climbed up. Because the gardeners found a very fine knife in it, and were exceedingly puzzled. But that was later."

Jewel wiped her streaming eyes. "So that's what happened to his old knife from our grandfather. A fishpond! Of course he wouldn't admit it."

I tried to maintain my dignity as the injured princess, but her helpless mirth was making my lips twitch. "I couldn't think of anything to say, and I knew I wasn't strong enough to fight him, so I pretended to go to sleep. Even tried to snore."

A whoop escaped Jewel.

"Well, your brother was laughing too, the stinker. But then we both yelped when we were thrown violently to one side. The coach had gotten outside the city by then, and as you'd expect on the side roads, hit a pothole and a wheel came off. As we picked our way out, Jaim was cursing and muttering about wanting to return it because he'd had to leave some ruby ring as insurance. He hadn't stolen the coach, then, he'd gotten it legally, so as not to raise the hue-and-cry. I told him—with great enjoyment—that only an idiot would take a city vehicle out on those cow paths."

Jewel mopped her eyes with her skirt.

"So Jaim told me to hold the horses—unless I was afraid of them—while he and that driver wrestled with the wheel, which hadn't broken, it had only come unbolted. We exchanged insults while he labored with the wheel, and while he was busy I was busy as well. I got one of the horses unhitched. Or almost unhitched. I was undoing the traces on the side away from him as I vented my opinions. I'd just gotten out a good one about how he was far worse than Garian when, to my dismay, he dropped what he was doing and came toward me."

Jewel snorted. "To snarl back at you?"

"He actually had the gall to warn me. He said, 'Take my advice and have nothing to do with him.'"

"Well, he was right, wasn't he?"

"Of course he was, but still, the sheer bare-faced audacity of an abductor warning me about someone else almost caused me to ruin my escape. But I said ever so sweetly that I thanked him, and he and the driver—who was one of your gang, I guess—were in the middle of lifting the coach to slide the wheel back onto the axle when I got the other horse unhitched. Then I hopped up and rode off, leading the second horse."

Jewel snickered. "No wonder he never told me about that. Graveled!"

"So I rode straight home and found that Maxl had dispatched the guard to try to track us on all the east roads. Even *he* laughed when I told him about the invisible knife and the wheel. Anyway I was so angry I went straight to Papa and said I would accept Garian's invitation and visit Drath."

Jewel's laughter died. "Oh no."

"Oh yes, I said I'd go, and I did. I walked into that mess all by myself. And though I am thoroughly ashamed of myself, I am also angry, because I wouldn't have if it hadn't been for *your brother* and his *idiot* plans."

Jewel wrinkled her nose. "Yes, I can see why you're angry with him. And so Garian had my other brother there, and what, they tried to make you agree to marry one of them?"

"Jason wasn't there at first. It was just the two of us—and of course an army of servants and guards. I should have been suspicious when we didn't go to Ennath, which is apparently a very nice palace on a lake. That's where Garian entertains and does his public governing. We went straight to Surtan-Abrig, which is a fortress on a mountain. His personal lair."

Jewel grinned. "Which is why Jaim picked the hideout he did, for proximity. Go on."

"Not much more. Garian tried to flatter me into marrying him so we could expand Drath, but it seemed to me his hints all pointed to getting rid of Maxl. I refused as nicely as I could. So then he changed tactics. He no longer courted me for himself. Instead he now wanted me to meet Jason in order to negotiate a marriage, and I refused that too. He locked me in the room alone for a week, and when that didn't make me any more amenable he tried sarcasm, and by the time Jason arrived, he had begun the bullying."

"I suppose Jason enjoyed slapping you too?"

"He never touched me. He was scarcely ever around. I suspect he found the whole matter tiresome, because he spent most of his time out riding."

"Looking for Jaim's hideout here, I dare swear."

"Ah! That makes sense. Well, I don't really understand what he was thinking—"

"Except that he desperately needs money as well."

I heaved a mighty sigh of disgust. "Don't they all? No, Garian doesn't! Drath is rich—and it all belongs to him. He likes meddling in royal affairs is my guess. Anyway, I bribed one of Garian's 'loyal' retainers who, I suspect, hadn't the stomach for what was going on, for this was right after the worst argument of all. That was the night Garian slapped me so hard I fell down. Got the black eye. It was warm—windows open—I think the servants had to have heard. Anyway I gave the guard all my gems, climbed down, got the horse, rode—but I did go too fast. The horse foundered, threw me, and that was that."

Jewel grimaced.

"When I think how close I came to being married, I feel like I escaped certain death."

"You did," she said with complete conviction. "Because as soon as the vows were made, Jason would *sweep* you back to gloomy, horrid Lathandra, where he could extort extra money from your family and then kill you off."

"Cheering thought. So now you see why I have to go home."

"I agree."

"That means I have to escape."

"I agree."

"You do?" I stared. I'd thought I'd have to sneak out alone and flounder my way down the mountain—somehow—by myself.

"I'll even help you escape. In fact I'll show you the way. And in turn, you can show me what life in a palace is like. Not a castle. No armies around. No bandits. Just..." She sighed. "Romance."

I laughed. "It's a bargain."

Chapter Six

It would have been fun to loftily ignore Jaim, if only he'd cooperated and noticed. But he didn't.

We all met for an early breakfast. Jewel tried her best to get us to talk to one another, with no success. He was preoccupied. Bolstered by the prospect of returning home, I was no longer really angry with Jaim. In truth, it was difficult to retain my hold on my righteous wrath because he gotten me away from Garian and Jason—even if for his own reasons—and because he made me laugh.

But I was afraid of betraying my plans, so I sat woodenly. And (I have to admit) Jaim didn't notice because he probably couldn't tell the difference between Flian the haughty captive ignoring him and Flian the dull princess who only attracts fortune hunters.

Jewel looked from one of us to the other, rolled her eyes skyward and finally gave up.

Jaim's group was going to run a raid the next day, and excitement gripped them all. As soon as the meal was over, they went off to one of the cave-chambers to rehearse the details.

By midmorning, Jewel's mood had changed. She was wistful when Jaim came by her room on his way to another practice run. He kissed her goodbye, gave me a sardonic bow, then was gone.

I said, "If you're regretting your decision—"

"No, I'm feeling guilty. And I know I'll miss him. Never mind. Let me write him a letter, and we'll go down and saddle Bard, and leave."

"A letter? What for?"

"Well, *I'm* not mad at him."

I thought about Maxl and nodded. I'd missed my brother and his good sense from the moment I'd reached Garian's castle.

She dug out a pen and ink, scrawled something on a scrap of paper, then straightened up. "It's done. Would you like to add an insulting postscript or two? No? Then let us get dressed and go."

"Dressed?" I looked down at my gown, which was clean enough.

Jewel grinned. "Haven't done much in the raiding way, have you? Travel about the countryside in a wedding gown and people will be talking for days. And if Garian has his people out looking for a stray blond princess in a wedding gown, it won't take too many guesses that you might be it—and a great reward forthcoming, too."

"So?"

"So you're going to be my maid. No one ever looks at servants."

She lifted the lid on her trunk and pulled out some very worn-looking clothes. She laid out a much-washed gray skirt, a heavy linen bodice and a very old cotton blouse.

"The bodice is still good because I got too big for it before it got the least worn," she said. "You are slim, though you're much taller. It should fit you."

"Just say no figure." I worked my way out of the lace wedding gown.

"Understated figure." She chuckled. "Elegant, in a severe sort of way. Oh, I hate to leave that lovely gown!"

"I never want to see it again. As for pretty gowns, I'll make certain you get enough of them at home."

I pulled on the unfamiliar clothes and laced up the bodice. We braided up my hair, bound it round my head, and tied a kerchief over it in the way of the mountain women.

When I was done, I stood back for inspection. Jewel narrowed her eyes, calling Jason unexpectedly and most unpleasantly to mind. "Nothing fits right, which makes it more convincing. You look like a gawky sixteen-year-old—as long as you're still. When you move, you're a princess again. But we're going to load you down with bags. And I know what I ought to wear."

She dove back into her trunk and soon had on an old-fashioned cotton-wool overdress with flowers embroidered at the square neck and the dropped waist. The overdress was a plum color, with laces of silver, and the underdress was fine but undyed linen. She looked like a merchant's daughter, for they have their own formal fashions, involving guild colors and symbols.

"We'll make up our stories as we ride down the mountain," she said as she thrust clothes and a hairbrush and some ribbons into a bag. "I think we'd best leave now. If Jaim is in one of his moods, he might come after us, but he won't ride too far inside your border."

"Good."

Jewel handed me the bag. "Wait here. I have to figure out how much we'll need from the gang's money stash, and there's the horse to get ready."

She left me near the entrance. After a time she reappeared, leading the horse and carrying a handful of coins.

She quirked a rueful brow at me. "Here's my inheritance."

We mounted up and began our escape.

I won't describe our ride down the mountain trails, pretty as it was. The scenery is there, unchanged, for anyone to see who wishes. Our trail paralleled a stream, sometimes crossing. At first we could only hear it, overhung as it was by the lovely willow and blue spruce and very old alders that grew profusely in the mountains. Also heard were birds and the occasional large animal—deer, elk.

We talked about a variety of things: romance, dancing, clothes, families. Our mothers. I had no memory of mine, but I knew my brother had vague memories of her languishing voice, her lack of interest in him. She had been seventeen—wraithlike, pale of eyes and hair, like a ballad princess—when my father, late in life, made a journey to Narieth and fell suddenly and violently in love. No, not in love, for they had absolutely nothing in common, but even my father, wise as he was, mistook that violent attraction for love. As for my mother, from what my great-aunt told me later there was no love or even attraction. She married to become a queen. However, few in Carnison's court liked her.

When, not long after I was born, she'd tried intriguing one of the coastal dukes and was refused, she'd threatened to drown herself by walking into a river in full ball dress. My great-aunt had maintained she'd only meant it as a dramatic gesture, and had been taken by surprise. She had no idea how heavy a water-sodden ball dress could be, and since she'd never learned how to fasten or unfasten her own gowns, down she went before anyone could get to her.

Jewel listened with sympathy. "At least yours wasn't drunk all the time. My mother was horrid! But." She turned around on the horse, looking at me with her wide eyes. "She was not nearly as nasty as our father, who was legendary for his temper. Which I inherited." She spread her hands. "You *need* a temper, to survive *my* family. But I have never, ever, ever beaten anyone or had them beaten. I promise!"

I laughed. "I believe you."

"Oh, I don't want to remember Father. I think Jason is exactly like him. Worse, if you ask me, because he never raises his voice. It's *inhuman*. Father was a bellower—like me. Ugh. Let's talk about something else. Like food."

And so we did, keeping ourselves entertained until we decided to stop.

The air was summery, pure, sweet, and only cold after sunset. We huddled into cloaks, making a campfire in a secluded grotto. Jewel had brought some of the outlaws' journey-bread, their staple on long runs, and some fruit. Bard was not the least sweaty, having ambled at a slow pace, so he just needed unsaddling and a brush-down, and he found plenty of grass to eat. We slept and continued on in the morning.

The second day's ride brought us into the lower reaches of Drath, above the border to Lygiera—and so we rode past ancient tiers of grapevines, tended by countless generations, to produce the gold and yellow wines that were justly famed.

Later that day brought us to flatter land and our stream began to meander, sometimes rushing over rocky falls. The trail finally met with a road and took us within sight of habitation—farmland, mostly. We were now in Lygiera.

Since two of us rode one horse, we did not proceed at any dashing pace. Slow is steady, and by the time the sun was westering beyond the far mountains, we had reached a market town. Jewel guided us to the inn as we talked about our roles. It seemed an adventure to play the part of the maid.

The inn lay at a crossroads on the outskirts of town. Jewel

sashayed inside to order her room and dinner. It fell to me to take the horse to the stable and carry the bags upstairs. There I discovered I was expected to make the bed ready.

Jewel had warned me that she'd give orders and not listen to see if I understood them, but what I hadn't expected was that the innkeeper, and her daughter who ran the stable, would do so as well. No one was cruel—not like Garian's exquisite sarcasm. They looked at me as an adjunct to the work. They issued an order, then turned away assuming it would be done.

Maxl had seen to it when I was a child that I knew how to care for any horse I rode, so it was no difficulty to curry down Bard and see him fed. The innkeeper's daughter glanced once or twice, gauged the amount of feed, and then left me alone. Once I got inside, the innkeeper, who was harassed with many customers, clearly expected me to fetch and carry from the kitchens and I had no idea where to find anything.

After the fourth trip upstairs—the last time with a heavy tray—I trod back downstairs. Finally it was my turn to eat.

I was given a plate of cooked beets, boiled potatoes and a small amount of spiced fish-and-rice, which was apparently the preferred dish of the paying customers, so there wasn't much left for us. A cup of ale or water was my only choice for drink.

Stiff from the long ride and the labor after many days of forced inactivity, I chose the ale, hoping it would help me sleep. Once I had my plate I discovered there was no table set aside for servants. They sat wherever they might around the kitchen, staying well away from the place where the cook and his two helpers worked.

I spotted a stool by the roasting-fire. No one else seemed to want it, so I sat down there.

A dark-eyed young woman said scornfully, "What are you? Lady's maid come down in the world?"

"What?" I looked around—to discover everyone eying me.

For answer she got to her feet and minced over to the ale pitcher. She poured out a fresh cup, her movements so finicky, her nose so high, that several in the room laughed. "Swank," she said over her shoulder.

My face and ears went hot. "Way I was trained."

A man snapped his fingers. "Dancer. Right?"

I nodded, relieved. And it was true enough: though I wasn't a professional dancer, I'd been tutored by one ever since I was small.

"I knew it."

The dark-eyed maid shrugged, looking a lot less confrontational. "I heard dancing is a hard life, unless you get some patron or a permanent placing."

"Or unless you can act as well. Or sing," said an older woman dressed in faded livery.

"I can't sing," I said. "But I've played the lute all my life. And the harp. Um, as well as dancing."

"Dancing has to be a better life than a mistress who's too fond of the stick," someone else spoke up, causing nods and mutters of "That's right." "She beats you, that black-haired weaver's wench?" He touched his eye.

Jewel was right. They do notice things.

"It wasn't she." I wildly considered different explanations, for we'd forgotten to account for my fading black eye.

But it was clear no one had any real interest. An old man cackled. "My auntie said, if they hit you, hit 'em back. You're like to either be turned off or else you'll teach 'em some manners. Her lady came to be known as the mildest in two provinces, after auntie was through with her."

They all found that funny. I smiled, sipping my ale.

"All those weavers, they think they're royalty," the older woman grumped.

"Silk-makers are the worst." Another woman waved a dismissive hand.

The old man grunted. "All of 'em the same. No more idea about how food gets onto their plate, and the costs during famine or fine weather, than a lord. Of course *they* get paid by the piece, come bad times or good."

"That's true enough," the cook spoke up, jabbing the air with his carving knife.

Several agreed, and I suspected I could name who had come from farm folk and who hadn't.

Hoping to steer the gossip, I said, "There's some I'd never hit back. Leastways successfully." My heart slammed; would that raise suspicion?

No suspicion, but general interest.

"Talking of your weaver?"

"No, but a cousin of mine was up in Drath, at G—the

prince's castle."

The old man whistled. "Now, he's a bad one, and no mistake."

"Pays well," said the dark-eyed young woman. "But you have to have a laced lip—you don't dare make a peep. My sister knows the cook's girl. She can afford to dress like a countess, but she daren't say a single word, lest the prince find out she was talking, my sister says. Servants who blab have a way of vanishing."

The other young woman stretched, then flipped back her red braid. "No thanks. Me, I'd rather take my mistress's old gowns, and listen to her chatter about her little dogs, and have my fun at festival time, with no shadow of a stick over my back. Or worse," she added, with a gesture toward the one with the dark eyes. "People who vanish don't turn up again, not if the likes of the Prince of Drath makes 'em vanish."

Several murmured agreement, and that ended the subject.

When I was done eating, most of them had left. I went up to Jewel's room and found her yawning. "Oh, good. It's so boring, sitting here! But the parlor is all men, except for those two old women, and all they talked about was their children. So I came away. How did you do?"

"Fine. Except for being accused of swanking." I demonstrated. "Do I really move like that?"

"No. I told you before, you move like a princess—like a toff." She pursed her lips, considering. "It's probably invisible to you, all those stylized gestures, the gliding walk, where you stand in relation to other people. You expect them to give you space. You've been trained to use fine posture and to move like a princess ought at all times, ever since you were little. It stands out, here."

I frowned. "I hadn't been aware."

She grinned. "I wasn't either, until I joined Jaim's gang. But your training far surpasses mine. Besides you really do move well, when one actually watches you."

I shook my head. "That is so strange to hear."

"Why?" Jewel put her chin on her hands, her eyes narrowed in a way that brought her brothers unexpectedly to mind. "I know. You're a watcher. Not a doer. Is that it?"

"I'm not used to it. I've come to see myself more like, oh, a piece of furniture. Proper, in its place, but silent. Noticed when someone wants it."

Jewel snorted. "I think court is going to be ver-ry interesting. So. Did you hear anything of use?"

"Garian's servants don't talk, according to the gossip. People are afraid of him."

Jewel fluttered her hands. "I am not surprised."

I looked at her tray of dirty dishes, and sighed. "I guess I'd better take that back down again."

"At least you don't have to sleep on the floor, or up in the attic." Jewel gave me a grin of sympathy.

We climbed into the bed, which was a lumpy hay-stuffed mattress, but there was plenty of room for two. Jewel blew out the candle with an exasperated whoosh.

"Something wrong?" I asked, trying to find a position that would ease my stiff back.

"I started wondering. My situation is going to—well. You know, my brothers are, um. Well, one really is a villain, and the other one, it seems has, ah, had a disagreement or two with your family." She coughed, and I looked away, trying hard not to laugh. But the urge vanished when she asked wistfully, "Will that make me not welcome?"

"I'll tell Maxl that you escaped too. And if need be, we can always make up some mysterious foreign alias."

"An alias! That sounds romantic." Her voice dropped back into seriousness. "But what if your father doesn't like me?"

"Oh, he will. You've only to behave with good manners, and he'll treat you the same. He's good and kind, and has always been very wise about trade and treaties, but in recent years he's become, um, somewhat unworldly. It's Maxl who is slowly beginning to rule, though Papa reigns."

"What if Maxl doesn't like me?"

"He likes everyone. My brother is known for his good nature."

"Is he courting anyone?"

"No. Not really. He *gets* courted, especially by that horrible—" I thought of Gilian Zarda, shuddered, made an effort to dismiss her from my mind.

"Horrible?"

"Just a court predator," I said firmly. Then smiled at the image of Gilian, who worked so hard at her dainty and sweet image, hearing herself likened to a predator. "My brother hasn't been romantic with anyone since he made his trip to Dantherei when he came of age, and he fell instantly in love with the crown princess, Eleandra-Natalia ru Fidalia. It's the only silly thing he's ever done, but he hasn't swerved from his devotion. I guess he's like father in that way. And since the kingdoms have to remain friendly, she's been officially considering his suit for four years. I think it all pretense—though I don't know her and haven't been there."

"Eleandra-Natalia," Jewel repeated. "Where have I heard her name before? I mean, besides her being Crown Princess of Dantherei and apparently the most beautiful female ever to walk in the world. I am certain I've heard her name in the context of some import, but what? Well, no doubt I'll remember it some day, when it's least needed." She yawned again.

We went to sleep.

Chapter Seven

Next morning we rose early, and again I had to toil up and down the stairs to get breakfast. After that I got Bard saddled and bridled. By the time I was done I was warm, and all the stiffness had worked out of my muscles.

Then I hefted up our bags and trailed behind Jewel, mindful of my walk. What was considered "swank"? Not since my first experiences with the girls of court, and Gilian Zarda's sweet-toned nastiness, had I been so self-conscious. As I slouched behind Jewel, hiding my face behind our armload of gear, I recognized that I'd tried to become invisible as a kind of defense since those painful early days.

In any case Jewel was determined to draw attention from me. She sashayed out to the stable, her nose up, her hips rolling so that her skirts belled from side to side. She exhibited enough airs and graces for a dowager duchess at a grand ball— a duchess with a splendid figure. The male stablehands never gave me a second glance.

We mounted Bard and rode out at our sedate pace.

And the next few days passed in much the same manner. The weather was so warm and sunny we put on bonnets to keep the sun from our eyes, me wearing the worn, limp one with the faded ties. We crossed westward over farmland, past meandering rivers and rice beds, and through villages and small towns, avoiding the larger ones, where hostelries tend to be more expensive. As I learned my role, I thought of my own maid, Debrec. A woman in her forties or fifties, she was quiet, mild of voice and meticulous in her work.

Did she like her work? She had not liked the prospect of going to Drath. She hadn't complained, but I'd been aware of it. And had paid no attention, any more than the people I dealt with during Jewel's and my journey across Lygiera paid to me.

From the alacrity with which Debrec had accepted Garian's invitation to go back to Carnison without me, I had discovered her dislike of Drath was more like hatred. Garian had met my brother's honor guard at the border and had insisted on his own escort, and his own servants. It had seemed more diplomatic to concur, especially with my maid so unwilling to go on. On our arrival, while he was still acting the courting swain, he'd assigned Netta as my maid. She had been kind, efficient and untalkative.

What did those women think? I had never thought to ask Netta, and I don't know that she would have answered, but I resolved to talk to Debrec on my return home.

Which was accomplished without any trouble. We had to wait out one day in a remote inn, while rain swept through. We spent it sitting by a cozy fire. I described all the prominent figures of court. Jewel listened with close attention, sometimes asking questions that I answered guardedly. I remembered how awful Garian's slanders made me feel. I tried hard to be fair to Spaquel, and I avoided naming any more of the people I liked least.

We ran out of coins on the last day, and so we arrived in Carnison's outskirts late after sunset, our insides gnawing with hunger, and poor Bard's head drooping. I was still wearing that limp bonnet, cast aside by some town girl and snatched on a raid by one of Jaim's fast-riding outlaw women.

As we wearily closed the last distance, I compared my journey home with the journey outward. I had never seen any of the towns or villages through which my closed carriage had dashed. I'd only seen some of the countryside, and then the well-ordered courtyards of royal posting houses. Servants had all deferred, smiling, where I walked; when I sat down, food appeared instantly, and the beds were down-stuffed, aired and fresh. I never had to carry anything more cumbersome than my fan.

The city streets were busy with traders, sellers, loiterers, running children who'd been freed from the day's labors, and savory smells drifted from every inn, hostelry, bakery. We passed a couple of the bake-shops that Maxl and I had explored when we were small and had ventured out into the city on our own. Time and duty had confined Maxl, and when he'd stopped the forays I had as well. My regret for those thoughtless, fun-filled days vanished when at last I spotted the towers of the palace.

We rode up the royal avenue of tall cedars, Jewel stiff and straight-backed, her breathing audible. I pulled off the bonnet and shook my hair down. I was Princess Flian, and I was home.

The familiar chords of the sunset bells echoed up the walls when we reached the stables. The stablehands stared at us in surprise and perplexity, some of them in the act of lighting the night-lamps.

"Yes, it is I, Flian. Take care of Bard, please," I added to the stable master, who bowed. "He's been a wonder." And, lest gossip race ahead and alarm Father, I said loudly to Jewel, "And so we win our wager, do we not?"

Her thin arched brows rose, but she said in an equally modulated voice, "Yes! We won our wager!"

I could see the mental shrug that passed through the stablehands. Oh, well, then, our odd appearance was accounted for by some strange bet, incomprehensible to anyone but the aristocracy.

We walked inside.

"Wager?" Jewel whispered.

One of Maxl's stewards approached and I breathed, "Later."

"Your highness," the steward said, bowing. "Would you like to be announced?"

Question infused his request—why was I here? Ought he to have known?

For a moment I envisioned the grand announcement and dramatic appearance, but that did not seem right. "No. I'd like to surprise them, thank you. Are they in the rose room?"

The steward bowed and permitted us to pass. The staff was going to find out about my appearance before Papa did. I didn't mind that. What I did mind was court.

The rose room was my father's favorite informal interview chamber—and sure enough, there was Maxl, helping Papa to rise.

"Papa," I exclaimed as soon as the door was opened. I ran

inside.

Papa sat back down, surprise creasing his tired face, gladness widening his brown eyes as I kissed his hand and forehead.

"Flian," he murmured. "Daughter. Did I know you were here?"

Maxl gave me a warning look. I straightened up, aware of the people in the room, all staring. Ignaz Spaquel, nosy old Duke Ydbar, Gilian Zarda—three of the very court people I'd hoped to avoid.

I forced a smile. "No. A surprise, all in fun. A wager."

"Why don't you tell us about it over dinner?" Maxl suggested. "We were about to part to get dressed."

"Why, certainly. I'm glad to be home, Papa."

My father patted my hand, and once again Maxl helped him to rise.

From behind I heard Gilian whisper to her friend Elta, "My dear. Will you *look* at those gowns. If you can bear it."

When I turned they raised their fans, but their eyes betrayed derisive mirth.

Jewel's cheeks glowed, but she said nothing.

Leaning on his cane, Papa started out, his own people closing in behind him.

Gilian minced in pattering steps to the side door, the little-girl flounces at the shoulders of her gown twitching. She was followed by Elta, who sent a scornful glance over one thin shoulder, as though memorizing details of our horrible clothes. Then they were gone.

I led the way to Maxl's suite, through the stately outer chambers to the room he called his lair—a room with shabby, comfortable old furnishings and lots of books.

He appeared moments after we did, looking tense and tired.

"Oh, Maxl." I ran to him. "I have so much to tell you."

"I figured that." He hugged me, giving a wry laugh. "Just because of the length of your typical lack of communication, I knew *something* must be going on. A couple days ago came word about your sudden, almost wedding. Lady Ordomar's message was incoherent. I'd been wondering what to do. Whether or not to tell Father. Then yesterday—well, here you are. How did you get away? And are there going to be repercussions I need to plan for?"

He sank into his old chair. I regarded him fondly—and with relief. That's why he's going to be king, I thought. He looks ahead. I barely notice the here and now.

Maxl turned to Jewel. "Ought I to rise? I am Maxl Elandersi."

"No, no bows or titles or trumpets. I am Jewel Szinzar." She uttered a faint, almost soundless laugh. "I've never had bows or trumpets, yet, and I shouldn't know where to begin."

Maxl's smile had reached his eyes and Jewel's tension eased.

"We met in the mountains," I said, and when Maxl's attention turned to me, Jewel gave him a covert head-to-heels scan. Maxl looks much like me: plain, medium height, slim build, fair hair, but his eyes are brown. "Life there is, um, somewhat rough and ready."

"It's true," Jewel said, palms out. "Rougher than ready, I confess."

"Trumpets you shall have, whenever you wish." Maxl smiled. "In the meantime, welcome to Carnison." He waved a lazy hand, a glance toward me expressive of question.

Jewel dropped into another chair as I began a swift outline of what had happened to me. Papa always dressed slowly.

When I'd reached the end, I sensed from the shuttered look to his brown eyes, which were so much like Papa's, that Maxl had his own news. So I ended, "...and Jewel and I rode here without incident. But you said 'yesterday'. And I am going to hate it, I can tell from your face. What?"

"The rumor reached us yesterday that you ran off from Drath with Jaim Szinzar for a romantic tryst. I'm afraid it's all over court."

"Of course it is," I said with cordial disgust, thinking: *Gilian is here.*

Maxl gave a brief, preoccupied smile. "Well, your showing up a day later, dressed like that, will scout the rumor"—he turned to Jewel—"or it might complicate it."

"I can be a lady of mysterious origins, if you like." Jewel's merry grin dimpled her cheeks. "I would love an alias."

"No need." Maxl laughed. "What worries me most is what Garian, Jason, or even Jaim will do next, when the rumor reaches them in turn that Flian is back here—and can tell us the truth. Begging your pardon, but the Szinzars have a long history of taking whatever they want—"

"The rulers only." Jewel crossed her arms. "Jaim has a sense of honor. He was *driven* to become an outlaw."

I held my breath, but Maxl was ahead of me. He did not argue, and Jewel relaxed again, seeing that he was not going to attack her beloved brother.

"What I need to find out is what your older brother wants," Maxl said.

"Power, of course," Jewel retorted. "That's an easy one. Conquer for the sake of conquering."

"Then why didn't he take Drath? Despite all Garian's wily games, or maybe motivating them, must be the knowledge that Jason could point his sword and send his army against Drath any time he wanted, poorly equipped or not. All those years of war games in your central plains make for a formidable foe even if the command is poor—and I don't get any hints that Jason would be a poor commander."

"No," Jewel grumped, elbows on her knees and chin in her hands. "Even Jaim says that."

"So what does he want? And what's behind the rumor of restlessness in Dantherei and Drath and Ralanor Veleth and Narieth—summer maneuvers and field exercises and couriers riding hither and thither? I can believe Garian would play games for the sake of the sport, but not Jason."

Jewel shook her head. "You don't know him."

"Maybe you don't," Maxl retorted, but with humor.

Jewel's lips parted, then she rubbed her chin. "Have you met him?"

"Yes. Once. Eight or nine years ago. Right before he took the reins of government from your mother." Maxl looked over at me. "You were spending the summer at Great-Aunt Delila's, learning from that old harpist from Sartor. Jason was on a tour. He was full grown, and I was only a short, yapping pup of fifteen or so, and I thought rather highly of him. He was quiet, but not contemptuous, even when I followed him around."

"Jaim did that as well," Jewel said. "Until he started to hate Jason."

"He was only here a couple weeks, but that was long enough for me to form a good impression. Next I heard was the news of the takeover, which surprised no one, since by then I'd comprehended how badly governed Ralanor Veleth had been. After that we heard about reforms. Real ones. The edict banning torture in capital crimes, and instituting the use of the truth-herb kinthus to get true testimony, was the first, and several centuries overdue. But he also granted civilians the right to civilian trials by peer, and the next thing we heard was that those warlord dukes were rising against him for cutting into their ancient rights."

"I vaguely remember those days," Jewel said. "That's when he turned so nasty."

"Next we heard he was preparing for war. And nothing has contradicted that since." Maxl shook his head.

I said, "All that will probably matter some day, but what I want to know right now is, what shall we do about Spaquel? I've sworn all kinds of revenge since that first week in Drath."

"The Duke of Osterog," Maxl reminded me gently. "Remember he has inherited. Everyone else in court remembers. He sees to it. As for what to do? Nothing," he finished with obvious regret.

"What?"

"The only good spy is a known spy. You are not going to tell any bad stories on Garian, either, only that you two did not suit, and we will continue to be unaware of Spaquel's true loyalty to his Drath kin. Until I can find out more, we will be very, very nice to him."

"*You* will be," Jewel huffed. "I am only nice to people I like, and I already hate him almost as much as I hate Jason."

Maxl studied her, then turned to me. "As well you are back. There've been changes in the music gallery, and Master Drestian has been fretting about making decisions without your approval."

"But that was why we hired him, because he's the best we could find."

"You'll have to deal with it all tomorrow."

"I will. How is Papa?"

"As well as can be expected. He's taken the notion that he's going to die soon. He wants to make one last Progress and then abdicate. He keeps saying that we young people are playing dangerous games, too dangerous for an old man, but we must learn to control power before it controls us."

"What does that mean?" I asked, clasping my hands tightly.

"I wish I knew. No, I wish I knew who's been saying things to upset him—or if, once again, he's seeing more than I assume he is." Maxl got to his feet. "Right now we have to get dressed and nip down to the dining room."

"Come, Jewel. I'll find something of mine to fit you and we'll have the seamstresses up here tomorrow."

"A wardrobe fit for a princess," Maxl said, turning around.

Jewel drew in a deep breath, her eyes wide with pleasure.

"So she's not going to be a mystery woman?"

"No. She's who she is—you met in Drath—because not only will it scatter the rumor about Jaim and you, it will be, oh, a message of rare ambivalence for our friends to the east." He smiled, a gentle smile, but his eyes, which were usually so good humored, were now rather sardonic.

"Ah." Jewel laughed. "I'm either a gesture of friendship—a visiting Szinzar—or I'm a hostage. Right?"

"That's it." Maxl's smile deepened. "You do not object?"

"Contrary." She snickered. "I adore it. Hostage! For once I can at least pretend to have some importance to somebody. What a change!"

Maxl laughed. "But you must be nice to the new Duke of Osterog, though in private we may continue to call him Spaquel. You must be ever so polite, and people will notice you being ever so polite, because a hostage is interesting, and interesting people are very popular."

Jewel sighed, but with an expression of delight. Maxl had managed to find exactly the right thing to say.

Chapter Eight

Though Jewel professed to have spent most of her life mewed up in a castle that was more of a garrison than a home, someone had seen to it that she was trained in courtly manners. I had only to explain some of our own usages and teach her the dances. Maxl served as a willing partner after she and I had traversed the steps enough to give her confidence.

Debrec efficiently took care of Jewel's wardrobe requirements, and found her a maidservant. Soon the clothes began to arrive: morning gowns, dinner gowns and a splendid ball dress. Every arrival delighted Jewel, but the one that rendered her speechless with ecstasy was the ball gown of lace over layers of gossamer, in white and gold and the same shade of violet-blue as her eyes.

Meanwhile the busybodies had of course been busy.

"Oh Princess Flian," Gilian said the day after our arrival, dimpling up at me. "Was that...unfortunate-looking female *really* Princess Jewel of the Szinzar? Of course we only had that one glimpse...*most* unfortunate, to put it delicately, but...why is she hiding?"

"She's in bed with a cold, Gilian. As soon as she recovers, I promise, you will be the first to receive an invitation to her welcoming ball."

"Oh, how diplomatic of your dear brother! But we all know he is so very, very kind to even the most... Well! I must see about ordering a gown suitable for so...*unique* a visitor."

And not long after, Corlis, one of Gilian's friends, stopped me on my way to the music school, sidling looks right and left before she asked, "Why did that princess ride in dressed like a dairy maid?"

Gilian should have had the wit to coach you to use another term if she doesn't want me to know she put you up to this. Out loud I said, "A wager."

Corlis shrugged, her thin shoulders rising abruptly. And to my surprise stalked right on to the music school as if she'd meant to go there, instead of scurrying directly back to Gilian.

Jewel's first appearance was not at a ball, but at an evening's concert, impromptu, that I arranged so I could hear a new quartet our music master thought of hiring as teachers. Maxl, who usually ignored such things, quietly invited a few people who were polite, reliable, and had a nominal interest in music.

Jewel wore one of her new gowns. I thought her mood one of anticipation until I saw her draw a deep breath and grip Maxl's arm before we entered the long drawing room. My observant brother had perceived what I had missed, that the courageous, outspoken Jewel was in fact afraid.

But the guests' calm politeness caused her to relax. I also observed that she had less interest in music than she had in people. I could not resent that as my own brother was the same.

She enjoyed herself so much that she ventured out with me on a walk the next day. Before we'd reached the lakeside we were surrounded by a crowd. The questions soon began, but Maxl had told her, *Least said, less to defend,* and so she only laughed with a mixture of mirth and hauteur that most of the fellows, and several of the females, found fascinating. That and her being one of those sinister Velethi added to her air of mystery.

On her fourth night, Maxl gave an informal dance. The fellows instantly took to her, for she was funny and pretty, and the new gown suited her lovely figure. I was relieved when my most determined suitors deserted me for her side; if they began fishing for information about her inheritance, she seemed capable of handling them better than I ever had.

And she was happy.

One night I was alone with Debrec, and while rain thrummed against the windows, I said, "May I ask a question?"

She paused in the act of rolling ribbons into the neat spools that kept them wrinkle-free.

"Your highness?"

"What I mean is, you do not have to answer if you do not like."

She merely paused, folding her hands, her dark eyes patient.

"What made you choose to be a lady's maid?"

"My mother served your grandmother, and her mother before that, your highness."

I was disappointed. "You never considered anything else?"

A brief flicker of humor quirked the corners of her mouth. "Not to any advantage, your highness. I grew up knowing the work. I like living in a palace. Your family has been, if you'll pardon my speaking freely, easy."

"I asked for free speaking."

"It can be asked, but the answers can be costly," she answered in a low voice.

So I had trespassed, then. "I spent the week after I, ah, left Drath as a lady's maid. One of the oldest proverbs our tutor gave us when I was learning to write was *The good king spends a year in his street-sweeper's shoes.* I'd always thought it hyperbole."

Debrec said nothing.

"Now, I'll never be a king, or even a queen, for my brother is healthy and I trust and hope he will live long and serenely, but now I see the wisdom in it. At least, it has made me reflect on things that hereto were such an unquestioned part of my life they were invisible."

Debrec bowed, looking somewhat nonplussed.

I said, "You did not want to go to Drath and I heeded your wishes not. It was very bad after you left—I won't go into it, but suffice it to say that my stay was nasty. I wish you'd felt the freedom to warn me."

Debrec looked from me to the window and then back. "Your pardon, highness, but in truth I knew only that I dislike travel and foreign places. The quarters are usually unpleasant, and there's the home servants and their quirks to deal with."

"So you didn't know that Garian is a thorough-going villain?"

"One hears things," she murmured. "But I fear my thoughts were confined to my own comfort, your highness."

"Thank you for talking to me, Debrec."

She curtseyed, picked up all my sleeve ribbons and took them out. She was going to roll them somewhere else.

Had I made her job impossible? No, for she would pretend nothing had happened. And either she was as good a dissembler as the best courtier, or she was not, in fact, omniscient about politics and personalities.

Two more days passed, with rain framing the grand ball we hosted. Jewel never got tired of wandering about the palace, pausing to observe the light through the high windows, or to exclaim over the carving and the shape of an old chair or table. She had learned, from somewhere, the names of the old styles, and she appreciated things that were so familiar to me I had ceased to notice them at all.

I saw our palace anew through her eyes: pleasing, airy, and unable to be defended, for the castellations had been gradually removed over the last couple of centuries, walls knocked down to broaden the gardens, other walls pushed out to make room for the winter conservatory and the summer terrace, windows widened to let in light and air. She adored the gardens, the drawing rooms and especially the ballroom. The only room she showed little interest in was the library. She liked people, not books—apparently their "barracks of a castle" in Lathandra possessed a good library, which was no credit in her eyes.

Every morning she scrupulously came to sit and listen to me do my daily exercises on my harp and my lute, until I caught her fighting yawns. I chased her out and bade her go riding or walking.

She also loved the food. Lygiera being a coast state, fish is often served, along with rice and the vegetables of the season. She spoke with loathing of dishes that mostly featured potato in limited guises. *Army food*, she declared.

Maxl seemed to find her as diverting as she found life at court, for I'd not seen him at social events so frequently in the past year as I did in that week. The two bantered back and forth, and she often made my serious, overworked brother laugh. As Maxl had predicted, she was increasingly popular. Particularly with the men.

And so came the night of her true introduction to Carnison's court, at the grand ball my brother hosted. Because she was the guest, she walked in on his arm, and though they were behind Papa—who escorted me—they were the focus of the room.

To my surprise, Gilian was one of the first to rush up to her, yellow ribbons fluttering. "Another handsome gown," she fluted. Then turned to me, her diminutive lace-edged fan flickering in butterfly mode—meaning breathless delight. "Oh, Princess Flian, are we to have a leader in fashion at last?"

Maxl smiled, as did most of the fellows, but almost all the women glanced covertly at me, because the insult was aimed my way.

Jewel said, "Do you like it? I'm so glad. Princess Flian picked the design. I think she was quite right."

Gilian pursed her pretty bud lips in an "O" of surprise. "Why, what wonderful taste! I hope this is a promise for a splendid season this year..." Blond ringlets bouncing, she tiptoed between Jewel and Maxl, shook her ringlets back, and turned her smile up to Maxl. "Do promise us." She wrinkled her little nose and pouted out her lower lip in the exact same way that had gotten all the adults laughing fondly and petting and cooing over her when we were all children.

"But it takes more than one person to make a splendid season," Maxl said, and signaled with a nod to the herald, who rapped his staff and announced the promenade. He added pleasantly, "I invite you to make your best effort as well."

Gilian curtseyed, Maxl bowed to Jewel—Papa bowed to me—and Gilian turned with a helpless flutter of her fan to Lord Yendrian, Maxl's best friend.

Of course he bowed. And, with her gentle guidance—I could see her small hand on his wrist—they took precedence of all the young heirs, behind the older courtiers.

Jewel's second dance was with Spaquel, the youngest duke. I saw her dash off with him, smiling and determinedly polite. At least he was a very good dancer, I thought. Then a hand touched my shoulder, and I looked up into familiar dark eyes, cleft chin, delightful lopsided smile.

"Yendrian!"

"Dance?" he asked.

"Of course!"

Yendrian had been my very first practice partner after I dared venture from the safety of practicing with Maxl, when we were in our middle teens. In fact, I strongly suspect Maxl had put Yendrian up to it—not that it would take much. He was always kind.

"How are your horses?" I asked.

Yendrian's eyes crinkled. "Is that a real question or a court question?"

I smothered a laugh. "I haven't blundered out with that question for years."

"It might be awkward, but it's true. At least, it seems to pop into my head more and more as the years swing by. But I don't say it aloud. Except to Maxl. Or you." He chuckled. "As for your question, get ready: there's a lot of news."

Yendrian's passion was horses and he raised the best. His family's lands lying next to Papa's summer home, which came to us through my grandmother, he'd been a part of our lives from early days, when he and Maxl used to build enormous mud cities on the side of the lake. Yendrian told a couple of anecdotes about his more eccentric animals as I watched idly; Jewel was smiling and I saw Maxl, observant as always, smiling to see her smile.

After that dance, I found myself dropping into my usual habit, prowling the perimeter near the musicians to listen for new talents, and avoiding my fortune hunters—who all seemed to have shifted allegiance without a backward glance. So much for my vaunted attractions.

Presently Jewel was surrounded by an eye-pleasing bouquet of lace-draped skirts. To my surprise, I recognized the diminutive figure in yellow next to her, walking arm and arm and pointing her fan hither and yon as they made a circuit of the room. Gilian's friends followed, all talking and laughing, some with partners, others not. Jewel really was becoming popular. I have to admit that envy constricted my heart for a moment, flinging me back into childhood memory when I'd tried wrinkling my nose the way Gilian did, but the adults didn't coo, they looked away, or I was asked briskly if I had my handkerchief.

If Jewel becomes a fashion leader, then everyone will enjoy court life. This cheering thought made envy vanish like fog in the sun.

"Come, Flian, you cannot escape." The newcomer was tall, his smiling brown face framed by curling dark hair.

"Althan," I exclaimed. Another of Maxl's old friends.

He grinned. "If I promise not to propose to you, will you dance with me?"

I laughed. "You, at least, have not mentioned my fortune once since we were sixteen."

"But my mother still does." He held out his hand. "Will you hurry up and spend it?"

We danced, our conversation mostly jokes, but he did ask an oblique question or two about Jewel, to which I firmly replied, "You must ask her." I did not blame him. His mother was notorious for seeking ways to expand the Rescadzi fortune.

And so the evening wore on, and I was in the balcony near the musicians, dreaming a new melodic line that I'd like to try weaving in with the old familiar tunes, when a rustle and a fan-snap broke my reverie. I looked up and there was Jewel.

"Are you enjoying yourself?" I asked, as no one was near.

Her blue eyes widened, reflecting the light of the chandeliers. "Oh. I cannot tell you how much. But I have some questions. First, is it so terrible to be fat, and second, *am* I fat?"

"Being fat is terrible only if whoever leads fashion isn't fat. Same as being thin. Look at the tapestries down the great hall, and you can tell something about who led style. Right now, well, we don't have any real lead in style, but there are those who want to lead…"

"You're not saying her name, but I think I know who you mean." Jewel frowned, not in anger, but in concentration. "I'm not familiar with females. How they think. How they act among themselves. My maid at home was a good person and she told me a lot of things, but I was young and stupid and dismissed most of what she said because she was only a maid. Then there are Jaim's girls, but all they talk about is fighting and riding, and though they do talk about flirting, well, I always stayed away. Thinking of my rank. Now I see I was a fool…" She fought a yawn. "I must get used to these late evenings! I've never had late evenings before. Anyway, Gilian came to me, and it was like having thousands of fragrant flowers dropped on me, her compliments. At first I couldn't see why you don't like her—I can tell, you don't—but after a time, oh, all those comments about how she regretted how tiny and fragile she is, how small and dainty, how difficult it is to be so very, very delicate, yet always in contrast to you, or the others, always women, never the men, though they are much bigger and louder, if not more clumsy. Did you know you are clumsy?"

I spread my hands. "Clumsy and boring and awkward and gangling. I've heard it all my life. So maybe it's true. She certainly thinks it is."

"Maybe—from a teeny-tiny perspective. Except you aren't clumsy. But you are tall and quiet, and probably don't lead. Am I right?"

"You are."

She nodded. "I think I see. So when she says that our court needs fashion and style, it's not just aimed at you for not leading, she's saying she should lead. Yes?"

"You have to realize that Maxl can choose his wife, unlike most princes. We are at peace and Papa promised us from very early on."

She observed Maxl in the middle of the pale peach marble ballroom floor, dancing with Corlis. "But he'll do his duty. Won't he."

"Oh, I don't know. We don't talk about such things, truth to tell."

Jewel put her elbow on the carved balcony rail and her chin in her hand. "Truth—and lies. Gilian didn't lie. She really is tiny. Those little eyes, but set well apart in her face. Tiny nose. Tiny bud of a mouth. Tiny ears, tiny feet, tiny hands, smallest waist in the room—and do you know she actually pointed that out, without saying it directly? Does it matter, how small a waist is? Jaim never talked about waists, but what sticks out, when he commented on girls' figures." She grinned.

"I think, from what I've read, that what girls like in other girls is not always what the men like, questions of attraction aside."

Jewel snapped her fan open. "So under all those flowers of compliments, the truth is that she wants to be queen, is that it?"

I spread my hands.

"My very dear Princess."

We whirled around—both being princesses—to find Ignaz Spaquel, Duke of Osterog, right behind us, having come up as silently as a cat.

Jewel sent me a look behind her fan—how much had he

heard?—before he bowed elaborately.

"I was delighted to discover that our charming visitor has a penchant for the art of the spoken word." He smiled and bowed again, but the corners of his mouth, the faint quirk under his long-lashed eyes, reminded me of Garian. I stiffened. Yes, he really was like Garian, the words so friendly, the tone so smug, the attitude of the body watchful and wary.

I turned to Jewel, trying to regain my inner balance. "You like poetry?"

She made a helpless little gesture. She'd uttered polite nothings while dancing, and now it seemed he was taking them seriously.

"I am come—I trust I do not intrude?—to invite you personally to our poetry reading the morning after tomorrow."

How could she gracefully refuse so direct an invitation? Some had the wit and skill, but Jewel was far too new to courtly talk, and so she said in a faint, rather wistful voice, "I would be delighted."

Spaquel's group of pretentious poets was long familiar to me, and I'd avoided them for years, and he knew it, but now he turned to me. "Surely, your highness, if your friend graces our gathering, you would not deny us a single visit? Your discerning musical ear—our efforts to please—I trust, I do trust, you will be surprised."

He smiled.

I felt uneasy, then mentally shook it off. This was Garian's cousin, not Garian, and though they had a few traits in common, Spaquel's smarmy flattery was hardly the same as slapping someone and laughing when she trips over a hassock and falls on her face.

And if I refused so direct an invitation, I would be rude. "Thank you for the compliment. And the invitation."

He bowed, Jewel curtseyed, I curtseyed.

He sauntered away and Jewel let out her breath. "Poetry," she muttered. "Well, how bad can it be?"

Chapter Nine

That morning Jewel came to my room. "What shall I expect?"

Pretension. But it did not seem right to say that. "I don't like what they do with words," I said slowly. "And even if I did, the way they read..." I shook my head. "Perhaps they are wonderful, perhaps there is a style in these things. But they sound like courtiers—the words saying one thing, the way they watch each other, and smirk—the meaning and the manner don't match up. I guess I trust music more. Words seem like ice in the springtime, leaving one uncertain where one can step."

Jewel gave me that narrow, assessing look, chin in hand. "That's it," she exclaimed. "I have it at last. You're so polite. So shuttered, you and your brother. I still don't know where his true self is, but yours is in your music. I saw you smile the other day when I found you playing that harp. A real smile. In fact, you tell your emotions through your music."

"I do?"

"Of course. Because you're inside it, in effect." She rose and shook out her skirts. "Most don't listen, so they don't hear it. It's time to go."

I made a sour face as I reached for my cup.

She crossed her arms, head tipped. "Oh, Flian, surely a morning of silly poems cannot be as bad as a morning spent in the company of Garian and Jason!"

"True! It's that I had a terrible thought. You're in a fair way to becoming a fashion, and if you make those readings fashionable, Spaquel will hold them even more frequently."

Jewel laughed. "He does have pretty eyes!" Her grin was mischievous. "If he's the worst thing I'll find here, I could stay forever. I am so glad we've heard nothing from the two villains."

"Jaim and Jason?"

"No!" Her brows drew together. "Jason and Garian. I confess I'm relieved I haven't heard from Jaim, much as I adore him. I'm afraid he wouldn't want me to stay for some pig-headed reason."

"He'd better not show up." I glared at the window. "Two abductions is enough. Even if one was a rescue."

Jewel tapped her fingers on the side of her cup. "You know, an idea occurs. Why should we wait for him? Or any of them? Why shouldn't *we* plan an abduction?"

I choked on a sip of steeped leaf.

She laughed. "Yes. We'll abduct Garian. Or Jason."

"And—?"

"And dump them into the ocean. Nobody would ever pay a ransom for *them*."

"Too much work," I said. "And no reward."

She waved her hands. "You're lazy. I shall have to consider this plan."

I set down my cup and rose, shaking out the delicate skirts of my new walking dress. "Oh, let's go and get this thing over."

"He said last night that the reading will be held in the gazebo in the rose garden since the weather is so fine. Where were you, by the bye?"

"Listening to the children's choir—" I was going to explain, saw her eying my gown rather than listening to my words, and suppressed a smile.

She said, "Oh, that is lovely. How I wish I could wear that shade!"

"It's one of the few that don't make me look as washed out as shorn wool." I smoothed the fine layers of midnight blue. An elaborate lace collar was the only added color. On impulse, to bolster my spirits for the boredom ahead, I'd also put on a diamond-and-sapphire necklace that Maxl had given me when I first appeared at court, and added diamond drops to my ears.

I glanced out the window. "Rain clouds! Perhaps we are saved."

"They're too far away. No rain before afternoon. You like my new walking gown? The rose garden is a perfect setting for it to be seen, if only by Spaquel." Jewel's gown was dusky rose with cream lace and gold embroidery. The sleeve ribbons were gold and rose as well. Obviously this was her favorite color—I had seen at least two rose gowns so far.

On our way out she brandished a rolled piece of paper. "Besides, I went to all the trouble of writing my very first poem, and I don't want to waste the chance of making you laugh. But I wonder if I ought to turn it into a song." She fluttered her eyelashes. "I really have considered flirting with dear Spaquel, if only to get him to let some of his secrets slip."

I laughed. "Mangle words all you like, but if you mangle music then I run away."

We were still joking when we crossed the little bridge to the rose garden, which was some distance from the palace. Spaquel was inordinately fond of "proper settings" for those readings, but most of them had been in the castle hitherto.

We entered the gazebo and found three older court ladies who had long claimed to be noble poets, one of Gilian Zarda's friends, and old Count Luestor, who looked like an tall, thin owl. Spaquel presided. As soon as he saw us, he swept forward, giving us an unctuous smile as he bowed most elaborately.

"Your highnesses," he drawled. And again there was something in his manner, a sense of hidden irony, of secret knowledge, that contradicted his gracious tone and low bow. The tone was too gracious, the bow too low.

I was being mocked, yet there was nothing I could think of to say except a bland politeness. As usual. "I have come to hear my friend's essay into poesy, your grace. And to delight in the works of everyone present."

They bowed. I bowed.

Spaquel peered out. "I believe we will begin. Latecomers will have to miss the pleasures in store. Lady Belissa?"

Lady Belissa rose with deliberate dignity and fussed with her paper, which a scribe had written out in exquisite handwriting for her. When she'd given us each a stern look to make certain we were attentive, her ladyship sonorously intoned, with quivering rhyme at the end of each line, a twenty-two-verse lament to her lapdog—which (it was rumored) had been overfed with candies by her ladyship, poor little creature.

My jaws creaked as I gritted my teeth against a yawn. Jewel, who'd stayed up even later than I had the night before, obviously fought yawn after yawn; the sheen of tears in her eyes made Lady Belissa smirk and flutter.

After polite clapping, Count Luestor rose, his knees popping, and muttered his way through something totally unintelligible.

Third was Corlis Medzar, one of Gilian's friends. She batted her eyelashes at Spaquel, lifted her fine nose, and launched into a loud, dramatic ballad dedicated to a lover. Judging from the astonishing list of his superlative qualities, a very imaginary lover. It was difficult to tell if she actually had a good singing voice because she added so many flourishes and trills that she sounded like a bag of demented parakeets.

Next was Spaquel's turn. He drew himself up. Jewel leaned forward, her gaze limpid.

Spaquel warbled:
I rise at dawn to watch the sun
Don the colors of the day.
Its sumptuous plumage melting into brightness...
I sigh in melancholy hope
That the colors will shine,
Reflected in her eyes,
Already the color of the sky,
Gazing humbly otherwhere
Like doves cooing on a rooftop
And flying, flocking to the sun
Like arrows
They rise to my face.
Oh yes! Oh yes! My heart cries
As dawn fills the skies of my mind.

Jewel fluttered her eyelashes at that reference to sky-colored eyes and simpered at Spaquel. He smirked as the polite applause ushered him back to his seat. Then he looked out of the gazebo. I wondered who else he could be expecting. Anyone wise had surely taken a detour and was on the other side of the gardens. I longed to be back inside and practicing my harp again. After my month away, my fingers had lost some of their flexibility, and I had two or three new songs forming in my head.

The second of the older ladies rose to sing a love song. The melody was a familiar one to which she'd adapted a popular witty, dashing old poem, and she'd gotten the cadence and the rhymes to fit. Jewel and I were enthusiastic in our clapping this time. But the third countess made up for the lapse into talent by unloading a forty-eight-verse epic dedicated to the summer song of her dove.

Then it was Jewel's turn.

Her voice sweetly intoned:

Elegant are the peacocks
In plumage glitt'ry and bright
Loudly the bantams strut about
Displaying raffish might.
Oh, the peacocks' display
The bantams gray
The sight, I say,
Display and gray,
A glorious bold parade

But making up this admirous flock
Are lesser and greater kind.
Some peacocks then, some plainly stout
Or plumed, mismatched dull you'll find
Oh, lovely as snow
Or distressingly low
Their numbers grow
The snow, the low,
All make a sumptuous show.

And with a melting glance Spaquel's way, she launched into her third verse:

The bantams too own fine and flat—

That's as far as she got, because the four arched doorways went dark.

Silent men in Maxl's new blue battle tunics blocked the exits, swords drawn. But I had never seen any of these fellows before and they did not act like our guards, unobtrusive and distant.

"No one move," said one of them. His gaze swept us all, stopping when it reached Jewel. He nodded and two more came in, passing their fellows in silence, and moved to her side.

"Stop it," Jewel exclaimed. And then, in utter disgust, "Oh, I don't believe it. I *don't!*"

The leader ignored her, frowning at each of the young women, his gaze turning my way—

And Spaquel gasped, waving a hand at me as though shooing away insects. "Oh, not *her highness!* Princess Flian, you *must* flee *at once!*"

I'd already gotten to my feet, but there was nowhere to go. The leader stared at me, motioning to two huge fellows. "That's t'other one, then. Right."

Moments later a thin dagger flashed near my neck. Over it I met Lady Belissa's terrified gaze. The countess with the dove had fainted. Poor old Count Luestor was wrestling with the dress rapier at his side, but the two strong young men had pulled me—struggling mightily—from the gazebo before he managed to get it free of its scabbard.

Down one of the paths to the shrubbery-hidden stream. I managed one glimpse of Jewel, who wept in sheer rage as she stalked between two big fellows in ill-fitting blue tunics.

I resisted as best I could, but it made absolutely no difference. I berated myself for refusing Maxl's offers to share his lessons in sword fighting because it cut into my music time.

All right then, if you can't fight, scream. I drew in my breath but one of the fellows in the blue tunics said in an embarrassed half-command, half-apology, "If you yell, we have to gag you."

I still couldn't believe it was really happening. The familiar garden, the nodding roses, the smell of jasmine, made the crunching martial footsteps, the subdued clink of chain mail absurd.

My thoughts raced around inside my head like frightened mice, squeaking: *Not again! Not again! Not again!*

And then we stopped.

Jewel gasped.

There, leaning against an oak tree, sword point resting on the ground, was Jason Szinzar.

Chapter Ten

"Clean job, boys," he said to the fellows in blue. And to Jewel, "It's been a long time, little sister."

Jewel stomped around in a circle. "How dare you! Oh, how I loathe you! Curse you! Norsunder take you!"

Several of the guards looked away, their expressions wooden. The biggest one blushed to the tips of his ears as he caught hold of Jewel again.

Jason gave her one sardonic glance, then saluted me with his sword. "We meet again." Was he trying not to laugh?

Since I couldn't think of an insult vast enough to express my irritation, I glared.

"You notice," Jewel snarled over her shoulder to me, while doing her best to wrench free, "the rotten coward slunk about here and didn't even have to listen to the poems."

"Perfidious," I declared.

"Let's go." Jason waved a hand and turned away. He was! He really was on the verge of laughter. And so were some of his men.

I glowered at his back, not believing what was about to happen.

But it did.

They ringed us so there was no chance of running (not that I could have run far or fast in that fragile gown) and someone came forward with lengths of cotton fabric and huge, heavy woolen army cloaks. Despite our efforts, Jewel and I had cloth wrapped round our faces as gags, sashes round our wrists, and the rest of us swathed tightly in those cloaks. When we had been wrapped like rugs, we were picked up and carried. It was hot and breathless inside our cocoons, making it impossible to struggle any longer.

We were deposited in something that was soon shaking and rumbling.

I suspect the binding and the cloaks were mostly to keep us busy. Jason, unlike Jaim, knew what he was about when he wanted to make off with a pair of princesses.

When we had fought our way free of the cloaks and gags, gasping and sweaty, it was to discover that we were in a chaise. The windows had been wedged shut and the door locked from without. From the rocking, I was certain that four, perhaps six horses pulled it.

Peering out the narrow windows showed outriders still wearing Lygieran blue. No one would stop us. I was angry—and amazed at the sheer effrontery, so audacious it was going to be successful.

"Here, help me get these knots undone," I said to Jewel, who wept in passionate fury. Her breath shuddered as she endeavored valiantly to suppress her tears, and we sat back to back.

We wasted a lot of time getting the sashes loose, and then we wasted more time trying to pry the windows open. At last we sank back, exhausted, angry, and I have to admit, afraid.

"Spaquel set us up," I said. "For Jason? I do not understand. Something's missing, I feel sure."

"Yes! His head! Or will be, when I get free and find myself a nice, big sword. Argh!"

"Spaquel or your brother?"

"Both! But especially Spaquel!" Jewel struck her fist against the cushioned seat. "That's another thing that makes me desperate. I thought I was so clever in flirting with him, and he was intending this *outrage* all along!"

"And probably saw to it that our real guards were nowhere near the rose garden or the gate beyond. And from there, with those fellows wearing our colors, no one will think to interfere. One thing, though, Maxl will get control of the guard at last when he finds out."

"If he finds out," Jewel cried.

"He has to. Spaquel might lie, but all those witnesses—"

"But what did they see, beyond us being taken? If Spaquel hands some lie to them as well, how will they know it for a lie?

None of those people would have followed us, much less tried a rescue."

"Poor old Luestor." I shook my head. "I'm glad he didn't try to rush one of those fellows with that old sword—and drop in heart failure."

Jewel's color was high, but now she looked determined. "Jaim says that the essence of command is to turn surprises to your favor. You get your perimeter outside the enemy's perimeter, and attack."

"What does that mean, exactly?"

"Oh, I don't know, some kind of military jabber. I was hoping you knew." She scowled. "I never paid attention when he tried to teach me—I was too busy daydreaming about balls and parties. Now I wish I had."

A very long ride ensued; it was dark when at last we stopped, and the door was unlocked and opened.

We climbed out, looking about cautiously. I was glad to stretch my legs. The silent liveried men closed around us and we crossed a moss-stoned courtyard into what appeared to be a fine house. The wall visible to us had diamond-paned glass windows amid ivy.

Inside, down a narrow stone hall, to a gallery whose portraits featured fine-featured, red-haired people in various fashions of long ago.

I knew where we had to be: Osterog, on our eastern border. Spaquel's estate. At first sight, that would argue for some kind of alliance—except Spaquel was not there. The courtyard of the stable was empty except for Jason's entourage.

We were led straight to an old parlor, where a new fire had been laid. Jason was there, taking off his cloak. The fire had not even begun to take the chill off the room. Jason, who had gotten rid of his mail coat and battle tunic in favor of a plain tunic-shirt, appeared to be comfortable, but I was chilled in my fragile tissue gown.

Jason dropped into a chair and stretched out his dusty riding boots. "Well, Jewel, what scheme is Jaim running now?"

I knelt before the fire and held my hands out.

"*Jaim?*" Jewel cried. "What? I haven't seen him since we left!" She paused, then said in a sharp wail, "Oh, you stupid fool. You think he *sent* us to Carnison?"

He stared at her and I could see his disbelief and question, even though at first he did not speak.

"Oh, murder." Jewel heaved a mighty sigh, flopping down onto the hearth. "I can't believe—what lies did Garian tell you about Jaim?"

I sat back on the hearth, thinking not of politics or war, but absurdly enough of my harp, which I wasn't going to see unless a miracle happened—and which I would have been happily playing right about now if I hadn't been a good princess and agreed to go to that cursed poetry reading. "Make that double murder."

"Where is Jaim?" Jason asked finally.

"I don't know!"

Jason's head lifted, and he considered her.

"I helped Flian escape and I haven't seen him since. I was enjoying myself for the first time in my life—"

"Do you know where his hideout is?"

"Somewhere in the mountains. That's all I know." She shrugged with her arms crossed. "If there's anything I hate besides a villain, it's a *boring* one. This is so unfair! You know I don't have anything or know anything, but you just love being a bully and a stinkard—" She launched into a loud, impassioned list of his rotten qualities.

Jason stared into the fire, then turned his head. It was a small movement, but his expression, his stillness, indicated sudden decision. "Markham. Take my sister to the adjoining parlor. See that she gets something to eat and drink."

Jewel gasped. "You weren't even listening to me!"

A very tall, silent figure, hitherto hidden by the shadows at the door, stepped forward and gestured to Jewel. She glanced back at me, angry, puzzled and now plainly worried. I rose to follow, but Jason held out a hand.

"Not you."

Jewel began to protest. The henchman closed the door and her voice faded away into the distance.

Jason said to me, "Where did Jaim take you? She was lying, but you have no cause to."

"I was blindfolded."

"But not when you left."

I shrugged. "His hideout was somewhere in the mountains

near Drath, some winding trail I could never find again if I tried for a year. Look. As far as I'm concerned you and Jaim can go make war on each other with my full approval. But I like your sister, and for her sake I won't willingly betray any more than that."

He looked at me meditatively for a long, neck-prickling wait. It wasn't a Garian-like mocking assessment, the false air of concern contradicted by the subtle signs of anger. Of threat. If anything, the one narrowed eye, the slight furrow in his long black brows that reminded me of Jewel, indicated ambivalence. He said, "I could get it out of you. I'm trying to decide if it's worth the trouble."

My heart constricted. My voice came out steadily enough. "I hope that means you could make me drink truth-herb. I understand you use it at your military courts now. But before you go to all that effort, let me assure you anything I'd say would be the same as I'll tell you now. Except you'll hear a lot more about how I hated that stay in Drath. Oh you'll probably get a couple of lectures on proper fingering, the correct method of tuning that preserves harp strings, and how the ignorant think there is only discipline in war and not in music."

He got to his feet. I tensed. His steps receded, the door opened and shut.

I whirled around—and there was a guard watching me, the fires reflecting in his eyes.

Presently the door opened again. This time one of Spaquel's servants came in, wearing his fussy livery. The man smirked at me as he set down a heavy silver tray. "Dinner, Princess. The Velethi king's orders."

I ignored the goblet of wine and turned my attention to the plate. Fish cooked in wine sauce, fresh green beans, rice and custard made the meal.

I set to with a will. When I finished, the man still stood there. "The wine as well."

"I won't drink any wine poured by any Herlester or Szinzar ever again." I was thinking of Jason's threat—and kinthus, the herb that makes one tell the truth, plus anything else a questioner wishes to hear. "There's *always* something nasty in it."

"Drink it," the man ordered. "Now."

Not *again!*

For answer I picked up the goblet and flung its contents in his face. And laughed as I said, "*You* drink it." I flung the goblet at him too.

He raised a fist, and I retreated round the back of the chair. Spaquel's minion kicked the goblet so it spun away, and left. The guard at the door was so wooden I glared at him suspiciously, but he neither spoke nor moved.

My heart thumped. It wasn't long before the weasel-faced Spaquel lackey returned and behind him was Jason.

"Care for some wine, Flian?" Jason was smiling—not the smirk of the weasel, but the sort of smile that verges on laughter.

"Not if it's got kinthus in it. I already told you the truth and I resent the implication that I am a liar—"

"Not kinthus. Drink it up," Jason invited.

"No!"

"Assist her," Jason said to the weasel, who grabbed and held my arms. I writhed, now mad at Maxl for not insisting that I spend my entire day training for war. But who would have known my life would end up this way?

The other guard rather fastidiously pinched my nose, and when I whooped in a breath, in went the wine. I coughed and after that realized I wasn't going to win, so I drank it, and then mopped at where it had splattered down the front of my gown.

"Very edifying," Jason observed.

"It's *your* fault," I said crossly, getting up to shake my skirts out. "Why this utterly uncivilized idiocy?"

Jason dismissed the weasel, who glowered in disappointment but withdrew.

"You'd better sit," he said. "While we wait for our friend to ride for the capital with word of what just happened."

"I will, I will." Then the words sank in. "You *wanted* someone to see me drink that stuff? *Why?*" I mopped at the gown, trying not to tear it. Already my hands felt heavy. Some officious soul had put in a hefty dose.

Jason moved to the window. Through it came the faint sound of a galloping horse, rapidly diminishing.

"My uncivilized idiocy serves a couple of purposes. We are going to make a journey, you and I. Of necessity I must cut down on the number of personnel accompanying us. So you are going to have a peaceful, relaxing ride."

"Ugh." Not kinthus, then—sleepweed. My jaw felt heavy now. "Wh-what about Jewel?"

"She's asleep in one of the other rooms. If I am right, when she wakens she will discover that she has been 'rescued' by Spaquel, and she will, no doubt, be escorted back to the capital by her hero."

"Villainous," I managed. "I mean, to make her grateful to that...that..."

His light blue gaze swam and swirled into darkness.

&

I woke up shivering. My face was wet. My nose hurt.

Smoke?

I struggled to sit up. I was bound in swaths of a heavy, sodden cloak.

My brain yammered *fire? Smoke?* I peered stupidly around me. I lay in an open carriage. Tall trees not far away whooshed and writhed, gigantic torches radiating hot, bright flame.

Danger!

I got a hand free and fought the cloak off, biting my lips against a scream of impatience. Just above, the burning branches weakened in the curling blasts of heat-wind, raining bits of flaming foliage on the wild grasses bordering the road.

I got free of the cloak and scrambled out of the carriage, stumbling from dizziness. I forced myself away from the carriage a few steps, then lurched to a stop when I discovered a human figure sprawled in the path of the flames.

The glaring, ruddy light shone on a face.

Jason.

A deep, neck-tingling *whoosh* overhead made me throw my head back in horror. A fiery branch tumbled down, landing with a crash of upward spiraling sparks not ten paces behind me.

I started to run. Looked back. Jason lay, either dead or unconscious, one arm flung out toward the ruined carriage, blood splashed across him. I backed up one step, two, my innards tight with anguish. I knew I could never leave anyone to burn to death, no matter how I felt about the person when awake and face-to-face. But was he already dead?

I stared down at him, uncertain what to do, as the world revolved. His head turned slightly. One hand groped, and fell slack again.

He was alive. But wouldn't be for long.

"I hate you," I screamed stupidly, over and over, as burning twigs rained down around me.

I sprang to him, grabbed one of his wrists, and tugged. He only shifted. So I grabbed at his sodden shirt, but it was summer fabric, and the rents already in it made it rip worse.

Another branch crashed ten paces away, sending up a whirling fury of sparks.

I leaped to the carriage, yanked out the cloak I'd been wrapped in, and flung it on the ground next to Jason. My hands trembled as I pushed Jason's ribs, trying to roll him onto the cloak. He woke briefly, turned over onto the cloak and went still. I tugged the sturdy wool about him, and yanked at the gathered hem. He moved—a pace, two paces, and as I backed downhill, he slid faster.

And just in time. A great branch crashed down where we had been. Weeping senselessly, I kept pulling Jason until I stumbled over an unseen root, lost my grip and rolled down a sharp mountain incline. I fetched up hard against a pine tree and lay for a moment trying to catch my breath.

Darkness shadowed the land around me; it was raining. Only the great fire gave light, though the fire began to hiss and send up steam.

I got to my hands and knees. The firelight beat with ruddy glare over a kind of rocky overhang not far below me. I looked back. The dark cloth fell away as Jason got slowly to his feet.

I staggered to the rocky shelter, and in. The cold wind and the rain abated, though my shivering did not. I essayed a step into the darkness, tripped over a stone, gouged my scalp nastily on an unseen outcropping of rock, fell again, then finally gave up. I curled in a ball and eventually drifted into a cold, uncomfortable sleep.

When I woke the second time, gravel ground my cheekbone. I stared in mute surprise into a pair of fever-bright blue eyes. Jason's face was bleached of color.

I closed my eyes. My face was stiff with congealed mud. I lifted a swath of my gown and rubbed it over my cheeks and forehead. The fabric felt cold and gritty, but at least it wasn't caked with mud.

When I opened my eyes again, I met Jason's gaze. He did not speak.

I looked around me at the fantastic roof of ancient, interlocked tree roots, grass and rock that formed the shelter. Just beyond was the steady thunder of rain.

I discovered I was thirsty. But the sharp pain in my head when I moved killed the thirst: the residue of far too much sleepweed. I was beginning to know that sensation all too well.

When I opened my eyes again, the pale light of day outlined the dangling vines. Rain hissed in sheets just behind. Jason was not going to go away if I ignored him.

He lay against a great rock, his left hand clasped below his right armpit. A sluggish ooze of blood seeped between his fingers. What remained of his shirt on that side was stained, a great, frightening stain. More stain darkened the ground under him. The rest of him was filthy with mud and moss.

I shut my eyes again, this time against an almost overwhelming surge of nausea.

When I had that under control, I looked down at myself. My gown was a sodden, mud-smeared mess, ripped beyond repair.

I looked up at Jason. "You're bleeding to death."

"Most likely." I could barely hear him.

"I can't look at that." My voice came out sounding accusing.

His eyes flicked toward the stream and beyond, and though he said nothing, the glance was clear: *so leave.*

"I wouldn't get ten paces in that storm."

His voice was barely audible above the rush of the stream. "Then suffer." I saw the briefest narrowing of humor in his eyes.

The ridiculousness of the situation overcame the sense of danger, making everything more unreal. "Well," I said. "Do you want some help?"

One shoulder lifted in a slight shrug, as if to say: what can you do?

Good question.

I looked about for something to staunch that horrible ooze. He had nothing, I had nothing. My gown was fragile and filthy— but my lace collar wasn't.

I found the catches, and shook it free of the gown. I moved to the edge of the overhang and held the lace out until the rain had pounded it clean of mud. Then I folded the heavy lace into a pad.

Wishing myself a kingdom away, I examined the blood-soaked wad of cloth pressed between his fingers and his side. His hair had come untied, black locks straggling down into the gore. I shuddered. My own hair had come undone, lying in a sodden mass down my back and on the mud and moss-covered stone ground.

"You're a fool," he murmured. "You should be making your way downstream."

"I don't know where I am," I said, as if that explained everything. "Move your hand."

"Why?"

The *Why* did not mean *Why move my hand?* but *Why are you doing what you're doing?* How did I know? I just, well, *knew.*

"I may loathe and despise you," I said as emphatically as I could despite my shaky, squeaking voice. "But I loathe my conscience worse. I'll leave as soon as I know I did what I could."

He hadn't moved his hand, so I reached down and tried reluctantly to pry loose one of his fingers. His hand jerked in resisting—which was his undoing. A spasm of pain tightened his features. His hand went slack and his eyes closed.

Gone off in a faint, I thought, triumphant. *See how you like it.*

I put his hand on his middle, flicked his hair out of the way, and pressed the lace over the long gash, wondering how to keep it there. His chest was bare where his shirt had ripped, and in the blood smears on his flesh lay a long silver chain. My eyes followed it, saw whatever was on its end was caught in his armpit.

As I tugged, it came free, but the object on the end was red and sticky. I dropped it, turned away and gagged dryly for a short but thoroughly nasty time.

When *that* passed off, I leaned back against the rock and fought to get my breathing under control. Since Jason was still in a faint, I pulled up an edge of his shirt and poked the thing on the chain down his other side.

Then I resumed my search for something to bind the lace over the wound, but he stirred, and his left hand came up again and pressed against his side, prisoning the lace there.

I moved away to watch the rain until the waves of nausea passed. When I turned, Jason said, "Ambush."

And he'd been taken by surprise, I thought, remembering the battle gear he'd worn the day of the abduction. He'd been ready for trouble that day. The chain mail and battle tunic were probably burning back there with the carriage and the rest of his luggage. "Where are we?" I asked.

"Border between Drath and Ralanor Veleth."

Almost to his homeland.

"Who did it? Garian's people? Or yours?" I added snidely.

"Enterprising independents, I believe," he whispered. "Of the sort my brother runs."

"Who were they after? Me—or you?"

"Not sure. You were hidden by baggage." He gave a brief, pained half-smile.

"So if they come back, what?"

"Won't come back. Dead. All of 'em."

"But if they have friends who come seeking them?"

"You tell 'em. Who you are. You'll be. Safe enough."

"*Another* ransom? Is that going to frame the rest of my life?" I asked the rocky ceiling. Seeing no answer, I faced Jason. "The fire?"

"Campfire. Most likely. Wind was coming up when they attacked. I used a stick from the fire. When my sword wouldn't come free of one of 'em."

"Ugh."

"Sent Markham for backup," he went on. "Didn't know about the fire."

"Markham?"

"Liegeman."

"How long have we been on the road?"

Another brief half-smile. "Couple days. Had quite a run. Your brother. Was commendably fast this time."

"But not fast enough, obviously. Well, at least when I get home Spaquel will be discredited for good."

"Talk himself out of it."

I sighed and braced myself to look at the lace again. There was white in it. So the bleeding was slowing. Time to go away.

I got to my feet, paused when I saw the gleam of a jewel not far from Jason. I bent. My fingers closed around the hilt of a long bladed knife. I said to Jason, "You lost my gems. This is a fair trade."

"Didn't lose 'em. Sold 'em. Get over the border faster."

Belatedly I realized he meant bribes. To my own people. Anger surged through me.

I glared at him, the knife gripped in my fingers.

The smile was obvious now. "Go ahead. This is the only chance you'll ever get."

Why was he taunting me? He couldn't possibly defend himself—even against me. I looked down at his blood-streaked flesh, the derisive blue eyes, and nausea clawed at me.

"You're squeamish," he whispered, and for the first time I saw him angry—really angry. "If I get through this one alive you'll regret the outcome."

Did he *want* me to stab him? I couldn't possibly figure out what he meant, but one thing was for certain: "Maybe I'll regret it, but I'm not going to do *you* any favors. Goodbye and good riddance."

I turned my back on him and stalked out into the rain.

Chapter Eleven

I figured that at least the hard rain would wash off the mud. But not ten steps away from the rocky overhang, the rain abated abruptly, typical of mountain storms. I walked a short way in the light drizzle, then sat down on a rock to let the pounding in my head subside.

Next time I made it to a trickling stream. I got a good drink, which made me feel somewhat better.

One step, another. Concentrate. It took all my thought, and all my effort.

I didn't go far or for long before I heard the sounds of a military horn echoing through the trees, followed not long after by the thud of horse hooves and jingling harnesses.

Thieves?

I looked about for a hiding place, tripped over something and fell into a mossy patch.

Horse hooves neared, someone dismounted and pulled me to my feet. Someone carried me and I was set down—not on a horse, but on a cushioned bench.

I was in an ancient traveling carriage smelling strongly of mildew. Jason lay on the opposite bench, that horrible wound wrapped with a hasty bandage.

As the forgotten knife was twisted from my fingers, he said, "I told you. Ought to have used it."

"I took it to ward thieves."

"Effective."

"You're stupid," I said, with as much strength as I could muster. "And ignorant. Mistaking scruples for cowardice."

He did not answer. Only gave me that faint, incredulous smile.

I made a sour face. "The ransom. You'll address it to my brother, I trust?"

"Of course... No use applying to your father... No worth in making him drop dead... But your brother doesn't know that..."

"You'll threaten to tell Papa?"

"Don't need to... Your brother jumps at shadows..."

I sighed in disgust, too sick to be angry. "It turns my stomach. Ransom me to raise an army to march on my own kingdom."

"Wrong."

"What? You're not after Lygiera?"

"No interest. No. Would be interesting. No intention."

He was in a fever. Would he ramble on about his plans? I studied him. His black hair hung down in his face, which was pale except for telltale red along the defined cheekbones that were so much like his siblings'.

"So whose is the fortunate kingdom?"

He did not answer.

I tried to think of something suitably scathing to say, but the carriage hit some kind of deep hole or root, jerked quite violently, and Jason shut his eyes, closing out the world, whether advertently or not.

I looked at the window. A pine-covered crag towered overhead. My skull and body ached. One of my more heroic ancestors might have been capable of leaping forth and making good her escape, but I did not know how to begin—or how to carry on if I did manage to get out of the carriage and past the escort whose gear and harnesses I could hear jingling at either side.

So I drew my knees up, tucked my sodden skirts around my ankles, put my head on my knees and went to sleep.

I roused when we stopped. Torchlight flared in the old-fashioned carriage windows. The door opened, and chill air puffed in, pure, cold, pine scented, and very damp. I discovered I was shivering.

A dark head and broad shoulders appeared in the doorway, outlined by the torches held high. A large male hand extended toward me. It was an offer—palm up—not a peremptory point, so I laid my own hand in it.

The silent liegeman guided me to the door then lifted me effortlessly out of the carriage, carried me a few steps, and set me down in what appeared in the leaping torchlight to be an abandoned woodcutter's cottage.

Mold and damp wood were the chief smells inside the small single room. Someone had spread an old blanket on the stone floor near a fireplace on which someone else was in the process of setting up a fire. I lay down gratefully and was vaguely surprised when someone cast another blanket over me. It smelled of storage herbs and moldy wood, but I did not care. I crooked my elbow under my aching head, content to watch the four or five dark figures moving in purposeful silence about the little room.

Voices murmured just beyond the open door. One of them was Jason's. Mumble-mumble-mumble, then a grunt of pain, followed by cursing.

Another voice: "Cut through the muscle, bone nicked. But the main blood vessel appears to be safe."

"What I figured." Jason's response was hoarse. "Or I'd have been dead by now."

Silence. I winced, trying not to think of what had to be happening in that old carriage.

The fire threw orange light on old plank walls, little shelves, and a moldy-green wooden trunk. An iron pot in a corner. Someone knelt at the fire; from the sounds outside others were rigging a shelter for the horses. Rain whispered in the high fir trees surrounding the cottage.

Cold puffs of rainy air blew in, making me shiver. My blanket did not hold heat, because of my sodden gown.

Two figures laid a heavy woolen cloak on the floor, covered it with two more. Jason came in, supported by that tall armsman from before. I noted with mild interest his dark, shoulder-length hair.

Jason lay down on the pile of cloaks, his breathing loud in the quiet cottage.

No one spoke. The tall man stooped to lay another cloak over Jason, who had been bandaged with ripped lengths from a cotton shirt. The tall man straightened up. I caught an appraising glance from dark eyes, then he vanished through the door.

More voices outside. Consultation, it sounded like. Someone came back in; I heard the muted clink of chain mail as he knelt at the fire. A creak, the door closed.

Warmth from the fire reached me, bringing lassitude. I had almost drifted into sleep when the door opened. Cold air rushed in, followed by footsteps.

A voice said, low, "Water?"

"Steaming," responded another in the same accent that Jaim and Jewel used.

"Good enough for now. Let's get the healer's brew into them."

Brew? My eyes closed. Very soon I smelled the wonderful, healing, summery aroma of steeped listerblossom.

"Here. Drink."

That long, bony face, the dark eyes and hair, firelit from the side—they were vaguely familiar. I remembered previous half-wakings when that same voice had issued that same command.

"No sleepweed," I protested.

A brief smile. "No."

An arm supported me, and a metal cup pressed against my lower lip. I drank the brew without pausing for breath. Then the arm withdrew and I lay down again.

"What happened?" I whispered. "Jason said it was thieves."

"An ambush," was the quiet reply. "Twelve against two seemed appropriate odds. An understandable error."

The man moved away, and I closed my eyes.

Woke when I couldn't breathe. I was shivering in spite of the warm air. The fire leaped and glowed. I moved toward it, felt its scorch on my face. The heat helped my shivering abate, so I crouched into a ball as close to the fire as I could, but soon I was much too hot, and so I moved away—and collided with that tall, dark-haired man.

"Lie down. Sleep," he said, moving aside.

"I'm hot."

"You've a slight fever. Too much sleepweed, too little food, and a chill. Lie down. I'll steep more healer leaf. You should shake it off by morning."

I looked at the scrunched blanket with its damp spots, and shuddered. The man had set the water pot on the hot stones near the fire. He then reached over my head. Fabric had been festooned above us to dry.

The man pulled it down—another of those heavy wool army cloaks.

"Here. This one is dry. Remove that gown and wrap up in the cloak. You will only stay chilled in those wet clothes."

I flushed as I looked Jason's way. He was utterly oblivious, his breathing slow and deep.

The man said in a quiet voice that didn't quite mask his amusement, "He won't waken and I'll go outside. Make it quick."

He opened the door and vanished. I wrestled my way out of what had once been a beautiful walking gown. Jason never moved—I watched him the entire time—as I wrapped myself in the woolen cloak, which was warm from the fire. It smelled absurdly of singed wool.

I spread my gown on the hearth, aghast at the mud and moss making it clot in wads. I scraped at the worst spots, knowing that I could never put it on again so dirty, and then stared down in horror as the fabric, so delicate, ripped like spider webs before a broom.

The door creaked open. I retreated to my spot. The dark-haired man came in and knelt before the fire. He checked the water pot and cast leaves into it. Again the wonderful smell of listerblossoms filled the air. I lay there looking up at the raindrops glistening on his hair and on his dark green long tunic. Firelight gleamed along the complicated pattern of his blackweave riding boots, and on the hilt of a knife at his belt. Who was he? His manner, some of his gestures, betrayed the sort of control that aristocrats get trained into them from birth. But he was dressed as an armsman.

"The steeped leaf is ready." His voice was a low rumble.

When I handed the cup back, there was movement beyond his arm. Jason sat up, his eyes bright with fever.

The man turned his way and wordlessly held out another cup. Jason took it one-handed, drank it, and lay down again.

I did as well.

My slumbers were uneasy, full of strange dreams of fire, and knives, and Garian's cruel laughter.

I woke to whispers. "...didn't eat for the two days previous. She has a mild fever, not nearly as bad as yours. Nothing that a couple good meals won't set to rights. But you—"

"I'll live."

"You won't if you try to ride. You lost too much blood."

"We'll see." That was Jason, sounding impatient. "I know I can't defend myself. We'll wait on Brissot."

"Good."

The next time I woke, people moved around me. The fever had turned into a head cold, otherwise I felt fine. Weak light filtered in from small windows in the four walls, the shutters wide. There was no glass in them; cool, pine-scented air drifted down in a slow breeze.

The voices ceased, footsteps clunked and clattered on the warped floorboards. The door creaked.

I smelled food.

Pulling the cloak close, I sat up to find Jason sitting across from me, leaning against the wooden chest. He still wore his muddy trousers and boots, but had someone else's shirt on. It was much too large for him; at the unlaced neck I glimpsed that long chain, now cleaned of bloodstains, and fresh bandages. His hair hung tangled in his face and down onto his breast.

Why did I laugh at his sorry, bedraggled appearance? Because ridiculousness made a repellent situation more bearable.

With his good hand he lifted a beat-up metal cup in a mocking salute. "At least I'm not blue," he observed, then coughed.

I looked down at my cloak and long, waving mud-streaked tangles of honey-colored hair. Blue? I poked one hand out. Oh. It was mottled and blotched with blue dye—from my gown, which had been intended only for civilized wear, after which careful hands would have put it through a cleaning frame.

"Were there a mirror we'd crack it." My voice was hoarse.

Jason turned his head toward the fire. He lifted his chin in the direction of the metal pot from the night before. Next to it was my ruined gown. "Markham is bringing extra gear."

I reached down, wadded up the gown and pitched it into the fire. Whoosh! A smell of scorched fabric, and it was soon gone.

I tucked the cloak more securely about me, and poured out steeped leaf. Then turned my attention to a pair of covered stoneware pots.

"Soup in one. Bread in the other."

I helped myself to the soup once I'd drunk the steeped leaf, since I saw no other dishes. The bread had a portion missing. It was still warm, having been baked in the ceramic pot. I helped myself.

"Can I get you something?" I asked, seeing Jason just sitting there.

"Ate." He coughed again.

"Then I will finish the steeped leaf. It's lukewarm anyway."

He gave a brief nod.

I sat back on my blanket, curling my legs under me, and sipped slowly. The taste, the warmth, faint as it was, felt wonderful.

When I was done I opened my eyes and set aside the cup.

Jason was watching me. "Markham corroborates that you did in fact pull me from the fire."

I shivered as the memory flooded back.

He seemed to be waiting for an answer. "And so? More helpful hints about my cowardice?"

He said nothing.

"I take your accusation of squeamishness as a compliment. I see no disgrace in finding oneself unable to hack apart one's fellow being. Nor in finding disgusting and reprehensible the kind of life wherein that is an everyday activity."

"Including self-defense?"

I remembered my short, intense (and totally ineffectual) wishes that I had had the skills of one of my adventurous ancestors. "No. I was shortsighted there." And, lest he think I was admitting defeat, I added, "Had I had the remotest idea that my life would be enlivened by all this violent effort to get hold of my inheritance, I would have forgone my studies of music in favor of all the sword-swinging and knife-throwing I could cram into a day."

"Music. You mentioned that before. That's what you do?"

"Is that so astonishing?"

Slight lift of his good shoulder. I read dismissal in that gesture, as though music was a foreign concept to be defined some day in the far future.

"Trying to pick apart from Garian's discourse what was truth and what was lies." He looked at the fire again.

"Garian," I repeated.

"I can't decide whether he's two steps ahead of me or two behind."

"What does that mean?"

The diffuse blue gaze returned to me, but he did not answer.

Puzzled, unnerved, mostly weary, I flopped down, my back to him, and listened to the rain on the roof.

Chapter Twelve

When I woke again, it was to the rumble of thunder. A flash of lightning had broken into my dreams. Rain roared on the roof of the cottage. A thin stream of water ran down inside the far wall, but at least it found another hole to run out of and our floor was not awash.

I sat up and sneezed. My head now felt stuffed with cotton. My throat was scratchy; I'd been breathing through my mouth.

The fire crackled, giving off welcome light and heat. Jason sat in the same place as before. Papers rested near his good hand, and a quill and ink.

He pointed with his chin behind me.

Neatly folded clothing lay to hand: a stout black linen shirt, and one of those heavy green woolen battle tunics. Under that was a handkerchief—a besorcelled one, I discovered, as I touched it. It had that same tingly feel as cleaning frames.

I buried my face in it gratefully, snorting and snuffling.

When I looked back, Jason's attention was on his papers. He too had one of the handkerchiefs. He set down his quill, picked up the handkerchief, coughed, snorted and then resumed his work.

I was embarrassed at the notion of asking him to turn around, for what if he refused? Or made some devastating comment? Despite having grown up with a brother, I was modest—private, in fact, and even under extreme circumstances such as these I did not want to change my clothes in sight of a man I not only did not know, but actively disliked.

Not that there was any hint of expectation, of desire, of the awareness of physical proximity from Jason Szinzar. In short there was nothing remotely romantic, flirtatious or even friendly in my present situation.

Jason's pen scratched steadily across his paper.

Though I'd exchanged the usual adolescent kisses and explorations, I'd come to distrust flirtation, wherein ambition was all too often masked by the sweet words of so-called love.

Since those days I had confined my definition of love to the strictly familial. Always, balanced against the romantic songs and the sights of flirting couples at balls was the knowledge of my mother's short, dismal life. Now, to me *she* embodied cowardice—not that I had ever spoken the words aloud.

So here I was alone with an enemy—the circumstances uncertain—and yet I had to dress.

I hesitated. Looked again. Jason was busy and I did not want to call his attention to me.

So I turned my back, pulled the clothes under the cloak and wrestled them on over my chemise and drawers, which I knew were grimy and as blue-smeared as my flesh, but at least they were dry. The shirt and tunic were so large that it was actually no difficulty.

When at last I shook out the folds, the battle tunic thumped straight down to the tops of my feet, forming an odd sort of gown above my walking slippers, which—mud caked and mossy—were still on my feet.

The laces on the shirt began well below my collarbones; ball gowns scooped only a fraction lower. I pulled the laces as tight as I could and tied them into a secure knot, though when I bent, an edge of my grubby blue-stained chemise peeked absurdly out. The shirt was also vastly outsized. I had to roll the cuffs back several times to free my fingertips, but I did not care. It was warm.

When I looked over, I saw Jason's gaze on me. He did not hide his amusement. "If Markham were any bigger, those clothes would fall right off you."

"Contrary." I sounded like a goose honking. So I dropped a dainty curtsey. "They are much too tight."

He gave me a sardonic half-smile, coughed hard into his handkerchief, and turned his attention back to his papers.

There was more steeped leaf, soup and bread. While Jason worked his way through his papers, I had a quiet meal. The only sounds were the fire, the rain, and our coughing and snuffling. Jason's cold, I noted with sour triumph, was far worse than mine.

When I was done eating, I felt for the first time that I might actually stay awake. I looked around the cottage, which provided little to view beyond warped planking and mossy patches. The thundering rain outside made venturing beyond the door a prospect of limited appeal.

So I sat down and fingered the worst tangles from my hair, then braided it. As I worked, I covertly studied my enemy, wondering what I ought to do, for I knew what would come next. He would go forward with the plans to extort my inheritance from my brother. Balanced against that I had only one small comfort: he did not intend to use it to fund an invasion of Lygiera.

Or, that was what he'd said. A lie? I could not remember him lying to me. None of the Szinzars had lied, whatever else one could say of their motivations. Unlike Garian, who in retrospect had enjoyed spinning out falsehoods just to see me believe them without question.

A stray memory recurred: Jason flicking my cheek with his finger, and saying, *You asked for it.*

Asked for "it"? Asked for what, a smashing fall from a horse? That was as close to a lie as he'd come, for I had never *asked* for pain and trouble! Did it mean he thought I deserved such a fall? But his tone had not been gloating, as Garian's had been. It had been more of a warning.

"Question?"

Belatedly I realized I was still staring at him. No, actually glaring. So I said, "You told me when I woke up in Garian's that I'd 'asked for it'. What did you mean?"

His brows lifted. "Neither of us expected you to climb down the trees and ride off at the gallop in the middle of the night. Put Garian in quite a rage, by the way." He smiled, obviously enjoying the remembered spectacle.

For a moment I dismissed Garian and his rage, contemplating the fact that Jason had not really answered my question. Why not?

"What happened to the man I bribed? I hope Garian didn't—"

"Took whatever it was you gave him and ran. What was it, your jewelry?"

"Yes. Maybe I was foolish to ride in the darkness—though it seemed a good idea at the time—but how do you make that out to be cowardice?"

"Didn't say it was."

"Yet you said I was a coward yesterday. Or whenever it was."

"So?"

Good question. Why *did* his opinion matter? It ought not to matter, not the least bit. I said in my grumpiest voice, "I don't know why I even bothered to remember. You are all selfish, stupid blockheads, every single one of you. That's the worst of what is laughably called courtship: men."

"So you females don't court men—or women—who have money, power, or the promise of acquiring them?" he asked.

I thought of Gilian Zarda trying to twine her little hands round Maxl's crown, and made a face. "Everyone is an idiot," I stated. "Except me. Because I don't court at all, and if I did, it wouldn't be for money, or power, or any of the rest of it."

Jason's mouth quirked. "Easy to say from the position of vast wealth."

"I'd say it even so." I hesitated, thinking, was that true? What would I be, had I not been born a princess? I would have found my way to music. Somehow.

"You'll be home soon enough, once your brother pays up, and you can spend the rest of your life reviling against me."

"You didn't tell me what you want my fortune for."

"No," he agreed. "Music. Now I understand why Garian was annoyed when you found that lute in his library."

"At first he denied me access to music. Playing or hearing. Just to underscore his authority. Another way to wear down my will and force me to accede to his plans, but after my memory blanked, I realize he was afraid that might bring it back."

"What is there in music that commands your attention?"

"That you have to ask that question—" I paused to cough, and then to catch my breath. "That you have to ask implies that you find music at best frivolous. Bad music, I'll agree, is frivolous. Worse, it jars on the spirit. Disharmony—" I shook my head. "Never mind. Good music is an art."

"Art being?"

I remembered Jewel's disparaging description of

Lathandra's barracks-like royal castle. Was he in truth so ignorant? No, ignorance implied no access. Art and army did seem contradictory ways of life; I could envision him dismissing the arts as irrelevant to the all-consuming passion for war.

Despite my increasingly hoarse voice, I said, "There are as many ways to define it as there are forms of art, but the best of it takes skill and insight to create, and it is not merely pleasing to the senses, but can have meaning for us. As individuals. As people." I stopped. That was usually far more than anyone would listen to.

"Go on."

"With music you can tell the truth about human experience. My great-aunt told me when I was little that every choice, a shift from key to key, a new melodic line developed counterpoint to a known melody, each becomes a personal, that is, a unique, response to universal experience."

"What about those who only hear noise?"

I hesitated, sorting his words, his tone, his expression. "Noise," I repeated. "So many have said that to me, in derision. Accusation. Defense. I don't have an answer, except for the observation that some people truly are tone deaf. Others, well, they haven't had access to music from childhood, which—this is something else my grandmother told me—is akin to a person who was never taught letters looking at a book and seeing hen scratchings on paper." I stopped again.

"Go on."

"That's pretty much all I have to say. For me music is true art, whereas words—so I've learned, growing up in a court—are at best artifical."

He gazed past me at the fire. I couldn't tell if he was thinking, bored, or just wondering when we'd eat next.

I sneezed, and buried my face in the handkerchief. Magic whisked away the nastiness of a runny nose and eyes. When I emerged, Jason said, "What I want to discover is whether Garian knew about your interests and dismissed them as frivolous, or whether he exerted himself to conceal them."

"Why should it matter? We all knew right from the start that your so-called courtship was an excuse to extort my inheritance by legal means. My brief lapse in memory hasn't obscured that."

"Had nothing to do with you."

"I should have known that." Pause to cough. "It never has! Just my wealth. Now I really comprehend why princesses—and princes—run away to become bards."

He cast the quill aside. "Leaving the field to the enemy."

Two against twelve, wasn't that what his armsman had said? As thunder rumbled across the sky, I comprehended that we existed in vastly different paradigms.

Instinct prompted me to say, *You won't understand.* After all, I held the high moral ground, as victim, and he, as villain, had to be in the wrong.

The words were there, my tongue ready to shape them, my throat constricted to utter them, but I couldn't. He'd listened to me talk about music, which was, as far as I could tell, so much hen scratching to him. Though we were enemies, we did sit at the same fire, with time's steady measure slowed to the movement of winter ice, and so I said, "You mean, making kingdom affairs into personal? I guess I can see the objection—if the princess who runs away to become a bard is the trained heir, abandoning responsibility because it's boring. But—" I shook my head.

He said, "But?"

I glowered at the fire. "But when you say 'field' and 'enemy' either you mean war, or figurative language that suggests you see kingdom affairs in terms of war. And where is the virtue in doing one's duty if 'duty' is defined as sending countless unknown people, on both sides, to death?"

At that point Garian would either have laughed or slapped me. It was just that kind of answer that had provoked him.

Jason Szinzar said, "What if every alternative you see ends with war?"

"Every? I'd say it sounds like someone is seeking an excuse."

He looked down at his papers. I waited, while the fire snapped and the rain roared, until I realized he was not considering an answer, that he was not going to make an answer.

Twice more this odd sort of conversation happened.

Once he asked abruptly if I disliked the rain, of all things—I said no—he said I was the first court woman he'd met who didn't, but his tone was not complimentary. It implied I was lying, and I retorted that most of the men I knew (I was thinking of Spaquel) hated rain. Anyone did if one wasn't dressed for it. Then we were off on court clothes (him: expensive and useless) and court behavior (him: as flimsy as the clothing) and before I knew it I was into my mistrust of words before I wondered if I was lecturing and stopped.

The second time he was even more abrupt, asking if I knew anything of Velethi history. Astonished, I stared—were his brains boiling with his fever? Taking up the implied challenge, I named their kings and queens going back three hundred years, and added in the major battles. It wasn't until I said that our tutors had exhorted us always to know the enemy that he stopped talking.

I turned my back and went to sleep.

I woke to the sounds of arrivals. The armsman once more offered me food and steeped leaf, and when that was finished, he said, "Can you ride?"

"Of course." I was annoyed at the implication that all I knew how to do was sit in carriages.

They were clearly relieved. The logistics of that big old carriage were daunting. I never did find out where Markham had managed to find it. I can only report that when we walked out of that cottage—which I fervently hoped never to see again in life, if I couldn't avoid it in nightmares—horses awaited, their coats glistening in the light rainfall.

As I mounted up, I caught several glances of amusement at my no doubt unflattering appearance. Yet there was no derision in those glances, or mockery. Just—humor.

The journey was sedate, down a narrow trail alongside a tumbling stream. Markham and the four silent men-at-arms were watchful of their master, whose only betrayal of weakness was an angry sort of grimness by the time we reached a camp near a great waterfall. They took him into a tent. We were all soaked through from the rain, a state that was to be constant over the next couple of days.

I did not see Jason again, except in glimpses, during that journey eastward.

Brissot turned out to be the captain of a military company that included a number of women. These latter took charge of me, at first trying to hide their considerable amusement at the spectacle of me—dyed blue—in Markham's battle gear. Or half of his battle gear. Once I was in their tent, one of the women produced some clothes that turned out to be for their young recruits. These fit me much better, right down to the warm softweave mocs—no riding boots for me. My long, bedraggled braid was coiled up and hidden under a helm.

And so we proceeded, an anonymous troop of Ralanor Veleth's army, riding on some kind of mountain maneuvers. Nothing was explained to me, but on the day or so it took to wind our way through the border mountains, we were met more than once by Drath's violet-clad guard riding on their own unnamed errands. No one gave me a second glance, even though at one point an entire troop of them lined up to watch us ride single file over a bridge. Jason was too far ahead in the line for me to see, but presumably they didn't recognize him either, for he was wearing clothing belonging to one of his warriors.

I had no desire whatsoever to cry out, or draw attention and cause a battle—which might end with me back in Garian's hands. So I stayed silent.

The clouds were low, heavy and gray as we descended into Ralanor Veleth. I hadn't a hope of escape. Just once, briefly, I envisioned myself managing to vanquish all these foes and galloping straight for home—except where would one possibly begin? "Vanquishing" has to start somewhere, but I hadn't a clue what the first step might be.

And wasn't vanquishing another form of war? Yes, I decided. So my weapons had to be my wits.

Use them.

While I tried unsuccessfully to figure out how, the journey was not unbearable. I watched diligently when we stopped, but I was always surrounded when we ate, and though I might begin an evening alone in the women's tent, the sound of laughter and the clash of swords outside made it clear their favorite campfire activity was dueling practice. Assuming I knew where to go, I wasn't going to sneak past that with any success.

Their conversations with one another were those of friends, punctuated by laughter, and their questions to me were at first tentative. When I recognized shyness, rather than the reserve of contempt, I exerted myself to bridge the gap between our two countries, and sensed them doing the same. Our talk was nothing political, or deep, or even all that interesting. But friendly in intention—mostly me asking questions about them, and their ready answers about a life that filled them with pride. But they didn't confine themselves to talk about war-related things. Far from it. Friends, horses, food—all the easy subjects were canvassed, with only a single reference to recent events. One of them muttered a remark about Drath's young guardsmen that caused them all to burst into laughter, but when I asked her to explain, she blushed, hastily said she had patrol duty, and whisked herself out of the tent.

By the time we reached Lathandra, their capital, we had established about as good an understanding as any captive princess ever had or was likely to get.

And so, after this journey I found myself with mixed feelings when we reached a formidable city built on a ridge and ringed with three sets of walls, their contours picked out by myriad torches. Silent sentries patrolled all the high points, and there were many.

We rode up the cobbled streets toward the central, highest rocky hill and the last ring-wall, which surrounded the Szinzar castle and the peak it was built into. Through a massive and well-guarded gate into a broad courtyard in which a great host could gather. The women who had stayed with me offered me salutes before they departed, which surprised me, but I gave them friendly words in parting, as if I was about to visit my elderly great-aunt and not about to get thrust into a dungeon. Or whatever form my prison would take. I was determined not to show how hard my heart hammered.

Everyone seemed to know exactly what to do, and did it with military efficiency. The company marched off one way, the supply people another, the stablehands leading the mounts toward a stable far bigger than ours at Carnison.

Out of this maze of ordered activity a liveried man appeared, and beckoned to me. "This way, your highness."

He led me through a heavy iron-reinforced door and up narrow stone stairs. My coughs echoed oddly. Down a hall, lit at intervals by torches in sconces. I remembered that dungeons could be above ground as well as below. In fact, I'd read that some stuck their prisoners in towers, and I'd seen plenty of torchlit towers standing squarely against the gray-black night sky.

But then the man paused by a door and opened it, bowing

slightly. I went through—and discovered that I was in what appeared to be the hallway leading into a residence wing. The floor was stone, but it was slate, cut and tiled, and the walls were a smooth cream-colored plaster, with doors inset along the way.

A woman appeared. Her eyes were wide-set and merry, her wild dark curls barely confined to a sedate braid. She too wore the Szinzar green and a fresh apron.

"Your highness." She dropped a curtsey. "This way."

I was too astonished to speak.

Numb, wet, I slogged after her, very aware of the squish, squish, squish of my mocs in the quiet hall, until she stopped at a double door, and bowed me into a spacious room with old-fashioned but fine walnut furnishings and what appeared to be a feather bed. There was even a rug on the floor, woven in pleasing geometric patterns of fish and birds and berries. Across the room a good fire in a huge fireplace made the air warm and mellow. In the corner stood a wardrobe, the right size to contain a cleaning frame.

"Your highness," the woman said, smiling. "Your choice is between a bath and a hot meal first, or sleep first."

"A *bath*?" I repeated, unable to get past that word.

She shook with silent laughter. "This way."

I followed, my vision of iron bars and a dark stone cell fading before the sight of a room with a tiled sunken bath, large enough to lie in. Steaming water waited for me.

As I skinned out of those clammy battle clothes, she talked lightly about the virtues of hot water, different types of soap. Always in that merry voice, respectful in word and tone, but mirthful in inflection. Not cruel mirth, or gloating, or contemptuous. It was obvious that this maid found my mute astonishment, like my blue-dyed skin, endlessly entertaining.

She massaged my scalp and rubbed ointments into my hair, combing it out until it lay like damp ribbons down my back. Whatever she had used had tamed the tangles, though it didn't smell like the flower-scented hair elixirs of home. I liked this astringent scent, I decided. It reminded me of summer fields.

Soon I sat, robed in expensive, soft-woven yeath-fur, drinking a spiced broth soup. After it came chocolate, warm with cream in it. I sipped it, felt lassitude steal over me.

Recognizing those waves of exhaustion, I finally spoke. "Drugged?" I set the cup down.

"No," she said, gulping on another laugh. "Hot milk makes a person sleep better. I always used to give it to her highness, Princess Jewel. She misliked the taste of plain milk, preferring the chocolate and honey. It's become quite a fashion, truth to tell, for ours is a cold climate, this side of the mountains— either wet and cold, or dry and windy and cold."

I finished the chocolate, and then she turned back the covers of the feather bed. A real bed, after days of cold, damp ground. As I climbed in, she removed two warming pans and set them on the hearth.

The bed was soft. Warm. Clean.

I don't remember putting my head on the pillow.

Chapter Thirteen

Her name was Berry. She had been Jewel's maidservant, left behind when Jewel ran away. She didn't say much about that—only that since then she had been working downstairs with the linens, repairing tapestries.

That second day she brought me a lute, a very old one, newly strung, saying that the king sent it with his compliments—a piece of politeness that surprised me. The third day, two sweating footmen muscled a huge harp into the room. It was old, but newly restrung.

I had ceased being astonished by then, and could only be grateful for the lack of threat or oppression. My duty was to escape, but I was uncertain how I'd even find my way out of this enormous castle filled with military people on guard night and day. I peeked out the door down the hallway on my first morning, to see a man-at-arms stationed there. There was no fighting my way past him, so the alternative was to wait and see what Jason heard from my brother—and plan from there.

I tried to make friends with the servants, and take note of my surroundings. When the weather was pleasant, I rolled the harp out onto the balcony to practice. This balcony probably had served some kind of military purpose long ago, but had been closed in, with potted trees set at the corners. Beyond the low, crenellated wall was a sheer drop to a garden that was bounded by the castle walls on the other side. Jaim might have been able to shinny up or down. I couldn't begin to figure out how.

Up behind me the castle reached, dark gray stone, with the ever-vigilant sentries visible along the walls and towers.

The garden was another surprise. Shaped like an L, it had been designed around a waterfall in the side of the peak into which the castle had been built. This garden, like the furnishings and the musical instruments, was old, for those trees had not been planted in my lifetime—or even in my father's. At any given time you could find courtiers wandering the garden in Carnison, but here if there were courtiers, they did not appear in the garden. I mostly glimpsed servants and warriors out on the paths, or sitting sunning themselves in the brief intervals between the bands of rain. Birds twittered in the trees, and in the distance, over the walls, I sometimes heard cadenced shouts and the clash and clatter of weapons drills.

Though this place was not like home, it was apparent that Jewel, in her loathing, had exaggerated to its detriment.

Berry brought a couple of gowns, soft, well-made cotton-velvet overgowns with square necks and full sleeves that fell from shoulders to the floor. Under them I wore a cotton underdress. I had no idea if these things were current fashion here or something left behind by another woman at another time, but that didn't matter. The clothing was warm in a very chilly climate.

Music kept my mind occupied; in fact, I tried not to feel guilt at the fact that this existence was preferable to court at home, for no one pestered me for poetry readings, riding parties or to dance with hopeful sons who needed to marry money.

There was no Gilian Zarda.

And so several days passed, one folding into another without any jolts of terror or dramatic pulse pounding. My cold, mild to begin with, rapidly dwindled to an occasional cough, and my blue skin lightened to its normal color. I spent most of my time out on the balcony with the harp.

I resolutely spent those first couple of days on elementary exercises to regain my fingering. Thus I learned the characteristics of each instrument. On the third day, at last, I gave in and played my entire repertoire. The lute, though a perfectly adequate drawing-room instrument, was nothing to the harp. That harp had been brought here by someone who knew and loved music. It was made of an extraordinary wood with brilliant resonance.

There was no communication with Jason other than the delivery of the instruments. I did not know what to make of that, except, perhaps, from a practical perspective that a happy hostage is a hostage not making trouble.

So since I couldn't parse his motives, I thought about him as I played the harp. What he'd done, and most of all, what he'd said. It was easy but not very enlightening to dismiss everything he said as the utterings of a villain. That comment he had made about quitting the field—the fact that it kept coming back to me meant that somewhere in it some truth must lie.

Quitting the field. As I brooded over the adventures into which I'd been unwillingly forced, the one common element was just that. I'd been forced. Garian, Jason and the others didn't get bundled along by others. They made things happen. Wise or shortsighted, for better or for worse, they acted. And I just reacted.

When rain came through, I trundled the harp back inside.

I sat by the fireplace as rain pattered on the terrace outside the windows, and ran my fingers through the chords, major, minor, major. Minor. So different, those chords, though both were required to make music. Could it be the same for differing views of the world? Passivity without strength created victims. Only where did strength cross over into evil? One answer was easy, the deliberate breaking of the bonds of morality, or of honor.

On impulse I opened the door and walked out.

The guard on duty approached and bowed, his eyes questioning. "I would like an interview with your king, please," I said.

He bowed again. Opened the hall door.

Surprised at not being put off, I followed. In silence we traversed what had to be the length of the northern wall of the castle. Before long we were passing by chambers wherein people worked, mostly people in military garb, though without the chain mail or weapons. Through a room in which I glimpsed maps and busy desks to a narrow hall, and then the guard motioned me to wait, which I did, while he went on alone.

Moments later I was ushered into a round tower room with an old carpet, and more of the walnut furnishings of the last century, plus two tall shelves of books. In fact, it reminded me so much of Maxl's lair a snort of laughter escaped me when I faced Jason sitting in an armchair next to a desk.

He wore the same plain riding clothes I remembered from

the days in Drath; if he was bandaged it was not visible. He eyed me with a kind of wary appraisal that I found unpleasant. "You have a complaint?" he asked, words that took me by surprise.

Since he had not invited me to sit I perched on the armrest of the other chair. "No. I thought of an alternate plan today. How about instead of your threatening Maxl I just *give* you whatever it is you want? I have controlled my own inheritance since my last birthday, except the land that came through my mother. We can't actually claim anything in Narieth. Since you say you aren't going to attack Lygiera, you can have it all. I go home, and there's an end to my wealth—and incidentally to my problems with wealth seekers."

"No," he said, but at least that wary expression was gone.

"Why not? Why does it have to be through Maxl?"

"It's the mechanics of transfer. I'm in a hurry. Your suggestion would take months." He added with that rare hint of humor, "There's nothing like judicious threat to bustle the bureaucrats along."

So much for taking action.

I left.

A long walk back, and I resumed my practice with the harp.

During the afternoon I contemplated throwing myself on Berry's mercy. She was kind—she clearly wished me well.

What would I say?

Will you help me escape? I am here against my will.

What would she say? She might not believe me, for to her eyes I had been in no danger. Had she a family? A lover? Would she want to begin again in Lygiera?

Was she loyal to the Szinzars, impossible as that seemed? Except I had seen myself that Brissot's company had not been unhappy or constrained by threat to carry out their orders. And Markham, who was Jason's own liegeman, appeared to be unquestioningly loyal. Jason'd had no doubt that Markham would return after he'd sent him off for help after the ambush. And so it had come to pass.

All right, then. The lesson here seemed to be that I had to rely on my own will as well as my wits. I would never use threat, but I wouldn't try to twist someone's sympathy to get me what I wanted, leaving them to face the consequences.

I was surprised later that day to observe subtle indications of unease in Berry. Nothing overt. Her hands moved about without their usual purpose—smoothing what was already smooth, straightening what was already straight, checking for dust on the old tabletops that shone from across the room.

And so I lifted my hands from the harp and faced her. "Is there something you wish to say?"

"Um," she said, blushing. "Your highness."

I laughed. "Uh oh. Whenever the titles come out, something awful is next."

"Nothing awful! But—presumptuous, perhaps. Have you noticed the crowds in the garden?" she asked in a rush.

"Of course! Who would not take advantage of a stretch of fine days?"

My own situation vanished like fog before the sun when she said, "They take advantage of your music." She pointed to the door to the balcony, which was open. "Some have urged me to request you to take the harp back outside. Now that the rain is gone. So they can hear better. If you can ask such a thing of a princess."

I laughed. When she looked upset, I waved my hand and shook my head as I tried to regain my equilibrium. "Oh! Oh," I said. "I was not ready for that. See, at home, I can't play for anyone. I would if I could—but the truth is, I'm not nearly as good as the professionals. Even that would not stop me from getting up musical groups, as happened in the old days, but somehow some stupid custom took hold wherein it's improper for people of rank to entertain."

Berry whistled.

"A *stupid* custom," I declared. "When my own grandmother can remember musical parties among the older people where everyone played to their own satisfaction, and they put together plays for the fun of it. Perhaps someone with the flair for leading could change the custom. Make it a fashion again..."

I was smitten by memory, when I had tried that very thing, not long after my first formal appearance at court at sixteen. How my heart had sped, my palms had sweated as I invited some of the other girls to a musical party, but not one of them brought an instrument, and how stiffly they'd sat, how politely they'd clapped.

119

And later, Gilian—whom I had not invited—asking in that sweet lisp she'd used ever since we were small, if it would become a royal decree to have to come listen to me exhibiting myself...

I shrugged away the embarrassing memory. "But I don't have that flair. So we must all be spectators. But here—" I laughed again. "Air goes where it will, and if the wind carries music as well as the scents of the garden, how can I object?"

I rolled the harp back out onto the terrace, and played for the rest of that day, pleased that for the first time in my life, someone besides me was listening.

Next morning a summons came in the form of one of those guards, a tall young man with big ears and a vague resemblance to one of the women of Brissot's troop.

"The king asks for an interview," he said.

"Well then, lead on." I set down the lute.

This time I met Jason in a small, plain sitting room that looked south over the assembly court and the far end of the garden. Sunlight streamed through the windows, outlining his form as he stared out at the garden. The old rosewood furnishings were spare and somber. As soon as the door closed behind the servant, he turned around.

"Your brother has refused."

"Refused?" My mouth shaped the word, but no sound came out.

The unexpectedness of his statement was followed hard with terror, and stars wheeled across my vision.

"Sit down."

He turned toward the windows again, his hands behind his back. "No one is holding a blade to your neck, so why are you acting like a trapped rabbit?"

He was irritated. *He* was irritated?

"So do you carry out the threat after the next meal? Or maybe next week?" I sounded like a mouse, not a rabbit, to my own ears.

He waved his left hand with a quick, dismissive gesture. "There was no real threat. Just bluff. And your brother seems to have figured that out. He learns fast, your brother. I'll remember that."

"No threat?" I repeated. "But—I don't understand. Then what am I doing here?"

"Spaquel was going to send you and my sister to Garian. I got there first."

"But—" I shook my head, bewildered. "Why did you—oh." I frowned at the wine glass, then looked up. "If you sent Jewel back with Spaquel, who was hotfooting to his house after you—"

"Then he either had to tell the truth to your brother, or make the best of it and pretend to be a rescuing hero, since it was you Garian wanted. Not my poverty-stricken sister. If Ignaz Spaquel tries anything more, he chances to lose everything he holds in Lygiera. Your father might be living in a dream, but I'm beginning to suspect your brother won't put up with treason."

"So Jewel was safe, and Spaquel thwarted. And you made me come here why?"

"To see who intercepted my ransom letter, and what would happen."

I glared at him. "What would have happened to me had Garian managed to make us marry that day up in Drath?"

"You were expecting to be strangled in the dark of night?" he asked, mocking.

"Jewel was certain that was your plan—if not sooner, certainly later."

"You ought to know by now that Jewel's imagination supplies more interesting convictions than the truth ever could."

"And so?"

He gazed out the window. "My original intention was to bring you back here and establish you in the rooms you have now until you conveniently followed your mother's path into a nearby river, as Garian insisted would happen before long—"

"Ugh! Never!"

"Yes, I realize now that the assumption was erroneous, but it's irrelevant because I have an idea that Garian actually had some treachery in line for both of us. I don't think either of us were meant to survive crossing his border. What I still do not know yet is if Garian was intending to come to the rescue of my empty throne, or my brother was." Again he raised his left hand, and turned around with a kind of rueful smile. "We can discourse on that later. It appears we are about to be enlightened in some respects, and misled in most."

He moved to a sideboard and poured out three small glasses of wine; I noticed he used his right hand very little.

Without any warning the door slammed open, smashing into the opposite wall, and in ran—

"Jewel!"

"Flian! I *hoped* you would not still be here." She whirled around, facing her brother. "You horrid, rotten, blast-mad villain! How *dare* you!"

"The Elandersi court started holding Flian's disappearance against you?" Jason asked as if he hadn't heard all those insults.

Jewel gasped. "How did you—"

"I had people there waiting, in case that happened. Their orders were to pull you out as soon as gossip started blaming you."

Jewel rubbed her eyes. "I don't understand. I'd rather stay there and face down the gossip, which is completely ridiculous—"

"You can spend the evening in ceaseless lamentations," Jason cut in. "Berry has your old rooms aired and ready. Here." He pressed a glass of wine into her hands.

To my surprise, Jewel took it and drank it down. "Ugh, my butt aches," she moaned. "I *loathe* riding like that, day and night!" She beckoned to me. "Come, Flian. I have so *much* to tell you." Her expressive brows lowered into a scowl line. "When *he* isn't looming around like a thunderbolt about to strike."

Jason waved at the door with his good hand. "She'll be along presently."

The door slammed, leaving us only with the mingled scent of Jewel's favorite perfume and the distinctive odor of horse.

Jason held out one of the wineglasses to me and sat down in the chair opposite to mine. "You're still looking like the trapped rabbit," he said dryly.

I took a fortifying gulp, figuring if they could drink it, the days of sleepweed must have abated, at least for now.

Jason drank his own, then set down the goblet. "How much does Maxl trust Garian?"

I tried to figure out how my answering the question might harm my brother, and Jason said, "This information will not aid me. I have come to believe that Garian will betray anyone at any time. He has wealth, so his reasons appear to be obscure. Does your brother know that?"

"He does now." I thought back to my arrival at Carnison what seemed a lifetime ago. "I told him everything that happened in Drath, but he said to keep it to ourselves until he knew more. He's hampered by not wanting to disturb Papa with added stresses."

"Jaim visited you there once, did he not?"

"Visited?" I laughed. "He tried to abduct me."

"He needs money too. Did he, during your brief acquaintance, ever mention Garian?"

"Yes! Said not to trust him." I sighed. "That's why I went to Drath in the first place, to spite him. But how was I to know?" My mind raced on ahead. "Don't tell me Garian and Jaim concocted that nasty little plan between them?"

"No. But Garian led me to believe that they had. Supposedly it was a bargain. Jaim would send you to Drath, and in return, Jaim got sanction to cross Drath while carrying on his lawless depredations in either my kingdom or yours. Garian represented himself as go-between, you see."

"So when Jaim came smashing in and carried me off, and you no doubt sent people like Brissot and so forth to find him, it looked like the two of you were betraying one another? Whatever for?"

"To keep us at one another's throats, and maybe get one of us to kill the other, so that Garian could find Jewel, force her to marry him, come over here and use his new status to take my army and march over the border into Dantherei."

"What? Why there? Does Garian want to be a king?"

"Either a king or a lover to the rescue."

I drank my wine off as quickly as Jewel had, and leaned forward. "Wait. Wait. None of what you are telling me makes any sense. Rescue who?"

"The queen's sister, Princess Eleandra-Natalia—"

"Her again," I said, sighing. "From what Maxl has been boring on about since his stay there, she already has as many suitors as I have gowns."

"You have never seen her," Jason observed.

That was all he said, but I had not spent a couple days in

his company without gaining a modicum of insight into the changes of his voice, his expression. "Oh no," I exclaimed. "Not you too?"

For the first time ever, I saw him laugh. "We have been secretly affianced for nine years, she and I."

My mouth was open. I shut it.

"Unfortunately there have been political intrigues that have become increasingly complex. Garian appears to have joined the complications."

"So...what is your part in those complications?"

"I promised her nine years ago that one day I would march in and remove her sister from the throne. At that time she would marry me and we could join the kingdoms. The benefits to Ralanor Veleth would be incalculable, for I've several generations of increasingly bad management to overcome."

I got to my feet and prowled the perimeter of the room. The mind-numbing power of surprise gave way gradually as I considered everything I had heard—bringing me to another surprising conclusion.

"You told me all this for a reason," I said. "What is it? Not another threat, I hope."

"A request. I promise, whatever the outcome, you will get safely home afterward, and I will never again interfere with your life."

I made another sightless turn about the room. The sunshine, the view out the windows, everything was blind to me but my thoughts and my memories. "You tried once to force Jewel to marry Garian. Is that true?"

"I did. Before I really knew him. He promised the money I needed, and at the time I believed him. Just like I believed the ambush was made by Jaim's renegades, as most were dressed in old green battle tunics. But Markham did not recognize a one. Circumstances being what they were, we only realized that later."

It all fell into place then, like the pieces of a stained glass window, only the whole was not nearly so pleasant to look at. "Garian was plotting not just against us, but against you, too?"

"Yes. As for Jewel, marriage for treaty or wealth is traditional in our family," Jason went on. "Our mother came here as part of a bargain between my father and his most powerful enemy among the regional lords. Not that the treaty held."

"Jewel told me much the same thing. To resume the original discussion, you want me to go to Dantherei, am I right?" I asked. "As your envoy? And you expect me to, what, do your courting for you?"

He smiled. "That was done nearly a decade ago. I can't cross the border now, not without international repercussions, and I don't want to turn my back on Garian. I would like you to go see her. If she intends to keep her part of the bargain, send her back here, and then you can go home again whenever you like—bypassing Drath entirely."

I frowned. "You really expect me to speak for you?"

"Say whatever you like, from your own perspective. But that's the message from me."

"And meanwhile?"

"Meanwhile I am going to find my brother. If my understanding of his real motivations is correct, I will offer him a new plan. Together we're going to seek our needed finances from Garian Herlester."

"The threat at last!" I laughed. "A real threat, yet how comforting to hear someone else threatened for a change, especially someone I loathe. Well, I shall consider this request of yours—and your promise makes it seriously tempting. I take it Jewel would be accompanying me?"

"I think she will like Dantherei's court."

I did not know what to say—I was not about to thank him for the prospect of my getting home safely as he was the one who'd brought me in the first place—so I left.

Chapter Fourteen

Jewel's rooms were the ones on the other side of the great tiled bath.

I knocked and Berry let me in. A couple of maids had just finished changing the bed linens and dusting. Berry told me Jewel was in the bath.

"Flian! Is that you?" came Jewel's voice.

I walked in, to meet a wide blue glare.

"Berry says all the servants are talking—saying that you saved his life. Is that true?"

I shrugged. "Yes."

"Why would you do such a demented thing? Did you delude yourself into thinking that he'd be grateful?"

"Not for one moment," I stated. "It never even occurred to me."

My calm certainty seemed to enrage her further. I studied her stony expression and black hair plastered to her skull. "You look exactly like him right now," I added.

Her jaw dropped. She ducked under water and came up again with her hair covering her face. "Is this any better?" Then she slung her hair back and laughed. "You must have been out of your mind!"

"Well, I was, but I'd have done it even so. Think, Jewel. You wake up seeing this huge fire and a live person lying in its path. Would you let him or her lie there, no matter who it was?"

She shook her head. "I'd say yes and good riddance, but I can't really imagine what it was like. What *was* it like?"

"Horrible. I didn't wake up after we left Spaquel's—not until that fire. In retrospect I think Markham and Jason were alone except for me, traveling by the fastest route in a racing carriage, and the rest of his people were either scouts or decoys. They gave me a couple of doses of sleepweed, so I slept through it all. We would have reached the border around nightfall, everyone gets a big meal, no harm done. Instead there was this ambush, which took them by surprise. The scouts riding ahead had been killed first, so there was no warning."

Jewel drew in a breath. "Oh, I hope the ambushers weren't Jaim's people."

"No. Garian's people, dressed up to look like Jaim's."

Jewel let out a sigh of relief.

"Anyway, they fought the attackers off, but Jason got stabbed. It was at night. When they were down to the last couple of 'em, Jason ordered Markham to leave us and fetch reinforcements, in case there were more ambushers to come. Markham took one of the horses. I was all wrapped up in a cloak, lying in the smashed racing carriage. Jason had probably passed out, and woke as the fire began to spread. It was dark by then. He freed the other horse, which was closer to the fire— yes." I closed my eyes, calling up the vivid images from that terrible night. "I nearly tripped over the traces. I think he was coming back for me, but he collapsed, for by then he'd lost a lot of blood. When I woke, the trees all around us were on fire and branches were falling." I opened my eyes.

Jewel gazed back at me in astonishment. "So what did you do?"

"Rolled him onto the cloak and dragged him out of danger. And when he first woke, Jason did his best to provoke me into running—either that or taking his knife and finishing the ambushers' job, and when I did neither, he scorned me for my cowardice."

"Eugh." Jewel grimaced. "He must have been in an almighty sulk. That's the only possible explanation."

"Maybe. But the truth is, I *am* a coward."

"A coward would have run and left Jason to burn to death."

"Then there are degrees of cowardice. I don't see that as an act of bravery, only one of moral necessity."

She snorted. "I see it as an act of insanity. And my stone-hearted brother thought you not only cowardly but stupid, or why would he snarl and snap at you afterward so nastily? Because I must say, his reaction sounds surly and uncivilized even for *him.*"

I knew by now that Jewel's perception of her older brother was limited by vivid childhood memory. Jason was opaque to me as well, but I suspected that he exerted himself to be opaque. It was his armor against his own harsh early life. Whatever his true motivations or desires or feelings, it would be a mistake to assume that because one couldn't fathom them he had none—or that they were uniformly evil. Especially in the light of his revelation about Princess Eleandra-Natalia.

Remembering that surprising revelation, I laughed inside. Jewel heaved herself from the bath. "Berry? You here? Where are my gowns?" She grinned as she swathed herself in a towel. "I made Jason's fools bring along my favorite dresses. And *they* had to carry them."

"They and the horses." I followed her into the bedroom, where Berry was in the process of laying out clothes.

I had forgotten Berry's presence, and wondered how much of Jewel's and my conversation she had overheard. Then I dismissed that thought with a mental shrug, remembering my days as a lady's maid. She'd heard, all right, and would probably relate all our words to whoever wanted to hear them— but that, I thought, was the Szinzars' affair. I would soon be going home, after my side trip to Dantherei.

I waited until Berry had collected Jewel's dishes and left before I said, "You are going to love the news I just heard. Only you better sit down first."

She was in the act of pulling on stockings. "Don't tease, Flian. You cannot conceive how horrible the past five days have been—" She paused. "No, actually, yours were probably worse."

I couldn't help a laugh. "Will you hate me if I admit that I did not find durance here very vile?"

"Impossible!" Jewel sat upright. "What is there to do? Nothing! No court, no flirts, no dancing—"

"But I had my music."

She shook her head. "Why do I like you so much when we are so utterly different? Never mind. Go on."

"I found out what Jason's raising money for."

"Which is?" She straightened her sleeve ribbons, admiring their loops.

I moved to where I could see her face best and said in my blandest voice, "He wants to take his army and march into

Dantherei to rescue his beloved."

She jumped as if she'd been pinked with a fork. "What?" She glared at me, narrow-eyed. "You're teasing! It can't possibly be true."

"Isn't it amazing?" I laughed. The revelation still felt peculiar, as if I'd stepped onto what I thought a floor, and found it was a boat. "What's more, it's that very same princess that my brother is in love with. And, it seems, Garian as well."

"Garian too? Oh, well, I don't see why Jason shouldn't have her, then," Jewel said, in one of her characteristic, dizzying reversals of mood. "Maybe afterward she'll keep him locked up writing love poems to her earlobes, and he'll leave the rest of us alone. And Garian can gnash his teeth and wail over his lost love for the rest of his life." She made a terrible face. "But I cannot, under any circumstances, imagine anyone in love with Jason."

"Especially for nine years."

"Nine? *Years?* I have to meet this wench."

"That's my next news. It seems that we are going to."

She whooped with laughter. "So we're going to Dantherei?"

"That's what he wants."

"Ow! Ow! Ow!" She shook with mirth. "My gut hurts! Stop. Show me what you've been playing during your durance vile, and I'll tell you all the latest gossip from Carnison. You are going to *steam* when you hear the horrible things that Gilian said about me, just because I danced with Maxl twice at the ambassadors' ball..."

She followed me into my room, where I sat down to the harp and played softly. Jewel related in colorful detail who had danced with whom, when, who was flirting with whom, and who was dallying with whom, making no attempt to be fair or objective. I listened to the tone under the brave words and laughing insults, determining several things. One: though Jewel had flirted with every handsome fellow who smiled at her, she had trysted with none of them. And second, she and Maxl had been circling one another with what sounded to me like mutual distrust—and fascination.

We were interrupted at sunset when Berry came back in, not accompanied by silent stewards carrying trays, as I had come to expect, but alone. "Your highnesses." She gave us a grand curtsey, and I wondered if Jewel saw the humor in it.

"The king requests your company for dinner."

Jewel's brows swooped upward as she turned to me. "Were you forced to *eat* with him?"

"Not until this moment." I was still smiling—trying not to laugh.

"Well, let's go see what the slimy villain is demanding now." Jewel looked in the mirror, flicked her curls back, twitched at her ribbons, and sashayed out the door, skirts swaying.

Berry's and my eyes met. She was biting her lip to hold in laughter. My own laugh escaped as I followed Jewel out.

Though the Szinzar castle had proven, at least in this wing, not to be a grim and dim barrack, I did not expect elegance and dazzle for a private dinner—and thus was not disappointed.

We were bowed into the same chamber we'd talked in earlier, and Jason wasn't even there. Jewel went to the rosewood cabinet in the corner, clinked around impatiently, then reappeared with two fragile glasses shaped like bubbles, filled with an aromatic amber liquid.

"Good mead." She brandished the goblets. "No one drinks it any more in Carnison, but it's so cold here, and mead warms you up better than those nasty Drath wines."

I took mine to the window where I could sip and watch the purples and roses of the sunset over the western mountains.

Jewel prowled about the room, swirling her mead in the one hand and picking up and setting down objects with the other.

Jason came in. Jewel stopped her peregrinations and scrutinized him. "You *did* get hurt!" she exclaimed.

"Markham will bring dinner directly. Unless you wished to socialize first?" he addressed his sister.

"Oh, most certainly. And a grand ball afterward," she shot back, arrow for arrow.

A few moments later Markham appeared, supervising the stewards who carried in the trays and swiftly and silently transformed the table near the windows. Cloth, napery, silver— unexpectedly elegant.

We all sat down, were served, and then Jason looked up. Markham flicked his hand, and the stewards filed out and closed the door. Markham stayed.

Jewel ignored them all and attacked her food with

enthusiasm. Jason said, "Markham is assembling your entourage."

"I'm not so sure I want to go," Jewel retorted with lofty scorn. "She's *your* princess. *You* go fetch her. *I* want to go back to Carnison."

"You can't. Garian has his entire force roaming the borders. It would actually be safer to go north into Dantherei and then southwest into Lygiera. Why not visit the capital on the way?"

Jewel groaned. "Doing your errands. I hate that!" She eyed him. "Unless you're lying. I can't see you languishing after anyone, except maybe a fast horse. Or a fine sword."

Jason's eyes narrowed in that suppressed humor, but all he said was, "Eat your food before it gets cold."

The food was trout in wine sauce, potatoes cooked in garlic-and-onions, and fresh peas dashed with summer herbs. It was delicious, but I was glad for the space to think. I had to consider the notion of Jason being in love, which I found oddly unsettling. I'd assumed that he wasn't capable of it—he was removed from all human feeling besides the martial ones.

Maybe I wanted to think of him that way? But that thought perplexed me even more. I decided to ponder the question later, when he was not sitting right there before me.

"Say we do go." Jewel waved her fork. "What are you going to do? Lounge about and recuperate?" She smirked.

"Find Jaim."

Jewel's smirk vanished and she glared at Jason. "You'll never find him. Never."

"Yes I will. I know approximately where he is. I monitored Garian's unsuccessful searches during my stay in Drath, while my own people ran around busily creating false trails. If I'm right about the general location, Jaim'll then find me."

Jewel threw down her fork. "And what, send your bullying border riders in to murder him like a rat?"

"I'm going alone."

"Well, I want to go too, to make certain you don't hurt him. And I don't want to go begging to some stupid princess."

Jason's eyes narrowed again, but not with humor. Their expressions were startlingly alike, and I knew he was about to say something cutting.

I said, "Please come with me, Jewel. Dantherei is supposed

to be lovely, and I would much rather travel with your company than alone. And afterward, remember, you can come home with me. And stay as long as you like."

Jewel studied me. "You don't want me to argue with Nastyface here." She poked her thumb toward Jason.

"Not over dinner. Argue as much as you like after," I invited.

She laughed. "Done."

I turned to Jason. "Sooner gone, sooner I'm home."

Jason slid his left hand into the neck of his shirt and pulled out the silver chain, from which swung an object. He lifted it over his head. "There's her ring." He tossed it onto the table. "Either she returns with it, or keeps it."

I looked down at the gold ring, a fine lady's ring, set with two deep blue sapphires twined in gold leaves. The last time I had seen it, there had been so much of Jason's blood on it I could not make out what it was. I was reluctant to touch it, but Jewel felt no such compunction. She grabbed it up, undid the chain's catch, then slid the ring onto her finger, admiring it against the last of the fading light.

"You leave after breakfast," Jason said.

Chapter Fifteen

I did not know what to expect—anything from another military company to Jewel and me departing on a pair of ponies with a pack of travel food between us.

What we found waiting after breakfast—which we ate alone—was a cavalcade fit for two princesses, all of it overseen by the silent Markham.

Jewel took one look at that tall, powerfully built, bony-faced man and said, in a whisper that was not very soft, "Figures my rotten brother would send along someone to spy on us."

I snorted a laugh. "It would hardly require a spy to overhear our conversation."

Jewel only grinned unrepentantly.

My own assessment of our escort was that they were warriors masquerading as servants; the woman, Lita, who was to be our maid, moved with a strong, trained efficiency that reminded me very much of my tent-mates in Brissot's company.

Jewel sighed, looking around the countryside. The road north wound up gentle, forested hills to the mountains that formed the border. The day had dawned without rain, and though there were clouds overhead, they were not—at present— a threat.

"If only I didn't hate Jason so much." Jewel lowered her voice. "The only way I can be certain he won't do something nasty to Jaim is to go along and watch him. Then there's the matter of being stuck doing his errands for him, fetching some obnoxious beauty—"

"She is obnoxious?" I asked, disappointed. "I was hoping we'd like her. Make for a much more pleasant mission."

"No, it'll be much better if she's awful." Jewel snickered. "Jason deserves a stinker, and anyway, would you wish a nice person a lifetime stuck with *him*?"

"Well, if she's in love with him," I pointed out, "she would want to be with him."

"A beautiful princess, popular with everyone?" Jewel's brows slanted up.

"But—people who are vastly different—can't they find one another interesting? I mean, I have so little experience. But it seems true."

Jewel affected a shudder. "Only a thorough rotter could have the bad taste to fall in love with him." She snickered again. "If she is indeed nice, let's talk her out of marrying him. What a score that would be. And if she's not nice, let's talk her out of it anyway. Then when he marches his army over to fetch her, they both look silly. Serve him right. Hah!"

I couldn't help laughing, and as usual, the more I laughed, the more Jewel's mood improved.

By evening we came to a guard outpost. Markham was waved through the gates, and within a short space of time we'd been shown to a somewhat spare set of rooms, clean and comfortable, but as plain as you'd expect at an outpost.

We dined early. I offered to while away the time by playing the lute, which I had requested permission—through Berry, because we never saw Jason—to take. Jewel listened for a short time, then danced about the room with an imaginary partner. But she was yawning long before I was tired of playing, and so she went off to sleep.

When I set aside the lute, Markham entered the room. Despite his size his footfalls were so soft one almost didn't hear him. "Do you have any orders for the morrow?"

"No. Thank you," I said, looking at those oblique, deep-set dark eyes. I wondered what he was thinking.

The man bowed and withdrew.

I sat for a while longer, contemplating my reaction. It was difficult to define. Was it Markham's unstated authority? Though he'd asked me for orders, I knew very well we were in his charge. The staff answered to him. Markham was unswervingly polite, but so unreadable it was like having Jason present.

At least we did have an intimidating-looking escort—most

of the men wearing those wicked-looking thin mustaches like Jason's. It would have to be a good-sized gang of thieves to waylay us; meanwhile, couriers had been sent ahead to apprise Queen Tamara, sister to the legendary Eleandra, of our approaching visit, and to order clothing in the current styles obtaining in Dantherei. All we traveled with was riding gear, though Jewel had insisted on bringing her favorite gowns from Carnison. I suspected they were a waste of space, for fashion did not flow from my homeland north, but the other way. Chiar-on-Tann had been built a hundred years before the market town of Carnison had been chosen as the royal residence by my distant ancestor; now the great capital of Dantherei was called Char Tann, a transmutation that evoked Eidervaen, the mythic capital of faraway Sartor.

ʒO

We descended from the rocky hills comprising the border to look out over broad, rich farmland. There was one great river to cross before we reached a well-tended royal highway that was busy with traffic from dawn to dusk.

Our cavalcade was nothing to be ashamed of. Our two scouts had returned and rode at the front as banner bearers. One carried a banner in my Lygieran blue, the other the dark green and pale gold of Ralanor Veleth. The liveried servants rode in columns behind Jewel and me, all of us on beautifully mannered plains-bred horses that were one of Ralanor Veleth's few enduring resources.

When we reached the broad and slow-running Tann, we crossed its splendid mage-built bridge. From its height were able to look over the entire city laid out below us, which appeared prosperous from our vantage. Built along the low hills parallel to the river was the royal palace, gleaming pearl white in the late summer sun.

Judging from the size, it was a little city on its own. Most of the buildings were obscured by tall golden chestnut trees, silver alders and well-trimmed lindens.

When we approached the city gates, Markham rode ahead. He was met by a woman nearly as tall as him. Her blond hair gleamed around the edges of her helm as she bent to hear what

Markham said, then she waved a gauntleted hand and we passed inside, up a brick-tiled street toward the royal palace. Very fine shops lined both sides, at intervals broken by little park-circles with fountains in their midst.

When we reached the gates round the palace complex, the female guards waved us on. Markham saluted as we passed, professional to professional.

We were met by liveried servants in gray and pale mauve and silver, who led us down a side path charmingly bordered by exotic shrubs that still showed blossoms, though the bite of autumn was in the air.

The vast gardens were carefully tended to convey an impression of artistic profusion, the tall flowering trees evidence of several generations of attention. Secluded buildings were visible here and there. The garden opened onto a grand parade before the royal residence itself, a great U-shaped building fashioned entirely from white marble.

A herald appeared from a side path. "Welcome to Erevan Palace, your highnesses. If you please to honor us by stepping this way, we can see to your refreshment."

Jewel cast me a look of half-laughing alarm.

As I dismounted, I found a tall, dark shadow at my side. I looked up into Markham's face. "Your highness. The king bade me request you to write no messages in this place. Any needs can be safely spoken through Lita to me." His deep voice was expressionless.

He took the reins of my mount. A little stunned, I gestured my understanding, and he bowed, his long hair swinging forward, and led the horse away.

Jewel and I followed the herald, who could not have been any older than I. Her walk was graceful, her manner pleasant as she pointed out the various buildings. Some of them were the private residences of those of highest rank and influence. Everyone else stayed in the big palace.

Up broad marble stairs, across a terrace shaded by potted trees with beautiful amber leaves, and inside. Up more broad marble stairs and midway down a hall. Later I'd discover that your importance dictated where you stayed: enemies or friends of high rank got the suites closest the stairs. People of royal rank who were regarded as neutral, their influence minimal (like Jewel and me, princesses but not heirs), stayed where we were. Those of less importance, or those who had lost royal favor, were consigned to the corners of the building farthest from where the royal family lived.

Lita had been brought up a back way. She was already busy supervising several efficient servants clad in soft gray-and-white livery, who were putting away the few things we had brought along for the journey. When we entered the murmur of voices abruptly ended, and the palace servants exited through an almost invisible door in one of the walls.

The furnishings, elegantly curved, were covered by satin cushions, the walls freshly papered. Everything was pale blue, or light, light gold, with crystal sconces to hold candles.

As Jewel wandered from room to room, exclaiming over everything, more of those quiet gray-dressed people came in with food and drink. After we'd eaten, Jewel expressed a wish to go out, but Lita said, "Your pardon, highness, but we will need to complete the fittings first."

Jewel's eyes widened. "Can you not pass my Carnison gowns through the cleaning frame?"

Lita shook her head and glanced my way.

I said, so she wouldn't have to, "I'm afraid we're hopelessly behind the fashions here, Jewel. And our first appearance is an important one."

Lita cast me a look of muted gratitude. "If it pleases you, your highnesses, Fanler, who came ahead to prepare for your visit, has hired local seamstresses. They've already begun the necessary work. We need only today to do the final fittings on walking and formal interview gowns."

"That'll get us through tomorrow," I put in.

Jewel flicked her eyes skyward, but submitted, and a little later the new clothes were brought for us to try on. Neither of us cared for the Dantherei fashions, which were mostly heavy brocade stiff with embroidery and beads.

Jewel whistled. "Are you sure you didn't pay off that ransom?" she asked when we were alone. "This stuff—plus that company of stitchers—must have cost my villainous brother the equivalent of a year's meals for the entire army." Her brows contracted. "Why the largesse? It isn't *like* him."

"But isn't it obvious? It's all to make us look good for his Eleandra."

"Mmmmm." Jewel grinned. "When I see Jaim again, I will

tell him our mistake was in not getting Jason paired off years ago."

I laughed, deciding not to point out that this romance had taken place before she'd had the least interest in such things. The ten years of experience separating Garian, Jason, Eleandra, and to a certain extent my brother from Jewel and me seemed like a generation.

The next morning Lita brought us word of the day's court activities. A herald apprised the guests' personal staff of general gatherings, which we were apparently expected to attend. More personal invitations would be spoken either in person or by messenger.

So we were to be presented to Queen Tamara out in the garden at midmorning. When the distant bells rang the carillon, Jewel and I were ready. She said, "Strange! I feel like a sixteen-year-old at her first appearance."

I smiled. "I feel like a stuffed cushion. If we do manage to meet any villains, we're not going to be able to run very far."

"Well, they won't either, if they're dressed like this." Jewel held her arms away from her body as she took a deep breath. "Whoop! This bodice is tight. In any case, villains can beware, because I did not come unprepared."

"What?"

In answer she vanished back into her room and reappeared with a long, wicked-looking dagger. "Found it in Jason's practice salle and decided I needed it more than he did."

I laughed. "Well, I can't imagine anyone needing a knife *here.*"

"So I would have thought at Carnison, and then my cursed brother came along. So I hid it under my chemises when I packed. No one will ever know." She chortled. "Unless I need it."

"Come, hurry. The bells did ring and we don't want to be late."

And so we trod sedately in our stiff brocade skirts down the stairway.

Lita had said that stewards along the pathways would make certain we did not get lost. "Spies," Jewel whispered, giving a surreptitious tug at her gown.

The bodices were unyielding fabric, embroidered with garlands of tiny beaded flowers and leaves, and they forced us to stand straight. Jewel insisted she couldn't breathe and cast me a look of envy, but in truth, the style flattered her curves. What little figure I had was flattened beneath that formidable bodice, making me feel fifteen again.

I found out quickly that I had to walk in a smooth glide or those stiffly beaded and embroidered skirts swung like bells. Poor Jewel, whose walk was characterized by an enticing swing of hip, kept batting down the skirts and then skipping or hopping to counterbalance the weight of the swaying fabric. Her fan knocked against her knees on its fine chain, and she swatted at that too, alternately cursing under her breath and spluttering with laughter.

A herald in fine livery appeared seemingly from the shrubbery, bowed, and ushered us through the crowd to a broad semicircle of people gathered along the manicured banks of a quiet stream. It was a relief to see that our gowns were indeed the latest style, and furthermore the courtiers, though daunting in their glitter and poise when seen as a mass, were all sizes, including those who had felt it necessary to cinch in their waists to accommodate the fashion. Not just women, for the men wore long, stiff tunics that were much the same style and fabric, sashed at the waist and then sashed again, baldric-style, over one shoulder. They did not look any more comfortable than the women. No one wore weapons; they were forbidden within the walls of the palace Erevan.

My mother had brought a die-away drawl from Narieth, a style my brother grew up loathing. Here in Char Tann voices were low, quick, almost a monotone—emotionless. Easy enough to emulate if one so wished.

Queen Tamara was tall and broad, about forty. She dressed plainly, leaving us convinced that the mysterious Eleandra led the fashions. The queen strolled along the riverbank with a couple of female companions, nodding pleasantly here and there as she contemplated the stream. The sweet sounds of stringed and woodwind instruments drifted from behind the flowered shrubs, where musicians had been concealed.

The beaded and gemmed brocade reflected sunlight into the eyes. I was not the only one overheated. People around us plied their fans.

A general, well-bred sigh of pleasure went up as a line of swans sailed with breathtaking grace down the water to vanish among delicate willow fronds. Those whom the queen had already greeted began drifting away.

So that had been the purpose of the morning?

Queen Tamara started our way. One of her companions was an older woman dressed in that splendid herald livery. She whispered and the queen nodded; when they neared, the herald spoke our names.

The royal eyes met mine. I looked into a wide, intelligent face, framed by thin brown hair expertly dressed under a pearl-edged, gold-threaded cap.

I dropped a curtsey, princess to queen. She acknowledged with a gesture. "How is my cousin of Lygiera?"

"My father is well, your majesty," I said, hoping that was true; I suppressed a pang of guilt. But even if I did write a letter, how would I get it carried through Drath to home?

"And Prince Maxl?"

"Quite well, thank you."

"You must give him my thanks for sending you at last, Princess Flian, as he once pledged. But I am disappointed that he did not return with you. I found him congenial and full of promise."

I curtseyed again, suspecting that this comment was, in fact a question: why did I thus come with Jewel and not from home? A question I was not even remotely going to answer! "My brother will be grateful for the kind words, your majesty, as am I."

"I entreat you to enjoy your sojourn here, child." She passed on to Jewel. "Yet another I have wished to meet."

"Thank you, your majesty. And I have always wished to visit." Jewel curtseyed with a flourish of her stiff skirts.

Queen Tamara tapped her on the wrist with her fan. "A remarkable family, yours." She drawled her words so subtly one could easily miss the glimmer of humor. "You must next visit insist Prince Jaim accompany you, and in the spring, when we hold our festival. I believe he might find our games and competitions to his interest."

Jewel curtseyed again.

Smiling, the queen passed on. Her third companion was a woman, slighter of stature, about the same age, her eyes a darker gray than mine. She was soberly gowned, though the fit and fabric were fine, and her gaze had that same quality of fast appraisal that characterized Tamara, Jason and Maxl. I stared, cold with shock. It was only now, as I gazed after Tamara, that I finally comprehended what our mission meant. We weren't reuniting lovers long separated. We were participating, however tangentially, in a plot to overthrow this queen.

Chapter Sixteen

Though we never again had private converse with Tamara ru Fidalia—if that can be considered private—I sometimes encountered her greeny-brown gaze over the next few days, and I was convinced that *she* comprehended a great deal. And I began to have misgivings.

During the two days that we waited for her sister, Princess Eleandra, to return, Jewel garnered a great deal of gossip about the queen—not that her life was very dramatic. She had been betrothed at a young age to a much older man who had fallen heir through the devastations of the last war to a vast amount of wealth and land. When she reached adulthood, the marriage was duly compassed, as were so many royal marriages—according to carefully worked out treaty, not according to inclination.

The king lived a secluded life on a distant estate, seldom coming to court; he was an artist, apparently, having never taken any interest in politics. It was his hand we saw in the new furnishings and the delightful design of the court theatre, whose balance of sound and space was exceedingly well devised.

The woman in the sober-hued gown was Lady Aelaeth—the queen's beloved. Once a scribe, she had been given title and land. In every way but treaty-ordained fact, she was the consort. The court knew it, ambassadors knew it, the country knew it. But, like most kingdoms in the world, tradition required one ruler of each gender, a man and a woman to symbolically represent the men and women who comprised the country's subjects.

Unless the queen chose to try the Birth Spell, and one could never predict if it would work or not, no matter what your rank in life, Eleandra was the heir. The queen led a staid, middle-aged existence; Eleandra, more than ten years younger than her sister, apparently led quite a dashing life.

"Of course," Jewel pointed out the third night of our stay, "gossip about affairs doesn't mean that they are serious, and sometimes they aren't even real. I heard what was said about me in my short stay at Carnison. All lies. Not that I care," she added in a brittle tone.

"At least we'll meet Eleandra tomorrow. And there will be a ball as well."

"I look forward to that." Jewel wandered toward to her room to get ready. "Not that I mislike plays, but I never realized before that court comedies are only funny when you know the local gossip. And we don't."

"True," I said, glad that I had not been invited to see this play a second time.

Jewel had already managed to make friends with some of the more stylish courtiers our own age. They liked her title, she liked their wealth and they all liked one another's looks. "I only said yes because Lord Darivei whispered to me that there will be impromptu dancing afterward," she called from her room.

Impromptu here meaning the same thing as at home: open to everyone instead of by invitation, and you don't have to tread all the way back and change clothing yet again.

I was glad that I had chosen to hear one of the choral groups instead; that ended well before midnight, consequently I woke early.

Because Jewel slumbered on and the dawn was fair, I decided to take a walk. By the third day I had learned my way around the gardens, which were divided into quarters by tiled paths. On this morning I struck out in a new direction, and drawn by the sounds of laughter, found myself on a terraced portion of the garden overlooking a grassy space on which people were engaging in sword fighting, wrestling and various sorts of target practice. At first I thought it was only the guards, for their silvery-gray tunics with the crimson edging predominated, but then I recognized some of the faces from court. Most of the guards were female, some exhibiting impressive displays of skill. One young woman in guard silver-gray disarmed two opponents, a man and a woman, both much bigger than her.

I followed the narrow path down to the grass, keeping to the perimeter until that young woman had finished and turned to a long table to get something to drink.

I followed. "Pardon, may I ask a question?"

She looked up. Her hair was much lighter than mine, her sun-browned face square and ruddy with her recent effort. She bowed. "Your ladyship?"

I didn't bother correcting the title. "I wonder, can anyone learn that? What you did to disarm those others."

She chuckled. "Begin in childhood and you'll know better tricks than that."

"Could I learn anything like it?"

Her face went serious. "Self-defense can be learned at any age—and ought to be, at least so our commander says. Come each morning, dress like this—in riding trousers and tunic— and we'll undertake to teach you as long as you wish. The dawn practice is open to anyone, no matter what your rank."

"Thank you. The sun just came up. Is it too late, or could I learn something today?"

She squinted upward. "If you are quick, you could get some of the basics over with." She grinned. "I warn you, though, you'll be stiff come morn."

"I'm not afraid of that," I said.

"I'll wait, then."

I fled, found that Jewel was still asleep. Good. I would not have to explain myself. Not that I really could. It was an impulse as incomprehensible as it was intense.

I changed into my riding clothes and ran all the way back, arriving breathless and damp.

She kept her word. She put me through some exercises that were not unlike those my dance mistress had taught me when I was young, which I still performed by habit. Afterward she taught me exercises for strength, especially in the arms. By then my muscles burned and trembled. But we were not done. She showed me eight arm blocks, four with each arm, and made me do them with her until I could deflect her attempt to strike me.

When at last a bell gonged and the practice broke up, my

body felt held together by strings—unraveling ones at that—but my mood was exhilarated.

There is little else to report about that day. Princess Eleandra did indeed return, sending a storm of whispers and interest through the court, but we only glimpsed her from a distance. Apparently she was even more difficult to get near than the queen.

The closest we got was when she was handed, laughing, into a canoe on one of the canals, by no fewer than three young, wealthy and handsome lords. And she was beautiful—probably the most beautiful female I have ever seen. Her hair was a compelling blend of shades that reminded one of all the richest woods of the world—heavy, waving and thick, partially dressed up, the rest hanging like a shining cloak against her skirts. Her coloring was rose-tinged coffee-and-cream, her lips delightfully curved and naturally red. From the distance I could not descry the color of her eyes, but guessing from the colors in her gown, they were a chestnut brown.

"She'll surely be at the ball," Jewel said with satisfaction. "We'll get to her for certain. The stupid part of our mission will be over with, and we can spend the remainder of our visit enjoying ourselves. All we need is an introduction. She'll make the time for a private chat."

I agreed, for Jewel's words sounded sensible.

They also turned out to be wrong.

We never got within speaking distance of the popular Eleandra that night. The grand ballroom was quite spectacular—almost barbaric in its splendor. It had been made in the far-north Venn style long ago, with golden mosaics and great carvings of fantastic bird figures above high inset arches. Color smote the eye from all directions as brocaded dancers performed for one another and for the onlookers.

We did not get within speaking distance of the princess for three weeks.

As those days passed by, I began to make a few acquaintances. The queen's formal affairs lasted a long time as they were conducted to exact ritual according to precedence. Since Eleandra tended to avoid them, so did we. For choice I attended music concerts, which did not permit much talk, or I went with Jewel to the less formal dances. Jewel had managed to make a great many superficial acquaintances, all one needs for dancing. We did not lack for partners, because she introduced me to her new friends, and most of those young lords were quite happy to dance with a princess—especially a wealthy one.

It was Carnison all over again. They talked of their holdings, their views, what they could do with some added wealth and power. A few questions to me, not from any interest, but to find out what I liked so as to make themselves sound better. If I mentioned music, I invariably heard something like "Oh, everyone loves music!" and a quick change of subject.

How many conversations like that have I endured while twirling down the line of a dance? Impossible to count. With the skill of long practice I nodded, smiled and scarcely listened. I could see in their polite, slightly bored faces that they found me a bland pudding of a princess, easily impressed. For my part, I listened to the excellence of Queen Tamara's musicians and rejoiced in my sore arms and legs.

From what coincidences are our lives shaped? After that first day of practice I might have gone right back to bed, but the knowledge of the hot baths downstairs, kept filled and warm by costly magic, brought me down to bathe. The soreness eased after a hot soak, leaving me ready to venture out to training.

My guard had become my regular teacher. Her name was Ressa. She knew me only as Flian, and free of the awkwardness of rank, we got right to work.

And so the three weeks slid by. Eleandra continued to be elusive. I was privately convinced that she knew who we were and was avoiding us, a notion I didn't share with Jewel. I was afraid Jewel would get angry before she and Eleandra had a chance to become friends. Then there were my own feelings to contend with. I did not want Eleandra to cause Jason to unleash a war against Tamara and her peaceful kingdom.

So I made no attempt to meet the elusive princess. Jewel was so busy flirting with two young men, I don't think she remembered our mission.

But I finally got tired of worry and avoidance. Over breakfast one morning, I said, "Maybe I should risk all the attendant gossip by requesting an interview from her household steward."

Jewel had been sitting with her chin on her hand, gazing out the window. She transferred her attention to me, and the bemused, tender expression altered to curiosity. "Tamara's?"

"Eleandra's. When she gets back from wherever it is she's gone this time."

Jewel grinned, reached over and tapped my arm. "What you need is a lover."

"No I don't."

She gave her head an impatient shake. "No one to *marry.* You'll marry to the benefit of Lygiera, if you marry at all—naturally. But someone with whom to flirt. The time passes much quicker with someone who knows how to kiss." She grinned.

"You're in love," I observed.

"No." Her answer was too quick. She blushed, pressed her lips into a thin line, then said, "Interest only, not devotion. Why not pass the time in agreeable flirtation here, where we're not known, and once we're gone we'll be forgotten?"

"I guess it's because no one I've met inspires me with the inclination."

"What? Don't tell me you did not find Krescan attractive? He's tall, has that pretty auburn hair, and he moves so well. He's even eligible! Krescan is a huge holding, and he has the title."

"He is handsome," I agreed, "and doesn't he know it. I swear he was watching his own reflection as we danced past the black marble insets. He certainly wasn't watching me."

"Rimboal finds you attractive. He told me as much—and he seems to partner you frequently enough."

I recalled Lord Rimboal's sweaty hands, his oppressive compliments on my hair, my sea-gray eyes, and shuddered.

"You can't say he's ugly. You can't."

Lord Rimboal was tall, as thin for a male as I was for a female, curling dark hair. Brown eyes, curved lips. He was attractive enough—in the way of a fine painting. I shrugged. "I don't know. I don't like his standing so close, and all those compliments. And some of his questions—" I made a face. "What perfumes do I prefer? That's so, so personal." *Personal.* For a moment I was no longer there, but stood in a tiny woodcutter's cabin. I was not looking at the handsome Rimboal, but a black-haired figure sick and feverish, whose derisive blue eyes stared straight back at me. Shoving away that unpleasant memory, I said, "There's no meeting of the mind. Not with *anyone.*"

"Well, but you don't have to have that to flirt. You just have fun. If you find the fellow attractive." When I made a face she shrugged, one of her dark brows slanting up. "No help for it. You're hopeless."

"Not hopeless." I tried not to laugh. "But probably much like my father. Who knows? Maybe I will fall in lust with a handsome, witless seventeen-year-old when I turn sixty."

"And I shall throw him in the lake if he hurts you," she declared. "But by then I hope I—" She looked away and shook her head, her lips compressed.

"Well, you continue to have fun, and I'll continue to—" I paused, stopped, thinking of my mornings with Ressa and the others.

"Continue to moon after the perfect harpist," Jewel finished. "Whatever you enjoy, which is the point, after all. We are here to have fun, and I mean to have it. I don't know what awaits when we leave. I don't trust those idiot brothers of mine not to make it impossible to go to Carnison with you. So I mean to please myself as long as I can."

"Fair enough."

Chapter Seventeen

"Good! Good!" Captain Voliz clapped me on the shoulder with a tough, callused hand. He grinned, gray whiskers bristling. "Again."

He came toward me with a knife, made a stab, and I used his motion to push him off balance, then hooked my foot round his ankle and yanked. He went down. I pretended to step on his elbow, grabbed the knife he dropped and held the blade to his neck. All as drilled.

"Excellent. Very, very good for a few days' work, eh?"

"She moves well." Ressa stood on the side, watching as she awaited her turn. "Learns quick."

A young guard said earnestly, "You ought to train with the rapier. You're fast—you might have fun with it."

I thanked him, adding, "My brother has been trying to get me to do that for ages. Maybe I'll surprise him and go along to practice with him one day when I get home again."

"Where d'you come from?" Ressa asked tentatively. "Your accent is coastal, unless I'm mistaken."

"Lygiera is my home."

Captain Voliz snapped his fingers, and Ressa did not look surprised. "You'll be the princess, then."

I laughed. "How did you guess that?"

He gave a nod. "You have a slight look of your father. Saw him once, back when we were having trouble from the north."

By then no one used titles, excepting the captains in charge of the practices. The free give-and-take was bracing; not one of them asked what land I would inherit, or whether or not I controlled my fortune. Not even the other courtiers at practice.

It was as if political questions had been set aside—while we drilled the elements of fighting. This contradiction sometimes amused me as I walked down in the cold dawn, or back when the sun had topped the gate towers. Still, I kept at it, because my goal was never again to be abducted against my will.

The very morning we finally met Eleandra, I went to practice in a prickly mood, for I had dreamed about Garian Herlester the night before.

I tried to see Garian's face on my first opponent and felt a corresponding determination that verged on anger. The result was a flurry of action too quick for me to follow, and I found myself lying on the grass, a blade pressed to my neck.

I smacked the grass with my hands, the signal that I'd lost, and the woman I'd been paired with straightened up. "You're quick. But you don't see the counterattack yet."

"That's dangerous," Ressa added. "You're at a bad place in training."

"Of which there are many," the taller woman put in dryly.

Ressa said, "Never lose sight of the fact that you're medium of height for a female and light of build. So until you've had years of special training you'll never be able to take on a trained person bigger and stronger. A hill ruffian who counts on surprise and shock, sure. But even then you have to act fast, because you'll probably only get one chance. Even the hillside ruffian is going to be stronger than you, and if he gets a hand on you, chances are you're going to eat mud."

"Or die," the other said.

I was in a somber mood when I returned to my room.

I had seen almost nothing of Jewel for two days. I let the door shut and kicked off my riding mocs, preparing to undress for the baths downstairs, when the connecting door opened, and Jewel appeared, her eyes red rimmed.

I gasped, my aches forgotten. "Jewel? What's wrong?"

"What's wrong is that I'm a fool. Never mind. Where have you been? Not following my stupid advice, I hope?"

"Just out walking."

"With grass stains all over your trousers?" She wrinkled her nose. "Not that you owe me any answers. Pardon if I intrude."

"I have been attending the dawn defense practices—something I've come to enjoy."

She raised a hand. "I'm glad. Jaim made me learn a lot of that, and I know I ought to keep it going, but—" A sob shook her frame. "But I'm a purblind idiot, and I never do anything right."

She whirled and dashed back into her own room.

I followed. "Jewel. I won't pry, but I wish I could help."

"You can't," she cried. "Unless you can really find a way to get us out of here the sooner. I hate, I hate, I *hate* being taken for a fool, but the truth is I *am* a fool, and the sooner we're gone the happier I'll be."

"Well, I guess I'll approach Eleandra-Natalia's steward, then. Someone at the practice mentioned Eleandra returned from her visit last night."

"They are *all* spies," Jewel stated with teary passion. "For— who knows who for? Maybe for themselves. Don't tell anyone *anything*."

I bit my lip. "This does not sound good."

She sobbed again, an angry sound, and dashed tears from her eyes. "I never said anything that can hurt Lygiera—or Ralanor Veleth. But it's simply because I don't *know* anything. Avars Darivei does, though. He had mentioned the ring before, but last night he tried to get me drunk. I went along with it. Curious. Truth is, we Szinzars must have inherited my mother's iron head, for she used to drink as many as four bottles a night, and she only got more sarcastic. I can drink and drink, and I'll get sick before I get drunk."

I waited; her words came, fast and breathless. "So between kisses he started in with the questions about the ring. I kissed back, laughing off the questions, and finally I outright lied. Said I'd taken it from our family collection because I liked it, and he was disappointed—I could *feel* it. He is a spy, and I don't even know who for."

"But your other friend can't be a spy as well," I protested.

She slammed her hand down on a table. "Oh, can't he?" she growled, teeth showing, and again she looked very like her brothers. "The only advice my mother ever gave me I can still remember. Mostly she was too drunk or too angry to make sense to a small child like me, and I know I bored her. But on my ninth birthday she said, 'When you start taking lovers, child, make certain you never have any fewer than two, and no more than four. One will assume rights not his; more than four

151

and they don't balance out their rivals.' I thought I was so clever to have the two, and besides, I liked them! But after I slammed out of Avars' apartments, I went to Begnin for consolation, and he was laughing at me."

"What?"

"Oh, not in words or tone. But I chanced to look at his face when he didn't know I was looking, and he was *gloating*. And his questions after the first two or three had less and less to do with my feelings, and more with what Avars had said—and why."

"Ugh."

"And so I lied to him, too. I don't care what happens to Jason or his stupid princess, but I do have some pride. No one brings the Szinzars to their knees unless they wish to be there!"

"I'm sorry, Jewel."

"Ah, there's no use in being sorry—or anything else. And here's the horrid thing. None of those fellows has the least importance. Not a one. They're *all* conniving to move up by influence and connections, by using secrets as well as skill in flirtation. Eleandra has all the powerful ones dancing to her tune. I want to get out of here."

"All right. Let's forget the steward. I'll bathe and we'll go to the morning swan-watch. Maybe Eleandra will come. If we exert ourselves, perhaps one of us might manage to get near her."

"Oh, we'll manage," Jewel vowed.

Jewel meant what she said.

At any court, the focus of attention is on those in power—or in favor. As the important people move about, noticing this person or talking to that, the watchers defer and then reform around them, little circles ever changing. You moved yourself forward by degrees, speaking to someone, being spoken to, everyone jostling by tiny roundabout steps either closer to power or closer to desire, for not everyone was there to political purpose.

Eleandra did indeed come to the streamside with her sister, supposedly to watch the swans, but when the queen moved away the princess lagged behind, talking and laughing with a tall, languid, cold-eyed lord who gossip said had supposedly fought four duels this year.

Jewel stood by me in silence, observing the patterns,

listening to the soft, well-bred murmur of voices, but when the princess was parallel to our position, Jewel smiled at the people before us, snapped open her fan and elbowed her way past.

I followed, aghast. If the princess gave us a direct snub (and we'd seen her do it, mostly to other women) we'd be the night's gossip—and the next day we'd endure turned shoulders and other snubs.

Jewel flung back her hair, her color high, and fetched up directly in the princess's path. I stopped next to her.

Eleandra looked down at us—she was half a head taller than I—with a sort of amused challenge. "You are Flian Elandersi and Jewel Szinzar, are you not?"

I curtseyed, my heart thumping. At least she didn't snub other princesses—under her sister's eye.

Jewel said, "We are."

"I trust you've found your stay agreeable?"

"Yes." Jewel smiled, snapped her fan open again, and plied it slowly, her wrist turned—and the sapphire ring glittered.

Eleandra's perfect bosom rose in a short breath. "Walk along with me," she commanded. Then forced a smile, and a more dulcet tone. "Though this is my home, it is refreshing to see it through a newcomer's eyes."

She stepped forward, her arms made a graceful, studied shrugging motion, as if she dropped a shawl, and the dashing Lord Galaki sketched an ironic bow of deference toward us, stepped away, and began a conversation with one of the other fellows.

For now the three of us were alone.

Eleandra turned to me. "Have you the same intent here?"

"I do." I strove to be diplomatic—to keep the promise I had made. "We are here to visit and to enjoy ourselves, which we have done. Your sister has been very gracious. But it is time to return to our duties in our own kingdoms. We are here to invite you to return to Ralanor Veleth."

Jewel said, "Shall I return to you this ring?"

The princess flicked her fan open, a quick gesture, almost of warding—obscuring Jewel's hand from the rest of court—and Jewel's arm fell to her side.

The fan waved slowly. "I am contemplating a journey," Eleandra drawled. "Have you ever seen the argan trees before they drop their leaves?"

"No," we said together.

"I assure you, it is a sight not to be missed. Accompany me on this little journey, and we will have more leisure to discourse upon the subjects that interest us."

I bowed acquiescence. Jewel bowed acquiescence. Eleandra bowed acknowledgement. Then glanced back—and the tall lord was instantly there, smilingly offering his arm.

A few more general comments about the swans, about autumn, about the prospective masquerade ball—and she turned down another path, surrounded by a crowd that had gathered without my being aware. We were left on its periphery as everyone again traded places in the endless dance-duel for precedence, but I no longer cared.

Jewel cast me a glance of triumph. "We did it. Now a boring detour to see these stupid trees, and then for home."

"Home?" I repeated as we walked along the garden paths. "You do not mean to Ralanor Veleth."

"No." She gave me one of those looks, her color high, her eyes wide and glittery with reflected light, her mouth pressed into a grim line.

Ah. I waited for her to say more. When she didn't, I left the subject for her to pursue or not. "At Carnison, court reconvenes after harvest. You'll like winter festival. We skate on the ponds, and there's dancing every single night. Plays, too. And our comedies will be funny, because you'll know who's being skewered."

"Beginning with Spaquel, I trust." She rubbed her hands briskly. "Oh, if he's still attending court, I shall write one myself." She spun around, the light winking and glittering off her embroidered gems. "We'll have to keep reminding ourselves of that pleasure."

"Why?"

"Because we're in for boredom until then, that's why. Beautiful she is, but did you see those eyes? About as much feeling as coins. She will not be any fun to travel with. But." She laughed. "You have to admit that she's *perfect* for Jason!"

Chapter Eighteen

Two days later we were gone.

Jewel's daring had turned into a social triumph because of that private conversation with the princess—witnessed by so many eyes. We spent those two days being courted by everyone in the princess's own circle. Everyone was either overtly or covertly curious about the subject of that conversation. I smiled, bowed, danced, ate, listened, deflected questions, and inwardly counted every bell toll until we could depart.

Jewel veered between excitement at being the focus of attention and moments of intense gloom when anything reminded her of her failed romances. She flirted more than ever, but refused to go off alone with anyone, even to drink a glass of wine. Consequently we were much in one another's company. Being with Jewel in an uncertain temper was like riding a little boat down a rushing river during a thunderstorm, but it was never boring.

Late the second day we departed. The queen sent one of her heralds with a gracious message charging us to carry greetings to our respective royal relatives. A great crowd turned out in the city to watch us ride by.

We did make a grand cavalcade, with long banners snapping from the poles in front, two for the princess (one for Dantherei and her own as heir) and one each for Jewel and me, and then the shorter banners of her chosen friends, in strict order of precedence.

Her own household guard rode next. Unlike her sister, she did not mix men and women. Her guards were men only, all picked for their looks as well as putative martial prowess.

We rode horses decorated with ribbons and late-season flowers. At the end followed a very long train of servants and wagons, including a carriage for when Eleandra was tired of riding.

We rode the rest of the day, though the wind became increasingly cold. We halted at a posting inn that, I suspect, outriders had cleared of any hapless travelers who had happened to be there, because the innkeeper and staff were all lined up waiting for us, and the entire place was empty when Eleandra's servants began carrying in baggage.

Jewel and I were given a suite on the same hall as Eleandra. I stayed there, waiting for steeped Sartoran leaf; Jewel went out and returned soon, flopping down into a chair opposite the fire. "Galaki has the room next to hers," Jewel said, wiggling her brows. "Ought I to tell Jason—or not? No, I won't." She let out a slow breath. "He won't care. He hasn't enough heart to be jealous."

I couldn't help laughing. "You really are cruel."

She grinned. "No, not cruel. I adore justified grudges, and you must admit that Jason makes a wonderful villain."

The door opened then and Lita carried in a tray of porcelain dishes for Sartoran brew. "Pardon, your highnesses, but Markham wishes to speak to you."

"Ugh." Jewel rolled her eyes.

"Is he here?" I asked.

Jason's tall liegeman waited in the doorway. I hadn't seen him during our entire stay at Tamara's palace.

"Please come in," I said. "Is there a problem?"

"Her royal highness has requested us to return to Ralanor Veleth. Her steward just spoke with me. They are trying to reduce the number of personnel, at least those whose functions are redundant."

Jewel smiled, for the first time looking directly at Markham. "Well and good. Tell Jason we'll be along soon with his princess."

"The king desired me specifically to remain with you, your highness," Markham said.

"But you're not needed." Jewel jerked her shoulders up and down, turned her back, and poured out steeped leaf.

I looked up at those dark eyes, feeling uncertainty. "Who all is considered redundant?"

"Cook and stablehands, as well as the outriders."

Jewel sent me an impatient look. "Since Eleandra is going back to Ralanor Veleth, why have the extra people cluttering the journey? Our own people can ride back to Lathandra and let Jason know she's coming."

"Though she hasn't actually *said* she's going to Lathandra," I pointed out.

"Well, she said she'd talk privately with us—and she can hardly do that if we have a hundred servants clashing around into one another like too many dishes on a table."

"She seems adept at being private when she wants to," I said.

Jewel rolled her eyes. "Do what you like." She flounced around in her chair and stared down into the fire.

I turned to Markham. "What think you?"

"I mislike this command. But if, in truth, her royal highness means to keep her troth, you will need at least a couple of us to ride on with you to Lygiera. Perhaps, if I may suggest a compromise, I can stay as well as Lita. I can see to your horses. They all know me. Between Lita and me, we ought to be able to oversee any unexpected difficulties." His soft voice was as oblique in tone as Jason's.

I couldn't understand him, but I had come to trust him after my experiences in the Drath mountains—that is, I trusted him to see to Jason's interests and to keep his promises. Including the one about our safety. Two against twelve...if anyone could keep us safe, it was he. "A good suggestion. Let's do that."

Markham went out, and not long after another knock came. One of the princess's particular female friends, a lively red-haired woman not much older than Jewel and me, stuck her head in. "Dinner downstairs. Come, Jewel, make us laugh. Tomorrow Galaki goes back up north and Eleandra is glum."

We set our cups down and descended to the great parlor, where we found the rest of the aristocratic company gathered. Fresh-cut roses in crystal vases had been set here and there, fine linen of a violet hue covered the plain tables, and the princess's own silver and plate had been set out. The room was as elegant as her servants could make it.

The redhead, a baroness named Siana, dropped down next

157

to her sister Eneflar, who had inherited a vast county somewhere in the west. Eneflar was an elegant, haughty woman. She had a light, drawling, very sarcastic sort of wit that kept them all laughing. Jewel responded with her own sarcasm, which was more passionate than witty, but the contrast made them laugh the more.

The two men besides Galaki were handsome, one dark, one fair, and their reputations for gallantry were matched by their reputations for dueling and gambling and risky sport. They made themselves agreeable to all, but their jokes were all reserved for Eleandra, all obscure references to their shared past.

I felt out of place in that company. Jewel and I were very much the youngest, as well as being the least experienced.

For a time Eleandra included us in the general converse, her manner gracious. But as the evening progressed her mood became more distracted. After dinner she said, "Let us make up a dance, shall we?"

Siana clapped her hands.

Eleandra summoned her servants, and within a short time we had a trio playing for us. The two barons were assiduous in partnering Jewel, myself and the two sisters by turns; Galaki never gave us a second look. He stood up only with Eleandra, and their murmured conversation was conducted below the strains of the music.

They left together at midnight, so absorbed in one another they scarcely heeded the others' polite words. I watched them go, feeling that unsettled sensation inside. I could not define why. It was clear that Jason was not on Eleandra's mind right now—but I had no idea how someone who had waited for nine years to be reunited with a lover would think and feel.

It seemed too easy that she would change her mind, and thus resolve my moral dilemma concerning her sister. Then I thought of Jason perhaps even now ordering his army to get ready for the march over the border, and I felt even worse.

Next day, Galaki was gone.

At dawn I was woken by sounds of readying departure in the courtyard below the windows: horses, people walking back and forth carrying things.

We discovered on arriving at breakfast that Eleandra

expected to depart the moment we were done eating; she was already in her carriage. Jewel was in a spectacularly bad mood, for she loved to lie abed of a cold morning, but we complied, presenting ourselves in our riding clothes about the same time as the others, all looking rushed and grumpy.

The sky was threatening, gray and low. By noon the increasingly cold wind brought spatters of rain. A downpour was due. Apprehensive looks turned skyward all up and down the line, for none of us had been invited to ride inside the carriage.

Eleandra paid no attention. The barons rode at the carriage windows. She talked and joked with both. Just as the rain began in earnest, we arrived at Siana's own home atop a hill overlooking the southern river valley. It was typical of many such places, an old castle turned by degrees into a palace: ancient walls torn down or made low to border gardens, windows widened and glassed, plaster and statuary or trailing vines masking the gray stone.

The place was small, but quite comfortable. Siana gave up her own suite to Eleandra. Jewel and I had adjoining rooms again. No sooner had I changed than Lita came in to say, "Her royal highness requests the favor of your company."

"Thank you." I had begun to wonder when that private converse would take place. That it hadn't in the capital made sense. Too many ears. The day previous she had spent entirely in Galaki's company.

Now, it seemed, she was finally turning her thoughts southward.

I went out, met Jewel, and together we passed down the hall of guest rooms to the great suite across the front. In the first chamber, we found some of Siana's staff busy arranging things under the direction of one of Eleandra's servants. The princess's steward escorted us to a pleasing little room where the princess sat quite alone.

The door shut. "Chocolate?" Eleandra offered, pointing to a silver service.

"Yes!" Jewel reached for the pot, pouring for three.

I took a sip of mine, enjoying a taste I remembered from childhood, and thinking that it might be time for a winter fashion when we got back home. Jewel would be pleased.

"How is Jason?" Eleandra asked.

"Yum! Excellent chocolate."

"Thank you."

Jewel's brows quirked, then she said with admirable diplomacy, "As for Jason, he is unchanged."

"So I surmised." The princess sounded wry. She transferred her gaze to me. Those eyes were so beautiful in shape and coloring, and so lacking in expression. "How comes it you are with Jewel?"

I had anticipated that question. "A long story," I said, in my most bland voice, and sure enough, she did not request it. "The end of which is that Jewel and I became friends. The idea of traveling together appealed to us."

"The ring." Eleandra glanced at Jewel's hand and Jewel began to twist the ring off. "No." Eleandra leaned forward. "Too many people might recognize it. Keep it for now. What I wish for is not the ring itself, but the message that must be with it, and I wish to hear it without other witnesses." She finished on a sardonic note.

I reported in as even as voice as I could, "He said, 'Either she returns with it, or keeps it.'"

"And?"

"And that was all."

"He did not discuss his plans for afterward?"

My insides lurched. The dilemma I'd hoped would neatly resolve itself was here at last.

Jason had promised nine years ago to marry her and send an army to remove her sister. Those words had had no real meaning for me when I heard them. Now, having met Tamara, and having seen a portion of her prosperous, well-governed kingdom, and practiced with her guard, the impact of that dispassionate statement was like a dousing of cold water over my soul.

"No." Jewel ran her finger round the gilding on her cup. "That was what he said. Either you return with it, or keep it. Isn't that right, Flian?"

"Yes." I watched her finger. Round and round and round.

Eleandra tapped her nails on the table. I blinked. Then noted that Eleandra's chocolate had not been drunk.

Jason's voice came to mind, when I was sitting beside the fire in Spaquel's house. He was saying something about making the effort to find out what I knew.

Kinthus.

That was how most people obtained truth in criminal cases these days, for the herb, when drunk, removed whatever boundaries the mind made against talking freely. It was used not just in criminal cases but in royal courts, it seemed. Where lying and lawlessness were practiced with style.

I set my cup down. Maybe I was wrong—but still, I'd lost the desire for chocolate.

Jewel poured out a second cup. She did not seem the least bit sleepy; on the contrary, her eyes widened. "There isn't much I can say for your court, but you people do know how to eat and drink well." She chuckled.

Eleandra smiled. "Tell me about Jason. Tell me everything."

"What is there to tell?" Jewel asked, making a large gesture. The sapphires on the pledge ring flashed. "I haven't seen him but for the day before we left for Dantherei, since Jaim and I ran away years ago."

"Ah. One day?"

Jewel wrinkled her nose. "Yes. His fools forced me back from Carnison, where I-I—" She blinked, her brow wrinkled, then she said, "Where I was almost coming to an understanding with Maxl. Dear Maxl. Lovely Maxl. He is everything Jason is not, but I believe he thinks I am just like my brother."

I tried not to gasp. She had never said anything about Maxl to me, though I had begun to suspect that she had some feeling for him. Was I in fact right about the kinthus?

"Maxl is a dear," Eleandra said in a smooth, soothing voice. "But we can discuss him later." She turned her gaze my way. "Flian. You do not drink."

I almost said, *You don't either.* The words formed themselves, but I bit my lip, hard, and said instead, "I do not care for chocolate."

"I shall order you some steeped leaf, then. Would you prefer it?"

"If you are having the good Sartoran brew, I will be happy to join you."

Her perfect brows arched, but she was still smiling as she rose, rustled to the door, ordered Sartoran leaf from someone standing outside, sat down again, her attention on Jewel. "So you favor Maxl," she said in that calm voice. "I like him well myself. Do you think you will make a match of it?"

"I would like that more than anything I have ever wanted." Jewel had plumped her chin on her hands, her wide, unblinking gaze on the pearls in Eleandra's hair. "More than anything." Her low voice carried all the fervency of vow.

"And so he sent his sister along when you returned home? That sounds like a promising gesture." Eleandra smiled invitingly.

Jewel blinked, opened her mouth—

I said, "Maxl often talks about his visit here—and about your kindness to him."

Eleandra's gaze turned my way. I kept my face bland, from long practice. Jewel blinked, looking confused, then her expression smoothed into dreaminess.

"Does he?" Her tone was kind, even coaxing. "Yet I have received no messages, much less embassies of suit, for at least a year, if not longer."

"Oh, I think he knows he hasn't a hope of winning your hand."

"Mmmm." The princess lifted her brows.

"Maxl's eyes are so beautiful." Jewel sighed the words on an outward breath. Then chuckled. "How often I wanted to kiss them! Especially when he was being cold. But he has much to bear, warding bad news from the old king, who sits and talks endlessly about the old days to his few remaining cronies, and to those sycophants who will listen to anything if they scent a reward."

"But that encompasses any court, yes?" Eleandra said.

"Not Ralanor Veleth. No court. Nothing but war games, and tribunals, and talk of land reform and raising money and then more war games. Horrid life, horridhorridhorrid."

"What can you tell me about Jason's war plans?" Eleandra asked.

"I don't know any. Ran away with Jaim...so long ago..." Jewel's eyes drifted down, then she jerked awake and smiled sweetly. "I am so tired. I want to take a nap."

"I will walk you back." I rose and took her arm. A nod of the head to Eleandra. "If you will excuse us?"

Jewel yawned.

Eleandra said nothing, only nodded back, politeness for politeness, but I felt her gaze on us as we left.

Jewel yawned several times as we proceeded back along the guest hall to her chamber. There we surprised Lita in the act of packing away her riding clothes from morning.

Jewel dropped onto the bed and curled up, her cheek on her hand, her eyes closing.

I beckoned to Lita and she followed me to my room. "The princess put kinthus in the chocolate. I am sure of it."

Lita's gaze did not waver. "May I ask what she found out, your highness?"

"She only found out Jewel's impressions of our court. She wanted to know Jason's plans if she returns with us to Ralanor Veleth. Not that either of us knows what those are."

Her expression did not change. "Thank you for telling me, your highness. I will inform Markham. If it is your wish, we will see to it that your food and drink henceforth pass through our hands."

"Please," I said, and she departed.

I sank down into a chair by the window, gazing out at the gray sheets of rain. Why not tell Eleandra everything I knew? I sensed that she was no ally of mine—but then neither was Jason.

Wherein lay the blame? Those two appeared to share evil intent. I could only consider an invasion of Dantherei as an evil act. Tamara was not a tyrant and her people obviously did not suffer under her rule. Everywhere I looked I saw prosperity— fine roads where in Ralanor Veleth there had been mud, except on the military routes. *Those* were better roads than ours, even, though we had been working on that. The cities clean and busy with trade, the people moving about freely. How could Eleandra or Jason better that?

Yet I was not without fault, for I'd blithely agreed to come here and perform this service, just so I could then go home. I could say that I'd merely agreed to court a princess, but the truth was that Jason had told me what had been agreed on their betrothal. I was, therefore, not innocent—only selfish and shortsighted. I had, in fact, consented to be drawn into politics, which was another word for betrayal, for war and strife and desolation—all to get an easy trip home.

Now I had to face the truth. If Jason married this princess

who talked of plans and not of love, and kept his promise to make war on Dantherei, lives would be lost and I would share the blame.

What was it Papa had said to Maxl? *You young people are playing dangerous games, too dangerous for an old man...*

I put my head down on my arms and wept.

Chapter Nineteen

The two barons departed, and only Siana and her sister continued with us.

On the surface our party was merry enough. I tried to do my part, smiling and pretending to be amused, but my inner turmoil continued. Jewel appeared to have woken without remembering the conversation, and I did not remind her. If she would not share her heart's desire by choice, I would not betray the fact that she had under the influence of herbs.

Eleandra did not seek any more interviews. During that long, distressing night at the baroness's castle I debated whether or not to tell the princess what had happened to me—to illustrate exactly what it meant to be drawn unwillingly into intrigues that had nothing to do with ethics or anyone's greater good. But even if I'd thought she might be sympathetic to my words, she gave me little chance for private discourse. With smiling, benign ease she avoided Jewel and me, except for the most general politenesses.

On our last night, at an inn, she stopped me outside my room.

"You knew about Jason's plans," she said.

Ice burned along my nerves. I so badly wanted to lie, to say something to end the threat of war. Yet I knew if she wanted war, she would find it.

And I also remembered that, whatever else I thought of his actions and motivations, Jason had never lied. "He told me what you promised one another on your betrothal nine years ago."

"But he said nothing about crossing the border to meet me?"

"No. Just what Jewel told you. Either go to Lathandra with the ring, or stay and keep it."

She gave a soft laugh. "Quite a game of risk he plays."

I wanted to say, *And you aren't?* But I kept my mouth shut.

"Yet you two are still with me." Her fan twitched like the tip of a cat's tail. Not a gross movement, but tiny, no more than a shimmer of the bright-painted silk. "A risky game. Good night." And she moved away.

I stared after, wondering if I should tell her that we intended to keep going west and then south to my home after we saw her argan trees, then decided not to. She had not asked our plans—and didn't need to know them.

So I retired for the night.

On the fourth day we descended into a gorgeous river valley—which meant we had ridden far more west than south. In the distance directly southward, sure enough, rose the northernmost of the great peaks that formed the border with Ralanor Veleth on the east and Lygiera on the west. The peaks that belonged to Drath.

There, to everyone's surprise, the princess bade her people raise the tent-pavilions.

Those had been brought against our being trapped on our ride by a sudden squall, but everyone had assumed we would be staying in some dwelling, even if only a posting inn.

As Siana stared about in unhidden astonishment, Eleandra said, "Is this not a profoundly beautiful place?"

"It is." Siana sounded more polite than convinced as she cast a puzzled, slightly weary look around.

Despite the court ladies' attitudes, the place really was beautiful. The campsite lay on raised ground above a fork in the river. All around us grew smooth, white-boled trees whose leaves were a brilliant variety of colors—crimson, amber, gold, pumpkin. And here and there the silver-leafed argan trees, rare in Lygiera's coastal air. Before their leaves fell, they seemed to take on a metallic glow that made them look like enchanted things, especially in the pearlescent light of dawn and in the slanting golden glow of sunset.

It was apparent that Eleandra had everything mapped out in her mind, for she did not trust her servants to the placement of the tents. She paced over the long emerald grasses, pointing here and there. It was not until the tents were actually set up that we saw a space near her own.

Eleandra expected someone.

Jason.

Some went inside the tents to change out of riding clothes. I wandered out on a palisade overlooking a waterfall just above the river fork. The two sisters had forgotten that tent walls block sight, but not sound.

"Who is coming?" That was Siana.

Eneflar drawled, "Whoever it is must be male, which would explain why she sent Galaki off in a huff. I don't know why you and I are here, unless those little princesses bore her as much as they do me. She's only happy when surrounded by men."

"She's not the only one." For once Siana sounded heartfelt.

"I wish she would tell me what she wants from me," Eneflar went on. "Then I could say yes or no, and go home."

"Where are you, Siana?" Eleandra called from across the camp, and the sisters fell silent.

As Siana emerged, I drifted around the back of their tent and made my way beyond wild berry shrubs so no one would see me and possibly be embarrassed. Though I suspected the only one who'd feel embarrassed would be I.

The horses and servants were all housed in plainer tents beyond the trees, well out of our view, along the riverbank. I could see the horses, some drinking, others grazing the sweet grass. Once I glimpsed Markham moving purposefully about, and I felt the urge to ask him how Jason would know to meet us here at this isolated riverside.

I squashed the impulse. Just because I didn't know about them didn't mean secret plans had not been made. So? I couldn't stop either of those two, Jason or Eleandra. My part was done. I had delivered the message, and I waited only to go home.

I turned away and wandered back to the tent that Jewel and I were to share. When I reached it, I found Jewel lying stretched out on one of the bedrolls. Lita was not there.

Jewel turned her head and studied me. "I wish I understood you."

No smile accompanied that statement, only a wide, appraising blue gaze that again called her brothers to mind.

I dropped down near her, murmuring, "I thought you did."

"I don't think anyone does," she retorted, her voice much softer. A hint of a smile warmed her eyes. "I will always be grateful to you for pretending nothing happened the other day—except whom were you going to tell? Maxl?"

So I'd been wrong, then. She did remember. I looked away, feeling a strong surge of sympathy. "No."

"Why not?"

"Because we don't talk about affairs of the heart. Not since his return from Dantherei, and he raved for weeks about Eleandra, and how he must have her. He didn't talk *to* me so much as talk *at* me. Then, when the years went on and she sent all these diplomatic messages but never actually came to visit, or invited him to visit her, he stopped talking about her at all. At least to me. What went on between Maxl and Papa, I don't know."

"So you two are as secretive as we Szinzars, for all your affect of sibling devotion."

"I do love my brother," I said in a low whisper. "I do. But he is private. And I guess I am as well, though there has been nothing in my life so far that required any exertion to keep private. Most people think me as boring as my interests."

"It's true," she conceded. "Some do. The ones with no discernment." She sighed, her eyes closing. "I love Maxl. I think I love Maxl. I am in lust with Maxl. Who isn't? He's handsome, smart and charming."

"Smart I believe, charming I don't know about—but handsome?" I smothered a laugh. "We're plain people, we Elandersis."

"Well, maybe attractive is the better term. It's his manner, the way he smiles with his eyes before his mouth does, the slight tip of his head when he's trying not to laugh. The way he'll rub at that cornsilk hair and mess it up when he's thinking." She paused, her expressive brow constricting. "Oh, I know some of his friends are better looking, like Yendrian. In fact I've met plenty of men who are handsomer, smarter, and a lot more charming. But Maxl is also in a position of power. Is it actually from that my supposed love stems? I can't say. I've never been in love before. I hope it's not the motivating inspiration, but I think he believes it is. I resisted it and resisted it, but now I wonder about myself."

"You are too hard on yourself."

"No one is hard on himself, or herself. Except maybe you two Elandersis. The problem is that you and your brother are good persons. Maxl has learned to live with power, but he very plainly regards it as his duty. Left to himself, he would sit in his lair among those old dusty books and that shabby furniture and read about history. And you have even less ambition than he does. We Szinzars aren't good. We all like power, and we're adept at finding ways to get it."

I shook my head. "Wasn't it you who said it's impossible to be all evil? I don't think it's possible to be all good either. We're a mix."

"I don't know. That's what I'm lying here trying to figure out. I feel very sure that Eleandra's motivation for her supposed love for Jason is his position of power. That's why she's here, isn't she? I mean, even I know that the Drath mountains are south of us now, and I remember what he said about going to Drath. The thing is, he didn't actually *say* he was going to come over and conquer Dantherei, did he?"

"No."

"He could be lying, but then he doesn't lie, my big brother. That's the problem! If he makes a threat, he goes right ahead and carries it out!" She grinned.

"He didn't tell us any plans, but that doesn't mean he doesn't have plans."

"Yes. Curious, how Eleandra picked this spot, when I would have staked my life she wouldn't cross a room to look at a tree, much less cross a kingdom. You think they set it up, all those years ago? Sounds kind of romantic, doesn't it? *If I send the ring, I will meet you at the river's bend. With my army.*" Jewel looked sardonic. "Have to admit the only part that sounds like Jason is the last bit. But would he really do something so disastrously foolish?"

"He did say that the resources of Dantherei would be of endless benefit to Ralanor Veleth, or something much like it."

"So why not trade? Surely a war is not cheaper."

"Not in lives, certainly."

She shrugged impatiently. "Lives probably matter nothing to him. All right. So their betrothal is a mixture of lust and power politics. What I want to know is, can there be real love in kings? Or does love have no place in those who command kingdoms?"

We were back to Maxl—though she did not say his name. "Tamara loves. Though they are not married." I had to admit the last.

"No, treaty marriages are expected of kings and queens. Are love marriages even possible? Would that be the test of a good king and a good person, marrying someone despite her lack of power?"

I shook my head. "My father is a good person and he married for love—he didn't need wealth, or treaties. What he brought back was trouble in the social sense as well as in the personal."

"Perhaps it means you're a bad person only if you know it'll be bad for the kingdom and you do it anyway," Jewel said, waving a hand.

"But what if one is so besotted one cannot see the signs? Oh, my Papa is so unworldly I don't think he would have seen the signs if they'd been painted on his nose."

"Did anyone warn him?" Jewel asked, leaning on her elbows.

"My grandmother did, from all accounts. If anyone else did, no one has said."

Jewel laughed. "Apparently your father was worldly enough to not listen to his mother! Well, that much is like Jason, who doesn't listen, he does what he wants."

"Yes." I thought of Jason wearing that ring over his heart for nine years. I remembered it hanging blood-smeared against his flesh that terrible day on the mountain. And I remembered him slipping it from his shirt and dropping it to the table. "Yes, he does."

We passed a quiet evening—five women waited on by a small army of servitors. I could see the campfires belonging to the servants glimmering downhill, though we heard no sounds. If they had their own amusements as the day passed, those were conducted quietly.

As for us, the three musicians played, Eleandra listened for a time, proposed a game of cards and then brooded, staring into the fire.

We departed to our tents fairly early.

Jewel lay in her bedroll without speaking. The silence was deep beyond the rush and chuckle of the river, and the sporadic sounds of birds. From the sisters' tent came the occasional rustle and low murmur of voices. From Eleandra's there was no sound.

I prepared for sleep, leaving the tent opening ajar so I could look out at the argan trees, stippled with silver light from the moon, and listen to the river. Our campfire was kept burning high.

Jewel wriggled to the tent opening, her bedroll around her, and lay with her elbows on the ground, chin in hands as she gazed at the fire, her features golden in the reflected light, the sheen of tears gleaming in her eyes.

She whispered, "What are we going to do? Sit here and risk launching a war?"

I scooted close next to her, my knees drawn up under my chin and my arms around them, the way I had sat as a child in my window seat, watching thunderstorms or first snow. "I have been thinking about the very same thing," I whispered back. "We could try, the two of us, to make it to Carnison and lay the problem before my brother." Only what could poor Maxl do, striving with Papa's old court as well as the machinations of those our age, and at the same time trying to shelter Papa from stress? "Should we break out, right now, and run for home?" I asked doubtfully.

"But we can't. We've got Markham along. You graveled us there, Flian. He'd be after us like a bolt from a crossbow, and no one outruns or outfights Markham. Even Jason can't beat him with a sword, Jaim told me. And there isn't anyone else that can whup Jason. I thought that was only a lot of male swagger, but Jaim said to believe it; in fact, that's why he ran away, really, because Jason kept making him stay in the practice courts for days and days, and kept sending all the biggest ones against him and they always thrashed him. Well, nearly always, there, at the end."

Jason must have done that as well, I thought, and contemplated the single-minded focus that would force someone to spend days and days "getting thrashed by the big ones" just to learn mastery. Supposing such a person liked art, when would he have had the time for it?

"Of course Jason had to," Jewel said cheerfully. "Just like

171

he grew the mustache. Jaim said it was to make him look older. I mean, he was younger than I am, when he took over! And you have to be strong to hold a runaway carriage like Ralanor Veleth. Well, look at the years after my father died. While my mother drank up Drath's vinery, civil war all over the place. Markham was a part of it, that much I know, though no details. And Markham, they say, was *always* terrifyingly good."

I remembered Markham's calm words about Garian's ambush, and how the thieves had made the mistake of thinking two against twelve a good balance.

"No, you're right," I returned. "We'd never be able to outrun Markham. Who is he, anyway, besides part of your civil wars? He's so, I don't know, different. Doesn't have the manner of a servant, though you can tell he's loyal."

Jewel waved a dismissive hand. "Some big mystery. Jaim wasn't sure of the details, or if he knew them, he didn't tell me. Who cares? I never want to see Markham or Jason again!"

"I suspect we'd better sleep before we have everyone listening outside our tent."

"Then I'll tell 'em exactly what I think of 'em," Jewel said, and crawled back inside the tent.

Two more days and nights passed. The first was pleasant enough. We whiled the time with walks. Eneflar had her maid bring paper and chalks, and she sketched the river fork, her skill unexpectedly fine. I asked Lita to bring out my lute, and I practiced, which made the time pass pleasantly for me, if not quickly.

At night the others asked me to play. They listened for two or three songs then talked as they had when the servants played, but I did not stop. I was only giving myself pleasure, but I was used to that, and I gave no one else any pain.

The second day was more difficult, partly because of a light rain that persisted through the day, but mostly because Eleandra's temper was uncertain. Jewel and I spent most of the day in our tent, playing cards—and it is a measure of the sisters' boredom that they asked to join us. Though I knew what they thought of us, I gave no clue, and Jewel's social manner was always easy enough. The sisters also made an effort to be pleasing, using their court manners, and so we managed to pass the afternoon until dinner was served in

Eleandra's tent.

After dinner, as the evening shadows began to meld and shroud us in darkness, we heard horse hooves.

Eleandra's head came up, her eyes wide, reflecting the light of the campfire that she had insisted be made each night and tended until dawn. I had my lute out again, had begun a ballad. I faltered, and laid it aside. Siana looked around, puzzled.

Eleandra swatted the tent flap open and walked out, her skirts flaring. The four of us followed as the sounds resolved into a great many horsemen.

He had come.

Anger burned through me—the anger of moral self-righteousness. Yet underneath that I was aware of a strong sense of disappointment. I had kept my promise, but I was not going to let Jason Szinzar spend lives without delivering my opinion of so evil an act.

The foremost rider leaped down, his long dark cloak swinging, and he threw back his hood.

The firelight made a golden-hued blaze of his long red hair.

It's not Jason, I thought blankly, buoyant with relief. Yes, and joy. *It's not Jason.*

"Garian," Eleandra cried. "You remembered!"

Chapter Twenty

"An invitation issued by you, Eleandra? How would it be possible to forget, when you are in my thoughts night and day?" He made an elegant bow and kissed her fingertips.

Her delighted laugh was the first real expression I had ever heard from her.

Behind her his guard dismounted. There had to be fifteen or twenty of them, all armed for war, and behind them servants.

Garian's gaze swept over the rest of us as he bowed. Jewel and I had gone as stiff as a pair of stalks. Garian's expression altered. "Is that Flian Elandersi?" He laughed. "And Jewel Szinzar. I don't believe it!"

"They came to invite me to Lathandra." Eleandra smiled, her tone teasing.

Jewel gaped with the same mind-numbing astonishment that I was feeling.

"It would, I admit, be strange to see Jason again after so many years," Eleandra went on, in that same tone: a little laughing, a little challenging.

"Seems a habit with you, meeting your suitors in secret," Garian retorted.

Eleandra glanced at us. This conversation was not following the oblique pattern that her court friends willingly followed. Siana and Eneflar were also staring in blank amazement. "Courtship is best done without an audience." Her chin lifted as she threw her beautiful hair back.

"But its completion requires one. Ironic, is it not?" Garian bowed once more, graceful and mocking. He saluted her hand with a lingering kiss. "It seems I shall eventually have to do myself the honor of calling on your sister again, but for now, we can while the time away here in this pastoral setting. What is it, watching the leaves grow? Fall?"

Eleandra laughed, and turned away. "If you've no liking for nature, then entertain us with wit."

"Now that is a challenge, is it not, Flian?" There it was, that nasty derisive tone I loathed so much.

Garian did not wait on my answer. He looked past me dismissively and instead asked questions of the sisters—who they were, how they liked their sojourn among the trees, and suchlike. They answered with court nothings, Eneflar's edged with sarcasm that made Garian laugh.

And so we stood about until the wind kicked up, blowing smoke into our faces. Eleandra gave the order for the campfire to be put out. It had been a beacon indeed, but not for Jason Szinzar.

Siana said, "I think I'll retire."

Eleandra responded with a polite wish for pleasant dreams. And so the party ended perforce. The sisters and Jewel and I returned to our respective tents. And though by then Garian's staff had set him up a tent in the space Eleandra had designated, he and Eleandra withdrew into hers, and occasional murmurs punctuated by laughter drifted through the cold night air until, at last, they diminished into silence.

I woke up feeling a whipsaw of emotions: relief that Jason had not come, wonder at how Jason was going to take the news, and apprehension at what Garian Herlester intended.

Rain pattered on the tent, promising another dreary day. Dreary and anxious. Lita brought us breakfast. She looked as tense as I felt.

As soon as she was gone Jewel muttered, "I won't stay with that nasty creature around. As soon as the weather clears, I think we should tell Markham to saddle our horses and we will leave. Now that Garian is here with her, our part is done. Markham ought to let us go on to Lygiera, whether he escorts us or not."

"I suppose we ought to tell Eleandra we're going. I don't want to make any diplomatic trouble for Maxl."

"You can do that. I won't talk to any of them. I hate it," Jewel grumped. "I hate rain and tents and boring companions, and I really, *really* hate Garian Herlester. Well, heyo, let's wander over and see if the other two want to kill time playing cards until Eleandra emerges and we can get the politesse over with and ride out of here."

There was no sign of Eleandra or Garian, so Jewel and I followed her suggestion. We sat in the sisters' tent and played cards in a listless, desultory manner until the sun came out late in the afternoon. Siana and Eneflar elected to take naps, and Jewel did as well. Eleandra's tent was silent, which could mean she was either occupied or else gone; good manners required us to wait until she wished to appear before us again.

I began to walk around to the other side of the fork where no one could see me, with the idea of practicing a little of what I had learned in Dantherei. I was about to slide my way down to the riverbank, which had a wide, flat space, when I heard voices below me.

Garian's and Eleandra's voices. They were walking at the water's edge.

"...afraid, my dear, you have no choice." That was Garian.

"What?" she demanded. "What do you mean?"

I was eavesdropping. Etiquette warred with expedience—and expedience won. I stayed right where I was.

"My invitation to return with me to Drath is more in the nature of a request. Send your friends home."

"But why? I told you I was going to break with Jason—if he doesn't break with me first."

"But you have not done it, my dear."

"Why bother? You know why I gave him that ring. I only wanted someone strong enough to oust Tamara. I'm tired of being second, of begging and pleading for money, of pretending this and that 'for the sake of the kingdom'. If I am queen, they have to please *me*. Jason said he'd put me there, once, but I don't believe he has any intention of making the effort now. Or he would have sent me word long before this, and not through a pair of twittering young princesses."

"Oh, he always keeps his word, the fool. I know that much. None better." His drawl tightened into anger. "He made sure of that when he and his damned brother visited me a couple weeks ago. He is quite predictable—and you, my dear, are famed for your fickleness."

She gasped.

"A compliment to the man who wins you and keeps you

constant." The smack of a kiss. "So yes, whatever he plans he will never fulfill, for I am already ahead of him. You say you wish to be queen? Then you must fall in with me. I take you to Drath. Your sister will not interfere, not with Lygiera and Ralanor Veleth on the verge of war."

"What? When?"

"Now. Soon. While Jason and his bush-slinking brother were busy helping themselves to the contents of my vaults at Surtan-Abrig and Ennath, my friends in Lygiera were busy filling the ears of Maxl Elandersi, in whom are combined the charming attributes of gullibility and earnestness."

"How can you provoke a war?"

"The same way you wished to. Turn the private passions of the monarch into a matter of state. I will spare you the details of that particular exchange, except for the delightful irony of the putative cause being your guest, all unknowing, here in this rustic retreat."

"Garian!" she exclaimed—laughing, admiring.

"Lygieran runners are probably halfway to Lathandra with their war declarations right now. You want a kingdom? Once Jason and Maxl have exhausted themselves in battle the winner will have to contend with me. I will give you"—another kiss—"an empire."

War? My brother?

I had been listening so intently that I forgot the surroundings and myself in them. I knew only that the voices were increasingly clear—so clear that they had closed the distance between us before I became aware.

Foliage rustled, and I stared up into Garian's face. "Flian." His eyes narrowed. "Doing some spying on your own? For whom, I wonder?"

My thoughts fluttered about like butterflies in a windstorm.

He stepped up to me. "You will be accompanying us, you and the Szinzar wench. I hope association with you has taught her some manners. You two will be useful, and that reminds me." He smiled, the gloating, hateful smile that made me burn inside with anger and fear.

He grasped my chin and forced my head up. "A piece of news that ought to interest you, if you've discovered a taste for politics. You are one step closer to the throne. The old man keeled over dead when my courier informed him of your abduction by Jason Szinzar and your subsequent disappearance."

A sun exploded behind my eyes.

Eleandra's voice came from a distance. "Jason did what to her? Why did I hear nothing of that?"

"You can ask for all the details on our ride. But get your people to pack. We will depart in the morning."

A cold frost solidified around my heart, quenching the impotent anger. The frost sent icy fingers up to freeze my brain, and like a string-puppet, I moved along when Garian gripped my arm, forcing me to accompany them.

He let me go outside Jewel's and my tent.

I walked in. I lay down on my bedroll—

How much time passed? I will never know.

My thoughts were far away, imprisoned in a terrible place. They returned briefly when I heard Jewel's voice.

"Flian? Flian. Are you asleep? Tomorrow we leave. There's a storm on the way, it seems, and Her Haughtiness does not want to swim aboard a horse down the river."

A voice spoke. "Garian is abducting her." Was it my voice?

"That so? Well, I must say it's a relief to have someone else get a turn for that!" She chuckled.

Time passed, or did it?

"...something wrong?" Jewel sounded anxious. "Oh, Lita, that gown on top. Otherwise it crushes into a million wrinkles..."

I dreamed. *Riding horseback, wearing Markham's clothes, Jason just ahead—*

The wind whisking, cold and pure and rainy, along mountain trails—

Memories of childhood. Of my first court gown, and Papa's pride. My first ball, and he danced with me himself. My first concert, Papa clapping the loudest at my choices, my hand-picked musicians, all of it spun through my mind, vivid, brittle, crystalline pictures, fragile as snowflakes, then they melted away. Maxl. Papa—

Papa.

The threat of war was not from Jason. It was Garian, and had been all along. Gloating. *Gloating* about my father dying, and sending Maxl and Jason at one another's throats, just so he could claim an empire...

Angry voices from outside the tent. Garian, Jewel.

"Apparently you have not yet attained a semblance of civilized behavior, Jewel. How tiresome you are, you and your fool brothers. How much pleasure I will take in being rid of all of you."

"You are stupid, and pompous, and rude, and a bore!"

Garian laughing. So confident, so cruel.

Lightning flickered somewhere to the west.

I groped my way to Jewel's baggage, neatly packed in the corner. Felt around, found the fabric of her chemises. Worked my fingers in—and there was the knife.

I was still in my gown. I took off the overdress with its tiny tinkling beads and lay down in the green linen underdress.

Closed my eyes.

Opened them, and the tent was dark, and Jewel's breathing was slow and even. Lightning flared, thunder rumbled.

Rain hissed down.

Time to act.

I slipped out of the tent and ran across the camp to Garian's. I crouched outside the flap, lifted it with a finger. Waited for lightning, which flared, blue-white and close.

He was there, sleeping alone. I saw how he lay, and a voice from far away said, *You'll have to act fast, because you'll only get one chance.*

Papa—he killed Papa. He intended to kill Maxl, as well as Jason Szinzar.

Not, though, if I could get him first.

I was going to take action, for once in my life. I eased in, my feet bare and soundless, and crouched beside Garian's long body. I raised the knife. When the next flash came it would guide my strike.

White and stark, the light ripped through the tent, revealing tousled red hair in his eyes, partially covered bare chest and—too late—a drop of water like a diamond falling from my wet hand.

I stabbed—an iron hand caught my wrist. It twisted with uncompromising strength, making me gasp with pain; this was no practice drill, each mindful of the other's safety. This was a duel to the death.

I dropped the knife into my other hand. Rose to my knees to throw my weight behind another strike.

Entangled in his blankets, Garian bore down with his hand and then yanked, throwing me off balance. We rolled over and over, winding together in blankets and my skirt as we each fought to stay on top.

We bumped against the other side of the tent. I writhed, desperate to free my knife hand, which was caught in one of the folds of cloth.

Garian's breath drew in. He swung a hand, knocked me backward. The knife flew free of my fingers, and a moment later he got me pinned down flat, hands on my wrists, and a knee across my own knees. I wrenched every muscle and bone in a desperate effort to get free, but his weight and strength and the enveloping mass of bedding kept me from moving.

"I wait only for the light to identify you, my would-be assassin, before I kill you. No one, ever, threatens me and lives." And he hit me again.

Then he shoved my wrists together over my head, and I knew he had the knife.

"Your wrists have a womanish feel. Which one are you?" He bent closer; I felt his breath on my face, and his hair brushed over my neck.

Lightning flashed. I saw his face above mine, mouth tight with anger. "*Flian?*" His eyes widened. "My very last guess. Too bad I will never find out what inspired you—"

He brought the knife down.

I tried, uselessly, to writhe free, but he was far too heavy and too strong, and so I closed my eyes—

At a sound from behind he jerked, something thudded against his arm—and the knife blade's lethal arc struck off center.

Cold fire flowered in my left shoulder. The knife yanked out, an oblique angle that caused the blade to scrape against my collarbone, and fresh anguish rent its way through me. I lay, gasping, trembling too hard to move.

Breathing, grunts—a struggle. Someone had entered the tent and attacked Garian from behind. I heard the sounds of violent exertion. Lightning glanced off that blade, now dark with blood streaks.

The sight of it enabled me to rise, stumble out and run.

Rain hit my face and I stopped, my mind clear for the space of one breath. My purpose had altered. War—betrayal—*He always keeps his word, the fool.*

I could not kill Garian, but I could warn Jason of Garian's plans.

Instinct aimed me, arrow to mark.

Jason would know what to do.

How did I get down to the riverside? Again my mind is blank. The next memory is the stark reflection of lightning in the horses' eyes in the makeshift pen. They were nervous and skittish. I don't know how I found mine or how I got away. I suspect the rain, and some wind-collapsed tents in the servants' camp, made it difficult to see one figure in a dark gown fling herself on a horse's back and ride out.

Lightning again revealed the mountains to the south. I held on to the horse's mane with my one good hand, for the other had gone fiery at my shoulder and numb below.

The horse bucked and sidled whenever lightning flashed. I kept my seat with increasing difficulty, until a flash almost overhead made the animal rear. The rain-slick mane whipped free of my hands.

I was in the air, suspended outside space and time. Not again, my mind wailed! *I am Flian Mariana Elandersi—*

Pain, and darkness.

Chapter Twenty-One

I woke to find myself gazing up into a pair of dark, deep-set eyes. The background was a hazy smear of rock and moss and close-growing pine in weak, early morning light.

"I'm Flian," I croaked.

"Yes." A deep voice betrayed mild surprise.

"You're Markham. I didn't lose my memory this time." I wriggled my legs. "And I don't hurt—"

I heard a soft laugh. "You landed in mud."

Gasp, when I wriggled my arms. "Shoulder. Pain. Pain hurts!"

"That was Garian Herlester's knife, not your fall from the mount."

Fire licked along my shoulder and arm and across my chest. "Uhn," I said, remembering what had happened.

The intelligent remark caused a narrowing of the dark eyes.

I struggled, found the words, forced them out despite the pain that each breath brought. "We have to. Get to. Jason. Warn him."

"Warn him?"

"Garian. Lied to my brother. To provoke. Attack from—home."

"An attack from Lygiera?"

I tried to get up. "Fast. We have to. Oh." I discovered that I had been bandaged, my arm fastened securely so that my forearm rested across my middle. It wasn't comfortable—but, as I grimaced and grunted my way into a sitting position, I realized that nothing was going to be comfortable. It felt as if someone had packed a burning cinder into the bandage. Every move of my shoulder was agony—but at least it was wrapped up.

"I took the liberty of dressing the knife wound," Markham said.

"Thank you." I thought of my no-doubt grimy chemise, and my face burned. At least I hadn't had to be awake for what must have been a thoroughly nasty episode. "Would you help me up?" Memories of Garian's gloating statements crashed through my aching head. "I must get going."

Markham bent and picked me up. But instead of setting me on my feet outside the makeshift shelter he'd made beneath a rocky outcropping, he carried me to a saddled, waiting horse. A big war charger, big enough to bear his weight and mine as well. He set me on the front of the saddle, then mounted behind me. He took the reins, but before we moved he reached into one of the saddlebags and pulled out a heavy flask.

"I suggest you try this, highness. One sip at a time. It might make the ride easier to endure."

He opened the flask and handed it to me. The aroma of strong rye whiskey made me sneeze. I took a cautious sip, for I had never liked strong liquors, and almost choked. The stuff tasted terrible, and it burned my mouth and throat. But the burn turned into a kind of glow, and the agony in my shoulder at every tiny movement eased enough to be bearable.

I took another sip. Again, the glow. My head buzzed, but it was preferable to the ache. "May I keep it?"

"Certainly. But not too much."

I was scarcely aware of his arm sliding round me. I sank my head against his chest as the horse picked its way down an incline and reached a path, then began an easy, steady canter.

Markham knew how to pace the horse for the best possible speed. Every time we progressed at a gait faster than a walk, I had recourse to a nip from the whiskey flask.

It was a relief to leave the effort to the silent armsman. I knew I would come to no hurt, and that was as far as I could think. Once I had an inner vision of one of my dashing ancestors galloping with courageous strength over the mountains on her own, despite weather, wound and lack of food; once again I found myself a dismal comparison.

No, my career as a warrior princess, short as it had been, was over, I thought morosely. Violence only works if you're good at it. Otherwise, it *hurts* too much.

At nightfall Markham found an old cave. He gathered firewood, made a fire, and when it was crackling merrily, he fetched from his gear a small, flat pan on which he pressed a handful of olives from the southern mountains, then fried some potatoes and shallots. I listened to the sizzle with happy anticipation, wondering how he'd managed to get all this accomplished and still find me.

I said, "What happened?"

"Lita saw you walking to Garian Herlester's tent. She came to apprise me, not certain what was your purpose. I judged I did not have time to return to my tent for a weapon but still I was just a moment too slow. I could not prevent him from stabbing you, for which I apologize, but at least I was able to knock his aim askew. He had two of his retainers sleeping in the tent behind. Lita held them off while I contended with Garian."

"Did you kill him?"

"No. The shouts of the others raised the camp, he lost his knife in the bedding. I tangled him in the quilts, and slipped out to avoid discovery. My purpose then was twofold: to get her highness safely away and to find you. Her highness refused to go with me."

I could imagine Jewel's response to Markham. "I didn't tell her the danger. It's my fault—"

"Her highness," Markham interjected with a hint of wryness, "refused to listen, maintaining that she was not about to ride in a thunderstorm at midnight. Lita will accompany her when the weather clears. She is resourceful."

"But Garian doesn't mean to let her leave at all." A wave of anxious helplessness made me feel cold and sick. "I didn't tell her. I couldn't. What he did to my father. He said he will get Maxl and Jason at one another's throats, and then form an empire. I tried to kill him first. But a raindrop fell off my hand—" My throat constricted, and I fumbled about and found the flask. I would not weep. Not until I could get home, and to Maxl.

Markham went on as if I were not snuffling and gulping. "When Garian Herlester appeared in camp the first night, I made ready for a fast retreat, should the necessity arise." As he spoke, he pulled the pan from the fire and spooned a goodly portion onto a plate, which he handed me, along with the spoon. He kept the pan for himself and ate with a knife.

"So you were waiting for Jewel and me to leave?"

"Yes. Though I was not certain that Herlester would permit that. My orders in any case were clear, to guard your safety but not to interfere with your freedom of movement."

"So Jason never intended to meet her at that river."

Markham gave me a considering look. "No. This journey took us by surprise, but as we moved westward toward Lygiera, Lita and I waited on your orders, whenever you wished to leave the princess's party."

"I wish I'd told Lita. I-I had misjudged the situation."

"So, perhaps, did we."

"How's that?"

"When Lita saw you return with Garian and Princess Eleandra during the afternoon, she was not certain what your intentions were. She said that you did not speak during the time she packed for the morning departure, not to her or to Princess Jewel. We had agreed to stand watch at night after Herlester arrived. It was during her watch that you left the tent and approached his. Again, she could not divine your intentions, but she came to me because you did not exhibit the manner of someone keeping a tryst, if you'll pardon the liberty."

I shuddered in disgust.

"After you left I spent some time in searching the grounds, but when I heard someone cry out that a horse was missing, I knew it had to have been taken by you. I departed at once in pursuit, fearing that the rain would destroy your trail."

"And you found me. But it's my fault that Jewel is in danger. All I could think was to warn Jason. I should have realized—remembered—warned her first."

"Do not distress yourself, highness. Princess Jewel is in no immediate danger. If she and Lita do not contrive their departure first, the king will assuredly find a way to bring her safely away." He gestured. "Eat. Drink. Rest. Three days of hard riding will bring us home, but you will need your strength."

As he predicted, so it came to pass. I had recourse to little sips from that whiskey flask with increasing liberality as the journey wore on. The terrible ache in my shoulder never seemed to abate. Despite my efforts to stay still, I managed to reopen the slash a couple of times, to sanguinary effect. The sight of my own blood made me reel with dizziness, and I drank the more, so that, on the third night, when the tired horse plodded down the road toward the torch-lit towers of Lathandra's royal castle, the whiskey flask was nearly empty.

We had ridden through every sort of weather, even snow, at the heights. It further twisted the warp of reality woven round me: the vision of softly falling flakes etched against the gray sky, the contours of the rocky peaks softened in their blue-white blanket, seemed unreal.

I arrived in Lathandra drunk, but I had stayed the course, and without making any complaint. That last was necessary to my own eroding pride, because my thoughts remained somber, veering between knowledge of my father's death and my disastrous attempt to summarily end Garian's plans—and his life—which had only made everything worse.

The tired beast plodded into the great stable yard, to be instantly surrounded with torch-bearing stablehands whose gazes followed us as Markham dismounted and lifted me down. Instead of setting me on my feet, he kept me in his arms as he crossed the court. A liveried guard sprang to open one of the iron-reinforced doors.

After the month in the rarefied atmosphere of Dantherei's royal palace, Lathandra seemed austere. Markham's pace did not flag as he passed through a military portion of the castle into the residence with its quiet colors, its spare furnishings of dark walnut or rosewood.

A footman appeared in a hallway.

"Where is the king?" Markham asked.

"In the salle. Shall I—"

"I will find him."

The footman lagged behind as Markham continued at a fast walk along the length of two hallways. The footman had enough time to duck around and knock before Markham kneed the door open to a large, mostly empty room, except for a table at one end, some chairs and a variety of weapons. Markham kicked the door shut behind him without a backward glance at the crowd of servants gathering in the hall.

Jason and Jaim were seated, Jaim on the table, Jason near it, drinking. They were sweaty and disheveled; two swords lay between them on the table. When they saw us, both got to their feet.

"Markham and—Flian?" Jaim asked, and turned to his brother, jerking his thumb in our direction. "Were you expecting them?"

"No." Jason's attention was on Markham as the latter set me carefully down. I tottered, the room swimming. Jaim was nearest; he shoved his chair behind me and I sank into it.

"Tell him, Markham." I clutched at my shoulder.

Markham said, "Garian Herlester met up with our party. When we left, he was about to force the Princess Eleandra to turn toward Drath."

Jason waited in grim silence.

"On learning of her father's death, and of Herlester's plans to initiate war between you and Lygiera, Princess Flian attempted to assassinate Prince Garian. When that failed, she wished to come here to warn you."

"So, what, Jewel is back with Garian?" Jaim grinned. "Pity him!" He then ran his gaze over me, his expression one of complete incredulity. "*You* tried to kill him? How?"

"Knife." I hiccoughed. "Crept into his tent. Would have made it. But rain dropped off my hand and warned him."

"Must've been a surprise, eh? I take it he tried to return the favor." He indicated my once-green linen gown, which was thoroughly nasty by then.

"Yes. Ran away. To warn Jason. Fell off my horse. But Markham saved me." The room spun and my voice sounded far away.

"...fever," Markham was saying to Jason. "Blood loss."

"Have a lot to tell you. But oh. It does hurt. Where's my whiskey?" I felt in my sleeve, where I had kept the flask, and pulled it out.

Jaim laughed. "I thought it smelled like a distillery in here!"

I uncorked the flask and was going to take a swig but Jason made a sudden movement and took it from my hand. "You did her no good by giving her that."

"She would not have made it otherwise."

Though Markham was a liegeman and always used titles with us, Jason spoke to him as an equal, and Markham answered back the same.

Jason went to the door, opened it, spoke an order, came

back in and addressed me. "Your news can wait. Now you must rest."

"No." I lifted a hand in protest. "Wait. You can't attack Maxl. Don't fight him, if he comes. Garian *wants* you to have a war—"

"I do not intend to attack your brother. Nor he me."

"But you didn't hear—"

"Your brother and I have been in communication since you left here for Dantherei. He knows the truth about my intentions. I promise you there will be no war between us. The rest can wait."

Someone else picked me up, for there was no chance I was going to be able to walk, and in a short time I was in Berry's governance once again. I will skip over the bandage changing, which was most assuredly disgusting, though the hot, herb-scented bath afterward was my reward.

But the warmth of the bath water, the warm listerblossom drink, seemed to melt that frost inside. "My Papa is dead," I said finally and began to weep, and couldn't stop until finally I fell into an exhausted slumber.

Chapter Twenty-Two

The next two days were spent veering between feverish sleep and dreams. On the last night I did finally fall into a deep sleep, from which I awoke feeling like a herd of horses had trampled my shoulder, but my head was clear and except for my shoulder, the rest of me was fine.

I was not alone long. Berry appeared, soft of voice and footfall, and when she saw me awake, she brought invalid food—all of it tasty and easy to eat, plus an infusion of strongly steeped listerblossom leaf. I felt immeasurably better after that, enough to endure another bandage changing.

Berry took the dishes away. When she returned, she said, "Do you feel ready for a visitor, your highness?"

"That means someone wants to talk to me. Yes? So it must be important. Let's do it right away."

Berry went out, and I thought, who could it be but Jason? All the worries and turmoil rushed back.

I looked down at myself in the nightdress, and blushed. I did not want to be found lounging in bed. The idea was, well, embarrassing.

One-handed I pulled on the yeath-fur robe, picked up the cup of steeped leaf that Berry had set aside, and walked out onto the balcony.

The cool autumnal air was fragrant with the scent of grass and fallen leaves. I sat next to the iron-wrought table and looked in bemusement at the ends of my hair brushing the stone of the balcony floor. The wheat-colored strands seemed unfamiliar. Except for that terrible first day in the woodcutter's cabin, I had not worn my hair loose since I was fifteen.

A bit of steeped leaf remained in the cup. I drank it and set the cup aside when I heard a quiet step in the open doorway.

I looked up. Jason came out and stopped a short distance away. "Berry said you were willing to see me."

"I owe you a report on what happened. Please sit down."

He sat in the chair on the other side of the table. "How do you feel?"

"Fine." Aware that I was speaking to a man to whom Eleandra had once been betrothed, I said quickly—suspecting that a lot of preparatory preamble would only make the news worse—and in as neutral a tone as I could contrive, "Eleandra took us to the river to see argan leaves. We thought she might be intending to meet you, and misconstrued. She planned to meet Garian all along." Jason said nothing, and his expression was as unreadable as it had ever been. So I added, "We did our best to keep the bargain."

Jason replied, "You may go home whenever you wish."

I found it difficult to talk. "Tell Markham thanks. For saving my life, I mean. I don't think I ever did."

"I will."

"My father—" I said to the cup on the table.

"He died almost two weeks ago. Your brother's letter to you must have reached Char Tann after you left on your journey with Eleandra."

I forced the next words out. "Garian said it was the news. About me. Someone told Papa I was dead—"

"Garian lied. Oh, he did send that message, and it was delivered. But I wrote your brother everything that happened the day you left, and sent my courier from the border when I went to find Jaim. Your father was falling ill when the courier reached him. Maxl maintains that your father did not even hear Garian's envoy, who came days after mine. In any case your father knew the truth—that you were happily dancing at court in Dantherei—and he died peacefully in his sleep." He added in a dry voice, holding out a folded paper, "I have your brother's letter here in case you do not believe what I say."

"I believe you." I turned my face toward the mountains and surreptitiously wiped the tears away. Then, taking a deep breath, I faced him again and told him everything. Tamara's kindness. Eleandra and the ring and the kinthus. Garian's gloating statements. All of it.

He showed no reaction, except a faint smile when I repeated Jewel's comment upon the news of Garian's intending to abduct Eleandra: *For once it's someone else's turn!*

"And so," I finished, "I don't remember much about the journey with Markham. I wasn't thinking clearly about anything, except the need to stop the threatened war. And that's that."

"Do not concern yourself over my imagined grief at Eleandra's machinations," he said with a sardonic lift to his brows that reminded me of Jewel. "The truth is, for the past few years I've regarded that betrothal as a liability, partly because I came to realize she'd never had any interest in anything but the immediate gratification of dalliance, and long term, the pursuit of social prestige, at whatever the cost. The man who takes her to wife will suffer a lifetime of trouble."

I stared at him. "Why didn't you tell us that before we left?"

"Because I knew that Jewel would never consent to go otherwise. And I wanted the two of you out of harm's way while I tried to find out what Garian's next move was to be."

I thought that through. "And you, what, expected us to talk Eleandra out of marrying you? You did. You *did!*"

He smiled again as he got to his feet. "I believed that the two of you would be fluent enough in my dispraise to inspire Eleandra to break off with me. And so would end a promise I never should have made."

I gulped in a breath. "So you never intended to march on Dantherei."

"Correct."

"When I think of how much I worried while trying so scrupulously to be diplomatic—" I groaned. "Well, maybe it will be funny some day, but now it's—"

Painful. I couldn't say it so I shut up, put my hands in my lap and kept my gaze on them. I was uncomfortably aware of him standing there, and though I did not look up, I could see him so clearly in my mind's eye: the long black hair swept back from his high brow, steady blue eyes, the sinister thin mustache that he'd grown to convince hard-riding, quarrelsome dukes and barons that he was older than twenty.

The conversation was over, so why didn't he go away?

He said, "You tried to kill Garian."

That surprised me so much I looked up. Not that I could

read anything in his unwavering gaze. "Yes. Of course it accomplished nothing—except to assure that the next time he sees me, he's probably going to want to finish what he started." I touched my shoulder and tried a joke, for the atmosphere had gone tense in a way I could not comprehend, had never experienced—not in Drath or the mountains or even in Dantherei. "I very much fear that Garian's and my courtship days are over. But then he never did need money."

Jason stood there before me, his hands behind his back. "Why did you not kill me when you had the chance?"

Good question. One that I had not thought to address myself. Anger had driven me into Garian's tent—but I had also been angry with Jason. I'd stood over both of them with a knife. Jason had even goaded me to strike. And unlike Garian, he probably could not have defended himself.

So...why didn't I? Because—because—

I did not know and needed time to figure it out. But not with him standing there staring at me so steadily.

Angry pride prompted me to retort, "Because I'm weak and cowardly. I thought we already established that."

He would have none of my petty evasions. "You tried to assassinate Garian Herlester. Whatever else it was, that was not an act of weakness or of cowardice."

"No, it was an act of passionate hatred, a thoughtless, stupid one. And yes, immoral as well, and so I did transgress against my own moral boundaries. I might have gotten a lot farther had I tried diplomacy—though I do confess I don't see how. I can't out-lie him any more than I can out-fight him."

Jason made a slightly impatient gesture; the subject was not Garian Herlester.

The subject was me—and Jason—and a knife.

Why? What had changed? "Why do you ask?"

"Why do you want to know what I think?" he countered, smiling a little.

But I found nothing amusing, there was no laughter in me to share. I just shook my head, unable to think at all, until he turned away and left.

Berry appeared on the terrace. She picked up the cup. "The king requested me to remind you to name the time when you feel able to depart for Lygiera, your highness. Preparations will be made for a suitable escort."

"As soon as possible. Right now." *I want to go home.*

She nodded, her round face somber. "Very well, your highness. I will convey the message."

Before midday I knew there would be no departure that day—or even the next. By early afternoon the roar of a terrific rainstorm drummed against the windows, continuing steadily through the night, rendering the morning light dim and dreary.

Berry was apologetic, especially since I couldn't play the harp—and I had lost the lute in Dantherei, along with the rest of my belongings. She said, "Would you like to visit the library?"

"The library?" I repeated, as if I did not know what one was.

"It's directly below us. You've only to go down the stairs and you'll find it."

As she spoke she laid out a gown that had to have belonged to Jewel. This gown was her favorite rose, too loose and too short, which made no difference to me. The rose color made me think of Jewel, and guilt wrung me; I hoped Garian was too busy dallying with Eleandra to torment Jewel.

When I left the room, there was the usual guard, but by now I had come to realize that he was there not as jailor but on watch.

Sure enough, he asked, most courteously, if I needed directions—I said I didn't—and I was on my way down old stone stairs, with a rail carved in stone that ended in stylized raptor faces.

The Szinzar library was mostly old books, in a gloomy room that had not been redone in at least two generations. I did find a small section of poetry and plays, none more recent than the century previous. One entire wall consisted of bound military reports dating back further than I cared to look, and on the far wall near a desk were some beautiful books, gilt lettering gleaming faintly in the dim light.

I made my way to them and discovered that most of them were personal records made by past monarchs of Ralanor Veleth. I pulled out a very old one, its pages gritty with dust along the top. The faded ink on the first page stated, in a slanting hand, *Being a history of the first two years of my reign. Viana Szinzar.*

Her name was familiar only as a name, some treaties and dates. This book in my hands had been written by the real woman. I leafed quickly through. The first several pages were a painstaking day-by-day account of a very young princess scrupulously listing all her accomplishments after the death of her father, the king. The regent, an uncle on her mother's side, set her various tasks, and she executed them conscientiously.

...at midday I had a few bites of seedcake and half a glass of yellow-wine. The wind kicked up outside. I could hear it in the trees below my windows. Aunt came in and sat down...

I skipped ahead to her coronation, which included a listing of all these military exercises and vow exchanges with the dukes, who were apparently military warlords then, too. A long letter from her uncle, the regent, had been diligently copied into the journal. It outlined current affairs and what a good queen should be.

I almost put it back, but the next page I looked at was written in a fast hand, and it was quite different than the careful print previous. Now she was analyzing conversations and considering the consequences of each action, each decision.

This time she outlined all the problems facing the kingdom, from Narieth's aggressive wish to expand—another thing that hadn't much changed—to her worries about famine. These were her thoughts, not a well-meaning regent's carefully considered advice.

I set the book on a table and flipped to the back page, where I read:

I am twenty-eight years old, and I know now what I suspected before, that I must rule alone and command the army alone. But I will never speak this vow aloud. The lords court me for power. I will return the favor and court them for balance.

I wanted to follow the career of this Viana Szinzar—but I had been standing a long time. My shoulder ached. So I replaced the book and made my way back to my room.

Berry came in bringing listerblossom brew at sunset. Once I'd drunk about half, she said, "Prince Jaim desired me to ask if you felt able to bear his company over dinner."

"My, that was polite." I felt an urge to laugh. "Not like the Jaim I remember. Tell him—very politely, of course—that he's preferable to boredom."

Berry chuckled and withdrew.

Jaim waited in that same south-facing parlor, the table set.

The Trouble with Kings

He grinned at me and waved a bottle of wine. "Some of Garian's best, taken right from one of his homes. Want some?"

"As long as there's nothing in it."

Instead of answering Jaim poured out a bit of wine, his gestures flourishing, and drank it off. He blinked. Then he rolled his eyes up, clutched at his throat, making terrible noises the while, and staggered back against the wall.

For a brief moment I believed he'd really been poisoned, then I saw the shadows of amusement at the corners of his mouth and the flush of perfectly good health in his face, and I laughed.

He opened his eyes and finished pouring out two glasses. "Good stuff, actually. In addition to being an exceptionally fine harvest, there is the distinctive savor of revenge."

"Garian did say something about you two raiding his vaults."

Jaim's smile disappeared. "That ambush on you and Jason was paid for by Garian—I'd finished tracing the hiring route when Jason himself showed up, cool as you please, and asked me if I wanted my rooms redecorated." He waved a hand overhead. "So here I am. That's what you were going to ask, wasn't it?"

"Well, no. I didn't think it was any of my business. But if it isn't inappropriate to say so, I'm glad you two appear to have resolved your differences."

"Communication"—he raised his glass to me—"is an amazing thing. Another one is growing up. When one removes oneself from a circumstance, events and their consequences—and their motivations—can suddenly make a lot of sense."

"I hope that isn't directed at me, as yet another hint about my wealth and my selfishness at resenting being repeatedly yanked from my worthless, boring, inconsequential life in order to further others' goals whether I like them or not—my opinion being the most negligible aspect of the business."

"Phew." He sat back. "But I guess I had that coming, didn't I? No, that was about me and my assumptions about my brother some years ago. You'll be relieved to know that I have no designs on your wealth. Jason's promise holds for me as well. From here on you are, to me, the equivalent of the most poverty-stricken princess on the continent."

I laughed again, though I did not feel any real mirth. "And

195

I, in turn, beg your pardon. I don't know why I said that. I feel—I feel unsettled. Perhaps it is my longing to be home, helping Maxl. It has to be horrible for him. And I miss Papa."

"Well, I don't blame you for an honest snarl. I'm a snarler myself, you may have noticed. Feels good." He smacked his chest. "Lets the heat out! And then there's this. Between the two of us, Jason and I've nearly gotten you killed three times over, which ought to be enough for anyone's lifetime—even for us evil, rotten, scoundrelish Szinzars."

I sipped at my wine, enjoying the gentle glow. "Evil and rotten. That's Garian. And a lot worse than scoundrel."

"My brother appears to be convinced that you regard the two of them as interchangeable."

"Well, he thinks I'm a fool, so I expect we're quits."

"Have you had another of your mysterious seeings? I've never heard him say any of that."

"Not a seeing. He said it, in plain words. Up in Drath, after an ambush he'd thought was yours. Not that I'd asked for his opinion of me."

"Is it possible that that conversation took place when Jason was not capable of using the clearest judgment?"

I thought back to that terrible day and shivered. "I don't know," I muttered, grimacing into my wineglass. "Not that it matters a jot what he thinks of me, since I will soon be going home, and none of us will ever see the other again." I raised my glass and drank off the wine, a reckless impulse that left my eyes burning.

"Here, let's hurry the eats along, shall we?" He strolled to the door, and spoke a few words to the footman I'd seen standing outside. "You aren't recovered enough yet to slap the wine back at so masterly a rate. Unless you want to emulate my esteemed mother."

"No." I set the wineglass down. "Neither yours nor mine."

Jaim grinned, going to the window and looking out. "Rain's abating. Hope the roads haven't washed away, taking the couriers with them."

I said nothing. The wine made my mind fuzzy and my lips numb. It had been stupid to drink it off like that.

"Jason's problem, as I see it," Jaim said, coming back around the table, "is that he doesn't lie. Never has. Doesn't mean he's always been right, but he knows that. He either says what he thinks, or says nothing. The problem with people like that is they are easy prey for clever courtiers expert in twisting the truth—like Eleandra-Natalia ru Fidalia. Who, I add, I would very much like to meet again. Despite the fact that, though I'm no longer a bored teenager, I know she wouldn't give me a second glance. I don't have anything she wants. And also for the likes of Garian Herlester, who is also adept at courtly jabber and turning it into outright lies."

"Garian does lie, easily and with great enjoyment." I frowned at Jaim. "So what you are delicately implying is that when we first met in Garian's fortress at Surtan-Abrig, Jason thought I was what Garian described me as—a worthless fool who had managed to inherit tremendous wealth that she knew not how to use?"

He turned his palm up. "That's about the sum of it. After all, Garian had spent time at your court, so he presumably knew you. He certainly brought you back, which argued at least some friendship."

I sighed. A lot was now clearer. "Why are you telling me these things?"

"Don't you like to know the why of matters that concern you, or have concerned you? I know I do. Which is why I listened when Jason showed up alone, arm bandaged, one rainy day, not very far from our hideout. Not far at all. And I'd thought myself so clever." Jaim rolled his eyes.

"Yes." I nodded, inwardly sorting through my reactions. "You're right. I do."

"Well, then. He said it turned him damn queasy when you hopped out with some cheerful assertions about trust, during the time your head and your memory had lost their acquaintance. In fact, about the moment Garian was offering the wedding toast and my merry band was preparing to swing down and smash in the windows of Garian's hall, Jason had been concocting a post-wedding plot for decoying Garian's nosers by sending his entire entourage east to Lathandra, escorting an empty coach with as much fuss and bother as possible, while you and he and Markham Glenereth rode secretly west to Carnison and your brother. The idea being to annul the vows on the grounds of your lapsed memory. And then plan from there."

I rested my arm on the table to ease the ache in my

shoulder. "So, what Garian intended was, either Jason contrived my death—in which case he'd be in trouble with Papa and Maxl—or he'd discover he was stuck with a wife with no intention of flouncing into a river and, what, Garian meantime could gallop to Dantherei and tell Eleandra that Jason had betrayed her and married someone else?"

Jaim grinned. "You figured it out faster than we did."

"With help from hindsight," I retorted, grinning back. Questions boiled around me, a thunderstorm of emotion-charged questions. "But that day Spaquel set Jewel and I up, when Jason grabbed us?" I drew a deep breath. "Spaquel is Garian's creature. So Jason sprung a trap of Garian's? He did drop a hint to that effect, which I didn't really pay attention to, at the time."

"That's about it. Garian wanted you as a bargaining piece— and as an excuse to create his war with Lygiera. Spaquel put together a plot to get you to Drath. Jason got ahead of him, but only just. He didn't know that Garian had gambled on that. As a test of Jason's real intentions, shall we say. Those hired knives of his were watching every single road from the west. We are fortunate he only sent them out in parties of twelve."

"Jason sent a threat—a bluff, he called it later, but still—to my brother."

Jaim twiddled his fingers. "Through a courier he suspected leaked news to Garian. Sure enough, Garian found out right away. And when Maxl saw through the carefully worded letter, Jason realized it was time to choose his allies and tell your brother everything."

I bit my lip. "But he didn't see fit to tell me any of these things."

It was Jaim's turn to study his wineglass. "Yes. Well. True. But you could ask him now." He waved a hand in the general direction of Jason's tower lair.

I thought angrily, *If he wants to talk to me, why isn't he here?*

Out loud I went on as if he hadn't spoken. "But that does not explain why Jason said, not long after the fire, that I would live to regret not using that knife on him."

While I had spoken, my words coming quicker and quicker, Jaim walked around the table, looking out the window, at the cabinet in the corner, down at the wine glasses, then at last at me.

Was he waiting for something more? I shut my mouth so hard my teeth clicked.

He said, finally, "I don't know. We talked little about that. I can only point out what I did before. He wasn't in any shape to make much sense. Perhaps you would do better to discuss that directly with him." Again the hand toward the tower.

I remembered Berry's voice from the day before. *The king requested me to name the time you would like to depart—*

I might have misunderstood—that what I assumed was dismissal of me and my disastrous mistakes was actually the opposite, an oblique invitation to continue the conversation, or not. As I chose.

If it was indeed true, what did I choose?

The door opened then, and servants came in bearing trays. The moment of decision was gone.

Jaim sat down. We served ourselves. His next question was about Dantherei, and my impressions thereof. The subject of Jason was never again introduced by either of us.

Chapter Twenty-Three

At dawn the next day, I wandered out onto the rain-washed balcony. A clean, cold wind swept out of the west, bringing the scent of wet loam. I faced into the wind and lifted my gaze beyond the castle walls to the distant mountains, stretching in a dark line on the horizon.

A flicker of movement resolved into a galloping rider splashing through great puddles. He vanished through the military gate. A courier? It was none of my concern.

I returned to the harp. Laboriously—trying not to jar my left arm—I tested and tuned the strings. Finally every one rang sweet and true, but by then my left arm ached.

Berry appeared, her expression anxious. Alarm kindled in me.

"The king requests an interview, Princess," she said. "If it's not too early—"

"Of course."

Terrible images chased through my mind like frightened birds. Maxl hurt—killed. Carnison under attack—

I forced myself to stop speculating and walked out onto the balcony, as if I could separate myself from imagined horrors and leave them behind.

I stood with my right hand gripping my aching left arm as I stared out at the mountains again. A long, low caravan of ragged gray clouds moved steadily across the jagged horizon, faint stars glimmering above.

A knock on the door.

"Out here," I called, my heart thumping as if I had run a very long way.

Jason came out and I looked anxiously into his face.

"The news is not from Lygiera," he said.

I groped behind me and sank into a chair. "Ah." I exhaled with relief. And then made a face. "Then it has to be Garian."

"He is holed up in his fortress at Surtan-Abrig. He sent a message. He wants to change Jewel for you."

I remembered the look on Garian's face before he brought that knife down, and shivered. Jason said nothing as he watched me. Wishing that I'd kept my reaction to myself, I mustered up my bravado. "Amazing. No ransom, for once?"

Jason's gaze flicked down to my bandaged shoulder and away to the west toward Drath.

"So what are you going to do? Make me go to Drath?"

"I leave that to you. I promised to send you to Lygiera, and I will honor that, if it takes half an army to see you safely to the Lygieran border." He turned back to me, waiting for a response.

This time it was me who looked away. "Do you have some sort of plan for freeing Jewel?" I asked the balcony rail.

"Nothing that I can promise is free of risk. Jaim is on his way there now, to evaluate the situation himself."

I frowned up at Jason. "Wait a moment. If Garian knows I'm here, he must know I told you what happened in his tent. What exactly did he say about Jewel? He must have—"

"Promised that if you do not appear he will kill her."

I shut my eyes. "Then I have no choice." I hugged my elbows against myself, but opened my eyes again. Being unable to see was not going to make the situation any easier. "It's my fault she's there. It's my responsibility to help get her out."

Jason made a sharp gesture outward with the flat of his hand. "I do not see that responsibility lies with you at all."

I said, trying for a semblance of humor, "Well, you could say it's your fault for sending us to find Eleandra, but you thought it would be a safe, easy trip. Yet you knew Garian too had a passion for that princess. Did you really not think he might go there?"

Jason looked away at the thin line of departing clouds. Then back. "I thought, should the worst happen and Garian did appear in Dantherei, that first it would be in the capital city, with you and Jewel surrounded by my guards as well as Queen Tamara's, and second you and Jewel would be so busy maligning me, Garian would see you two as useless as tools against me."

"Oh, no." I understood at last what had occurred outside my narrow perception of events. "So by overhearing his plans— and by trying to kill him—I really did make everything worse. For everyone. But especially for poor Jewel."

"You are in more danger than she," Jason said.

"But I have to go. There is no choice! I can't go home and leave her there to be killed, especially when I see myself at fault. It was I who chose violence over diplomacy—" He shook his head. "No, don't waste the time arguing with me about who is or is not at fault. Make your plans. I'll abide by them." I spoke as forcefully as I could, though my insides had cramped with fear.

"In that case, the easiest plan would require your presence. We would trick Garian into releasing Jewel. You could then continue on to Lygiera from there."

"Trick. You mean double-cross him? Not that I am criticizing. It's what he deserves, I believe with no shadow of doubt."

"Yes. Jaim and I discussed the possibility. He will set things up. Get as much rest as you can, for we will travel fast. Also remember Garian is brandishing Jewel as a lure to get you, but through you he wants to get at me."

He left.

At the time, I did not delve for more than superficial meaning. I was too preoccupied with worries about Jewel—what I ought to have done differently—Papa—Maxl, far away in Carnison, no doubt wondering what was happening, but unable to act because he was tied down by all his new responsibilities.

After breakfast the next morning, Berry brought me a very fine travel gown, deceptively simple in design, elegant in fit. More important for my present purposes, it was quite comfortable, a soft, sturdy cotton-wool of gray and maroon that harked back to the old style of overdresses that hung in panels to show the undergown beneath. This was one piece, the elegant skirt divided for riding, high-necked, which hid my bandages—and it fit me, which meant some unknown hands had been working on it so it would be ready.

"This is very fine, but I did not order a new gown. More to the point, I did not pay for one." I felt a twinge of regret for all those fine gowns I'd worn in Dantherei, paid for by Ralanor

Veleth's treasury—which was not all that capacious—and then abandoned.

Berry smiled happily. "It's a gift. From the others down in linens. Do you like it?"

"It's wonderful," I replied, surprised at a gift from people I had never met. "Please convey my thanks."

"They wanted to thank you for what you did. Saving the king's life."

Thoroughly embarrassed, I made a fuss of smoothing out the gown and admiring the flow of the skirt. "I just hope that this lovely gown will not soon be covered in mud!"

"You will not be riding, I was told, Princess," Berry said as she braided my hair up into a coronet. "But in case, I did pack a second riding outfit in the valise in the carriage, the more practical tunic and trousers."

"Thank you," I said again.

She gave me a nod, then her smile vanished. "We wish you a safe journey." She whisked herself out the door.

When I got to the stable yard, I found waiting a high-structured racing carriage, built for speed and comfort, of the sort that hot-blooded young lords and ladies drove in races, only it was not open, but had a roof and sides and two windows. In front there were traces for four horses. As I walked round to the door, I saw fine gilding enhancing the smooth lines. The thing was evidence of wealth and I wondered who Jason had strong-armed into relinquishing it.

A footman about my age appeared, bowed to me and opened the door. "May I offer my wishes for your highness's successful journey?"

"Thanks." I tried to sound light. "I hope your wish comes true."

He shut me in, then said through the open window, "I hope we put in everything you might need."

I looked about me. The carriage seat was filled with several down pillows, hot bricks, another of those yeath-fur robes, and a basket of things that turned out to be bread fresh from the oven—so fresh it was still hot—and a flask of steeped leaf. Some fruit and cheese wrapped neatly in linen completed the contents.

"Thank you. I think I'm ready for a journey to Sartor!"

He gave me a serious look. "You saved our king's life. And now you go to save his sister."

Then he was gone.

The little window darkened, and there was Jason. I busied myself with rearranging all the good things in order to hide my red face.

He said to my bandaged shoulder, "Is there anything you require before we set out?"

"No." I lifted my hand. "I didn't expect such luxury! I thought we needed to make speed, and I am perfectly willing to ride."

"This rig is fast enough," Jason said.

"I suppose it's inappropriate to ask, but did the owner get a choice in loaning it out?"

"It was offered for your use."

"Oh."

"If you have reason to stop, all you need do is wave. Markham and I will ride at either side."

The courtyard behind him was full of activity. The coach jounced and moved as the driver mounted, and the horses were hitched up and the traces checked. Beyond them what seemed an enormous number of mail-coated and armed warriors were busy checking saddles, girths, weapons and bags. Some mounted up, others ran back and forth. Above the noise were occasional calls and laughs, the tones full of suppressed excitement.

"I'll be fine," I said to Jason, who seemed to be waiting for an answer.

He rejoined the others. He too was dressed for battle in the plain green long tunic over mail, and beneath that the quilted black-wool garments of his warriors. There was nothing in his outfit to mark him from the rest of them—he wore at his side the same long knife of plain black hilt, and his sword was stashed in a saddle sheath. His head was bare, his long hair tied back with a ribbon; that was the only difference, for most of his warriors had shorn hair.

He lifted a hand, and the stones rang with the thunder of hooves.

The carriage rolled out, picking up speed. Well sprung, it

made me feel that I was floating over the roads. Long autumn grasses sped by, and the rocky terrain, marked occasionally by walled towns and distant hilltop mounted castles, became an ever-changing scene. Westward of the capital began the hills that would eventually rise into the mountains of the borderland in which Drath lay. Three times we stopped to change horses, and I did not get out of the carriage. By afternoon we rode in and out of deep needleleaf forest, and alongside rivers overgrown with cottonwood and willow.

At nightfall we stopped in a crossroads town below a great castle. Markham, windblown and dusty, opened the carriage door and helped me out.

A stout woman innkeeper awaited me, respectable from her clean white apron to her pleasant smile. She took me upstairs to a room that had a fine fire crackling merrily and a clean bed all turned down.

"I'll have food and hot drink along directly, mistress," she said. "Will the cleaning frame serve, or do you desire a hot bath?"

"Cleaning frame will suit me fine, thank you," said I.

Mistress? I thought after she had left. Jason must be doing one of his decoy tricks, sending all those warriors off in one direction, and we were riding anonymously. I thought about our appearance—two dark-haired men in plain warrior garb, escorting a young woman. We could be anyone, for warriors in Ralanor Veleth's colors were certainly common enough.

The innkeeper came back bearing the tray herself.

I stepped through the frame and sat down to my lonely meal. I had napped off and on during the long drive, and I did not really feel like sleeping. There was nothing keeping me in that room, but when I thought about going downstairs I was reluctant—and my shoulder ached enough for me to excuse myself from examining the reasons for that reluctance.

So I sat on the hearth staring into the fire, but my thoughts were not good company. Finally I slept.

Early to bed means early to rise. When the soft knock came in the morning, I was already up and ready, my hair braided, and I'd stepped through the cleaning frame again. After a hasty meal, I trod downstairs to the carriage, which waited at the door.

And so went another day, ending with a night at another

inn, only this time the curious innkeeper was an old man.

But the next morning the routine changed. When I went downstairs at dawn, slinging on the yeath-fur cloak against the cold, it was to find Jason and Markham in the stable adjacent to the inn yard. Three saddled warhorses waited, one of them pawing the hay-strewn ground. The two dark heads turned at my approach, and Jason said, "Here she is. We'll ask her."

Markham turned to me. "I am afraid, Princess, that you are not yet recovered enough to ride." He glanced at Jason. "We will not be making great speed, for our route now is steep and treacherous."

I pointed at Jason. "He made this same journey in the very same place not so long after *he* got stabbed, and his cut was much, much worse than mine."

Jason turned away, then back to me. "We can call a halt any time you say the word. But from here on, it will be safer if there is no carriage."

"I'll go back and change into sturdier riding clothes."

Chapter Twenty-Four

The air was sharp and cold and smelled strongly of pine. I breathed deeply as I pulled the cloak close. Markham handed me the reins of the roan. The horses sidled and tossed their heads, fresh and ready to go. We mounted up. At a word from Jason, they sprang at the trail winding up westward behind the inn.

The trail, or path, was narrow and difficult, zigzagging along the sides of great rocky cliffs and under tunnels of thickly branched trees. We passed through dark grottos where the air smelled so lushly of greenery you could imagine the legendary maulons passing through, singing down the sun; the sound of water, running, splashing, chuckling, was constant, though its source was as often as not unseen. We rode single file, with Jason leading. I noted he now had his sword slung across his back, and besides the knife at his belt, there was a hilt at the top of each of his riding boots.

Markham rode behind me, similarly armed. From time to time one or the other of them would make a quiet remark, Jason turning or Markham looking up at us. Neither of them talked past me, nor, at first, did they address me directly but I realized very soon that I was included in the conversation—if I so chose.

Though I'd avoided their company previous to this, now that we were all together the constraint I'd felt vanished. We whiled away the long morning with quiet-toned talk so our voices would not carry over the sound of tumbling streams or calling birds, or the constant sough of tall, wind-tossed pines brushing the sky overhead.

Not that the talk was anything memorable. Weather—snow early on the mountains—which types of horse best for trail riding—horse shoes—a couple references to history, to which I contributed my own observations. Easy talk, on insignificant subjects, the atmosphere quiet, amicable, curiously removed from danger, threat—or emotional turmoil.

I found myself enjoying Jason's commentary, uttered in so dry a voice my reaction to his occasional humorous observations was sometimes delayed—which he and Markham in turn found funny. Markham's prosaic responses were an entertaining contrast. Once I made them laugh, with a reference to the absurd red wigs that for some reason had been courtly fashion down in Sarendan, next to Sartor (in those days still under that terrible enchantment)—neither of them had known that, but my father had seen them on his single journey to the southern continent, when he was a prince.

Ordinary conversation, but it seemed to take on life of its own, no matter how insignificant the topic. The quiet, acerb humor brought Papa to mind, reminding me of his better days when I'd been younger. I still missed him, but the news that he had died in his sleep had eased some of the pain of his death.

But. I had forgotten the jolts and lurches of horseback riding—even when one didn't have to constantly duck under low branches. After a time I put the reins in my numb left hand and slid my right up under my cloak to hold my shoulder. My responses were fewer. I was content to listen, wishing the pleasant talk would never end, even as my physical discomfort grew steadily worse. Mentally I chanted over and over: *You can hold your own. You can hold your own.*

Late afternoon began to blend the shadows, making it difficult to see branches overhead, or ruts and roots. I was breathing slowly against occasional washes of faintness when my horse stumbled over a root on the edge of a precipitous drop. The horse's head plunged, yanking the reins, which in turn wrenched mercilessly at my shoulder.

I might have made a noise. I thought, *ugh, not again* as clouds of darkness boiled up before my eyes and I began to waver in the saddle, clutching tightly to the reins until hands gently lifted me down.

When the blackness cleared, I found myself lying on a nest of cloaks in a mossy cave next to a campfire being set up by

Jason and Markham. My shoulder ached with the sort of jabbing throb that I'd felt after Garian stabbed me, but otherwise I was unhurt. When the fire caught, Markham suspended a pan of water over it by a contraption of wires and good-sized rocks, then sat back. Jason dug in a pack and handed Markham something.

Slowly the throbbing receded. At last I heaved a sigh without even realizing it, and both heads turned.

"Flian," Jason said, his voice the sharpest I'd ever heard. "If Markham hadn't been watching you would have done Garian's work for him."

"I thought I could make it. Would have." I grabbed onto my other arm, determined I would *not* whinny. "If my horse hadn't stumbled."

Markham moved between us, holding out the steaming water pan into which he dropped a pinch of leaves from a packet. I smelled strong listerblossom brew and gulped a stinging sip. My eyes burned, but as always the fresh steeped leaf felt so good going down.

Markham sat back.

I blinked the tear-haze from my eyes. Jason said, "I apologize. But why did you not speak up?"

I recognized the sharpness in his tone: not anger, or judgment, but worry.

"Because I hate. I loathe. I *despise*. Being weak." My voice trembled on the last word. I looked away, at the fire, and drank more steeped leaf.

Markham murmured something about horses, obtaining fodder for the next stage of the trail. Jason responded in a low voice, occasional words like "outpost" and "courier" discernable. Their attention was on one another, leaving me to finish my steeped leaf in peace. Much of the worst pain eased, and I lay down again. My mind, released from the ache, seemed to float somewhere between my head and the fire.

I looked beyond the hypnotic flames to the two men. Jason was almost in silhouette. The ruddy gold flames fire-lined his cheekbone, an edge of his thin mustache, the veins and knuckles of one of his long hands as he raised a cup to his lips. On a couple of strands of his fine, straight hair that had come loose from his ribbon and lay, unnoticed, across his brow.

Markham was taller and broader, his long, bony face firelit, but his deep-set eyes remained in shadow. His hair was also black, but heavy, waving, worn loose to his shoulders in the style of an aristocrat ten years ago. They conversed in low tones. Neither had a cloak on—I probably had theirs under me. The fire highlighted the contours of their arms in the heavy black cotton-wool garments. A thin ribbon of fire gleamed along the edge of the sword lying next to Jason.

The fire leaped. Ghostly shapes formed in the flames, and faces. My brother's. Jaim's. Garian's. The latter made me hiss.

Jason's head turned, and again he spoke sharply, but this time I clearly heard the worry: "What is it? Are you ill?"

"No. I saw faces in the fire. Garian's," I added.

They exchanged glances, and Jason shook his head. "I don't know what to make of that. Can you control it?"

"No. At least, I've never tried. It only happens sometimes, when I'm looking at water. Or fire."

"Do you hear thoughts?" Markham asked.

"Never." It took no special abilities to know that they, as well as I, were thinking back six years to the strange period during which the entire world had been under enchantment, during the Siamis War. We had learned that such abilities as mind-travel and mind-talk really had existed in humans before the Fall of Old Sartor many centuries ago.

I said, "My grandmother told me that mind-talk is called dena Yeresbeth—*unity of the three*. Body, mind, spirit."

Markham retrieved my empty cup. "It's awakening in the world again."

Jason sat back. "Never thought any of those ancient legends were anything but hyperbole about the good old days, and all the fabulous powers our ancestors had."

Markham said, "Fabulous or not, our ancestors nearly destroyed themselves."

Norsunder. Damnation. And our ancestors, for some reason none of us knew, had invited it into our world.

Bringing the question: if our children, and our children's children, were born with those amazing abilities re-emerging in the world, would that in turn bring Norsunder back?

Jason's face had gone remote again. He rose to his feet. "I'm going to ride the perimeter. Markham, make up a supper, will you? I hear rain coming. We're far enough along that we can continue tomorrow morning, soon as the sun is up."

I woke to find Markham sitting nearby. He put a cup into my hands. It was not listerblossom brew this time, but strong coffee, laced with honey. It was deliciously aromatic. Wondering how he'd managed to fix *that*, I sat up and drank it. The warmth spread to my fingers and toes, leaving me feeling refreshed.

"Do you feel that you can continue on?" he asked.

"Of course I can."

"The king wishes you to ride with me, if you will consent." He made it a question only in form—I knew an order when I heard it.

"I hate being a burden." I sighed. "I'm sorry, Markham. I'd rather try to ride alone, but on the other hand I'd as soon not make any more dives from moving horses. Oh, if only Jewel was as good at escaping as she is at dancing!"

"Jewel," came Jason's voice from behind us, "is only good at one thing: complaining. Her expertise there is unmatched." He entered and dropped a saddlebag near the fire. It landed on the sword with a muted clank.

"Only about you. After all, you did try to marry her to Garian." I pronounced his name with all my pent-up loathing.

Surprisingly, they laughed.

"Would've served her right if I had," Jason said. "Both of 'em. Let's go, before the rain gets any worse." He held out a hand to me, but embarrassed, I pretended not to see it, and got to my knees and then my feet, my left arm pressed against my side.

I pulled my cloak on, feeling a strong but unexpressed relief that I would not be riding on my own, then wandered out, dusting my riding trousers off with my good hand. Behind were the sounds of the two breaking camp. The horses waited, trained and patient; there was no nipping or nudging, only the whuffing of noses, flicking of ears, as they exchanged signals with one another that were impossible for me to interpret. I went to the roan and patted its nose. These attentions were suffered with a good grace.

Markham kicked dirt over the fire while Jason strapped on the bags. He put the sword into its sheath and shrugged it over his shoulder across his back. Then he mounted up, leading the roan, who now carried most of the bags.

Markham waited for me to mount and swung up behind me onto the second horse. He slid his right arm round me. He was warm and comfortable and strong enough not to mind my weight; I knew this journey would be easier for me, if not for the horse, which was that same big, barrel-chested gray we'd ridden from Dantherei.

Beyond the close-growing copse of trees a soft rain fell. The early light was blue-gray and diffuse, with fog drifting down gulleys and over streams. Again we talked, and I discovered that the dullest topic came alive. No, there was no dull topic. No courtly wit or innuendo, just an easy exchange of ideas from three different viewpoints and ranges of experience.

We rode through two very old cave-tunnels that Markham said were probably left over from morvende travelers a thousand years ago. At night we stopped in another of those caves.

Once again I got the pile of cloaks. When I woke up, Jason was gone. Markham had made a breakfast of toasted bread with cheese melted onto it, and more of that delicious coffee.

Not long after we ate, noises outside caused Markham to slide his own sword from its sheath and step to the cave mouth, but a moment later he was back, smiling faintly as he resheathed the weapon.

Jason appeared behind him, along with Jaim and several of his followers.

"Heigh ho, Flian! You look grim," Jaim said with great cheer.

"I was fine until I saw you," I retorted, and he laughed.

"Any more of that coffee?" Jaim passed by me to Markham. Near the entrance to the cave some of Jaim's followers encircled Jason, talking in swift, low voices. One of them I recognized— the woman with the masses of curling brown hair, now compressed into a single thick braid down her back.

When the circle broke, she turned toward me. Our eyes met, she smiled and came over to squat down next to me. "We didn't have a chance to meet before. I'm Vrozta. How are you feeling?"

"Oh, fine."

Her brows contracted slightly. "Oh? Well, we ought to be all done by midday. It's only a short ride from here. Prince Garian apparently doesn't know about these old morvende caves, which is how we've managed to get about so deedily."

"Is there a plan?"

Vrozta lifted a shoulder in Jaim's direction. "He said he'd tell you. Meantime, you can ride with me, if you like. I'm strong, and"—she lowered her voice—"I know that I would rather let my arm fall off than permit all those arrogant males to act like I'm one step from dead while *they* go riding around with wounds ten times worse than a hole in the shoulder." She tapped herself on the left side.

I grimaced. "Am I so obvious, then?"

"The pain lines are." She grinned as she lightly traced her fingers on either side of my mouth. "Don't you feel how set your jaw is?"

I waggled my jaw as a flush burned its way up from my neck to my face.

Vrozta's grin turned rueful. "But even so, we all know what happened. Jaim said everybody in the Lathandra castle, from company commanders to the kitchen runners, was dying to do something for you—didn't you even notice? You *didn't* notice. Jaim was right! Oh, my! Now, you can be sure if *I* ever had the guts to pull a king out of a fire and go after a villainous prince with a dagger, I'd strut it for all it was worth. How often does a person get a chance to be a heroine?" She looked closely at me. "You really don't see it," she marveled.

"But there is no heroism. In fact, if my mistakes are seen as heroic, what does that say about real heroes. Are they all fake?"

Vrozta wrinkled her nose. "Good question! One thing for certain, I'd hate to meet the sort of fellow—or female—who brandishes a sword and blusters out heroic statements, knowing they're heroes. Wouldn't that be tiresome to be around?"

I couldn't help laughing. "Only if they really are tiresomely perfect. And remind you of it all the time."

"I think," she said consideringly, "heroism is doing what has to be done. Despite perfectly normal fear. And, well, maybe regret. Like you did."

"I appreciate your kindly meant attempt to bolster my faltering courage, Vrozta. Were there any mite of heroism in my actions so far, be certain I'd swank about as happily as any heroine has a right to! The truth is, the one thing was instinct, and the other I nearly killed myself because I was too slow and untrained, and in short my own worst enemy. Everyone's enemy—it's the reason we're up here."

"I think it's quite possible we would have been up here anyway. But as for you... Hoo." Vrozta fingered her braid. "This is worse than I thought."

"This what?" Then I remembered what she'd said previously. "What did Jaim say about me?"

"He said the whole royal castle thinks you walk on clouds, and you are too, um, austere to notice."

"Austere." I pursed my lips. "He didn't say that. He said silly, didn't he."

"No!"

"Frivolous."

"No!"

"Boring. It's fair—I'm boring at court in my own kingdom, so I must be twice that here."

"No." She was laughing now, a soft sound.

"Weak." I could barely get that one past my lips. It did seem to gall me more than a simple word ought.

"Never, never, never." She sidled another of those looks at me. "Innocent."

"Ugh." It was my turn to grimace, my face now flame hot. "I would rather be called silly."

"No you wouldn't," she contradicted with cordial assurance. "Silly is always silly, but innocent is easy enough to fix. Why, I could name half a dozen fine fellows who would volunteer with overwhelming enthusiasm to help you amend that any way you wish!"

I laughed and she did as well, but then she said, "You are one of those who can't dally where they don't love, am I right?"

"I don't know." I flung my hands wide. "I don't even know what love *is*, outside of that for my family. And dalliance—flirting—for the sake of passing the time or for power or for pleasure doesn't come much in my way—everyone is too busy trying to get their hands on my inheritance. That's the inevitable result of being a rich princess, I guess." But Eleandra had shown that she was quite capable of getting exactly what she wanted, and when. "No, that's not true." I sighed. "It's mere self-pity. I'm afraid I'm being silly after all."

"No. Innocent. But the word can be a quality, and not mere lack of a certain kind of experience. You might lack the latter, but the former stays with a person all her life, I think. Or his. It's an admirable quality—like honor. It is as much a part of you as your hair or your eyes." She gave me a comradely pat on my good shoulder. "And you, you wear it as gracefully as a crown."

"You two done gossiping?"

We looked up, equally startled, to find Jaim standing nearby, with Jason beyond him.

"Sure," Vrozta said, springing up.

"Saying fine things about me, I hope," Jaim added with a false smirk, sliding his arm around her and squeezing.

"No, because there aren't any." Vrozta shook her head, and leaned up to kiss him. "I told her that you eat with your knife, and that you snore."

Jaim lifted his hands and turned away. "See? I get no respect from anyone. Come, Flian, you can ride with me."

I pointed to Vrozta. "She offered to share her mount."

Jaim shook his head. "No respect."

Several people laughed and Vrozta helped me get up. I was soon seated before her on a horse. Her arm was strong and steady.

Jaim rode next to us.

After a short time he looked across at me, the humor gone, the appraisal in his narrowed eyes reminiscent of his brother's. "You'll ride up to Garian's lair with Randal and Terreth, who'll be in my brother's livery, because Garian will be expecting at least that much. The only way this plan will work is if you stay with them and do not dismount. Use whatever excuses you can think of, but don't leave that horse, at least until you see Jewel move away from his minions. Get Garian's attention away from Jewel, because as soon as she's out of their reach, we're going to attack his hidden ambushers." Jaim grinned, his anticipation evident. "Because you can be firestorm sure that *he* plans a double-cross as well. Your part, then, is to keep Garian talking, get Jewel in range so one of the three of you can get her on horseback, and then ride for freedom. Leave the rest to us. I've had people sneaking into place all night long."

"But what if he doesn't let her free?"

"Oh, he will, if only because she's no possible use to him. He wants you—and Jason. But if he doesn't let her go, then

Randal and Terreth will get you away again. It's not your responsibility, it's ours. Jason's and mine. Your business is to get as close to Jewel as you can."

"He'll have arrows trained on us," I said.

"Yes, but he's going to suspect that we have them on him, and he'll be right. But don't think about that. You get Jewel, stay out of his reach, get away. Simple. Got it?"

I tried to swallow, but my throat had gone dry as old wood.

Chapter Twenty-Five

The highest towers of Garian's castle were visible above the treetops.

Memory made my insides cramp. I did not want to be there again. We stopped in the mouth of the ancient morvende tunnel, beyond a long waterfall that hid the access path, and prepared to leave.

The two young men closed in behind me: Randal, a big, broad redhead, gripping and regripping his sword hilt, and Terreth, a dark-haired, slim fellow whose build was a lot like the Szinzars', staring with narrowed dark eyes through the falling water at those towers. Both fellows wore the Ralanor Veleth warrior gear.

Vrozta gave me a quick hug, gentle on my left side, then wordlessly slid off the horse.

Jaim and his people all withdrew, for Jaim wanted them in certain places, leaving only Randal and Terreth.

Jason stepped up to the side of my horse, and absently stretched out his hand for the animal to whuff and nudge with its muzzle. His brow was tense. "Remember what Jaim said."

"You don't think I can do it?" My voice came out strained and accusing.

Color edged his cheekbones. "I don't like this plan. I don't like you in it."

"But it has to be me. It's the direct consequence of my own action." I paused, making sure my voice would stay steady. "Garian would never have bothered with me if it hadn't been for what I did to him."

Jason looked up, then down, then away. "I don't like you in it," he repeated. "Should have asked directly for me."

"But he wouldn't believe you'd go." As I said it, I knew it was true—Garian would assume Jason'd behave like him. Had Garian a sister, he'd shrug off her death, and take revenge at his leisure if it suited his plans. Trade her for another hostage, maybe, if the plan seemed interesting enough.

It was then I truly understood the differences between the two. Oh, I'd seen them right from the beginning, only now did I comprehend what they meant. All along there had been two reasons for everything Jason did, and most of the ambivalent words and actions had been Jason's own way of throwing dust into Garian's eyes. But he'd not actually brought anyone to harm, except by accident, and here he was, determined to rescue a sister he found more exasperating than fond.

Everything he had done had obvious reasons—except his statement in that cave the night of the fire, *If I get through this alive you'll regret the outcome.*

That was the threat of a villain.

Jason said, his mouth grim, "Given my preference I'd run an attack right now. Put 'em all to the sword."

Would he really have done that, had I refused to come along? "Then many would die."

"Jewel the first," he agreed—making it clear why he'd consented to this plan at all. "I don't trust Garian. Don't you either. Stay with the plan."

"How many times must I say that I will?" My voice wobbled, and I turned away, fiercely angry with myself, because I could see how my tension made the others more tense. "Let's get it over."

In silence we rode out of the cave, the falling water gracing us with gentle spray.

Randal led us up a slope. There was no pathway. The horses' hooves sank into the mulchy ground, still colored with the falling leaves. I glimpsed movement at the line of my vision; Randal and Terreth looked up.

One of Jaim's people high in the tree, holding a cocked crossbow, lifted his fist in a salute.

Terreth nodded, Randal waggled his fingers surreptitiously and I forced a smile. I was terrified, my mouth dry, my armpits and palms damp. My shoulder ached, my heart thumped in my ears.

We emerged from behind a great thicket onto the road, and

within moments heard a whistle that was not quite a warbler's call.

"Signal," Terreth breathed, without moving his lips.

So enemy eyes were indeed watching.

We rode up the fine road to the drawbridge. Below, water thundered over the rocks and away downslope. Overhead, the sun broke through the clouds, and I felt its warmth on my shoulders and the back of my head.

Movement from the direction of the castle. It resolved into a small procession on foot, first Garian, and then Jewel—her hands bound and her mouth gagged, her brow a dark, angry line—and last several armed men.

They stopped at the other end of the drawbridge, and Garian took hold of Jewel's arm. Even across the bridge I could see that it was no easy grip. But Garian smiled his courtly smile, his green eyes were wide, their expression triumphant; I thought, *I will never again like jade.* He was dressed splendidly in his house colors, with a gem-hilted knife at his side.

He took his time surveying us, turning that nasty gaze of ice-cold amusement last to me. His smile widened. *I am in so much trouble.*

Terreth stirred, as though about to speak.

Garian jerked Jewel up against him and drew the knife.

"I've an idea, Flian, that the only person who wants her alive"—he pressed the knife-blade to her neck—"is you. Dismount, come here and I will let her go. If either of your swains steps onto this bridge, she dies."

Silence. A bird—a real one—somewhere up above twirtled happily, but none of the humans moved. We might've all been carved of wood except for the breeze flapping at cloaks, hair and clothes.

"I don't believe you." My voice came out squeaky. "You've never told me the truth. Let her go. First."

"You can believe me now." Garian favored me with another of those gloating smiles. He was obviously enjoying himself. "You know I have no scruples whatsoever, but a very fine sense of play. And you, my very dear Flian, made yourself a part of the game, there on the riverside in Dantherei."

"So I learned," I said, anger helping me control my voice. "A steely tutorial. Let her go."

Garian laughed. "An attempt at wit! You have changed, Flian. I wonder who is the inspiration? We shall have leisure to discourse on the verities, and I almost think that what you say might be interesting."

"Let her go."

"But I am running out of patience," he added softly, and his hand tightened. I'd thought I was already at the limits of horror, but I discovered how wrong that was when I saw Jewel's face contract in pain, and a thin red trickle run down her neck from the blade.

"Now. Or watch her die."

Again his hand moved, and there was more blood.

Uttering a cry, I threw my leg over the saddle horn and stumbled onto the bridge, running as fast as I could.

A heartbeat before I reached them, Garian flung Jewel away from him. She thumped onto the wooden bridge directly in the path of Terreth and Randal, who'd hot-footed after me.

As I passed, Jewel shook her head at me, tears spilling down her cheeks. She tried to say something, but five relentless fingers closed on my arm, and Garian yanked me against him, the bloody knife pressing under my chin.

Terreth pulled Jewel across the bridge to safety.

Randal froze not two paces from me, hands out. As Garian's grip on the knife tightened, Randal backed up slowly, his face pale with fury.

Silence. No one moved, no one spoke.

Garian stirred against me. "I was hoping that Jason might take an interest. Have I miscalculated?" he murmured into my hair. "We shall experiment."

And he paused, his red locks blowing against my cheek. Disgust tightened my throat. I was already trembling too violently to shudder. He did not move—he was waiting. The knife now pressed up against my jaw, forcing my head back against him. Over his shoulder, I glimpsed one of the towers, and on it a wink of sunlight on steel—the jointure of a crossbow.

I hoped Jason and the others saw it too.

Five, six long, painful breaths, and Garian said, quite annoyed, "I must have misread the situation, then. Jason does not seem to be here. Where is he? If you tell me where he is, and what he's minded to try, I will forego the pleasure of your company for now."

I said nothing.

"Where is Jason, Flian?" he asked, in a low, intimate voice, and his grip on me shifted so that his thumb stroked over my left shoulder where the stab-wound was.

"Lathandra."

"Then—I shall—make do with you."

So saying he dug his thumb into my shoulder. I yelped with pain. He kept up the inexorable pressure, until my knees buckled. I knelt at his feet, the edges of my vision going dark.

I felt Garian shift position as he looked around, and then he gave an exclamation of disgust, reached down and backhanded me across the face.

When I next became aware of my surroundings it was to find myself dumped into a tower room. I lay on a bed, my left armpit sticky. Heavy stone walls circled around me, but the room was warmed by a substantial fire. The only other piece of furniture was a fine table at the foot of the bed. At one of the long arrow-slit windows stood a female figure.

Familiar sun-touched dark hair and the silk-draped contours of an enviable figure: Eleandra.

"Unh." Experimentally I eased myself up on my right elbow.

Eleandra whirled round, her skirts flaring, then falling against her long, shapely legs. *Here I am.* Hysterical laughter fluttered inside me. *Alone with the princess all those men are warring over.*

She came toward me, the glitter of tears in her glorious brown eyes.

"Did Jewel get away?" My voice came out a frog-croak, but that was better than the squeak of fright.

"Yes."

"But you haven't."

She made an ironic gesture, as if presenting herself.

I gulped in a breath, trying to calm my middle, which was boiling like a nest of mad snakes. "We have to think about escape."

"He's got warriors all over the place. You can't step without some castle-sized fellow armed with a crossbow glaring at you."

Her fingers slid up her arms and gripped tightly above her elbows. I recognized that posture. I'd used it a lot of late.

So Eleandra had normal feelings, then. I also noticed that her face, even full of tears, was more staggeringly beautiful than ever. Whereas when I wept, I got puffy pink eyes and a glowing nose.

Life is *not* fair.

I said, "I got out of here once before. I can do it again. I think. If I can stand up. Why did he have to dig his soul-blasted fingers into my shoulder like that, if you'll pardon my language?"

"To force Jason out of hiding. His men were to shoot him in the knees, so that Garian could have him to play with."

I shuddered and fell back on the bed. "Ugh."

She tossed her long gorgeous hair back and wiped her wrist across her eyes. "I have been pretending to fall in with Garian's plans in hopes my sister will investigate my disappearance and send someone here. Preferably an army." She gave a bleak smile. "But I don't know if Siana or Eneflar understood the situation—or if Tamara will care if they did."

"Of course she will. She's your sister. I know my brother would care, very much, if he knew I was here."

Eleandra's pretty mouth pressed into a line, and once again she wiped her eyes. "She might think that I deserve what I get, for she's going to know what he's really after. I never, never, ever thought Garian would go to these lengths. He was always so affable, and very amusing as a lover—few better."

"Faugh."

She gave me a wry, lopsided smile. The more human she acted, the more I began to like her. "He'll never forgive you for that, by the way. He might sound so dispassionate, but in truth, he was very much stung by the fact that you made it very plain you don't find him attractive."

"No. Never have. He has a fair form, but an evil mind. It shows in his face."

"Yes, I see it now. I see a lot of things more clearly. There's little to do up here but think, when Garian doesn't demand one as an audience to his cleverness." Again the wry smile. "Where is Jason?"

Probably halfway down the mountain now that Jewel is safe. Aloud I said, "I don't know."

She drew in a shaky breath and came to the bed to sit down. Then she made a quick gesture with her hands, almost like wringing them. "I don't blame you if you don't trust me. But you must believe me. The only way for you to stay alive past this day is to convince Garian that Jason lurks somewhere about, so he can use you to trap him. Just lie. Say he is indeed here and wants you free for your money, or something."

I shook my head. "I can't do that."

"Why not?"

Because there was the vaguest chance it might be true.

No, I only hoped it was true.

If I get through this alive you'll regret the outcome...

I sighed. "I'm no good at lying, Garian sees through it. I may's well not even bother. I don't know where Jason is."

"Don't you understand? Garian keeps threatening to *kill* you if you don't tell." She lost control of her voice then, and I felt real pity for her—more than for myself, actually, but only because I was so hazy minded. Now that I was actually *in* trouble and not anticipating it, I felt almost detached.

"He will anyway, if he's minded to." I touched my shoulder tentatively. It throbbed fiercely. "Either that or he'll keep piling on the threats, and smacking everyone who can't hit back. He does like to play with his victims. Augh, I am so thirsty."

"Water or wine?"

"Water. Please."

She moved to the door, opened it, spoke to someone outside. Guards. Probably more than one.

The door shut. Eleandra wandered to the window again, running her hands up and down her arms. When the pitcher and glass was brought, she poured my water, which I gulped down.

She said, "I'll tell him you said Jason's here."

"No. I can't think of a convincing excuse why he'd be here. The money one is less believable since Jaim and Jason helped themselves to a good part of Garian's movable wealth."

Eleandra snorted a laugh. "He did not tell me that."

"Well, they did. Are you certain that Garian doesn't know you want to leave?"

"As certain as I can be about anything. I'm very good at flattery, and all the rest, when I have to be." She arched her brows at me. "It's why I'm here—he believes I can winnow from you Jason's whereabouts. Though I wouldn't tell him the truth if you did tell me," she added in haste.

But he'd get it from you just the same.

Out loud I said, "Then you are our key to freedom. Tell him that you want to take a walk, and I'll dress as one of your maids. It's the only thing I can think of, only I'd hope it wouldn't endanger your maids even if they don't know what is going on."

"Garian wouldn't bother revenging himself on servants." Eleandra waved a dismissive hand. "Not his style. Tormenting the powerless is boring, for they have no choices. Peers can be forced into terrible choices, which affords him exquisite pleasure. So does forcing the powerful into powerless circumstance. He calls it *the game.*" She drew a deep breath. "I admit I'm terrified—but I don't see what else can be done. Let us try it, then. I will go see what I can arrange."

She went out.

I watched after her, thinking better of her than I ever had during all those interminable affairs at her court that were designed to impress the impressionable. Then I was going to take another sip of water, when I remembered my conversation with Jason and Markham.

Could I do it on purpose?

I sat up, holding the glass close to my face so I could look into the distorted reflection of the flames, which leaped and sparkled in the liquid. There was Jason's face, staring at me through fire and water. His light blue eyes were narrowed, his mouth pressed in a line. He was angry.

I blinked—and it was gone.

Again. I stared through the glass into the leaping flames, and this time thought of Markham. His face flickered, expression thoughtful. I blinked him away and tried Jaim. He was talking, and though I heard no sound, I saw the intensity in his face, and his hands gesturing.

Jason. This time—it's difficult to explain—I called to him in my mind.

His head lifted, his eyes widened, then he looked behind him. As if he'd heard!

But my vision was beginning to flicker around the edges, and so I drew a deep breath and set aside the glass.

I lay back, trembling, my brow damp with sweat. How

foolish, to wear myself out on such uselessness. Looking at faces in the glass was the kind of thing to play around with when one was not hurt, faint with hunger and under threat of death.

I closed my eyes.

Chapter Twenty-Six

Before I could drift into sleep Eleandra returned.

"What did you find out?" I asked.

"Garian is convinced that Jason is indeed here, lurking about somewhere close by. He wants to conduct a search himself, which gets us rid of him for a time. It really seems to disturb him that Jason has a knack of getting in—and out—of places at will, no matter how well guarded. Is that true?" She regarded me curiously.

"True enough He abducted me right out of our palace. Well, the grounds. In the middle of the day. Seems to have taught Jaim his tricks, because when I was a prisoner here the first time, Jaim and his gang came crashing through the windows to rescue me."

"I only met Jaim once. He was a gangly, ill-behaved youth. This was almost ten years ago, when I first met Jason." She paused, and when I didn't answer, she gave a faint shrug and went on. "Like all men, Jason came if I crooked my finger, but he was otherwise so very different from my other suitors. Never bothered dressing in fashion, but he beat *all* the best duelists at the games. Delightfully intense in private. But so boring in court—never opened his mouth. His training was clearly military, and that was what I wanted for my plans."

She paced about the room. "What a short-sighted fool I was! I've been thinking and *thinking.* All I've sought is someone strong enough to unseat my sister from the throne. She's fat and dowdy, and I've always envied her being first. I thought a queen should be a graceful leader of society, so I ought to be queen. I suspect she knew all along what I was doing because she said once or twice that ruling meant endless paperwork, and the least she could do is make certain that no one saw any of it. That's as ornamental as she was capable of being. And so when the years slipped by and Jason didn't come, I shrugged him off, and turned to Garian—"

She lifted her hands and whirled around, her skirt flaring. "I seldom saw this side of politics. I wonder if Tamara knew something of this sort would happen to me eventually." She gave me a sad smile. "Alas, I never paused to consider the men themselves—and what it might be like to spend a life with them. I think, with Jason... Oh! I'm dithering at you like a sixteen-year-old, but here's another truth. I am so very much a coward. I will never forget you jumping off that horse to keep Garian from slitting Jewel's throat. How long does self-abnegation last? Probably not long. I was standing at the window down below, calling to you *Ride out! Save yourself!* In short"—she whirled again—"I would have let her die."

"But you weren't there, and the choice was not before you. I too am a coward. It's just that I was five paces from Garian and Jewel, and I saw that blood on her neck. There was only one thing to do so I did it. No time to think about bravery or cowardice or anything else."

"Instinct, you're saying." She came over and stared at me, frowning. Even her frown was lovely.

"I guess it was."

"But, see, my instinct would have prompted me to run and leave her behind. I'd run faster so I wouldn't have to see it." Tears gathered. She wiped them away then gazed at me through those tear-drenched, tangled lashes. "I think what you are saying is that instinct is like habit."

"I don't know, am I?" I carefully touched the side of my face. It was hard to think, truth to tell. "I guess I am."

"Well, then, it's obvious." She flung her hands apart. "Your habits are to make the right choice, so your instinct prompts you that way. My habits—" She shrugged, her mouth crooked. "Are to choose whatever pleases me most."

Now I felt on surer ground. "But you can begin to make the right choices here. Today. Now. And tomorrow. And the day after that. Except," I felt obliged to add, "sometimes we make what we think is the right choice, and it isn't. For example, when I tried to stab Garian, there at the riverside. I made a terrible choice, but thought it right at the time."

She drew in a deep breath. "So you really did try to kill him."

"Yes."

She laughed softly. "I cannot tell you how angry he was."

"What happened?" I asked. "I mean, after I left?"

"The guards closed in round us, and he wouldn't let anyone move from their tents until morning. He sent searchers after you—and whoever else it was who'd been in the tent after you left. But when they returned and hadn't found either of you, he sent Eneflar and Siana off in a flurry, and issued orders to pack up for instant departure. Jewel was ordered to come along, and they had a towering fight. Raised voices—they make me ill, I've heard them almost never—and I cowered in my tent, but she squared right up, and the *things* she said! Told him what she thought of him—he knocked her down—she got up and went after him again—then he had his guards bind and gag her. That restored his good mood enough to give the order to leave. For a time he made Jewel ride with the servants."

"Was that supposed to be an insult?"

"Yes. Until the sound of talking and laughter from the back caused him to halt the entire entourage. Then he had her gagged again, and she had to ride with us. And the rest of the journey he'd say these horrible things to her, laughing, and she would glare at him. It made me feel *sick*." Eleandra walked to the window and whirled around. "So when you talk about making the right choice, what is right? How do you know it's right? No, no, I'm trying to talk myself out of knowing that I would have left Jewel to die, and I would have found excuses for it afterward—I didn't like her—she would have died anyway, for you have no idea how much Garian despises her—oh, no use in talking about it. You ran right into danger to save her life. I couldn't do that."

"You could if you knew her, like I do, and if you knew it was your fault she was here."

"No I wouldn't." She gave me a sardonic look. "I don't know her because I never wanted to, and it's my fault all of us are here. It was a moral choice," she said in a low tone. "And I know I have no morals—or at best what I have is amazingly adaptable. Maybe Garian and I are two of a kind after all." She wiped her eyes again and shook her head. "Only why do I keep weeping? He only gloats."

"Tell you what." I sat up wearily again. "Is there any chance of getting me something to eat?"

"No." She gave me another of those strange looks. "And that's another thing I do not comprehend. Garian got angry when he discovered some of his own servants putting together a tray for you. Healer's brew and some bread and cheese, but he was furious because they were going to sneak it up here."

"Uhn," I moaned. "Why did you have to tell me that? My middle is hollow!"

"Because I have not gotten anything but reluctant obedience from his servants, and yet they risked his fury, unasked, to make a tray in case *you* might want it. He's forbidden them to come anywhere near this room on pain of death. I can't imagine them doing that for me. Why do they do it for you? What is it about you that places you here, opposite me, that I am not descrying?"

I touched my cheek again. Yes, a bruise was forming. "There's no mystery. I'm here because I tried unsuccessfully to rescue Jewel, and Garian got his knife at my neck. And you and I are not opposites—or enemies. Garian and I are, not that he cares."

"You don't see it, do you?" A distant bell sounded, and she swung about. "Oh! I forgot! There's the dinner bell, and he will expect me to dine with him. I must hurry and dress." She glanced behind me and her face blanched.

I turned my head and felt dizzy when I saw the dark blotches on the quilt where my left shoulder had been. "Ugh. Trust Garian to reopen his handiwork."

She covered her face with her hands, and I remembered that this woman had laughed in anticipation when Garian talked so blithely about leading two, no, *three* kingdoms into war. She wasn't evil—she just hadn't known what that really meant. Oh, she knew she'd be the beautiful empress of three admiring courts, but as for the war beforehand, it would be a distant battle. She'd only hear about the glory and banners and charges.

I couldn't blame her, I reminded myself, because I'd easily agreed to go to Char Tann and send her back to Jason, knowing what he'd promised. At that time, the idea of an army marching into Dantherei hadn't seemed real to me, either.

When she lowered her hands and stared at me, I thought:

Yes, we have both learned that when you cut people, they bleed.

Her eyes were huge. She opened her mouth, then shook her head and left with a hasty step.

Time to find a way to escape. I'd ask Eleandra on her next visit if she would go along with my plan of dressing as her maid. I couldn't figure out how to get past the guards on the grounds but if we could get out of the castle, that would be a beginning.

I went to the corner and stepped through the cleaning frame there, which at least cleared away the grime of the mountain journey, and the stickiness from my shoulder— though that latter wouldn't stay long if I was going to be moving about. Well, there was no help for it.

I lay back down, closed my eyes, and this time fell profoundly asleep.

And woke when I heard a sneeze.

I opened my scratchy eyes. Someone was sitting on a chair next to the bed.

My lips were dry, as was my throat, or I would have exclaimed, "Eleandra? What did you find out?"

As well I did not, for when I turned my head the flickering firelight highlighted long red hair, a bony face and the physical contours of a man.

Garian.

"Pardon me, Flian." He smiled. "And you were sleeping so peacefully."

"What a horrible sight to wake up to."

He laughed. "Think how much more unpleasant the surprise will be when Jason sneaks in here to rescue you."

He'd stayed, then?

He stayed.

"You'll have to wait a long time, because—"

"Don't bother trying to lie to me, Flian. One of his men was rather clumsy in attempting to break my inner perimeter right after midnight. I regret to say that we were unable to apprehend him, or I would not have to bore myself in this manner, but—" He shrugged, waving a hand with a knife in it, firelight reflecting on steel. "The exigencies."

"So, what, if Jason manages to show up, you'll knife me, is that your plan?"

"This time," he said with his courtly smile, "I'm unlikely to miss."

Firelight glinted on the dagger as he made a fencing gesture.

At least he'd cleaned the blade.

"So I have been sitting here listening to you snore. Salutary, I assure you."

"I don't snore."

"You do," he contradicted, again with that mock-apologetic air. "It's a very soft, quite proper little princess snore. But you are not at your best." He indicated my shoulder with one of those nasty smiles.

"No thanks to you. So why haven't you finished the job?"

"Because I don't know why Jason wants you. I would like very much to find out. There is a chance, a slim one"—his voice went grim—"that you will be more useful to me alive."

I said nothing.

"No tears? No lamentations or accusations? A refreshing change from Eleandra." He stared down at me and gave a soft laugh. "Such hatred! And no fear. How could I have misjudged you so completely, or have you changed? I suspect you are the only one of us all with unexpected depths."

As he spoke he touched my cheek. He was on my left side, or I probably would have struck at his hand—but he would like that, I thought. So I stayed still, willing myself not to react as his fingers stroked, back and forth, down my cheek to my neck, and then traced my pulse down to my collarbone above the edge of my riding tunic. Stroke, stroke.

I did not move.

"Too thin," he murmured. "Ordinarily I prefer women with some flesh. Between Jason and I, we have almost ground you to dust, have we not? But your spirit grows brighter."

He bent, as if to kiss me, but I turned my head, and again he laughed, his breath on my cheek.

He sat back. "Even I am not villain enough to seduce someone and then threaten to kill her. Or attempt to seduce, for you'd have none of me, would you?"

"No."

"It might be worthwhile to postpone our accounting. The temptation to exert myself to win you to my cause is tantalizing, except you seem singularly ambitionless. Or is that another of your hidden depths? What do you want, Flian?"

"To go home to my brother."

He shook his head. "What do you want?"

I didn't know what I wanted, but one thing for certain: were I to discover it, I would never tell *him*.

"Peace."

He sighed. "Well, if it were that easy to get a true answer, the question would not be nearly so interesting." He leaned back, the firelight reflecting on the fine silver embroidery of his dark tunic.

A faint blue light glowed in the window. Dawn was near.

Garian said, "Then tell me this—"

He stopped at a soft tap at the door.

"Garian?"

Eleandra.

Garian's mouth hardened. "One moment."

He went to the window, looked out, and then to the door, which he unlatched. "Come in."

Eleandra slipped inside, and Garian relocked the door.

Eleandra looked around, shivering. Her beautiful hair was disheveled; the gold silk gown she wore was in fact a wrapper. "Your man told me you were in here." Her tone made it a question as she glanced at me on the bed.

Garian said, "What do you want?"

Her voice trembled. "There are people gathering down in your hall—servants—heard noises at some of the first floor windows. My maids are in hysterics. Can you do something about it?"

Garian walked up to her and took her chin in his hand, forcing her head back. "If you are lying to me, Eleandra, you are going to regret it."

"Please, Garian." Her voice caught. "We are all frightened."

"Show me." His hand now gripped her arm, and they crossed the room. I heard it open, close and latch.

I think I counted fifty breaths, during which I sat up, fighting against dizziness. It had been too long since I'd eaten. What now? What now? I thought wearily.

But then the door unlatched and opened. Running steps, and Eleandra bent over me. "Quick—we must be quick. I don't know how long my maids can weep all over him."

As she spoke she tugged on my good hand, and I got to my feet, and staggered as the tower room revolved.

She gripped me against her and together we ran from the room, outside of which there were no guards.

Eleandra said, "All the inside guards are searching round the outside of the castle. It won't take long, so hurry."

I gritted my teeth and forced myself to match her pace. Down, down, down, then into a hallway. The whole castle seemed to blaze with lamps, torches, candelabra. Garian had not left a room unlit, except mine.

Into a small, elegant chamber—the room with the mirror in it, I realized. From my almost-wedding day. The mirror was blocked by Jaim and four men.

"Good work," Jaim said to Eleandra, and saluted me with a casual wave.

"Here," Eleandra gasped. "Help. She's so heavy."

As Jaim's strong hand slid under my elbow Eleandra stepped back—and then raised her fists to her mouth.

Garian stood in the doorway with several of his men behind him. He laughed in surprise. "Jaim? Well, well."

They advanced into the room, the men fanning out. Jaim let me go, gave me a gentle push in the direction of the beautiful carved desk, and pulled free his sword and knife.

Clang! Clash! Blades met, whirled, met again.

Eleandra's eyes widened with terror. She backed to the window, turning to a beautiful silhouette in the strengthening dawn light. No help there.

Door. It was maybe six or seven paces away. I readied myself for a sprint.

Three battles raged furiously in that room, deadly weapons arcing and slashing in all directions. Jaim fought against two men, grinning with bloodthirsty joy as he held them off. One of the men staggered my way. I retreated—and found myself near Garian, who gave me a distracted look as he battled one of Jaim's men. He shifted—to block my exit!

I closed my hand around the nearest object on the desk, a heavy carved box full of letter seals. I flung it at him. The box hit him on the forehead and the wafers spilled down the front of his tunic like giant snowflakes.

He struck out with his free hand, slapping me back against the wall. A whirl of the blade, he jabbed the point into the side of Jaim's man, and then turned on me, white-faced with anger. "You're far too much trouble." He shoved me against the table. I fell backward, and he pinned me down with one hand. "Goodbye, Cousin." He raised his sword, watching me all the while. For what, words of surrender? Begging and pleading? I glared back, my teeth clenched against making any sound at all.

Before he could bring the sword down a thin strip of shining silver flashed across my vision and rested against Garian's upraised hand.

Garian turned his head, and so did I.

Jason lifted the blade in salute.

Chapter Twenty-Seven

Garian's blade arced straight at Jason's head, to be met in a smooth deflecting beat that sent it harmlessly to one side. Jason's tip whirled in, to be blocked by Garian's dagger. This battle was going on within arm's length of me, understand. I was still lying on my back across that desk, helpless as an upended turtle.

I finally got the idea of heaving myself onto my good side, though by then it felt as if my spine had cracked in two. I pushed myself away from the desk and made my way dizzily to Eleandra's side. She clutched a curtain in one hand and watched Garian and Jason, her eyes wide in her pale face. Wide, but no longer in terror. Her expression was—ardent.

She was enjoying that battle!

I just wanted to get out of there. But Jason and Garian fought their duel between me and the door. No one was going anywhere, either in or out.

Jason forced Garian to stagger back a step or two, then flung his blade up into the air and caught it with his left. Clearly his own wound, which had been far more spectacular than mine, had not yet completely healed.

Garian tried again and again for the advantage, using both blade and dagger. Jason beat, blocked, once using a foot to kick the dagger-hand aside. Then he altered his grip, his eyes narrowed with intent, and struck the flat of the blade across Garian's face, leaving a red welt.

Garian snarled a curse and pressed to the attack—and at the door a crowd of his men appeared.

They'd win now, out of sheer numbers. Jaim and his foes stopped fighting; everyone watched Garian and Jason. The man whom Garian had wounded staggered to the corner, breathing in harsh gasps.

Garian seemed to realize that he'd won, for he laughed out loud, as he traded blows with Jason. You could see the triumph in his white-flashing smile.

But Jason had been driving Garian steadily toward the cluster of Jaim's men, while keeping his own back to a wall. Jaim moved two steps to Jason's shoulder to shield him from those at the door as Jason's eyes narrowed again and the blade flickered, a maneuver so fast it was a blur. Garian's weapons went flying out of his hands—blood ran down his fingers on his right hand—and he staggered, Jason's swordpoint pressed in the hollow of his throat.

One step. Two. Jaim and the men were ranged all around them.

Garian's men froze.

Everyone froze.

Garian struggled for breath, flexing his bleeding hand. Jason gazed straight into Garian's eyes.

One move, and he'd thrust.

"Well." Jaim's voice was startling in the sudden silence. He waved his sword at Garian's armsmen. "You know what happens now. Retreat—nice and orderly—or your master will be shopping for a new head."

The men backed from the door.

Jason glanced once, then flicked the sword to the side of Garian's neck, against the main blood vessel that I had learned about during my lessons with Ressa a hundred lifetimes ago. "Move."

Garian started to walk, Jason matching him step for step.

Jaim bowed outrageously to Eleandra and me, then twiddled his fingers at the remaining Drath warriors. They backed out, one or two glaring over their shoulders.

We followed, and so a strange procession made its way through the castle. Eleandra's servants followed behind us and Lita (who'd been disarmed back in Dantherei, so perforce had to watch for her chance to act) silently joined behind Jaim. She had taken a sword off of one of Garian's men, which she held, now, at the ready. Jaim and Lita were on the watch lest anyone try a countermove against Eleandra or me.

Down the steps and out into the courtyard, which was bleak in the blue-gray early morning light.

When all had left the castle, Jason must have increased the pressure of the blade against Garian's neck because Garian stopped, his hand jerking up then dropping. He could never touch the sword blade before Jason could rip it across that blood vessel.

Jason said, "Your men will remain here. We will proceed alone. It is the only way you will live."

Garian was furious, the sword-welt on his cheek now purple. As I watched Garian debate within himself, I recognized that the welt on his face corresponded with my own sore face. The sword had struck him where he'd struck me the day before. *Fair trade*, I thought with sour triumph.

Garian's mouth tightened, then he made a staying motion with his unmarked left hand.

The warriors faded back.

And so we walked on to the drawbridge, where several of Jaim's and Jason's people waited, some with crossbows, and Vrozta with horses. I noted the bows were sighted on various portions of the castle: a balance of threat, then, with those hidden above.

In low voices, Jaim and Vrozta got the servants sorted among the horses, and they began mounting up. Eleandra stayed back, and perforce I had to as well, for my knees were too watery and my balance too uneasy for me to walk on my own.

Jason looked our way, then abruptly lifted the sword and sheathed it.

"You will regret that decision," Garian said.

"I already regret it," Jason replied.

Garian turned around and walked slowly back toward his people; one sign from him, and though we might die from bolts, he'd be the first one down from Jaim's people. And he knew it.

Markham was holding the last two horses. Mounted, Jaim led the train of servants down the trail. Vrozta followed, her sword out, but she kept looking back from Eleandra to me. An intent gaze, as if containing some meaning or message that I could not read.

Jason crossed the drawbridge in three quick strides, and Markham said in an undervoice, "Vrozta and Randal hobbled their horses and slashed their gear. It'll take them some time to mount a chase."

"Ah. Thank you, Markham."

Eleandra clutched at Jason's arm. "My dear, I believe you should send one of your people here to help Flian. She can barely walk."

Jason did not answer her. Step, step, then he was next to me, and his arm slid round me—checking when he felt the new stickiness down my left side.

He picked me up and put me on the saddlebow of the nearest mount, then got into the saddle behind me. The world was revolving gently by then. I closed my eyes as we began to ride. My aching head rested against Jason's shoulder as he gave the sign to ride out.

We moved, slow at first, then faster. At some point they turned off the road, and the horses slowed again, making their way down the slope. Sounds—birdcalls, the rustle of trees, the rush of water—were unnaturally clear. Close sounds, too: Jason's breathing, the rapid tattoo of his heart.

Scents: pine, horse, the perfume of late jasmine, sweat. His, not mine, though I was clammy from my exertions and my earlier fear. The smell was not at all unpleasant. No, not at all. I fought against the urge to breathe in his scent, for his proximity was so reassuring. So warm. So...so *compelling*.

And then at last I knew what the unthinking part of me had known for some time, making me dizzy with overwhelming sensation. I was acutely aware of the contours of his arms, the feel of his fingers through the heavy fabric of my riding tunic; I realized, with a kind of hilarious despair, that I had at last managed to fall in love, or rather in lust, for how could it possibly be love with someone I did not know, who had once threatened to make me regret sparing his life?

I kept my eyes closed, my cheek pressed against the rough wool of his tunic, glad that I had at least the duration of the ride in which to get control of my mental state—and also, I thought weakly (knowing it was weakness, but right then I did not care at all) to bask in the fire of his proximity, a dear and burning brightness I would never again feel.

Time passed, and I smelled the cold wet stone of the morvende cave.

Jason said, almost too soft to hear, "Flian, are you awake?"

"Yes."

"Did you endure any more of Garian's maltreatment?"

How to act, to sound normal? All my emotions as well as my senses had kindled to flame. Only pride stayed steadfast. Pride would keep my voice even, would reason for me, would not betray me.

"No." Because he stayed silent, I babbled on, "But I haven't had anything to eat since breakfast yesterday. I guess he didn't want to waste a dinner on the doomed. Did you know he was sitting at my bedside waiting for you?"

"Yes. We sent a man under his window to provoke him into action. I had counted on something like it, and I apologize for once more putting you directly into danger, but it was the only way Lita could get Jaim and his boys in through the back way."

"Well, I spoiled the plan, so I guess it was my—"

"It was not your fault." He interrupted me, low and quite sharp. "The blame was mine, from the beginning." He hesitated, then said, "You did not tell him that we were at hand."

"No, for I thought you might have gone back to Lathandra, once you had poor Jewel safe. How is she?"

"Fine—angry but fine. You will no doubt hear more of her experiences than you have interest for, if not patience." Humor warmed his voice, but then it was gone. "You expected us to abandon you?"

I struggled with words I could not say, and words that I could. How to trust words, when I couldn't even trust my own emotions?

Start with where we are, and leave out the messy emotions completely. Be calm and rational. "How could I know? I saved your life once, and you were angry at me for it. Now you don't owe me anything, if that's what made you angry, because you have saved mine."

His voice was flat. "So what you mean is, now we are quits."

"Yes."

He said nothing else.

A short time later the horses stopped, and we were once again deep inside the long morvende tunnel. Jason dismounted, lifted me down, set me gently on my feet, and walked away. I leaned against the horse, bewildered and miserable. *Now we are quits.* My attempt to state exactly where we were had become a chasm that I could not cross.

I heard his voice, giving orders for the organization of a camp. Then Jaim's cheery tones, followed by Vrozta's low laugh. I opened my eyes, and saw Eleandra's golden form gliding through the camp in the direction Jason had gone.

I turned my face into the horse's side, my eyes aching, until a familiar deep voice murmured, "The king sent me to see to your comfort, Princess Flian." Markham. "Come. You will soon have steeped leaf and something hot to eat."

I clung to his arm as we traversed the uneven, rocky floor toward an alcove divided off from the carved tunnel by a great, slanting slab of granite. Its edges glistened in the firelight. Markham handed me into a kind of small chamber and withdrew, vanishing behind me. The fire blazed and crackled, giving off welcome warmth. Jewel waited, pointing with pride at a nest of rugs and blankets. "Come in. Sit down, Flian. I made this ready and built the fire against your return."

Jason had sunk down. He looked tired, his expression the old winter stone one. Eleandra settled herself close to him, as one whose presence would be welcome. She put aside her cloak, shaking back her gleaming hair. She did not seem the least self-conscious to be sitting there in silken wrapper and nightgown, but she looked superb even when disheveled.

Jason poked at the fire with a stick, and got to his feet. "I will see what there is to eat and drink."

Eleandra looked up in surprise. Jewel exclaimed in protest, "I told you I have that coming!"

Jason stepped past me and disappeared.

Eleandra shook her hair back again, combing the fingers of one hand through it. She held the other out. "Thank you." She smiled. "For holding my pledge-ring for me. I believe I will have it back now."

Jewel's eyes widened. She looked down as though discovering the sapphire ring for the first time, twisted it off and handed it to Eleandra.

The gems sparked and glowed in the leaping light as the royal heir to Dantherei put it on her heart-finger, then held it up to admire it.

"Handsome stones, are they not?" She lifted her head. "Flian. You must sit down. You look dreadful." She pointed across the fire from where Jason had been sitting.

Jewel winced, touching her neck as though the movement hurt. Her eyes were concerned. "Flian! Euw, is that blood on your sleeve?"

I dropped down on the blankets that Jewel had set for me. "Never mind." That was all I had strength for.

Jason appeared, carrying a steaming pot and four mugs hooked by their handles through one of his fingers. "You were right," he said to his sister as he stepped past me. "Good job."

"I'm not completely useless," Jewel said, huffing.

"Well I am," Eleandra stated, smiling. "And I have never regretted it more than today. But it was truly splendid, my dear, seeing you defeat Garian."

Jason knelt before the fire, positioning the steaming pot on a flat rock. He seemed absorbed in the task.

Eleandra reached up to touch his arm. "Was it your version of justice, or mere caprice, that strike with the flat across his face?"

"A warning," Jason said.

Eleandra looked across the fire at me, a slight frown marring her brow. Then she lifted a shoulder in a shrug and flung her hair back with a grand gesture. Strands of shimmering chestnut drifted over Jason's arm.

"I take it Garian is not dead?" Jewel asked.

"No." Jason poured out the last mug. "Here, hand this to Flian, would you?" He gave two mugs to Jewel.

She pressed one into my good hand. "Why ever not?"

"Because he didn't kill any of you." Jason drank some of his own. "I expect I know his limits now."

"He came very close to stabbing Flian." Eleandra looked from Jason to me and back again.

I remembered Garian's expression, and the table's edge grinding into my spine as I waited for him to strike. "No he didn't," I said. "Not today, though I believed he would. It was different than when I tried to kill him. That time he really meant to return the favor, and except for Markham, he would have." I flicked my good hand, trying to express my relief. "To be perfectly fair, I can't really blame Garian for that one, for I'd just tried to stick a knife into him. But last night...this morning...he made the threats, but he didn't seem in any hurry to carry them out. Even at the end there."

Jason sent me an appraising look, and then turned his attention to the fire. "True. He waited too long. He could have finished the job with the dagger at the same time as he blocked me with his blade, but he didn't do that either. Truth is, he talks a bad line but unless he's in a rage he seems to prefer to stop short of murder—at least with women. I expect it would have been different if he had gotten his hands on me."

Eleandra gave a delicate little sigh. "You do take the romance out of it."

I tried to hide a grimace. Jewel made no attempt to hide her disgust—not that Eleandra paid her the least attention.

"No romance in him killing me." He smiled faintly.

"No! No! I meant—"

"Or in my killing him and having to contend with uprisings all over Drath." Jason lifted a hand toward the back of the cave, taking in the entire principality. "He'll be looking for ways to get back at me, but that's less of a headache than the prospect of settling Drath."

"I'm glad you have the strength to do that." Eleandra scooted close to him again, and this time laid her head along his arm, her hair draping over his sleeve like a shining cloak. "All I know is, I longed for you to come to the rescue." She sighed, her shapely bosom rising and falling. "I am, at last, safe."

Jewel turned my way, rolling her eyes and making a face like she was going to be sick. I tried to smile, but the wretchedness I felt at the sight of them was worse than the pain in my shoulder. I got to my feet and walked out; behind me I heard Eleandra's voice, tender with affection, and her musical laughter.

I wandered, scarcely seeing anything, until I reached the cavern where they stabled the horses. There I found a familiar tall, dark-haired figure.

Markham turned. "Princess Flian?"

My eyes ached, my head, my heart. "Markham, you can act on your own, can't you?"

"Yes."

"Take me home. Now. Don't tell them. Just—take me home."

"You're not well." He frowned. "You really ought to rest that shoulder."

"I can't." I covered my face with my hands. I had lost everything that mattered—including pride.

"I will," he said at last. "But not now. The searches will be too thorough. Here. I have a place. I will bring you food, and you can rest. I will tell the others you are asleep, for they all know your wound reopened. And we will leave before dawn, when the search-lines have moved their way eastward. The search to the west will be at best desultory. Herlester will expect us to ride home."

Home. I gestured my thanks, my throat too constricted for words.

And so that's what happened. He led me to another side-alcove in that great, ancient warren, which was spread about with numerous bedrolls. I sank down onto the one he indicated, and waited there until he brought listerblossom leaf and food. I ate and drank, and fell into an exhausted slumber from which I woke at the touch of a hand.

I rose, my head aching abominably, and followed Markham's silent form through the quiet camp. I could not see Jason—or Eleandra. I realized I was looking for them, just to make myself feel worse, and confined my gaze to Markham's broad back.

Down the tunnel, away, away. I wept, for there was no helping it, but at least no one would see it now, except for Markham, and I trusted his silent impassiveness.

Markham had prepared a couple of mounts. He and I shared one, because I was not able to ride, and he led the other. We traversed several tunnels, only lit by the torch he bore in one hand.

We finally emerged behind a great waterfall and rode down a narrow, precipitous trail that afforded occasional glimpses of the farmland of Lygiera.

And so we journeyed westward, with no further adventures. It was a quiet trip, each of us absorbed with our own thoughts. Markham saw to everything; each day I was substantially recovered, at least in body, if not in spirit, and presently I was able to ride by myself.

Thus we arrived in Carnison at last. Markham stayed with me until we reached the courtyard of the royal castle. "You are now safe. I believe I will return home."

"Please come in," I responded. "My brother will wish to thank you and to repay you for the money you had to spend."

"It is unnecessary." He smiled faintly. "Do you wish me to be the bearer of any message to the king?"

I thought of Jason, of Eleandra and the ring she had decided to wear again. I remembered those last horrible words that had divided us, and shook my head. More words would only make the hurt worse.

Markham took the reins of my horse, wheeled his and rode slowly back down the royal avenue.

I stood where I was until I had control of the tears, and walked past the shocked stablehands, past the footman at the courtyard entry. *Home*, I thought, *I'm home. I'm safe, I'm home.* It didn't make me feel any better.

Not long after I stepped into my bedchamber, there was my brother's step behind me. He looked worried.

"Oh, Maxl," I cried and threw myself into his arms.

Chapter Twenty-Eight

"I've spread the word that you were caught in that bad rainstorm a week ago. Got chilled, which turned into a lung fever," Maxl said the next day.

We were alone out on my terrace, overlooking the rose garden. The morning was balmy, almost summer-warm, the breezes carrying the fragrances of late blooms.

Beyond the roses, atop a hill, I could see the gazebo where Spaquel had set Jewel and me up to be taken by Garian, beyond which Jason had stood, counting on Spaquel's being too arrogant to notice that the men in blue weren't his, and trying not to laugh at the absurdity of the situation...

I turned in my chair, so my back was to the garden.

Maxl frowned. "What is it, Flian?"

He sat on the edge of my table, his hands absently fingering the ironwork edging. I knew he needed to be elsewhere—probably half a dozen elsewheres.

"My arm aches." I forced a smile. "Go ahead to your morning's work. I'm certainly not in any danger here."

"It can wait. I'm more concerned about you."

Instead of answering that, I asked, "What happened to Spaquel? You didn't say."

"Nothing. I let him know that he'd be fine as long as he confines himself to court socializing and to governing Osterog. One step beyond and he'll get an escort to the border, and his land reverts to the crown."

"Ugh. I wish you had thrown him out."

"He's actually a good governor—if for no other reason than because he needs the revenue. But that's going to have to satisfy him, unless his taste for mixing in royal politics is so insatiable he wants to indulge it by being lackey to someone like Garian. He won't give up a dukedom and his family's lands lightly, though."

"I would have thrown him out. But then I already know my judgment is poor, so we can be glad that you were the oldest, and the heir, and that I am a disposable symbol for useful wealth."

Maxl got up and turned all the way around, then he sat down next to me, his restlessness gone. He frowned at me. "I've never heard you so bitter," he said at last. "It's not like you. It pains me. What have I done? What have I missed?" In that moment, he looked unexpectedly like Papa. "What did you not tell me last night?"

I blinked my blurring eyes. "I told you everything that happened."

Maxl ran his hand through his hair and gave me a puzzled frown. "Something is missing."

"You reminded me of Papa just now. The news of his death is recent for me. And Maxl, I feel so badly that I was not here."

"Except he was quite proud of you. When I told him you'd gone to Dantherei, his face lit like a candle. Like this." He opened his eyes and smiled. "He was so very pleased that you had taken an interest in what he regarded as a diplomatic mission to strengthen the bonds between the two kingdoms."

"I'm glad of that, but I can't help regretting he believed a lie."

Maxl sat back, crossing his arms. "Not a lie. When Tamara wrote back after my envoy carrying the news about Papa got there too late to reach you, she said several flattering things about you. And she wrote herself—it was not some unknown scribe who is employed to hand out empty compliments."

"Empty—do you have any such scribes?"

"Yep. Four of 'em." He grinned. "And they're good at what they do, which is greasing the wheels of the social..." He waved a hand round and round. "What? I was going to say 'intercourse' but that's a fairly nasty image."

I choked on a laugh, most of it kindled by surprise, because Maxl had never spoken to me that way before.

"Social carriage race? I like that. Everyone racing around in a circle. Sometimes it seems we don't actually go anywhere, but then Papa did hammer on the fact that the path of least resistance gets the job done better. I've since experienced resistance, and what I assumed was tired-old-man talk has convinced me that he was quite wise."

I nodded. "He was, wasn't he?"

Maxl got up, and his fingers were restless again, tapping on the balcony rail. The breeze fingered his blond hair, hiding his profile. "He also talked about how power and position warps otherwise normal human interactions. Feelings. Relationships. He said, 'Better for the monarch to be beloved than to love.' I used to think that was just bitterness about Mother. But of late I'm coming to see the wisdom of that. What can happen when a ruler throws royal strength and resources into acquiring what he or she wants most passionately, be that another kingdom— or a person."

"A good ruler suddenly turns into a bad one?"

"Well, more like a good ruler makes a bad decision. Papa fell in love with our mother, and it was his single worst mistake. Though we wouldn't be here. But there are some who would consider us mistakes as well." Maxl's brows lifted in irony.

"So you're saying it's better for us to marry without passion? To marry for political need?"

"It's one path. Not necessarily the best. Look at the Szinzars. The old king forced his biggest rival into treaty by marriage, and that did not save his life or his kingdom, nor did it—from what Jewel said once or twice—make for a very enviable home life."

"Did Papa want you to marry? Or is all this discussion meant for my edification?"

"For us both. I am trying to figure out what I ought to do in that regard." He lifted a shoulder in a rueful shrug. "Supposing the opportunity comes my way. As for your situation, I've been trying to follow it from a distance." He gave me a comical grimace. "Since you won't write letters."

"I still don't trust words." My voice started to go high, and I got an internal grip. "So far, experience has borne me out."

Maxl moved restlessly to the rail, staring down at the late, autumn-blown roses nodding in the morning breeze. "I wish I understood why, because I sense something missing. Never mind. Specifically I have been wondering if, balked of her plans with Garian, Eleandra is going to remember that I am now a king, and come courting me. And if she does, what I ought to do about it. Is she still beautiful? I'd probably look at her and become a rabbit before the wolf."

So why are you looking like a trapped rabbit—

Argh! Go away, memory.

My hands were in my lap, lying there loosely. Pride had reasserted itself. I would not burden my brother with my foolishness. "I'm afraid you're too late. I told you last night only that she was safe, along with Jewel and their servants, when I left the border to come west. What I didn't tell you was that she managed, in the time it took for everyone to dismount from their horses, to get to Jewel and reclaim the sapphire ring she'd once given Jason. That and some of the things she said while we were alone together make me fairly certain that her interest in Jason rekindled when she saw him circumvent Garian's plans."

Maxl whistled.

"No," I corrected myself. *Let your words be true.* "I'm not being fair. I think her interest in him as a person rekindled as well. She said, um, things about him that made it clear she hadn't considered him a completely bad bargain nine years ago, despite his lack of fashion."

Maxl grinned. "And what Eleandra wants Eleandra gets, eh? Well, that's been true all along, so why not now? I'm not sure I like the idea of her as Queen of Ralanor Veleth. She might seduce old Jason into thinking a war against us not a bad idea after all. I know she has ambitions, and I know he would like sea access. Huh. Well, so much for me thinking myself such a prize." He laughed and pushed away from the balcony. "On that most salutary note, I will get downstairs to the work I ought to have been at. We'll dine together. How's that?"

"In truth, I am tired of my own company," I admitted.

Maxl gave me an apologetic smile. "In truth I would like my own company for a time—I wasn't really ready for Papa to die—but then we Elandersis seem to be adept at wanting what we can't have." He bent down to kiss my forehead. "Sleep well. We'll eat in the lair, just like we used to. How's that?"

"You still use the lair?"

Maxl grinned. "I had a door from the king's study knocked into that back wall. When you're a king you can do that sort of thing."

It was a joke, and he paused, looking hopeful, so I smiled.

"So you don't have to go through Papa's outer rooms." He whistled softly. "'Papa's rooms.' I think of 'em that way even now. I wonder what he felt when he first moved into 'em? Enough chatter from me. I have to get to work." He flipped a hand in a wave, and left.

I looked out at the roses once more, wondering if Jason and his entourage had yet reached Lathandra. I remembered that huge battalion assembling in the courtyard, waiting at the Drath border. That impressive gathering would close safely around all three Szinzars, and Eleandra. And accompany them home. *Their* home.

What would Jaim do then? How about his gang?

What would Jewel do? The one regret I permitted myself was that I had not said goodbye to her.

I turned my attention to the crystal water glass on my tray and stared down into it. Sunlight gleamed in the water, catching and scattering the light.

Jason?

He was there, clear and not clear, for the light flickered across and through his image. Sunlight sparked in his eyes. He looked up, and then his gaze went diffuse, as though he shifted his focus to the horizon.

I closed my own eyes, knowing that this trick with the glass, however unexplainable, was just another form of spying. I had not been given leave for so intimate a connection, and so I put the glass aside.

ॐ

"Many have asked about you," Maxl said several weeks later, when we dined together in his lair. His room was cozy and warm, while outside another autumn storm raged against the walls and windows. And there in the corner was the new door, to the king's chambers—silent evidence that our lives, after all, had changed.

"People have asked about me?" I didn't hide my skepticism.

"Some of them even wanted to hear the answer."

I snorted. "Swains who need wealth to fully realize their

ambitions being the loudest, no doubt."

"Well, the music master. And Mistress Olith."

"The music school runs itself. They need my funds, not my person swanking about as presiding princess."

"They want you to hear the new children."

"I will. Soon," I promised.

"You've been saying 'soon' to me every day for what, a fortnight? Is 'soon' going to be another word for 'never'?"

I made a sour face. I did not believe anyone wanted to see me any more than I wanted to see them. But I'd kept busy: in between trips to the archive for reading on recent history, treaties, diplomacy...and personalities, I had taken up my own music again. I wanted music as a conduit to feeling. My studies of the intricacies of diplomacy reinforced my conviction that music was *safer* than words.

I had also—slowly—taken up some of the exercises I had learned at those dawn practices in Dantherei, for I missed the feeling of strength that I had begun to enjoy there.

My thoughts fled eastward, to that salle where once I'd seen Jaim and Jason, and were they, too, practicing?

"Flian?"

The reverie broke. I looked up.

Maxl said, "You've been buried in here either playing your instruments or reading for the past week. What have you been researching?"

"Knowledge. Answers to questions."

"Such as?"

The history of Ralanor Veleth. But I would not say that. "Well, for one thing, the meaning of truth. Diplomacy seems so often the opposite of truth—is there any truth in a court? Then I wanted to find more about this trick I have of seeing faces in glasses of water."

Maxl snapped his fingers. "Dena Yeresbeth. Not that, but some kind of precursor to it. Did you see that book from Bereth Ferian that Papa ordered after the Siamis war? It explains a lot about that."

"I found it first thing. There still really isn't much information."

"That's because the whole subject is new. But it's something our children might be born with. And in turn, that means we must think about…" He shrugged. "Everything."

About who the other parent will be—and what the person's influence might be. But I forbore saying anything.

Words.

Just as I had not said anything about my own disastrous first attempt at the danger-fraught and ungovernable realm of passion, so had my brother kept to himself whatever emotional difficulties he was enduring.

We passed the rest of the meal talking amicably about those current records that he'd been able to get. Maxl's recent reading projects had been to find out why various ancient kingdoms flourished despite war and conflict, like Sartor, and why some sank into mediocrity, like once-glorious Everon.

But as he talked, his hands betrayed a tension that I had not seen since that morning after my return. I did not ask; I did not want to risk breaking the calm good fellowship that we shared.

The next day dawned bright and clear and cold.

Midmorning I was sitting at my music when Maxl came in unannounced. I looked up in surprise, for this was the customary time for his interviews downstairs in the audience chamber. His eyes were wide. "I do not know if this is what you will like—"

I heard a quick step in the hall outside my parlor. Moments later a figure in rose dashed in, arms wide. "Flian?"

"Jewel!" I exclaimed.

Chapter Twenty-Nine

"Oh, it is good to be here again," Jewel exclaimed, looking about at the old family dining room, to which we had gone for refreshments. "How pretty this room is! Enough of the blue and gold trim on the carvings to make the white attractive and not plain."

Maxl and I preferred the lair, and its lack of formality, but unspoken between us was the wish to compromise for Jewel's sake. Now, sitting with her in the room that my great-grandmother had had redesigned, we saw its artistry anew.

"You have different rooms for different seasons," Jewel went on. "I *love* that. In Lathandra, all that military barricading makes the place impossible any time except in winter, when the light is low enough to be direct. And there's only one decent room for socializing. Ugh." A reflection not quite true, for I vividly remembered mellow summer lighting—but I said nothing.

She reached to pour out more steeped leaf, pausing to examine the cobalt blue pot with admiration.

"Are you here for long?" I asked at last.

"I," Jewel preened, her nose in the air, "am an Official Diplomatic Envoy—and I shall want to be Presented." She cast a glance at Maxl. "Jason said he did write to you about it."

Maxl rubbed his hands. "He did, and I told him you'd be most welcome." He smiled across at me. "I didn't say anything to you because I thought you might like the surprise."

"I do. It's wonderful to see you, Jewel."

"It's wonderful to see you too, but why did you leave us so suddenly? I feared you were angry with me for not managing to escape, and thus landing you back into Garian's clutches." She pinched her nose. "I know *I* would have been. But I assure you I couldn't sleep, couldn't even eat. I had to know you were safe. I kept screaming at Jaim and Jason to hurry and get you out, until Vrozta finally dosed me with sleepweed. That's why I didn't come along to help on the rescue run." She shivered. "There was this, too." She flung back her carefully draped curls, exposing the hairsbreadth pink line on the side of her neck.

Maxl's mouth tightened.

Jewel pulled her hair forward again to hide it. "I still have nightmares about that day. I probably always will. Ugh. Don't let's talk of that. I am so happy to be here again, and *not* as your pensioner. I have my own household for which you must find space, and even my own seamstresses. Like this gown?" She twitched her shoulders back and forth, showing off the clusters of cherry-colored ribbons up the sleeves, and the round neck with its fine embroidery. She then gave me a perplexed glance. "You, on the other hand, look like one of your housemaids in that old brown gown. Don't tell me you're yet recovering?"

"Oh no, I'm fine. Nothing left but twinges if I swing my arm too hard at sword practice." I touched my shoulder.

"*Sword* practice?" She sighed. "Has everyone gone mad? Jason's gone completely mad. You can*not* imagine what a *relief* it was to get away from the hideous boredom!"

"What, boring? With Eleandra there? I would have thought she'd have reorganized your entire kingdom by now," I said in surprise. "At least the social side."

"You'd think that, wouldn't you?" Jewel gave me the sardonic Szinzar smile. "There we were, up in Drath, free at last, and my, *how* she chased after him all over those caves. It was simply stomach turning." She brandished her cup.

I leaned forward, willing her to go on—but afraid, too, of what I might hear. All the feelings I had thought I'd defeated came back, like a pack of ravening wolves.

"Go on," Maxl said. "So Eleandra was courting Jason, is that it?" He sat back in his chair.

"Courting! She was so sweet and charming, and, and..." Jewel gestured down her own pretty figure. "And so alluring, that I think half the escort was stunned by her. Oh, I don't have to think, because they *were*. Everywhere she went, they watched her, practically licking their chops, and didn't she adore it. Ut-terly revolting! And all of it aimed at my rock-headed older brother, for she totally ignored Jaim. You'd think Jason would be smirking worse than that stinker Garian did all the way up into Drath—when he wasn't honing his sarcasm on me—but Jason kept everything organized, often going off to talk with his company leaders or Jaim, after Markham left so unaccountably with you." She jerked her pretty chin at me. "But Vrozta said it made perfect tactical sense, to take you home to the west while we drew all the searchers east. Since tactical sense has nothing to do with common sense, of course I don't understand it. But I'm glad it worked."

"So you did have a safe journey out of Drath, then," I said.

"Oh, perfectly safe. When we got out of the caves, there were all Jason's people waiting, hordes of 'em. When Garian's people inevitably caught up with us, there were far too many to attack. They ranged along the mountaintop and watched us. Eugh, that was creepy, but Eleandra apparently didn't think so! Turn me into a cookpot if she didn't look up at them and smile! Can she *not* stop flirting? Well, I suppose people say that about me, too, even when I don't mean anything by it." Her smile was contrite.

I smiled back. Maxl studied the ceiling as if reading a secret history.

"Anyway, when we got to Lathandra, did Jason get out the old silver and have the nasty old barracks furbished up a bit and maybe get the play-season begun early, for Eleandra's sake? Not he!"

Maxl slid his hands over his eyes. I saw his shoulders shaking.

"He left all her entertainment to *me*. You know what he *dared* to do that first night? He sat there in the south parlor with us, and he read *military supply reports* all evening! Why, you'd think he didn't want her after all—and if I'd known *that*, I never would have gone haring off to Dantherei in the first place, you may be *sure!*"

Maxl made a muffled noise.

Jewel glanced his way. Her cheeks glowed with color.

"Sorry." Maxl coughed. "Sorry. It's so unexpected. Please go on."

"You're just like Jaim. When I told him I couldn't figure out what Jason was about—I expected him to hustle her off to his rooms and stay there a month, especially with her dropping all these hints about as subtle as boulders that she was ready and willing—Jaim laughed so hard I thought he was going to fall out the window." Jewel's brow contracted in perplexity. "What is it with you men? You are all idiots, that's what it is."

"I'll agree to that." I glared at my brother, who instantly assumed a sober face—if one didn't look at his eyes.

Jewel turned back to me. "I did what I could, but she was so *bored.* So *obviously* bored. Two days of that, and she started writing letters. Constantly. Must have sent half the garrison couriers north to Dantherei, but Jason let her do it. He stayed in his rooms almost all the time, except when he was over in the garrison. After Markham came back, Jason was scarcely even home. When he was, he always had work in hand."

"I don't understand," I said. "Perhaps he was annoyed with her for choosing to run off with Garian rather than with us. Yet I can't believe he didn't even talk to her."

"He did spend time talking to her after a couple weeks of excruciating boredom. Seems like it was a year! He didn't seem angry with her, or really much of anything. Just..." She pulled a blank face. "Impervious. I don't know what she did at night, and I don't want to know. All I can tell you is that he wasn't there to do it with. Oh, I didn't mention that her pretense for coming with us instead of going home with the escort Jason offered her was that she had been made ill by her experiences and could not face that long journey."

She crumbled up a fresh apple tart. "So. We three had dinner that last evening. Now, I'd been reminding him—well, nagging and whining and threatening, truth to tell, because he did promise to send me here, and I saw no harm in bringing it up again because I didn't know if he was about to go off and leave me to yet another week of boredom. So I said, 'When are you going to keep your promise and send me to Carnison?' He'd said initially that I wouldn't go without a staff and accoutrements, but Berry had already seen to that. Took her two days to get things organized!"

"Is Berry with you?" I asked, hoping that she was.

Jewel shook her head. "Stayed. Says that if there's ever a queen, she will be the queen's head steward, and meanwhile, she doesn't like to leave home. Imagine anyone wanting to stay in that gloomy old barracks who doesn't have to!"

Maxl was also crumbling an apple tart. "So did Eleandra offer to bring you here, is that it?"

Jewel turned her attention to him. "Do you want to marry her?"

"No." He grinned. "But I wouldn't mind her showing up with her full armor of allurements and battering at my door, I confess."

"Huh." Jewel gave him a reluctant grin. "So anyway—where was I?"

"Dinner. With Jason." As I spoke I felt my brother's gaze, and I wished I hadn't spoken.

"Oh! I asked when he might keep his promise and send me, and he said he would when you had recovered enough to resume your court duties." She cast a glance my way. "He added that your four-day ride after leaving Garian's had probably dealt you a setback. And Eleandra gave him one of those *looks* that she gives men—half the candles in the room melting to puddles." She made a face, poonching out her lips and fluttering her eyelashes. "We saw enough of that at their court, didn't we?"

I nodded, my clammy hands now hidden in my skirts. "Go on."

"That's really it." Jewel lifted her shoulders in a careless shrug. "Oh, Eleandra said something like, 'So you know her progress?' and Jason's answer was typical for him." She shrugged again.

"Typical like..." Maxl prompted.

"He gave her one of those stone-faced looks of his own— and we know *those*, don't we, Flian? He said something like *Of course*, or, no. It was, *Can you doubt it?* I think. Who cares? Anyway, next day she was gone, and no hint of coming here. Whsssst! Just like that!" Jewel flicked her fingers in the air. "Back to Dantherei, with the escort she'd turned down before. Good riddance! But the important thing is, as soon as she rode through the gates—I was congratulating myself on having seen the last of her—*then* Jason turned to me and said I could name my departure day. He told his own steward to see to my orders, and so you can be sure Berry and I scrambled it all together as fast as we could, before he could change his mind—which he's clearly lost—again." She laughed, hands wide. "And here I am!"

"No problems through Drath, I take it," Maxl said.

"Not a one. But they were watching," Jewel added. "I felt the temptation to wave at walls and trees, but there were all the banners, and the armed outriders and servants, and we never veered a step off the Treaty Road—and yours truly rode at the head of the cavalcade, being an Official Diplomat with all her might. That means I behaved myself."

Maxl and she exchanged grins.

I hardly listened. Of course I was thinking of what concerned me most. "How could Jason know my progress?"

Maxl said, "I didn't tell you, since apparently you didn't get along with him. He's written to me a couple of times. About Jewel's coming and about border concerns. Trade issues that I'm hoping we're going to hammer out. Asked if you'd recovered from the stab wound."

"Well, that's very polite," I said, trying for the same casual tone.

So Jason had rid himself of his one-time beloved, the old passion gone despite her strenuous attempts. Did that leave him heart-free? What matter if it did? There had certainly been no message for me.

Of course there wasn't. Didn't he always keep his promises? There was his promise, made before the horrible rescue journey to Drath, that he would send me home and never again enter my life. *And he always keeps his word, the fool.*

"That's enough of my boring, stupid brother," Jewel commanded. "Now that I am here, it is time to have some fun, and that means the subject of Jason Szinzar—and Lathandra—will never be raised again! And you, Flian, are going to stop roosting like a molting bird. It's time to put on a nice gown and come to court."

Her Presentation gown was not her favorite rose, but green velvet, gold edged, with black silk beneath—Ralanor Veleth's colors—relieved by pearls looped gracefully across the bodice, the ribbons all green silk, long and exquisitely tied.

While that was being made up, the three of us worked out the details of our story. Maxl was quite firm about insisting we say nothing whatsoever about Garian Herlester. As far as court was concerned, Jewel and I had traveled together to Dantherei and then back to Ralanor Veleth on diplomatic visits. Only I was taken sick and came home early; Jewel followed upon receiving notice that I had recovered.

Simple—and dull. No one would want to pester us for details of a dull story—which meant no one could use our story for their own purposes.

In other words, diplomatic lies—and this time I was telling them.

The day of Jewel's Presentation was at the weekly formal Interview, the first day of the autumn season, which meant a grand ball that night. Maxl insisted that I host it with him, establishing our positions in court, or rather mine as heir.

We were going to host the reception afterward, too, until Maxl received a charming note saying that as a surprise, all the senior nobles had clubbed together to give the reception for us, as a salute to the new king.

Organized—the note written—by Gilian Zarda.

"Here we go," Maxl said in an undertone as we stood side by side on the dais in the great throne room, which was used at most half a dozen times a year.

We wore our sky blue and gold. Along the perimeter, in strict hierarchical rankings, stood those Lygieran nobles who were at court for the season.

I watched Jewel approach, and felt strange. As if we were playacting. But when she swept a perfect formal curtsey to Maxl, princess to king, my vision rippled and underwent such a change I was almost lightheaded. For the first time in my life I was not, in fact, the young princess playing at the grownup games.

It was now *us* in charge. Papa and his generation no longer held the real power while we played at it around them. We now held the reins. The older people in the room watched us go through the rituals, and I wondered how it must feel to the older people to watch power pass on to the next generation.

A wash of shame burned through me at my self-involvement. Maxl had been so very forbearing, only hinting at how much he needed me to do my part, while I'd lurked in my rooms for a month feeling sorry for myself.

As I watched Jewel rise from her curtsey and turn to me, I resolved not to shirk my duties any more. Whether I liked them or not was immaterial. A selfish queen would be like my mother—or Jewel's—and a responsible one like Tamara, who didn't care for court either. Surely that went for princesses too.

Jewel curtseyed to me, princess to crown princess, for I was now heir. Her mouth was grave, but her eyes merry, sapphire-bright in the candle-glow, as she glanced at Maxl.

Maxl spoke the formal words of welcome, and she curtseyed again and withdrew.

Three more people were presented: the first, a daughter of an earl on her first visit. As I looked at that sixteen-year-old face, almost green with terror, I felt very old of a sudden, and I made a few comments, nothing of any import or even interest, just enough for her to be able to respond, and to relax, and finally—tentatively—to return my smile.

Again, how strange, for I had grown accustomed to thinking of myself as the youngest, the gawkiest, the most awkward and inexperienced. But that was no longer true.

Next were a couple of coastal aristocrats, here for their yearly visit. There were no inheritance-fealty vows to be spoken that day, which were long and tedious, so the formal ritual was soon over.

Maxl held out his arm to me, I placed my hand on it, and we walked out, leading the way to the reception chamber.

And so began the autumn season.

The real work takes place year round, in the judgment chambers, and in the heralds' rooms where the Lord Officers rule: the revenue office, the trade office, the farm office, the guild office. And in the archive, without whose scribes decrees do not get copied into law books and distributed throughout the kingdom.

In court the social and diplomatic work follows its own rhythms, dictated by the seasons. As I walked down the center aisle, I wondered what goals were in the minds of the people we passed. Political, personal, known, secret? It would all unfold over steeped leaf, or wine, or dances, or games, or on sledding trips over the snowy gardens. Or in private rooms.

Not in mine. The lips I wished to kiss had, the last time I looked on them, been grim, the arms I wished to walk into had set me down and withdrawn. The gaze that fascinated me had not looked on me with fascination, and the mind that I had begun to comprehend a little, had comprehended me and found little of merit.

That was the truth, I decided. But it was also true—for I did not believe all those old records would lie—that mere passion would eventually die away, and perhaps I would be able to look about me for love. After all, what I felt for Jason was mere attraction, silly, superficial, it couldn't be anything else. But until then—

"Blade at guard, sister," Maxl breathed. "Engage."

Gilian Zarda and her closest crony, the Baroness Elta—who had inherited at far too young an age—minced toward us, twinkly court smirks on their faces.

Gilian carefully fingered one of her blond curls as she said in her most caressing voice, "Oh, Flian, it is so *good* to see you on the mend!" She linked her arm through mine. "You shall stand with us to receive. So many people have waited for word on your recovery. What a *long* bout of lung fever! But I can see at a glance that you have *yet* to fully recover."

All this said in the sweetest voice, just to make certain even stupid Flian understood that she looked dreadful.

I knew what I looked like—which was no better or worse than usual. But Gilian was preoccupied with appearances—always had been, ever since we were children, and she had cheated at games and gotten round anyone older by batting her lashes and pouting about how small she was. She had learned early that if she couldn't win, she would claim not to be a player. And those who did play were stupid or clumsy or common.

She tucked her other arm through Maxl's, and the three of us entered the west parlor, which had been beautifully decorated with hothouse lilies and pale, peachy-yellow roses. Elta, her chin elevated to a supercilious level, firmly thrust her arm through that of stocky, stolid Daxl Nethevi, heir to the powerful dukedom of Bharha, and fell in behind as Gilian pointed out the lemon cakes with warm custard, and the punch she'd concocted with her own hands—so very tiny!—pausing only for praise.

Maxl gave it to her. I said nothing, not that she would have listened. Her entire focus was on Maxl.

The rest of the guests arrived in order of rank, Jewel in the lead. Gilian took the primary position as hostess to the reception, the center of attention—with Maxl standing at her side.

All of those hints he'd made, about courtship and marriage for the benefit of the kingdom, coalesced into a sharp fear. Was he considering marrying Gilian? How could she have contrived so startling a change between the time I'd left and my return?

The reason why was obvious. Maxl was now king, and she did not have to deal with my father, who had loathed the Zardas and would never have permitted any of them to gain more power than they already held.

Maxl has been facing this threat alone, I realized, watching that little hand firmly tucked round his arm. *While I cowered in my room feeling sorry for myself.*

One of my duties was to help him. How? I had relied on music as my safest form of expression, but no one listened. I'd tried action, but just got hurt.

Maybe it was time to venture at last into the realm of words.

This resolution had been made when the doors were thrown open one last time, and the herald announced, "His highness Prince Ersin Aldi of the Three Kingdoms."

A tall fellow with long wheat-colored hair stepped in, threw his hands wide, and said with a rakish smile, "I take it I'm too late for Presentation?"

Maxl hesitated, for we were no longer in the throne room. Gilian exchanged a look with her sharp-faced, sharp-eyed father, who smirked; she scudded forward, her baby-pink ribbons bouncing, and tucked her hand around Prince Ersin's arm as he looked down at her in polite surprise.

"I am Lady Gilian Zarda, and this is my party," she lisped in her sweetest little girl voice. "Permit me to present you to Maxl—I beg your pardon. King Maxl." She tittered, guiding him straight past Jewel and pausing near me. "And here is his sister, the Princess Flian..."

Just like a queen.

Maxl welcomed the newcomer as if nothing untoward had happened, though a faint flush along his cheeks betrayed a hint of emotion. Jewel, next to me, whistled softly.

Chapter Thirty

Frost from my breath bloomed in the air as I hurried across the courtyard toward the guard wing. A flicker on the edge of my vision brought me to a stop.

Something arced through the air and landed at my feet. I bent, picked up a rose. The petals, cream-colored with a faint blush of pink, were still tightly furled.

I held the rose to my face and looked up to the balcony above. Golden hair flashed, lit by the rising sun as Ersin bowed, grinning.

I lifted the rose to my lips, swept a deep court curtsey. Ersin laughed, for I was not gowned for court, but dressed in old riding garb. He waved a hand and vanished back into the royal guest wing. On the other side of his balcony, Jewel's windows were curtained. There was very little that would force her up at dawn.

There were faces at two or three other windows, one sour and spade-chinned: Elta. She turned away, no doubt to rush off and report to Gilian.

A shiver tightened the outsides of my arms and I resumed my walk, tucking the rose stem (from which patient fingers had removed the thorns) behind my ear.

I was soon in the big practice salle, where the smell of sweat and the echoing clash of weapons smote the senses. The new recruits were already at work at the far end, their faces crimson with effort as they were put through their drills. My brother was busy in one corner with the sword master as I crossed to get some practice gear.

I watched bouts until one of the minor trainers was free. When I was thoroughly drenched and my muscles felt like old lute-strings, I found Maxl standing at the side watching. "You are coming along nicely," he said.

"Yes. Who knows, in five years I might actually be able to engage in a match with some youngster without embarrassing myself," I retorted with mendacious cordiality.

Maxl snorted. "What standard are you holding yourself against? You are ahead of the new recruits, who will be sent out on their first tour in three months."

"And hopefully they will not be required to do much more than rescue mired carthorses or chase after some half-drunk bandits for at least a year or so."

Maxl shrugged in rueful agreement.

Lest he think I was poking fun at his favorite project, I added in haste, "But I think it is working well, do not you?"

"All the reports indicate that the plan is a success," Maxl agreed, his smile genuine now. "New recruits sign up almost every week—in fact, the captain says they can now begin to pick and choose. If this keeps up, in ten years I'll have a trained militia among the citizens, should the need arise. Yet no standing army eating up our revenues and getting restless for action."

I nodded. Maxl had implemented his plan around the time I returned from Drath. This was the plan that previously had been thwarted by Spaquel at every opportunity. At first he'd been limited to the city guard only, but on Papa's death he'd decided to go ahead and expand the plan to include the entire kingdom.

It was simple enough in outline. Any young unmarried person who committed to four years of guard duty came out with enough pay to start a business or a family or reach some other dream. Yearly drills were to be organized in all the main towns each season. Spring recruits would drill in spring, summer in summer, and so forth. All who came to yearly drills would earn extra pay. The revenue that in former days used to go to housing and feeding a big army now would go back into the economy more directly, in the hands of four-year veterans— and as Maxl said, if the need in future arose for mobilization, he'd have a ready-trained army.

So each season a new crop would be put through training here in the city and sent out the next season on a tour of duty. The groups would rotate round the kingdom, ending with city duty in Carnison; only the palace guards were hired for life.

The autumn season had seen the first batch. Now that winter was nigh, he'd installed the next group, and so far everything was running the way he wanted it.

Maxl rubbed his hands as he started back across the court toward the residence wing. A clatter of horse hooves rang through the open gate that led to the royal stables. Some of the men raced off—Yendrian, as usual, in the lead, but Ersin wasn't far behind. Althan, a close third, was laughing some sort of challenge, and behind him a group of five or six jostled for position.

Maxl's longing to be with them showed in his face, in his arrested posture as he watched them vanish, but then he turned away. I said nothing. It was easy enough to see his thoughts: no more morning races until the winter season ended. There was work waiting.

He said to me, "It's cold. That rose must have been the very last one."

"Probably," I responded. "A shame to have it plucked."

"Oh, it has to be seen, and it wouldn't be, out in the garden." Maxl fell silent as a footman opened the door.

Maxl walked me to my chambers. Debrec set down the tray she'd brought, bowed, and silently left.

I sighed.

"Something wrong?" Maxl lounged over to pour out some hot chocolate from the pot; Debrec always brought two cups in case Maxl joined me, as he occasionally did now that early morning practice was becoming my routine as well as his.

"Oh, I embarrassed her once with some personal questions, and she's been wary ever since."

"Who, Debrec?"

"Yes."

"Want a new lady's maid?"

"No. It's my fault. If she wishes to leave, let it be her decision, not ours."

Maxl cast himself into a chair. His hair was tousled, his shirt unlaced. By the time the midmorning bells rang, he would be immaculate, dressed like a king, busy with state affairs, but until then, he was my brother. These mornings alone were no little part of my reasons for continuing the training in self-defense.

As if his thoughts paralleled mine, he said, "You didn't take a turn on the mats—only swordwork. Trouble with your shoulder?"

"No, that healed months ago. I twinged my other arm a bit on the mats last time, and mean to let the knot work itself out before I do it again."

"Wise." Maxl saluted me with his chocolate, then drank some. "Ah!"

I sipped my own chocolate and got up to find a crystal vase. I poured some water into it and set the rosebud in, placing it near the window.

"You like Ersin?" Maxl asked.

"Yes." I turned around. "And so does everyone else. He and Jewel made the autumn season fun. In turn he likes everyone. Especially Yendrian."

"You saw that, did you?" Maxl grimaced. "Here's a coil. Ersin sent to find a treaty wife, and instead finds love. And Yendrian, too, my oldest friend. And the most loyal."

I agreed. "If anyone deserves a prince it's he."

Maxl stared past my rose out the window. The sky, reasonably clear at dawn, was slowly going gray and bleak. "I think we'll have First Snow by afternoon. I'd better get downstairs soon. The coast people are restless, and this will make them anxious to be gone."

Except for Gilian. She was definitely a part of Maxl's biggest current political snarl, but she wasn't interested in the harbor versus fishing-fleet problems. She was gambling for much higher stakes.

I was unsure how to broach the subject of Gilian. It was one thing to resolve to be more open—and quite another to break past the boundaries of my brother's reserve. All autumn long he'd deftly deflected any discussion of her at all, and I had not wanted to intrude.

Maxl said, "Ersin has to make a treaty marriage. That's his official reason for being here. And he appears to like you a lot."

"I think he does." I stared at my brother, wondering if he was about to break our unspoken embargo on personal subjects. "I'm not in love with him, though he's fun to dance with, ride with. Talk about court nothings with."

Maxl shrugged. "I wondered—-but you didn't have to answer. I won't pry, I know how much you hate personal talk. Right now, so do I. But I do want to say how much I appreciate how you and Jewel have taken up the social duties, leaving me more time for kingdom affairs. Don't think I haven't noticed."

I smiled. "It comes naturally to Jewel. She's so good at it. I just stand behind her and smile, and everyone has a good time."

"Strange, that a Szinzar would be more adept at court than you or I," Maxl observed. "When we've been bred to it."

Szinzars. My thoughts winged eastward. What was Jason doing now? Was he studying plans for his river-diversion project? How would he pay for it, since he'd sent Eleandra away and thus lost the prospect of her considerable wealth?

I had learned to accept how some little, unrelated thing would remind me of Ralanor Veleth, or its history, or its king.

It was foolish to be angry with myself for these reveries as I sat at endless court affairs. At least I embarrassed no one by speaking of my passion, and if my spirit remained stubbornly faced eastward, well, I could be patient. There was no answer, in spirit or flesh, and in time this... I refused to name it as *love*—say, *subject.* Yes, a dispassionate word. Eventually it would wither without the sun of a light-blue gaze, and maybe, maybe, some day I could hope that someone else's smile would be preferable to loneliness.

Maxl gave me a pensive glance, and left.

I sat down to my harp and lute, practicing until the midmorning bells. Then it was time to get ready for the afternoon choral presentation sponsored by an old duchess. One of the few court occasions I looked forward to: no talk, just pleasant music.

I'd just left the private wing and was heading toward the stairs to the public rooms when voices echoed up to the landing. Feminine chatter some laughter—a familiar titter. "Oh, but I *never* listen to gossip. Birdy is one of my oldest friends. People might say she's as fond of wine as her mother was, but I insist that's just her unique manner. I've known Birdy since she was little, and thought I didn't know—well, after all, she's a friend."

And Elta's sweet, languishing voice, "Oh, Gilian. You're too kind."

I peered over the balcony to the marble-floored hallway below. Gilian and Elta led the way down the hall, followed by Corlis Medzar and a half-dozen ladies my age, some looking uncertain, and one hesitating before the archway leading to the north wing.

I remembered Lady Milian Torquel's wine-tasting party. Milian, known since we were all coltish twelve-year-olds as Birdy (ostensibly for her high voice, but actually for her birdwits) was as handsome and empty-headed as her twin brother Malnaz. She'd never been any friend of mine, but followed after Elta, her cousin.

I began to walk away, relieved because I'd already turned down the invitation on behalf of the chorale, and because Gilian had not seen me.

Rapid images flitted through my head: Jewel sinking into my chair the night before, telling me about the masquerade after I'd sneaked away—the Torquel twins dancing—Ersin and Maxl making some kind of laughing bet on who would sit down first, trading off dancing with Birdy and Jewel—

But Birdy always danced all night, if she could. Everyone knew that. So...was there a problem, or not?

Gilian pattered ahead with her baby steps, her ribbons and curls dancing with the quick mouse-pouncing turns of her head right and left, as she led her crowd of party-dressed females toward the far door.

Gilian's step faltered. She looked around, made a sad little face, and said, "I just cannot. Though I was bred to respect politeness, even at cost of my own comfort. But I fear I am too delicate—and I do apologize."

"Is it the wine?" Elta asked in a penetrating voice.

"Naming no names—nothing whatsoever imputed—but just in general, moderation is so important to me, it gives me no peace, how high my standards are. I wish you all a pleasant afternoon, but believe I might just view the end of the horse race, and cheer for our dear visitor from Three Kingdoms..."

Gilian was definitely up to something nasty.

This was not a situation music could resolve, nor swords. *Gilian just used words to imply that Birdy's a drunken sot. Use your own words to deny it.* I started down the stairs. "What a pleasure, meeting you here," I called, and all those faces snapped upward, surprise and varying degrees of guilt on some, anger on Elta's.

Gilian twinkled. "Oh, Flian," she said in her sweetest tones. "What brings you away from your singers?"

I mimed surprise, probably looking as false as Gilian sounded. "The chorale is mostly for old people. Isn't everyone in fashion going to Birdy's party?"

Gilian's mouth rounded in an "O". She flushed.

"Who's joining me?" I asked before she could speak, my heartbeat thundering.

And I did not look back. But I heard them. One or two, then three or four, and soon all of them but Gilian and Elta.

I chattered more emptily than Birdy ever had, all the way to the party—races, horses, dancing—whatever I could think of. But we arrived.

Birdy looked surprised to see me, then a brief flicker of frustration, quickly hidden. I said, "I apologize for not responding to your invitation—where are my wits?" Though we both knew I had.

But at least now she had an excuse for the wrong number of places. Her smile broadened in relief as she ushered us in.

I pretended nothing was amiss, and when Jewel arrived moments later, I figured out why Gilian had suddenly chosen harmless Birdy as her newest target. She'd gathered all the guests, intending them to skip the party at the last moment, leaving Jewel to arrive alone at Birdy's empty rooms while gossip circulated about Birdy being a drunk...and Jewel condoning it. What better way to make them both a laughing stock?

In other words, Birdy wasn't the target. Jewel was.

So I endured a very silly party that never became either fun or natural, despite extremely fine samples of the year's gold wines. Voices got louder and sharper as they chattered about the usual empty court nothings.

Instead I veered between relief at having fumbled my way into circumventing a cruel trick, and dread at how Gilian would get back at me. She always had—had always won, too, ever since we were children and my father, right in front of everyone, had chastised me gently for slapping someone smaller than I while Gilian pretended to snuffle and smirked at me behind her hands. And I'd been too humiliated to tell my father she'd repeated something her father had said about how old kings should have the decency to drop dead.

Jewel flopped onto my couch after the play the night of Birdy's party. She smoothed out her rich satin skirt in her favorite rose, observing, "Does Gilian always have something nastier to say, right at hand, if someone speaks up to her?"

"Always, in my experience. Did you tangle with her tonight? I did not see it."

"No, not directly. I'm an ambassador." Jewel grinned. "It's all indirect. So every time she makes little comparisons to the fellows about how tiny she is and how huge, fat and lumbering I am, in case they aren't quick enough to get the comparison, I remember I'd feel much worse if Maxl had to send a letter to Jason saying I'd set your court afire by pushing her into a fishpond, and I must go home."

We laughed, then Jewel began pulling the pins from her hair. "I told Jaim all about her on that long ride to Lathandra. And you know what he said?"

"What did he say?" I smiled at the memory of Jaim's pungently expressed opinions.

"That a sharp tongue requires as much training as a sharp blade."

"Huh! I never thought of that." And, for the first time, I told her about our childhood as she set her pins aside and began braiding her long, thick curls.

She glowered. "So is that why you permit her to grip your arm that way, whenever there's an informal reception line? I've wondered why you don't shake her off. I probably would. And she'd be nasty and make it into an incident!"

"I've been watching Lord Zarda. The way he smirks whenever she does that, and I think of all the trouble Maxl is having with those northern dukes about the Ghan Harbor plans. I don't want to risk making things worse."

Jewel finished braiding her hair, and flung it back over her shoulder. "Do you think her father loves her, then? Or is it just ambition?"

"How do you define love? Did your parents love you? I don't think my mother cared much for us, except in the abstract— when we were all dressed up and behaving prettily, not acting like small children usually do."

"What about Lord Zarda's wife? Was there a grand passion,

do you know?"

"My great-aunt told me he was set up from childhood to marry the wealthiest young lady in Narieth, a second child. Not an heir. The treaty was considered a real coup, she said. The Zardas were desperately poor, especially once they built their new palace. After they married and she came here to live, he not only derided her for being slow, he actually started a series of jokes beginning, 'You know what's even more stupid than my wife?'"

"That's horrible!"

"And so it went on until he'd gambled away several years of revenue, all in one season. He tried to woo more money out of the Narieth family, but the heir turned him down flat, reputedly with a real ripper of a letter beginning, 'You know there is nothing more stupid than a duke who cannot manage money.' And he was forbidden the court of Narieth."

Jewel got up. "Have you met the duchess?"

"Oh, just once. He won't let her come to court any more. Or their son, who supposedly stays on their land to learn governance. I rather liked her. She was very quiet, very placid. Mainly interested in food, as far as I could tell."

Jewel lounged against the couch. "Strange."

I sat back. "What are you thinking?"

"That despite all Gilian's little remarks about how tiresome it is to always have the tiniest waist in a room and how dreadful to be so dainty, none of the fellows ever seem to show much interest in tiny waists or frailty. It's only her friend Elta and their followers who coo over her. And yet she goes on speaking as though she's the center of fascination."

"The fellows are too busy watching you cross a room. And Gilian knows it."

She laughed, blushing, and bent to pick up her pins. "For a time this evening I considered fighting fire with fire—you know, making little comments about scrawny females who could be wearing a barrel or four kingdom's worth of gemstones and never catch the eyes, but that seems a false road."

I shuddered. "Very."

"Not only would she probably have a nastier comment all ready to tongue, but what about all those silent young ladies hearing these things, who have large waists—or small—who, through no fault of their own, look this way or that? And for that matter, why is it always the females who seem to talk about looks? Why not the men? That is to say, they might, but we don't hear it, just as the worst of our personal chatter is in private."

"Maxl told me once that the fellows all had private nicknames for one another. And for some of us. Like they called Gilian Babyboots. It got out, too."

Jewel wrinkled her nose. "You mean those awful things we all wore to steady us on our feet when we first walked? And you say it got out?"

"Oh yes. Everna Medzar, Corlis's little sister, told her right out at her very first party, when Gilian had been especially nasty. Everyone laughed. I mean everyone. She was wild with anger. But she got her revenge, never against the fellows, only on any girl who said it, and eventually it stopped."

Jewel said slowly, "That's what I was missing until recently. She gets people to fall in with her out of fear. So she makes her view of things turn real."

"Huh! That sounds right. Though I think she really does see herself in the center of the world."

Jewel started toward the door. "I have an idea. If it works, it won't change court, but maybe it'll work as an antidote to that particular poison."

On the sound of her laughter, she went out, and I headed wearily to bed, trying not to dread yet another long day of courtly festivities.

The next morning, Maxl was quiet, tense, and left practice early. So I wandered back alone, taking the long route through the garden.

As I crossed a little bridge toward the gazebo where my life had taken its sudden change, I paused, leaning on the rail, to wonder what might have happened had I refused to go with Jewel to that reading.

If I get through this alive you'll regret the outcome.

Everything else he had explained—but that.

I sighed, watching my breath cloud. I looked up. The sky was covered by a thick white blanket. I wished the snow would fall.

"Looking for the first flakes?"

I turned. Ersin of Three Kingdoms strolled up onto the bridge, smiling at me. His smile was easy and warm, his long golden hair lying unbound over his black cloak.

"Yes," I said. "Thank you for the rose. It's up in my window."

He leaned on the rail, his long brown hands dangling loosely. I glanced up, saw his profile, the clean line from brow to jaw, strong bones, features regular, countenance characterized by intelligence and good humor.

He glanced down at me, his brows quirking. "I wanted to speak with you alone."

"Please do. How can I help you?"

"Will you marry me?" He said it simply. No extravagant gestures, no cynical smirk.

For a long moment the words opened up my life to a new path. I continued to stare at him, as though the future would be writ in his steady gaze.

He waited, patient and polite. Consideration followed after a long space, long enough to register as embarrassing. I felt my face go hot. "I'm sorry. That was unexpected."

"It was, wasn't it?" He gave me a wry smile. "And— unwelcome, I gather?"

"I don't quite know how to answer that. Shall I be courtly?"

"Be true. Please." He added disarmingly, "I will begin with the truth, if that makes it easier. It is my branch of the family's turn to seek a spouse from outside the Three Kingdoms. A duty with which I did not find it hard to reconcile. I came to this kingdom to court a princess, my third such quest. Here I found one with whom I could share my life, if she found she could share hers with me." He took my hand, bowed over it and kissed my fingertips. "You're honest, smart, kind, and when one can get you to talk, interesting."

"That really is a generous compliment. I wish I could respond with more grace—"

"But?" He made a courtly gesture, full of humor. "Is it 'but' or 'yet'?"

"'But', I fear." I thought of Maxl and shook my head. I could not leave now, not until he had established his kingship—and though my help might not be much, he needed everything he could get. But I did not want to say it out loud, lest it seem to disparage Maxl.

"Is it a lack in me? You know you would have perfect freedom. And though courts are courts, Three Kingdoms does have plenty of attributes."

"I'm sure you do. There is no lack in you. It actually makes it easier that you are not in love with me—"

His smile was regretful.

"—or pretending to be. That would merely make it unbearable for us both. In truth, I suspect your heart lies elsewhere—"

"As does yours," he interrupted, his voice gentle and tentative, his eyes, for once, completely serious. "It's one of the reasons why I thought my proposal might meet with your approval."

I gazed at him in stricken silence.

"Perhaps it takes a lover to recognize a lover. I don't think anyone else has noticed. I have heard not one jot of gossip to that effect—and I delved for it, as discreetly as possible."

My breath went out, freezing in a soft cloud.

"You are in love." His voice was gentle, gaining in assurance. "But with no one here. And your old companions, possibly blinded by ambition or their own overriding concerns or by having known you from childhood, do not see it. But the fact remains that you are, and that it seems to be unsuccessful or you would not be here, alone. And so I thought that my proposal might suit you not only for the exigencies of good will between our kingdoms, but also for companionship. It would suit me quite well having you to smile with, to ride with, to watch the gardens with, to talk with on long summer evenings or short winter ones, when we were not presiding over the court at Three Kingdoms."

My eyes stung. "That is the most generous speech anyone has made me yet. And I thank you especially for doing me the honor of being truthful."

"It's why we are here, with no witnesses." He kissed my fingers again. How different from Garian's mocking salutes! I had always wanted to scrub myself after his touch. Ersin's touch gave me no inner spark, but no disgust, either: it was the warmth of human friendship.

Jason had touched me three times. Twice before that interrupted wedding at Drath, and not again until that very last day, also in Drath...

273

I shook my head, trying to banish memory. "It seems so unfair that kings—or queens—have less freedom of choice in so personal a matter than anyone else."

"We choose very carefully in the Three Kingdoms. We have three royal families presiding. This alliance has kept us stable since our treaty. There is enough trace memory of the bad old days to make us reluctant to tamper with the form. And so I seek a princess, or a lady, who is intelligent, and kind, and interesting to talk with, and my own sense of honor requires me to seek one who is not in love with me." He touched my hand lightly. "Only who, I feel constrained to add, could be so blind as to not see your worth?"

Pain constricted my heart. I turned away, wiping my eyes.

"I'm sorry," he said again, his voice husky and contrite. "I'm sorry, and not only for my own clumsiness."

"No." I pressed his hand, and let go. "It's all right. We'll go back and dance and smile, and I'll wear your rose in my hair tonight, and before long you'll find a princess who might suit you better than I."

"I very much fear my search for such a person would take me round the world," he said, and I laughed at his gallantry.

And together we walked back toward the palace as above the first snowflakes of winter began to drift down around us.

Chapter Thirty-One

Ersin stayed only until the day after Midyear, and then he rode south, accompanied partway by Maxl and Lord Yendrian Redesi.

Maxl returned before the evening bells, looking tired and dispirited. I followed him to the lair, ringing for hot chocolate. When he reemerged into public, he'd have to squash down Maxl and assume the outer demeanor of a king. I would help him find that balance if I could.

But he did not want to talk, only stood staring down into his fire, until the ting of the suite bell recalled him to the time.

"We'd better get ready for the Barons' dinner," I said. "And wear dancing clothes—apparently Jantian Weth returned from his journey south with the spring and summer dances from Sartor."

Maxl commented, "It might be midsummer in Sartor, but here we've got the longest nights of the year!"

He wasn't talking about our being in midwinter's dark. I knew what he really meant, and I felt the same.

But the Barons' dinner for the Guild Chiefs went quite well. The Weths had brought back not only ideas but things: there were scented candles placed before mirror-bright silver panels so that each candle flame was magnified five times, and the candles themselves brought a faint, fresh scent of some astringent herb into the room.

The foods, we were told, were the latest rage in Sartor. The older people who grew up knowing Sartor had lain under a century of enchantment were impressed. They were also cheered at this evidence of another defeat of Norsunder's evil. The atmosphere was lighter than I remembered since before

Papa died, the oldest talking about what their grandparents had said about Sartor before it was enchanted. Sartor's court was now full of young people surrounding a young queen.

Jantian, pressed to talk about his interview with Queen Yustnesveas, last of the Landises—the oldest family in the world—said she had the characteristic Landis protruding eyes. She was tall, and kind, and had brown hair. He didn't remember what her gown was like, which disappointed the girls.

He'd also brought back a singer-musician from Sartor, who'd been busy teaching our musicians (the ones who customarily played for balls and dances) the newest songs. I resolved to talk to Jantian later about getting them over to the music school, and then it was time for us all to assemble.

The promenade was old—everyone according to rank, moving round in a circle—but the music was new to us, cascades of exquisitely sung triplets under the melody, which was played by a combination of harps and silverflutes, the percussive counterpoint marked out by a whisk applied to a hollow wooden tube and shaken gourds with seeds in them. The songs were all in Sartoran, which none of us knew—but it has a lovely sound, and those triplets were a recognizable Sartoran flourish that had died out of fashion over the century Sartor was inaccessible.

Next was a complicated line dance, full of braidings, twirls, changes of partner, still in triple-beat time. Some had prevailed on Jantian for secret lessons, for they moved with assurance. Gilian was one. But she'd always done that. I don't think she'd ever made a single misstep no matter how many new dances were introduced.

Jewel's mistakes caused her to laugh, and she got the idea of kissing her partner's hand in apology, a gesture which made Althan blush right up to his hairline. He promptly bowed and kissed her hand right back.

And that started it off—errors were opportunities for gallantry, a happy gesture that filled the room with laughter until the dance ended, and there was Gilian standing near Maxl, plying her fan so her curls blew, and she tipped her head back and said in Jewel's direction, "What a burlesque!"

Jewel went on talking to Riana Dascalon and handsome, silly Malnaz Torquel.

Althan blushed again. "Not all of us had practice beforehand. I think we did pretty well, considering." He looked around, and several signified agreement.

Gilian flirted her fan, then spread it flat in intimate mode. "I thought we did wonderfully. But Sartor, so ancient, so sophisticated—its dances so graceful, really requires the most graceful figures." A pause, a coy twitch of her head.

Lord Zarda shifted his smirking gaze from his daughter to Maxl.

"...but I have long accustomed myself to the dreary truth. We tiny people never are seen, for few look over the rooftops, but alas one cannot make that claim for the lumbering bovine." She finished, tittering, with an artful flick of her fan Jewel's way.

Jewel had never been prettier, the candle light making a blaze of her yellow gown with its gold and peach embroidery, her splendid coloring heightened by the dance, her lips curved in a smile full of mischief. Maxl gazed as one besotted.

"To see a cow dance in a royal court!" Elta laughed without mercy. "Oh Gilian. You are too absurd."

"Alas," Gilian said airily. "The absurdity is not as bovine as reality."

Jewel's brows rose. She snapped her fan open with a crack, drawing all eyes, and she said, quite mildly, "Beg pardon, what did you say?"

It was completely unexpected.

Jewel was on the verge of laughter, and with an inward flutter against my ribs I realized what she was going to do. "I didn't quite catch your remark, Gilian. Were you addressing me?"

Now either Gilian retreated—insults are never funny if they have to be repeated to the recipient, especially one as stupid as that—or explained. Gilian, no weakling when it comes to malice, whispered, "I was not. I was making an observation on clumsy dancing. If you wish to claim the attribute, I can only bow in polite acquiescence." And she gave a dainty curtsey, every line a mockery.

Jewel just kept looking at her with a puzzled air. "Bo—?"

Several of the men muffled snorts of laughter, and Riana and Birdy giggled. Even Corlis's thin lips curved in a tight smile.

Jewel looked around, her hands making a helpless gesture.

"Bo—vine? Is that what you said?"

Half-smothered laughter spread through the circle. I had never seen such a clear division of reaction. Most of the young were laughing, most of the old, at least Zarda's many allies, looked disapproving. How had he gotten so popular? No—not popular—that's when people enjoy you. *What was that Jewel said about leading through fear?*

Jewel rounded her lips.

I nearly gasped out loud. She really was going to moo.

It would be devastatingly funny, it would serve Gilian right.

But it would also divide the court. And I could not let Zarda's allies get any advantage over Maxl. Even social.

I snapped my own fan open, walked right through the center of the circle, took Jantian's arm. "Please? May we try it again?"

Jewel cast me an arrested glance, her lips still parted, then the disastrous moment was gone. She held out her hand, a random gesture, and no fewer than half a dozen fellows stepped forward offering to partner her.

Gilian tucked her tiny fingers possessively under Maxl's arm, smiling up at him wistfully. I could feel him taking in the entire room—what he had missed, the fact that he'd missed it—with a kind of internal slap.

He bowed to Gilian and led her into the dance.

That night Maxl followed me to my room. I had stayed in case there might be a need to attempt to avert any more disasters. Maxl prowled around the perimeter of my room, touching things. When Debrec entered, looking enquiry, he said to me, "Let's go to the lair."

Hot cocoa had been made in anticipation.

My brother prowled around the perimeter of this room, too, gazing sightlessly into the dark outside the window, tapping his fingers on the back of the old sofa, the chairs, and on the mantel as he stood at last beside the fire, the stylized wheat pattern embroidered on his tunic gleaming like threads of molten gold in the ruddy light.

"Power warps our lives," Maxl said finally. "Tradition—treaty—put on thrones, kings and queens who are too seldom bonded by any regard outside of power, or expedience. Like our mother. And the Szinzars' previous generation."

"There are exceptions," I said. "And compromises."

"There seem to be two natures," Maxl observed in a slow voice. "There's the one that can find consolation—and pleasure—wherever it is offered, and then there's the other that chooses once, and once that choice is made, no compromise is possible." He looked over at me. "Do you agree?"

I thought of Eleandra, dancing from lover to lover. And of myself, in whom mere memory of the all-too-brief ride in one man's arms was far more compelling than all the graceful words, the ardent smiles, the caressing hand-kisses and oblique offers of more, from numberless men of four different kingdoms and one principality.

"Yes."

Maxl turned around to face me. "Did Ersin offer marriage to you, then?"

I nodded.

Maxl wandered back to the window. "I thought he might have."

"And you didn't want to influence me."

"No. I could see advantages either way. You would get a fresh start there. You might even like it. But I would miss you here. Yet you aren't happy." He turned to face me again.

I said, daring, "Neither are you."

"No." He spoke to the fire and not to me. "But I cannot leave."

A knock at the door.

Maxl answered it himself.

Jewel stood there, her dark blue gaze searching his. "Do I intrude?"

"Of course not." He held the door wide.

Jewel entered, her gown rustling, her scent lightly perfuming the air. "I love the new dances. And would probably like the songs if I could understand 'em. A lovely evening, considering Ersin's departure. I'd thought they'd all be glum as a row of crows." She sat down next to me. "Though I must confess I am too angry with our favorite swain to admit how much he will be missed."

I laughed. Only Jewel could get away with such blithe illogic.

Maxl's lips twitched as he cast himself into the worn old armchair on the other side of the fire.

"I really thought he would propose to you in form," Jewel said to me. "How very romantic that would have been! I did not take him for a trifler. At least, not with you."

"He was fun," I said.

"That he was," she agreed, and she glanced over her shoulder at Maxl, who had taken up his letter opener again, and was playing with it. "Not that he ever took me seriously for a moment. Not with all those outrageous compliments!"

"That you returned. More than Ersin himself will I miss your preposterous flirtation."

"He told me that last night. That I'd made him laugh, and he'd always be grateful." She grimaced. "Jewel, the royal clown."

"But you were not serious with him either. Admit it!"

"Easily. I'd thought—I'd hoped—he was serious with you." She frowned in perplexity at me, but then her eyes narrowed. "And he was. Wasn't he? I can see it. *Some*thing happened."

I shrugged. "Nothing but a wish for friendship."

"Friendship," she repeated. "No. Don't tell me if you would rather not. But friendship was what he offered me—and most of the people here in Carnison. He was more, oh, *tender* with you, especially the past week."

I could see the hurt behind her smile, and so I said, "He spoke in private, and so I kept our conversation private."

She moaned. "Oh, Flian! That's what I was afraid of. Are you impossible to please?" She ran her hands over her face. "Or is there more political subtlety at stake than is obvious to the barefoot princess from Ralanor Veleth?"

She did not look Maxl's way, but I felt the intent of her question veer and aim straight for him.

Golden light flickered along the steel of the letter opener as Maxl spun it into the air and caught it. He looked toward the fire and twin flames burned in his widened pupils.

"Ersin was not any more attracted to me than he was to you. His heart lies elsewhere, but he did me the honor to be honest when he offered me a treaty marriage."

Jewel's brow cleared. "Yendrian. I thought there was something there!" She sighed. "Oh, how romantic. And tragic, for Yendrian is an heir, and Ersin from another kingdom."

"More examples of love thwarted by political expectation," I said.

"What I was thinking." Jewel tipped her head. "But you did make friends with Ersin. You will write to him, I trust?"

And when I made a gesture of repudiation, Maxl said, "Flian doesn't write letters. As I can attest, waiting and waiting to hear all last summer." He grinned at me.

Jewel looked from one of us to the other, and I said hastily, "I had a very bad experience once. When I was a young teen. And someone—she's married now and living happily in the south—entrusted me with a secret. But my letter was intercepted. And the contents spread all over court."

Jewel looked askance. "I can imagine by whom, but how could you be so clumsy? You have a castle full of servants surely you can trust."

"I didn't know how to arrange a private correspondence." I flung out my hands. "It never would have occurred to Papa to tell me, and, well. I don't write letters. But after he safely finds his princess, perhaps I'll go visit Ersin. That would be fun—and diplomatic as can be."

I glanced at Maxl, and perceived that his mood had changed. He wanted to be alone. Moments before he had been restless, brooding. Now his brow was furrowed with intent as he impatiently tossed the letter opener onto the desk. "I think we will liven court a little. Let's give a masquerade ball, shall we?"

"We?" I asked.

"Yes. You and I." He spoke with decision. "Next month. Dreariest part of winter. People will have something to look forward to. So order your very finest gown. Begin selecting your music now." His voice turned ironic. "I will see to the dangerous and terrible words of invitation."

I laughed. "Very well—and I wish you all the enjoyment of your having to write all those dangerous invitations over and over. But then you've got those four wheel-greasers with the good handwriting, eh? Good night."

Jewel accompanied me to my room, and cast herself on my couch, her expensive yellows skirts lustrous in the firelight. "I thought I would scream! He is *so* unhappy! Yet he does nothing while that horrid little monster ties her ribbons of spite and ambition around him."

"Gilian." I made a sour face. "I'll tell you this: if he marries her, I will leave Carnison."

"She would like nothing better," Jewel stated. "She hates it when you speak once and dissolve a nasty moment, like you did tonight. She hates it and I love watching you do it."

"It works only because she respects rank. And I'm now the heir."

Jewel nodded, a glitter of unshed tears along her eyelids. "You also dissolved my own nasty moment."

I could not help a laugh. "It would have been funny. But wicked, too."

"Am I wicked?" Jewel asked, pressing her fingers against her brow. "I was so proud of deflecting the bovine comment—and I got them kissing hands—but then I got angry. I'm never sensible when I'm angry. I know it, I scold myself to remember." She sniffed. "I try to be so good, but I wasn't brought up good, so what terrible things might I do, if I get power? Maxl is right to avoid me. You saw he didn't dance with me again. I know it's because of that disastrous moo that I didn't make, but everyone heard it anyway, in their minds."

I shook my head, thinking, *he doesn't trust himself.* The subject being Maxl, one could not separate the man from the king. "I'm hoping Maxl can face down these Zarda alliances with his patience. They aren't—can't be—natural alliances. The Zardas lead through fear. And I suspect Lord Zarda's current alliance is also based on promises he's making among his cronies if she comes to power."

Jewel bit her lip. "But you're suggesting it's all political. It isn't. I think she wants *him.*" She shivered. "How could he possibly want her?"

"He doesn't. She doesn't see his distaste, but I do, even though he says nothing to me whatsoever."

"He doesn't?"

"We still don't talk about private matters."

"So it's not only me you hold at a distance." Her brows puckered, and again she looked hurt.

"Jewel, I don't talk because there's nothing to talk about."

"I wish I knew why. You said once that everyone courts you only for your money, but that is not true of Althan. And one or two others."

"Althan is good and kind and funny, and we agreed there

would never be a courtship years ago. And we have exactly nothing in common—he loathes music. I get bored hearing about horse races."

"All right, that's Althan. But you turn them *all* away, with the same absent air, only you're not content to be alone, I can *feel* it." She grinned, and got up to pace restlessly around the floor. "I apologize if I trespass some boundary that is invisible to me. I can't hide anything I think! But I do wish I could see you happy."

"And I wish the same for you."

She clapped her hands to her arms and hugged them, her head bowed. "I know what I want." She stared down into the fire. "But what I want doesn't seem to want me. Or wants me, but not as—"

Not as queen?

She flounced onto the sofa again. "So what you think is, Maxl might give in and marry Gilian because if she and her father are powerful enough to make a faction that can stand against him, he cannot afford to have them as enemies?"

"That's the only reasoning that makes sense."

Jewel put her chin on her hands. "I would never dare to speak to him about my own feelings, lest he think me another Gilian."

"Oh, he could never think that."

"Oh, couldn't he," she retorted. "I don't interfere with the coast factions or the guild problems or any of the other monsters." She faced me, her wide eyes reflecting the fire, the sheen of tears that had not fallen gleaming. "I could even flirt with the new Lord Dascalon, and Jantian Weth, and the north coast faction, and try to find out their secrets. But—strange as it may seem—I do have a sense of honor. I stay strictly with the social round. And if that cannot be recognized for what it is—if I am adjudged superficial because of it—"

"True." I rubbed my aching temples. "I tell you what, Jewel. If he does marry her, I will buy a house on the sea and begin a music school, and if you like you can come live with me there."

The tears fell. "I see what you're doing. Whatever happens, you are offering me a home."

"Yes."

"I wish I deserved it," she whispered, and went out, and closed the door.

I stared into the fire, but then I felt that pull again, and I knew if I made that little bit of effort I would see Jason's face among the flames.

Trespass. Unwanted trespass.

I doused the lights and turned my back on the fire so I couldn't see anything at all.

The next morning, I went to the music school for my weekly visit. As I rounded the corner I heard a fine tenor voice soaring up the scales in a warm up. Standing in one of the window alcoves to listen was a familiar figure: Corlis Medzar. I looked around quickly. No Gilian.

To my surprise, Corlis stepped toward me.

"Princess Flian," she said, her nose elevated.

I bowed. What could she possibly want here? Or to be more precise, what could benefit Gilian to send her here?

She sidled glances both ways, then said something in a quick, low voice, too quick and too low for me to hear. All I made out was *Mistress Olith*.

"You wish to see the mistress? For what? To hire the singers? Or do you have a candidate to be interviewed for the school?"

Her fingers played with her fan, then up went the nose. "Yes."

"Well, all you need is to ask. You don't need me."

I started to pass, then she whirled about. "It's myself."

I stopped, staring.

Her thin cheeks flushed, and the nose went higher than ever. When her expression was human—even embarrassed—instead of supercilious, she was rather pretty. Prettier, in fact, than Gilian, despite the latter's fondness for her own babyish contours.

"I know what you think of my singing. I saw you at his grace's reading, months ago—you and that Princess Jewel. So very refined!" She drawled the last word in an angry mockery.

I turned away.

"Wait. No, I apologize, I take it back. I-I got angry, because—look. I know I don't sing well. That governess we had, she was a terrible teacher. I know I can sing. I *know* it. But how to learn to do it right?"

I faced her, wondering what sort of plot lay behind this amazing conversation. "You can hire anyone to teach you." Corlis flushed. "No I can't. Mama says every coin goes to maintaining us here, and until one of us marries appropriately, there is not a tinklet to spare."

I was about to say that a tinklet—the slang for a copperpiece—would not buy her much beyond a pastry tart, but then I looked at those dark eyes, and I did not see derision or superiority or anything except stark fear.

"You're serious." The words slipped out before I could think.

Again she flushed, and her lips soured. "You think you are the only one who loves music? Sitting up there in your royal rooms with harp masters whenever you want to whistle one up?" Her thin hands wrung on her fan.

"No. But I play for my own pleasure. It's against custom to perform, unfortunately."

"I can tell you why," Corlis said. "It's because your great-great grandmother had no talent whatsoever, and so when she took the throne, she declared that it was bad form for aristocrats to entertain one another at court. She brought in master players and singers. All we could do was dance. She almost ruined that, too, because she was so bad at it, but she knew no one would come to court if dancing was forbidden. It's in the records if you don't believe me. Your own archive—right here in the palace."

"No, I believe you. My grandmother told me what happened, though not the reasons. I've never known how to change it."

"Because you already have everything you want."

"So it appears. But to keep coming back to me is to go round in circles. What exactly do you want? Lessons?"

"Yes. No. If Mama knew, she'd—" She gripped her fan again. "I stand out here and listen sometimes, but I can't always hear the mistress. And singing in my head doesn't really teach me much. If I could stand at the back of the classes. Pretend I was there to listen—" She gestured in the air, and dropped her hands.

"Come," I said.

She followed me inside Mistress Olith's office. We found the tall, white-haired woman busy with one of the younger teachers, who was dismissed with a nod.

"Your highness? Your ladyship?" The mistress curtseyed.

"I came to discuss music for a masquerade ball my brother wants to host next month," I said. "And I want to arrange lessons with the musician the Weths brought—or maybe we can hire her for as long as she is willing. I'll get that set up."

Mistress Olith looked pleased. "That would be excellent for us."

"I would also like to request, if I may, that Lady Corlis be permitted to attend the singing classes. She thinks of hosting a school on the coast, you see." To my considerable surprise the lie came to my lips as easily as, well, any of Eleandra's court finesses.

Corlis's cheeks burned, but the tension in her eyes and lips eased to relief.

"Ah." The mistress glanced from one of us to the other, then back again. To Corlis: "If you will follow me, your ladyship, I will introduce you to Master Balan, who can outline the schedule, and what we teach..."

While they were busy, I slipped out again, to spare Corlis and me any more awkwardness.

Chapter Thirty-Two

The sky was clear overhead on the day of Maxl's masquerade ball, the air sharp and cold as I glided along on the ice. Laughter and whoops etched themselves in frosty clouds. Today's impromptu skating party had been Jewel's idea—and it was open to the whole court, whatever age. No exclusive party. I was there representing Maxl, who was away from Carnison, as he had been for a week.

Younger brothers and sisters not yet officially presented were busy on the frozen pond, chasing, whirling, playing daisy chain. The rest of us skated about, most in couples, some swooping and gliding round the others with athletic grace.

I proceeded slowly. The garden lay under its wintry blanket of white, its contours smoothed almost into unrecognizability.

In the center of an admiring group, mostly of men, Jewel whirled about, one foot lifted with grace, an arm arced. She'd told me she had little else to do during those long winters in the mountains with Jaim. Vrozta and some of the others had made frequent parties up to one of the frozen lakes to skate and sled race with the mountain-village Drathians, who had no idea who they were.

Several people looked on in envy. Gilian Zarda sat at the side with two friends, Elta at her post on one side and Harlis Spaquel, the duke's cousin, on the other. Gilian's hands were hidden in a blue-white yeath-fur muff, her blond curls artfully arranged to escape her bonnet in ringlets.

Gilian pursed up her little mouth as she glared at Jewel skating so gracefully, making it look effortless.

"You aren't skating, child?" Lord Zarda addressed Gilian as he walked by, arm in arm with one of the coast dukes. Though he was a head and shoulders shorter than his companion, his manner, as always, caused him to dominate.

"Alas, Papa. This sport is not designed for those cursed with refined tastes."

Two or three people nearby faltered. Unhearing, or unheeding, Jewel and those surrounding her skated on, swirling and swooping. I pushed grimly on, not wanting to hear whatever the Zardas were saying to one another behind me.

Althan Rescadzi zoomed close, turned, his blades sending up ice shards as he came to an expert stop at my side. His nose was red, his curling dark hair dotted with ice-frost. "Flian." He grinned, looking around to make certain we were not overhead, then jerked a thumb over his shoulder. "What'd you do to my cousin?"

Corlis and Riana Dascalon skated with several of the coastal fellows on the other side of the pond. Her back was firmly turned Gilian's way.

"Me?" I asked. "I haven't done anything to Corlis."

Althan shook his head. "She's changed of late. Couldn't account for it. Thought she had a hankering for someone or other, the way she's begun standing up to my monster of an aunt in favor of Everna and Jantian."

I picked out Jantian Weth's thin form amid the cluster.

"They want to marry, is that it?"

He snorted. "They've wanted to marry since they were sprats. He was supposed to forget her and bring back a rich Sartoran bride, but instead he wisely brought back all the very latest fashions."

"Ah." I laughed, understanding now. The Weths, despite their lack of fortune and their being a cadet branch, always had to be in fashion. My grandmother had once told me in her day they'd been exactly the same.

"And there is no chance of a fortune unless Ghan Harbor gets widened—and even then who's to say Baron Weth will hold Ghandri-on-Sea?"

One of the northern harbors was to be widened for great trade-ships. The debate was over who would be appointed to govern. Lord Zarda was campaigning to make certain that would be he or one of his allies.

"So what did you do to Corlis? It can't be Everna's return to court that makes her so different."

"It has nothing to do with me," I said.

Althan's bushy brows went up. "Something does. When Babyboots made one of her customary charming remarks about you at the Zarda card party last night, Corlis gave her a flat denial. It was worth being in that stuffy room yawning over cards all night, just to see Gilian jump like she'd been stung by a wasp."

I snickered. "My compliments to Corlis. But in truth, there's nothing."

"There is something, and what's more, you're protecting her," Althan contradicted, grinning. "You getting into intrigue at last?"

"No." I smiled. "That's why I know nothing."

Althan laughed. "Well, continue doing nothing, and see if you can win the monster-mother over to the Weths. Jantian's as good a fellow as he ever was, and a staunch supporter of your brother, whatever he decides in the harbor matter. But old Auntie Medzar is seeking money first and power last, and won't let Everna out of her sight until Jantian is married to someone else."

He saluted and with a few strong running steps whooshed along the frozen stream out of sight beyond a clump of winter-bare yew. I followed more slowly, soon passing by Gilian and her entourage again.

"Oh, do be careful, Flian," Gilian called, waving with one hand crimped in its tight mitten. "You look so...so unsteady."

"As unsteady as I feel," I replied cheerily. "Well, I'll not spoil your view. See you tonight at the masquerade."

"If your brother returns." She rose and shook out her skirts. Elta half-rose, but Gilian patted her hand, and she sat down again. Elta and Harlis watched Gilian follow me.

"Oh, he'll be back. After all, this masquerade was really his own idea."

She walked on the side of the stream, kicking her way through the snow as I skated. We were, for once, eye to eye. It was strange looking straight into her face—and from the way she looked back, she appeared to find it strange as well.

"I don't suppose you know where he went." She dimpled at me. "Oh, I'm sure it's great state business. But—" She made one of her dainty little gestures. "Business waits here on his return."

"Border inspection, he said."

"That couldn't wait?"

Did she actually think I was stupid enough to give her a real answer?

She turned her attention back toward the iced-over stream. "They all seem to like Princess Jewel's charming idea." She waved at the stream and the pond beyond.

"It was a good idea, wasn't it?"

"If you like this sort of thing. So how much longer are we to be delighted with this visitor from Ralanor Veleth? Many wonder if your brother is contemplating some sort of...alliance with that great warlike kingdom," she went on. "It is not a comforting prospect."

"You would have to ask my brother."

"But he's not here." Another dimpled smile. "And Princess Jewel is *your* guest."

"She is a royal envoy. You were at her Presentation. Jewel finds her stay agreeable," I said finally. "I find her company enjoyable. Maxl feels her presence aids the progress of the trade talks between Lygiera and Ralanor Veleth."

"Dantherei is said to be a charming place," Gilian lisped sweetly. "She would probably do quite well there, with her style of being an envoy."

She made her way with dainty steps to where a clump of the older generation watched the skaters. I stared after her. Had Gilian Zarda just made a threat? Yes she had.

I didn't talk to Maxl about emotions, but this was a political matter.

It was time to get ready for Maxl's masquerade ball.

Debrec was finishing with my hair when a knock came at the door. Jewel entered, looking dazzling in sky blue and gold. She walked around me, nodding in satisfaction. "Maroon really is your color," she stated. "And you look graceful as a swan with all those loops and loops of ribbons and lace. Are those silk roses holding up the flounces?"

"Yes." I spread my skirts in an extravagant curtsey.

She curtseyed back, then added with a brilliant smile, "Maxl's getting ready. We passed in the hallway."

"I knew he'd return on time. This is his party."

"I don't understand why he had to tour the eastern border this week." Jewel sat with care on a hassock. "I trust Spaquel is not making some kind of trouble."

"Contrary, Maxl says he's been as deferential as can be. I love your gown."

It was a great bell of delicate tissue, artful drapes bound up in lace. A sash at her waist set off her lovely figure. Her mask dangled from her fan-cord, a pretty confection of blue and silver; her hair was elaborately done up with pearls and silver threads braided through. She put her head to the side. "I hope there is no great danger that the troublesome envoy from trouble-causing Ralanor Veleth cannot hear about."

"I don't know either. Honest. Maxl said only that it was state business, could not be postponed, and when I admitted to my worry that Garian was planning something nefarious and Maxl was protecting me from the knowledge, Maxl promised it was nothing dire. You know he talks at his own time and in his own way."

"He doesn't talk at all," she said with a catch in her voice.

"But he laughs." I turned around to face her. "You made him laugh and laugh the night before he left. He hasn't laughed like that in months. It's so good for him."

"Any fool can make people laugh," she muttered.

"But not every fool is witty. You are."

"No, wit is well read," Jewel said. "Wit quotes poems and plays and all I do is make exaggerated jokes that bind one subject to another."

"That's a form of wit. And Maxl likes it. He doesn't like cruel wit, and he gets bored with the studied competition of quotation-capping."

Jewel groaned. "Oh, Flian, how I *wish* it were true!"

"Come. Let's go to the lair. He ought to be ready. The three of us will go down together, how's that?"

"No. He doesn't need the social grief." She drew in an unsteady breath and rustled out, shutting the door quietly.

Maxl knocked only moments later. I wondered what had happened during that meeting in the hall.

He came in, looking his best in an old-fashioned long robe with a baldric and sash.

"That suits you," I said.

"And that gown suits you as well. Let me guess—great-great, how many greats? Many-great grandmother Angel, famed for her harp compositions."

I smiled. "No one will recognize this gown, which I copied from the portrait upstairs, but I liked the idea." I wondered if I ought to tell him about Gilian's threat, then I decided to wait. His brow was tense, his hands restless.

"Shall we?" he asked, holding out his arm.

I picked up my mask, which was entirely made of lace and ribbon, and we walked out together.

Maxl was silent until we reached the great gallery above the grand ballroom. Along one side were the windows; beyond them lamps flickered and flared as guests' sleds pulled slowly up to the terrace below the carved doors. Foot servants ran back and forth, torches streaming.

Maxl slowed, and I obligingly slowed as well. He looked down through the window. "I arranged a surprise," he murmured. "I hope it is something you will like."

I thought of Sartoran musicians. "I am certain I will."

"Though you've been an excellent help, you have not been happy." His manner was odd—restless yet hesitant. I could see why Jewel had been upset. Something was definitely wrong.

"Neither have you."

He exhaled slowly. "No, I haven't. Time will tell. For us both."

With that he pulled on his mask, and I did as well. He squeezed my hand with gentle pressure, and we walked down the curving stairway where so many of our ancestors had once walked, and as always I wondered, what had they thought? Had they approached their own grand evenings with trepidation? With pleasure? With anticipation, triumph, secret sorrow?

We reached the first landing, and the trumpets pealed out the king's fanfare. Down we trod, in time to the music, as I scanned the room, which was already filled. Gorgeous costumes from a variety of eras graced the guests' forms. Some were instantly recognizable, some not. I found Gilian right away, gowned all in white and gold, tightly corseted. What queen did she emulate? It didn't really matter; the costume enabled her to wear a crown, even a false one, but that was enough for her—and though she was no longer the youngest, she still had the tiniest waist in the room.

Then we reached the marble floor, the herald announced the promenade, and as we were all masked, the guests formed up in any order. My excellent musicians' horns echoed from one side of the ballroom to the other in heart-racing trumpet calls, and the dancing began.

There is little to report about the beginning of the evening. People danced, flirted, laughed, ate and drank. Some tried to find out who others were. After the first dance with Maxl, I danced with Yendrian, and then with Althan. And after that I chatted with Yendrian, who had been corresponding with Ersin, and reported the latest on his search for a queen. When Riana appeared, begging Yendrian to partner her, I drifted over to listen to my musicians. My idea was to sneak out once the ball was going successfully and sit up in the gallery where I could hear the instruments better.

But as I made my way through the swirling couples, I became aware of Maxl moving parallel to me. I lost sight of him as my way was blocked by a chattering group. I sidestepped, and almost ran into a tall male figure. I was about to go the other way when the man held out his hands to me.

Puzzled, I stepped back, surveying the dark blue velvet tunic and long trousers tucked into blackweave riding boots, the fine gold embroidery down the arms of the tunic. An arresting presence; the mask was dark under a wide-brimmed, plumed hat, his dark hair simply clasped back.

He did not move. His hands were out, palms toward me. My brother reappeared a few paces away. He nodded to me, one hand open in a brief gesture of encouragement.

So I stepped into the waiting man's embrace and felt the cool grip of his right hand clasping my left. His other hand slid gently round my back.

We were not the fastest couple. There were no fancy dips or swirls. Yet my feet were leaf-flight, my senses alert as we whirled straight down the middle of the floor.

That hand. Warm, the palm rough as if from years of sword-work. I looked up, to be met with the barrier of the mask. But behind it the jaw-line was square, a familiar line that sent tingles along my nerves. I leaned close enough to sniff his scent, a complex scent that was familiar, so familiar, making my heartbeat tattoo its rhythm faster than the dancers whirling around me, bringing me an internal flare of lightning, of joy.

This time I perceived the faint line of mustache at the edge of the mask.

Jason.

Did I speak? I might have stumbled, but his grip tightened, steadying me. I said, numb with shock, "Why are you here?"

"To see you," he said.

Chapter Thirty-Three

I caught sight of Maxl again. He danced with Jewel, but his mask was turned in my direction.

Maxl's surprise! So he *knew.*

I looked up again—to find that mask once more walling me from seeing Jason's face.

Jason murmured, "Objection?"

"Only to the mask." I managed not to squeak.

"Have we not masked ourselves hitherto?"

That low voice. The quiet irony, so familiar, so unexpected. Again tingling swept through me, and I felt myself tremble.

"I have to know," I whispered. Braced myself. Looked down. "Is this yet another plan for securing my fortune?"

"I made you a promise about that once," he replied, just as softly. "I am here only at your brother's invitation, or I would have kept that part of my promise as well." A slight hesitation, then he added, "And one word from you will send me back again."

Whatever the word was, I did not speak it. I dared not speak at all.

Turn, step step, turn, whirl, step step. The music spun its enchantment around us. My thoughts reeled, directionless, between physical sensations and emotional reactions. Comprehension came, like our progress down the room, in sidesteps.

Jason was *here.* That meant he had left his kingdom to come all the way to Carnison. He was here in my home, wearing a costume, dancing on our ballroom floor, his arms around me, instead of tending to the countless chores of kingship in a difficult kingdom. He had chosen to be here, in circumstances I would never have ascribed to him.

I could not think past those facts; my mind seemed to whirl in endless circles as our bodies twirled in slow progression round the room.

But the music ended, and so did the dance. Jason's hands lifted away from me, and he stepped back. My childhood friend Daxl, stolid, humble, stood at my shoulder. He spoke, but I was too distracted to hear the words. I was being invited to the next dance, a prospect I found impossible to address.

Jason said, "I'll wait."

And so the evening sidestepped yet again, and then whirled me on through time.

No one but Maxl and I knew who Jason was. My comprehension ventured out by degrees: Maxl had planned this evening with precisely this result in view. He had gone himself to meet Jason and bring him back to Carnison.

Jason had willingly returned with him.

We danced again—three more times. No conversation took place in that crowded room. Too many people gathered round, for Maxl and I were not anonymous, though we left our masks in place, signaling that there would be no official unmasking. Some unmasked after midnight anyway, laughing and flirting as they willed. The teens were fast turning the masquerade into a romp.

I cannot name any of my subsequent partners, and though they must have spoken—and I am certain I responded—I cannot recall their words. I cannot recall if Gilian got Maxl to dance with her, or Jewel's partners—Corlis—Jantian—I forgot them all.

Our last dance occurred when the ballroom was almost empty. Once more I felt his arms around me, my body alive with joy, though my mind was too tired to think.

My brother appeared at my shoulder.

"Bring him up to the lair, if you like. I've ordered something to drink." He vanished into the crowd again.

"This way," I said to Jason when the dance was over, feeling intensely self-conscious. And when we reached the quiet hall above, I pulled off my mask, though as yet I couldn't even look up at him to see if he'd removed his. The moment—the symbolism—overwhelmed me.

By the time we had reached the back way upstairs, my senses were sharp and distinct: the pools of yellow light, the scent of burning candles; the sounds of our breathing, the hush of my gown over the floor, his almost silent step on the woven carpets. His proximity.

We had reached our hall when I heard a quick step and a familiar rustle, and we were face to face with Jewel.

"Flian? I hoped we could—" Her eyes rounded in horror. *"Jason?"* She gasped, and then she began to scream, "How *dare*—"

Jason moved quickly. One hand clapped over her mouth and the other held her. She struggled violently for a moment or two, as Jason looked over her head at me. "Flian. Do you want me here?"

"Yes," I whispered.

Abruptly he let Jewel go. She yanked violently at her gown, which had twisted out of line through her efforts.

"I'm sorry, Jewel." Jason reached to disentangle her fan from a lace flounce, but she slapped his hand away and gave us an angry, confused glare. "But it won't help Maxl if you start screeching and bring half that court pounding up here."

"Flian, you must be *sick*," she stated with fierce loathing and marched down the hall.

When the last of her train had twitched out of sight, I sighed. "Maxl's lair is this way."

Soon we were inside, to find that Maxl had already arrived.

"Coffee?" he asked, as if this were a normal day—and a normal time, instead of right before dawn. "Few but Flian and I like hot cocoa." I sat on the couch, and Jason seated himself at the other end.

"Coffee. Black," Jason said.

"Thought so." Maxl flashed a quick grin.

Their calm familiarity, the homeliness of the task, intensified my sense of unreality.

Maxl poured out hot coffee first, then chocolate into porcelain cups for us. Still with that weird sense of detachment, I watched his slender hands. Jason's were longer and stronger as he took the coffee cup; firelight glowed along his fingers, outlining tendons, knuckles, and highlighting the whorls on each fingertip. At the thought of those hands clasping round me again I shivered inside and closed my eyes.

"Is Jewel a problem here?" Jason asked.

"No." Maxl shook his head, his eyes turning to the fire.

I opened my eyes. The time had come to think—to risk words instead of leaving the risk to others. "Gilian wants her gone. I believe her request, uttered today at Jewel's skating party, was more in the nature of a threat when she said Jewel would 'do better' in Dantherei."

Maxl lifted his head, scowling.

Jason leaned back, the cup in both hands. "That'll be the Zarda heir, yes?"

"Not the heir."

Both turned to me. "Zarda has refused to declare an heir. As far as I knew," Maxl said.

"Then I am gossiping. I—overheard someone close to her remarking on it." I thought of Corlis, who had happened to let the fact drop during a conversation about music the week before.

"The heir has to be Gilian," Maxl said, looking skeptical. "Zarda despises his son Vadral as a dullard, too much like his mother."

"It's the opposite, actually. What we didn't know was that her father apparently told her after Papa died that she will never be heir to Zarda, that she's smart enough to find her own fortune, and double the family's power. Vadral is good enough to stay home and act as steward to the family holdings. Leaving Papa Zarda free to spend."

Maxl lifted his hands. "Explains a lot."

"But doesn't amend your problems." Jason gave Maxl one of those ironic smiles. "I take it you don't favor the easy solution."

"What, assassination?" Maxl's tone matched Jason's irony. "If anyone is to have the pleasure of strangling her, it would be myself. No, let's say I suffer from moral constraint."

"Then you use her weaknesses against her. Exactly as she does you."

"Weaknesses," Maxl repeated. "Yes, the Zardas would see me as weak." He stared down into the fire again. That was the first time Maxl had been so forthcoming about Gilian.

Jason said, "So shall I remove my sister? If she contributes to your difficulties, I can bring her visit to a close."

Jason did not know about their attraction, then. To spare my brother having to answer, I said, "Please don't. Jason, what you saw in the hallway was only her temper—I'll wager anything she thought you were here to take her away. She loves it here so much, and she does not make problems. Quite the opposite—she's been wonderful. Maxl, Jewel saw Jason and me coming upstairs—and misunderstood. There was no time to explain."

Maxl finished his cocoa in a gulp then rose. "I'll go make things right. If you'll pardon me?"

He was gone a moment later.

I was alone with Jason Szinzar, right there in Maxl's lair. We sat at opposite ends of the couch, the fire crackling merrily two paces away.

I poured more chocolate just to keep my hands busy. "Who rules in your stead?"

"I straight-armed Jaim into taking on some tasks, and Markham rides rein on the army," Jason replied, the fire reflecting in his dark pupils.

He set aside his coffee and rose, his back to the fire, his attention wholly on me. I sat silent as a stone, staring up at him.

"I don't express myself well," Jason said. "I suspect that you don't either. Not unless it's self-defense." He gave me one of those Szinzar smiles.

"You mean not unless I'm angry," I said, trying to find my way to the truth. Once pride had kept me silent, and he had turned away from me. "When you were angry with me, you were direct enough as well."

"I've never been angry with you."

I shook my head. "Perhaps you don't remember. But I do—in fact I have never stopped thinking about it. It's why I—"

"Why?" he prompted.

My face heated up to the tips of my ears. *The truth,* I thought. *Silence left you sitting alone in your room.* "After Garian's ambush. And that fire. You told me I'd regret it if you lived."

"Oh. I'd hoped you wouldn't remember that," he said with a wry smile, his hand making an apologetic gesture. "The idea seemed right at the time. Either you killed me or I would come courting you. Even though you'd just stated how much you loathed and despised me."

I gasped. I had expected—braced myself for—anything but that.

"It's true I was angry," Jason admitted. "But though I directed it at you, I was really angry with myself. I was experiencing, not for the first time, remorse. I think—" He frowned down at his hands. "I said it to drive you into petty action, so that you would conveniently fit my previous judgment. It would have made my life so much easier." He grinned. "That is, assuming I survived any attempt by you to actually stab me."

"Because?" I already knew the answer, but I desired—oh, so intensely—to hear it. As intensely as I remembered all his words to me.

"Because every moment I spent in your company I wanted to prolong, yet I knew you did not, could not, possibly reciprocate. It's the real reason I took you over the border myself, instead of sending Markham and a few trusted men."

Jason smiled a little, clearly thinking back. "Those two days you slept so peacefully in the summer carriage, Markham kept asking me my real reason for such an act of madness. And when he finally guessed, he didn't stint in outlining, with a wealth of detail, just how much I was going to regret what I'd done. That was before the ambush."

Ambush. He meant what I'd said to him just after. I'd discovered early on that he did indeed have emotions like anyone else. Now I had to face the fact that I'd hurt him. "I apologize for those hateful words. Even then I knew they were not true, though it took me a while to see it. Yes, now I see why you thought your courtship would be about as welcome to me as Garian's knife-waving."

He opened his hands. "It had seemed such a good plan at first. Get you away from everyone else. Trim Garian's claws and those of his kinsman as well. Then it would just be you and me, only where would I begin? I haven't any skills at courtship. And so, once we got home, I left you up in that room while I tried to figure out what to say. Days slipped by as I wondered if I was less loathsome than Garian—or more. And all the while I was aware of that accursed entanglement with Eleandra to resolve."

I couldn't help a laugh. "Was it easier courting Eleandra nine years ago?"

A brief grin. "She did the talking for us both."

I laughed again, thinking of what she'd said about him.

"At first you talked. Once about trust, and again about music. Every foolish subject, no matter how irrelevant, came alive when you talked to me. Then you stopped," Jason went on. "You talked to me when we were in the mountains, but in my home, you didn't. I had come back to the conviction that I was indeed more loathsome than Garian."

He hadn't moved. The width of a woven rug separated us, he standing by the fire, me sitting on the couch with my wine-colored gown billowing all around me.

"I never thought you worse than Garian. Ever. But...well, it was more convenient, if unfair, to think you a villain."

"I have regretted my actions, and my words, ever since you left us, there in Drath. And I apologize for them all."

"I said far more hateful things to you. Let's say we're quits with the insults."

He flashed up a hand, palm out, in the old gesture of truce. Then he gave me a considering look. "The worst one for me was when you maintained I could never understand your perspective, just when I was coming to realize that your perspective was so close to my own, or close to the perspective I was trying to achieve. You were already there, looking back at me from unassailable moral and ethical high ground, and it was so clear that I was, to you, on the lower side of a gulf impossible to bridge."

"I tried to think it, though I don't think I really believed it." My throat had gone dry. "That wasn't clear vision, it was only pride."

Jason shook his head. "No, it was true enough, for there remains the matter of my actions, which had seemed so reasonable and rational, previous to my meeting you. But became less so the more I began to see them through your eyes."

"I never understood my own actions." I tried to laugh.

He smiled, and went on. "I thought I'd graveled it forever, but Markham was convinced otherwise. He said we are too alike, you and I. Not in upbringing, but here." He touched his heart. "But he said that after I had promised never again to interfere with your life."

I began to see then how farsighted not just my brother had been, but Markham—and how much I owed them both.

"The ride up the mountain to Garian's." He made a gesture. "I don't even have the words, the idea was so new. Not just passion, which I had learned to distrust. But the meeting of minds."

"Of friendship," I whispered. "It was like I'd known you and Markham my entire life. I think that's why I almost fell off the horse, because I wanted that talk never to end."

"And so did I."

I drew in a long, unsteady breath, wondering why Jason stood there unmoving, his face so blank. But tired as I was, amazed as I was to hear what I had never permitted myself to hope, I began to think past myself, for I was learning that to make a relationship work one *must* think past the self.

Jason's regrets held him back. He would stand there and explain himself as long as I wished to listen, but he would make no move toward me at all.

So the move must be mine.

I set aside my cup. My heart was now beating fast, so fast I heard it in my ears, but it was only anticipation, for I knew that there would be no turning away, no cold looks of indifference or rejection.

Jason had made all the verbal efforts to bridge that gulf between us. It was time for me to complete the bridge, and close the gulf that had left me so desolate.

Two steps took me across that rug, and I held up my hands. He stepped into them, and then moved swiftly, pulling me against him. I turned my face up, and ah, how can one adequately describe the sweet and consuming fire of a first kiss?

Chapter Thirty-Four

The day after the ball, Jason and Maxl went riding together on a tour of the city. As if they splashed across a river, the widening ripples of Jason's presence in Carnison spread outward and outward, until, by evening, everyone at court knew, for they all showed up for an otherwise undistinguished play that Maxl had said he would attend. Not only were the audience seats crowded, others gathered along the back walls. Jason sat on the other side of Maxl from me, impassive, dressed plainly as always. He was probably the only one who watched the stage, for Maxl and I were covertly enjoying Lygiera's courtiers staring at Ralanor Veleth's infamous wicked king.

It had been Maxl's idea, as a protection for me. A foreign ruler who arrived in great state had to have a state reason. Maxl had felt that if his surprise was to be a mistake and Jason rode right back home again, the inevitable gossip swirling behind him could be twisted to intimate a secret conference between kings, and not touch me at all.

So directly after the play Jason moved into the royal guest suite upstairs, next to his sister—who had vanished earlier on a sudden visit to friends.

The second night after the ball, Jason walked into the concert hall with Maxl. I was already there, so I saw all the faces following them, like so many flowers marking the course of the sun. I wondered if anyone listened to the music the children had practiced for so many weeks.

I left first, as was customary. Whispers about Jason were inevitable, but as yet it had occurred to no one to include me with the speculation. I was far too unexciting.

At the gathering in the grand parlor after the concert, when Jason left Maxl's side and crossed the room to sit near me, they all watched as well.

"Music," he said, dropping down beside me on the windowsill. "Once you said it functioned as a symbol for the heart of a people, or something very like it."

"What did you hear in that concert?" I asked, smiling.

"Court mask." He smiled back. "Children well trained, and performed well. Afterward, all that flourishing with the strings, the five melodies tangled, that was flattery aimed at your company, unless I miss my guess." He pointed with his chin over his shoulder.

I tried to subdue a laugh. "You're right."

"On the ride west. Before I met your brother. One of the old posting houses. I'd stopped early because of snowfall, and mindful of what you once said about music, I listened to the singing in the common room. Old ballads, mostly. Past glories of war, that's what my people seem to hold in their hearts—" He stopped, making a slight grimace.

He was too well trained to ever turn his back completely on a room, so it was I, and not he, who was taken by surprise when Gilian's familiar voice gushed next to me, "*Dear* Flian! How *very* fine was the concert this evening, did you not think? Of course you have *ever* been a leader in *that* regard. Some even say that you play *yourself*. Why, you could start a new fashion! Except for us poor females who are cursed with hands too small to compass an entire chord." She sent a fond smile down at her fingers at this mendacious self-criticism, and as Elta and two or three others crowded around, making noises of protest, Gilian looked expectantly through her lashes at Jason.

"That's a curse?" he asked, rising politely, because she was waiting for an answer. "You don't consider it a blessing?"

I winced, feeling the doubled edge of that thrust, but her flush was entirely triumph, judging from the way she preened. She sent a covert glance at me, her expression so easy to read: did I see how easily she'd won his attention? How much he admired her delicacy?

She chattered on, keeping the conversation strictly on her hands—and how simply awful it was to be too dainty for so many robust activities—until she seemed to realize that though her faithful followers were responding to her hints for compliments, Jason hadn't said anything more. He just stood there politely, hemmed in by Elta and two or three others.

Maxl came to the rescue. "We've spiced punch over here, but it has to be drunk hot. Any takers?"

Gilian's eyes flickered between the two kings, her mouth a moue of triumph. Which would she pick? In her view of the world, she had only to choose.

The familiar won over the exotic. She slid her hand possessively round Maxl's arm, but cast a coyly apologetic look up at Jason, as if to console him for his loss.

They moved away to the refreshments, which broke up the circle. Jason and I followed last; several people vied for Jason's attention, asking questions about music, and Ralanor Veleth.

I drank a glass of punch and excused myself. My early departure would go entirely unnoticed, so used everyone was to it. If any of the more astute courtiers marked the private signal between Jason and Maxl and myself for our subsequent meeting in the lair, they gave no sign.

Gilian certainly did not see. The last thing I heard as the footman opened the door for me was her complacent voice, in a loud whisper to Elta and Harlis. "Did you hear his compliment about my hands? A blessing! How charming! Why is it that the men all notice them first thing? He's no different from all the rest, despite that awful reputation..."

Maxl and I strolled along his own balcony a few days later. The sun was warm as long as we stayed out of the shadows; new snowfall lay over the garden, a soft white blanket with blue shadows here and there indicating where summer's favorite pathways lay.

It was the first time we had been alone together since the masquerade ball.

"You are, at last, happy," he observed. "I have only to look at you, and see that it is so. Yet I want the pleasure of hearing you say it."

"I am happy." Once again joy suffused me. "Though I have difficulty believing it is real, or understanding how it could come to pass. Our backgrounds being so vastly different, and our first meetings disastrous."

Maxl smiled.

I said, "But you did not invite me to walk with you to hear

me extol at length about my bliss."

Maxl glanced back along the great balcony. "I had an idea Jason's presence might strike through court like a thunderbolt. What I did not expect was for each faction to attribute his presence to its own reasons."

"Ah." Here at last, and it was inevitable, the personal crossed into the political. "His unusual appearance?"

"His sudden appearance," Maxl corrected. "I did not foresee that the Zarda faction would see his presence as an oblique threat."

"A threat to equal theirs to you?"

"Greater. Zarda has been most assiduous during the past few days—even when it became apparent to him, if not to her, that his daughter was not going to net Ralanor Veleth's crown."

"Interesting," I said. "And, I hope, prospective good news."

"As good as I've had since I took the throne." Maxl closed his eyes for a moment, face up, as if tasting a rare and exquisite wine. "Whatever transpires, I shall always cherish the memory of Gilian's attempts to glamour Jason. His rocklike blindness has been...masterly."

I grinned. "Oh, but she will never see her efforts as a failed attempt. She sees what she wants to see. I will wager anything you wish that she believes he's secretly attracted to her. And will continue to believe it, and talk about it, long after we've gone."

Maxl opened his eyes. "Only Gilian could think herself the superior choice to Eleandra of Dantherei. I don't know how that gossip got started—that Jason had turned Eleandra down—but even that has redounded to our benefit."

I strongly suspect that Jewel had been behind that particular rumor, from her distant vantage, but I said nothing. Some sort of rumor had been inevitable. Eleandra was too famous for it not to have been noted, even if the motives behind her journey to Ralanor Veleth were completely misconstrued.

Here was another discovery. I was used to going about unnoticed, protected by my reputation for being boring. But the safety of being unnoticed and uninteresting was lost as soon as someone interesting paid attention.

Jason was interesting. Ralanor Veleth's history of violence added to the reputation he'd made early in his rule. Most of the rumors about those early years were true, I discovered over our nights of private talk, though his motivations were completely misunderstood.

"When you come from violent people," Jason said to me one night, "you have to strike fast, and hard. Be relentless. Afterward compromise is perceived as mercy, and not as weakness. To begin with attempts to compromise is to be perceived as weak, and an open invitation to a lifetime of trouble." He added somewhat wryly, "I told your brother this insight. Though I expect he's already learned it."

Maxl brought my focus back to the present. "I really believe Zarda thinks that I can whistle up Jason's army if I want to. He can't see an alliance based on economic need. He sees everything in terms of power, or force."

"I hope you won't disabuse him of it," I said.

"I've learned my lesson. I used to believe that if I tried to explain my own motives—proving that they were to everyone's best interest—others would in turn give of their best. Not true. They translate it into their own terms and act accordingly." Maxl grinned at me, a hard grin. "A sizable detachment of Jason's most restless hotheads coming over here to participate in some sort of spring training exercise will underscore that impression. As well as be good for our militia in the long run, though I foresee some bruised pride as the immediate consequence."

"Jason's people are good at all that." I swung my arm in a block and riposte. "Though he maintains they aren't the best, that their training is generations outmoded. He wants Jaim to go to some other country down south, where they have this war school, and bring back new ideas."

Maxl's brows drew together. "Marloven Hess?"

"That's the one." I added, seeing Maxl's concern, "I know that place has a terrible reputation, but Jason says their present king is trying to make that country over into something that doesn't need to look to war to exist. Readiness, defense, patrolling against pirates and the like, is how Jason explained it to me. He's been writing letters for the past five or six years to other monarchs with problems like Ralanor Veleth's."

Maxl thumped a fist on the rail. "I knew about the letters, from a brief reference."

"You have to ask. He doesn't mind answering," I said. "I have learned that it isn't in his nature to offer information. He's so used to action, and survival made him good at hiding reaction."

"Ah." Maxl gave a nod. "In that sense all three of us are alike, are we not?"

I smiled and shook my head. "I didn't talk because I couldn't trust words."

"You spoke in music. But only I listened. I guessed at the cause. And I must say I come quite well out of a gesture I had meant only for your good."

I said, greatly daring, "I know you did, and I can only wish you the equivalent of my own happiness."

Maxl's smile disappeared. "I do not know if that's possible. The two of you are much alike, and I can see that it's a real match, not merely the heat of attraction. For me—" He shrugged.

"For you what? Please don't tell me you are going to have to marry Gilian."

Maxl grimaced in distaste. "No. Not that. I have come to see that this sacrifice, made for the best of motives, would have been the worst of mistakes, for she would never be my ally. A crown would mean she would exert herself to the utmost to rule through me. Every day a battle. What a life! And I came so close."

The coldness of fear trickled through my veins.

"Why did you not speak?" I asked.

Head bent, Maxl spoke to the snow. "Because I knew what you'd say, and I also knew you would not understand my reasons. But since that time I have come to see that my own reasoning was at fault."

Maxl sighed, and his breath froze and fell.

"No. Gilian will never rule, and I might see a way to curtail her attempts to ruin Lygiera. Assuming that I am stuck with her presence at court for the rest of my life, as Papa was stuck with her father. How did she get that much influence over me, despite my straining against it?"

I said, "Fear. And her conviction she's the center of the world. People went along because it was easier, but I don't think anyone believes her. I don't think even Elta believes her, but Elta is desperate to marry, and she's courting Gilian's brother through sister and father."

"Zarda will never let his son marry Elta. I realized when I was about twenty that he can't stand the sight of her, but he tolerates her because she pays for Gilian's good will."

It was the first time he had talked so straightly to me.

So I said, "What about Jewel?"

Maxl turned away, but not in anger. He kicked at snow piled between the carved supports of the stone rail, and shook his head. "She's good-hearted, but as volatile as fire. She never bores me, ever. And every time I look at her I want to lock us up together for a week." He grinned, and I was grinning as well. "Yes, you know that spark. What is it between the Elandersi family and the Szinzars? But—well, try to imagine you had the spark for Jaim."

"But I could never—" I stopped as my perspective shifted. "Oh. I see what you mean."

"Good-hearted, volatile, and not the least given to a single love for a lifetime, that sums up them both, does it not? Yet I— like you, and Jason, apparently—we seem to be impervious to everyone but one."

"But Jaim is loyal in his own way to Vrozta. I think, as much as one can predict, that he will always come back to her. She's first in his heart."

Maxl nodded. "I could live with that if I was first to Jewel, and not my crown, because then she might take on the occasional flirt, but they would not be forced on me as favorites, which would create endless political strife. But I am not sure. And I don't think she's sure."

Suddenly Jewel's own comments came into perspective.

"No," I said. "She's not, and she hates herself for it."

Maxl looked pained. "You see my dilemma. It's too much akin to what Papa went through with Mama, and I won't deliberately put myself into that kind of nightmare."

"But unlike Mama seems to have been, Jewel is honest. And you yourself said it has been a mistake not to talk. Jewel likes to talk things out. Her silence of late, I suspect, is not just because she's waiting—hoping—that I send Jason back home, but because she's trying to very hard to live by what she thinks are your own rules. And mine."

Maxl pursed his lips. "You think so?"

"I'm sure of it. She does have a very strong sense of honor. And she understands the workings of a court."

"Understands?" Maxl laughed softly, making a cloud of white crystals. "More than I can say for myself at times. I comprehend the blend of tradition and habit that makes kingship work. How court serves the double purpose of keeping those who serve as my eyes and ears bound here so that I can watch them—and they can watch me—and also serves to transform ordinary humans into mythic figures. A yellow-haired fellow of medium height and no particular brains or ability could come to a conflict and hand out orders, and both sides would turn on him. But I come—not Maxl, but King Maxl Elandersi—and I hand out orders, and everyone scrambles to obey. It is the gilded custom of court that imbues me with that power. Me, a mythic figure."

His brown eyes were quirked in irony.

"You're a good ruler," I said.

"No. I am trying to be a good ruler. Maybe I will become one—if I survive the learning process. The first lesson has been the hardest, to compromise my own standards. I had believed until very recently that if I had to be first in the kingdom, then I must be first in virtue, in wisdom and in brains. The first I can manage, but the rest?" He shrugged.

"But you've picked good help."

"Yes. And I have to learn how to deal with the ones who aren't good, the ones I have inherited. Because maybe they are good from someone else's perspective. That at best is the balance of power, when you strip out personality. But we can't strip out personality, can we?"

"No," I said. "So you talk to your allies."

"And know how far you can trust them, Jason told me." Maxl flicked out a hand and dashed more snow from the railing. "His advice has been an enormous help."

We watched it fall into the garden below. I thought about this conversation with my brother, the first time he had been so straightforward. It couldn't be because I would be leaving soon.

No, it was because I would soon be a queen. A king talking to a queen, brother and sister; once again we were completely equals, and could share one another's burdens. When I had come home so unhappy after Papa's death, he had done his best to hide his burdens from me, and to resolve mine. The actions of a king.

"I wish I could find out how Jason managed to make

Markham Glenereth into a liegeman," Maxl mused after a short pause. "I expect it might shed some insight. But he doesn't talk about it."

"I asked him last night what is Markham's story, and he told me that that rightly belongs to Markham. All I know is that he has a young child, a son, stashed somewhere. He's polite and loyal, but so very intimidating!"

Maxl grinned. "He is, isn't he? Jason said he'd send him as his commander this spring, and I very much look forward to watching Zarda attempt to intimidate Markham." He whistled softly, his breath clouding. "The little I know is that Glenereth was the biggest holding on their eastern border, and I only know that from old records. Same as I found out from reading some of Father's early dispatches that Glenereth was the leader of the faction out to destroy the Szinzars—but this was some years ago, and the mention was of a female. Nothing since. Whatever Jason did when he took over isn't in any records that I've seen."

A distant bell chimed. Maxl smacked more snow off the railing. "Curse it! Already our time is lost."

Jason came through the parlor door just then. He sent an inquiring look from Maxl to me, and my brother said, "It's time to plan the engagement." He whirled a forefinger in imitation of dueling, making of the word *engagement* a pun.

Jason smiled. "Gesture of solidarity?"

"Precisely." Maxl rubbed his hands. "We can make the official announcement at Interview tomorrow. Be prepared for the resultant storm. And related to that, which do you prefer, a big, elaborate betrothal, or a big, elaborate wedding?"

Jason looked to me, and I spread my hands. Jason said, "My preference would be to marry at home."

"I like that idea," I said.

Jason's eyes showed his reaction, not that there was much of one, but I was beginning to be able to read him. His pleasure suffused me in turn with my own pleasure—much more than the prospect of Maxl's big, elaborate affair.

"Betrothal it is." Maxl pointed the Royal Finger.

"I have only one request," Jason murmured.

"Which is?" I asked.

"That you invite Garian Herlester."

Maxl grinned. The two exchanged a look I could not interpret, unless it was to define it as anticipation and comprehension, but even that doesn't quite encompass it. Something male? Probably.

"Wouldn't think of leaving him out." Maxl smacked his hands together again and rubbed them even more vigorously. "Leave it all to me."

Chapter Thirty-Five

Meanwhile, Jewel was still gone.

She had been, it seemed, invited to visit the ancestral home of Riana Dascalon.

I found it interesting that Jewel had formed friendships with Lygierans who had no connection with me. I wanted it to mean that she was going to become Maxl's queen, but I knew—even in the midst of my own happiness—that real life seldom works out so neatly.

It troubled me most that she had gone with no word to me.

But the word did get to her, as was inevitable, after the shock of the announcement of Jason's and my betrothal.

What's to say about the announcement? Courtiers are courtiers. Maxl made the announcement at morning court. The congratulations were all fulsome, some heartfelt and others false; quite suddenly I stepped from the background into the foreground, and many did not know what to make of it. By this prospective alliance, Jason's interesting aura now extended outside me. I found myself the recipient of more speculative glances than I'd had in all my life, for Jason had made it plain to the more discerning that it was no mere match of political expedience. Not that he said anything, or behaved with courtly effusion, for that was not his way, and he seemed to be incapable of false fronts. From that day on, whenever there was dancing he simply refused to dance with anyone but me.

The days passed quickly. My time was divided between the courtly rounds and with choosing or discarding the accumulations of my life so far, and packing for the move east, a task that gave me pleasure. I offered Debrec the choice of going to Ralanor Veleth or a pension, and I was not surprised when she accepted the second choice. Having overseen the last of my things on their journey east, she bade me fare well, and we parted.

Bringing me to the day of the betrothal celebration. With it arrived Jewel. Though the winter weather was grim, freezing and gray, the aristocratic houses all down the royal way shone lights, and so too did the guest wings of the palace.

I was thinking about Jewel and her long absence as the last touches were put to my gown and hair, when I heard her familiar tap at the door.

"Come in!" I cried, rising.

It was indeed Jewel. She sailed in, resplendent in blue and white and silver. She paused and looked around, her expression perplexed. The oldest pieces of furniture would stay, but the last of my things had been packed up and sent, for we would depart in the morning.

"It is so empty here." She rubbed her hands up her arms. "I-I know this will seem very odd, but this is the most convincing evidence that you truly mean to leave Lygiera. By your own choice."

"An act of madness?" I laughed and embraced her.

She flung her arms round me and hugged me, hard, then she stepped back. "Oh, Flian. I have felt so terrible."

"Not on my account, I hope."

"Yours and Maxl's, but mostly my own." She grinned wryly, then looked around again, as though seeking someone.

"We are alone. You may speak freely."

Tears gleamed in her eyes. "I had to go away. You see that, don't you? Maxl came to me that morning after the ball when Jason first arrived, and said that I was to make a pretense of welcome, or withdraw."

"Ah." I gave her a hug of sympathy.

She nodded, one side of her mouth lilting up in a very lopsided smile. "Oh, did we quarrel. It was a merry brangle, quite long and loud and awful, but he wouldn't budge."

"It had become a state question. That's the way our lives are defined."

"I know that." She shrugged sharply. "He told me that he had the good of the kingdom, and your happiness, as his priorities, and he stuck steadily to that position while I raged and stormed and stamped and declared that no one could possibly love Jason—that it was only a momentary madness on your part, and your inexperience had dazzled you but it wouldn't last out a week, that Jason only courted you—if he did—to make inroads into Lygiera, that—oh, who cares?" She gulped and drew a shaky breath.

"You don't have to tell me."

"But I do, because you'll soon be gone." Her face contracted, and tears spilled over. "Gone! And I wasted what could have been our last weeks together in brooding far away."

"Because you wish to stay here, do you not?"

Again a gulp. "Yes."

"And so you should," I stated.

She sighed. "I will, but first I had to think. I see now that my position was really this. I wanted Maxl to make me, and my feelings, his first priority. And he can't. He never can. Ever."

Again I embraced her.

She trembled in my arms, and then whirled free of my grip, and dashed her fingers across her eyes. "That's the true meaning of monarchy, isn't it? The kingdom must come first. Why didn't I see it in Tamara, who is supposedly so powerful?"

"And so?"

"And so, if I want to win him, then I must make Lygiera my first priority, instead of merely loving it because it is not boring, gloomy, dreadful Lathandra!" She smiled, and straightened up. "So I will smile, including at Jason—though I shall wish forever that you had fallen in love with Jaim. But." Her brows drew down. "If I ever find out that Jason has been cruel to you, I will come and kill him. I swear it."

I said, trying not to laugh, "If I thought such a vow needed, I would not be going away, Jewel."

She shook her head. "I don't believe it. But no matter." She smiled through the last of her tears. "I want you to prove me wrong."

And so she joined the three of us in the throne room for the troth ritual, which defined the treaty that our marriage would sanction. I scarcely remember what words I said or heard. That part of my mind stays numb. What I do remember is the expressions on their faces: Maxl's pride, the light reflecting steadily in his eyes; Jewel's passion, making her more beautiful than ever, and Maxl's gaze straying her way; Jason's steady regard, and the warmth of his hand clasping mine.

Then my mind is a blur of candlelight, of brilliant reflections off crystal and silver, of the smells of hothouse blossoms and the fresh sprays of greenery. We were dancing alone, watched by uncountable eyes. I could not imagine what went on behind those courtier gazes. Even Gilian Zarda was coy but cooperative, her false joy expressed in dimpled smiles divided equally between Jason and me. An effort in friendliness due to the reputation of Ralanor Veleth, to the fact that I was going to be a queen, and to her hopes, not the least relinquished, of Maxl.

But I did not speak to her, for I no longer had to pretend even a social regard. By the end of another day I would be gone, and we would dwindle to unloved memory in each other's mind.

What I do remember, with the distinct recall impelled by intense emotional response, was my first glimpse of Garian Herlester. For he was there, having arrived that day. Dressed splendidly in his house colors of violet and gold, he looked exactly as he always had: sardonic, laughing, and a little angry.

The second dance was the signal for everyone to join, Maxl leading it with me.

When it ended, and Maxl led me back to the thrones, Garian appeared at my side. He held out his arm, a gesture of grace and imperiousness that made me take a step back.

But Maxl bowed and relinquished my hand. Jason's smile was amused, betraying no alarm whatsoever. It was my choice, but I suspected that he wanted me to dance with Garian, and to listen to whatever he might inadvertently reveal.

"Come, Cousin." Garian slid his arm around me. The dance—I realized too late—was a waltz. Garian's hazel eyes glittered in the blazing candlelight. He had been drinking. I could smell it.

My heart slammed, and I felt sick. Maxl had vanished among the swirling, flashing velvets and gems. He danced with a foreign diplomat and did not glance once our way—but he was near, as was Jason.

Three steps, four. I felt Garian's breath stir the top of my hair, and dropped my chin down to diminish the sense of proximity.

He said, "Tonight you are as beautiful as Eleandra, and you always were more interesting. I wish I'd realized that sooner."

"What?"

Of course he'd intended to take me by surprise. I looked up into that mocking, passionate jade-colored gaze, the edgy smile that presaged cruelty as easily as it did humor.

He steered us expertly between two couples. "Meaning I would be marrying you instead."

"Never," I said. "Never."

He laughed, a soft laugh, and tightened his grip.

I stiffened, seized with the longing to rip free of his grasp, but I knew that it would cause untold political consequences—even if I could actually get free.

"On the other hand, since I intend to destroy Jason Szinzar, doing it through you has a certain appeal of completeness. But you might not survive it. We shall see."

I took a deep breath. "If," I stated, "you are going to spend the entire dance gabbling threats like a fool, I'll thank you to let me free, because I don't want to hear it."

"You will stay with me until the music ends," he retorted. "But pull your jaw in. I have spoken my warning."

Another glance. He smiled down at me, a strange smile that went beyond anger or revenge or pettiness or cruelty.

He said more softly, "You do not feel it, do you?"

"Feel what?" Though I knew, because his grip, his breathing, the rapid beating of his heart through his velvet and linen and my pearl-encrusted satin bodice all buffeted me with his desire.

"Amazing." He frowned, for a moment more puzzled than angry. "I can have any woman I want—half of them will be chasing me before evening's end—except you. Is that, and that only, the lure? Or is it that innate sense of honor, even in the face of the worst intimidation, that doesn't exist for the rest of us? The attraction of opposites?"

I almost said, *Except Jason has the same sense of honor,* but I knew better than to say anything about Jason at all that could be used against him.

So I returned a blank face.

"So why Jason?"

Possible answers whirled through my mind as we whirled

across the ballroom floor, ending with the conviction that I did not owe him the truth, for it would be twisted to his own ends, and that, joined with his careless cruelty, was why I could never have loved him.

"I am marrying Jason for his taste in clothes," I said loftily.

Garian laughed, sparking speculative glances from the couples near us. And as the music was ending, he brought us in a series of tight whirls to the edge of the ballroom, where I discovered with profound relief Jason stood.

With a gesture of deliberate grace Garian placed my hand on Jason's, bowed to me and vanished in the crowd.

Jason led me out onto the floor. "He threatened me," I began.

"Too many ears now." Once again we danced.

Later, when we were alone at last in my nearly empty room, I told him what had happened.

He listened closely, his face unreadable, and at the end he nodded. "I know how to deal with Garian," was all he said, but it was enough.

Chapter Thirty-Six

We arrived in Lathandra at night, riding side by side at the head of a spectacular honor guard—most of whom had chosen to ride to the border and meet us. Had Garian wished to cause mischief, he would have found a war on his hands. I expect his own guard—and his hired swords—watched in silence from the heights, no doubt in relief that there had been no orders to waylay us along Treaty Road, for a good portion of Ralanor Veleth's high-ranking regional commanders and their own guard had joined our party.

Everyone was on horseback. The roads were still bad except along certain well-guarded military routes. I had left Carnison's exquisite, perfumed palace and found myself surrounded by people in military dress, weapons polished, helms gleaming, chain mail jingling. But this was where I had chosen to be, and so I looked past the warlike image and contemplated the faces of the men and women who looked back at me.

And what I saw was not the trained mask of empty politesse of home. I saw speculation, curiosity, cautious approval, sometimes wariness. The approval, I was glad to note, appeared most often.

The night we arrived in Lathandra, we discovered the entire city turned out to stand in the snow, holding torches. Two thin rivers of fire led up the road to the castle, which was ablaze with light and streaming banners.

"This is all for you." Jason's breath clouded in the frozen air.

How long had those people stood in the snow? I met their gazes as we rode past, and I smiled and waved until my fingers were numb and my face ached. But I didn't want to pass one of them without some kind of acknowledgement.

Markham met us in the great courtyard. His face, in the torchlight, was as expressive as I had ever seen it. He bowed to me, actually smiling, and held out his hand as a gesture of welcome.

Jason said, "Markham will take you inside. I'll finish up here and be along."

I took Markham's arm and we walked into the corridor so familiar from summer. How different were my emotions now! The residence wing was all lit and warm, with scented boughs put over doors.

We walked in silence, but it was a companionable silence. I can't say how or why I knew, for Markham was even less expressive than Jason, but I felt his approbation, and I wondered if he felt my trust.

Markham led me down the main hall, past the stairs that would have taken me up to my old rooms next to Jewel's. Instead, we walked to the end, and up a carved stairway that harked back hundreds of years. I had never known where Jason's rooms lay; as we trod up the stairs I contemplated Eleandra walking where I had walked. Where was she now? Either in the arms of her cold-eyed Lord Galaki, or else courting some prince I had never met, her sojourn in Ralanor Veleth rapidly fading to mere bad memory.

How strange life is, I thought as Markham opened two great carved doors onto a marble-floored vestibule. Two more grand doors awaited us. Markham opened one and bowed me inside.

I walked into a huge sitting room, where all my things had already been set amid old rosewood furnishings. I turned around. Markham stood there, watching my reaction.

"I take it this will be my room?" I gestured.

"Queen's private sitting room," he said. And, "Welcome."

It was his tone that made me blush, for it conveyed more real greeting than any prepared speech might have.

"I'm glad to be here." Because it was Markham, I added, "It feels strange. But right."

He bowed again, a smile narrowing his deep-set eyes.

I drew in a breath. "I have a question, but it does not concern the kingdom, or Jason, it concerns you. So if you don't want to answer it, I won't be insulted."

Markham gave me a thoughtful nod. "I believe I know your question. I also believe you would not want to hear the details," he said after a long pause, during which his eyes had gone diffuse, as if he looked into a very dark past. "Suffice it to say that once, at a time when all the evidence was most damning, Jason Szinzar trusted my word. I lost everything I had once possessed, for that was justice. Any alternative would have destroyed the kingdom, in time. But I was left with my life, and more important, my honor. They belong to him. And now to you."

My palms were damp, my mouth dry. The quiet voice was exactly as emotionless as always, but I'd learned something about masks, and the cost of maintaining them.

Do I thank him? No. "I understand."

"Yes. I thought you might," was the response. "Is there anything else I can do for you?"

"I thank you, but if you've other things to see to, don't think you need to stay with me. I'll be happy to explore around these rooms. Get used to things. Until Jason is finished with his own tasks."

He bowed again and in silence withdrew, closing the door behind him. His past was his own to keep. But there was one gift I could give him, if he chose to accept it, and I would speak to Jason about it once I had settled in: I would invite Markham to bring his little boy to Lathandra, and I made a mental vow that the child would be treated exactly as any children Jason and I might have.

That resolved, I looked about me once more, then walked the perimeter of the room, touching things. My porcelain statues of horses, inherited from my great-aunt. The portraits of Papa and Maxl and me as children, made once for my grandmother, and now mine. My crystal vases, which would be filled with flowers in spring. I came to the floor-to-ceiling window-doors, and opened one. Cold air blasted in, but I glanced out long enough to glimpse a terrace lined with pots awaiting plants once spring arrived. Beyond it was the garden, seen from a different perspective than the one from my old room.

I closed the door and moved on. The sitting room opened onto a smaller sitting room, this one with desk and shelves already set with my books. Someone had worked very hard.

Next over was a room with musical instruments. The harp I knew. Added to it was a fine lute that had to be recently made.

Through that into a dressing room, which connected to a room with a sunken bath.

One more door remained—but when I reached for it, the door opened and Berry stepped through. We both backed away in surprise. She pulled the door tight behind her and swept a deep curtsey.

When she came up, she was so close to laughter I felt the urge to laugh as well. "You cannot go in, Princess Flian. They would be so disappointed if you did."

"They?"

She waved a hand and then brushed it down her spotless apron. "The house. Jason's own people. And now yours." She did laugh then, that merry laugh that I had liked from the beginning. Unconsciously I had ceased to believe myself in danger when I heard that laugh, though it had taken a long time to acknowledge it.

A moment later I heard Jason's step behind me, coming in through the new music room. "Won't let me into my own bedroom." He gave me a humorous grimace.

"You too? I was trying to nose about."

Berry curtseyed again—snorting on another laugh—and left.

Jason said, "Markham, it seems, has taken everything in hand, leaving us little to do but wait for supper. They're all gathering down in the great hall. Want some wine beforehand?"

"Thank you."

He opened yet another door, this to his own private study, where he found the wine and glasses. We stood before the fire. Jason did not drink his, but held it in his hands as he looked at me.

"Last chance," he said, "to back out."

"I'll not back out." I set my glass down, took his and set it down. "Hold me. Better than wine."

His arms slid round me, and I nestled there, bathing my spirit in happiness, as my nerves sang with anticipation.

"Is everything all right with the kingdom?" I asked, my voice muffled in his arm.

"The kingdom is quiet." Jason's smile I couldn't see, but I

could hear it in his chest. "A certain amount of speculation about the alliance with your brother, an unexpected benefit. No one fears his little army, but they do his mighty wealth, and his diplomatic reach. This alliance—the prospective trade route through Three Kingdoms to Lygiera's northern harbor—might help revitalize the entire western region."

"And so the plan for the east is what?"

"Soon's spring thaw begins, I want everything and everyone in place to begin the diversion of the rivers. We'll make the eastern plains into farmland again, though it might not be a success until we are old."

"I'll wait."

"And you—you are to civilize us. They all look to you for that. I am very much afraid you have become a legend here."

"Impossible." I laughed.

He shook his head. "Truth. Honor and mercy—you saved my sister's life, you saved mine. Justice with the knife when it was just."

"But—if that refers to my clumsy attempt to rid the world of Garian Herlester—I failed!"

"You tried. The people are yours. I am yours."

He kissed me. And again.

What more is there to say? The great hall was then as it is now, hung with banners testifying to past glories. I think not of the anguish and bloodshed of those glories, for I'm happy enough that there is no war now.

Before all his regional commanders we spoke the marriage vows. There was no coronation, no layers of social artfulness, as my brother would say, to transform me into a queen. That was done by Jason himself, his words and his tone, as he performed his part of the ritual. I had first become his beloved. Now, before his people, he made me his partner.

In this kingdom one had to prove one had the strength to hold what one promised to keep. Now there were two of us, each with different strengths.

Afterward we retired, for it had been a very long day and the night was ours. I stopped in my new dressing room to divest myself of my traveling clothes and was in the midst of taking down my hair when I heard a laugh.

Jason very seldom laughed out loud, so I had to know what was the cause.

I flung on my wrapper, with my hair half-pinned up, and opened that last door, to see a large room with walnut furnishings. Jason sat on the edge of the bed, still in his riding clothes. He was laughing, though silently now, as he hooked his thumb over his shoulder at the bed.

I looked past him and discovered the sheets strewn with roses. Roses! In winter! All the thorns carefully removed, the flowers perfuming the air.

"Someone has been nursing these in some hothouse for months. Are we that predictable?" He held out his arms.

I walked into them.

ॐ

And so, time swiftly passed. Good days and difficult days.

Never between us. I have had no moment of regret for my choice. It was my sustained happiness that inspired me to write this record, my children, when you were born.

Liara Viana, our blue-eyed, black-haired sprite! And Jaimas Maxl, our blond-haired dreamer of a son! Some day one or both of you will wish to know the inner reasons for our being here as well as the outer, and so this record is for you.

There is so little to add! Markham did indeed bring his little son Lexan to live with us, and just as we promised, he has become a much-loved brother to my own children.

But before that—just before my first child's birth—Jewel returned, angry and passionate, storming tears and cursing Jason and even Jaim, who had returned from his sojourn abroad.

It seemed she had fought with Maxl again—and had run away.

A week of talking later, and she disappeared as suddenly as she had come.

My next communication was a long letter from my brother, ending with the announcement of their forthcoming wedding. It was a spectacular wedding, one that will probably be remembered for several generations. Even Tamara broke her rule of isolation and attended, along with royal representatives from all the surrounding kingdoms.

Jewel has been back twice since, both times angry and teary; we talk, and she calms down, and then returns to Carnison, and to Maxl's arms. It seems that Maxl's wish to never be bored has come true.

So how can I finish? I guess what I want to say is that there are many roads to happiness, and that happiness does not depend on power, but occurs in spite of it. And that we who are growing toward middle age were once young and passionate, and uncertain, and determined. One day you will be taking the reins of government, and you will at the same time probably be trying to fashion yourself a life with love, and though I hope I am there to see it, in case I am not—power also means great uncertainty—I share my heart with you here.

About the Author

To learn more about Sherwood Smith, please visit www.sherwoodsmith.net. Send an email to Sherwood at Sherwood@sff.net or join her LiveJournal Community Athanarel http://community.livejournal.com/athanarel/profile to join in the fun with other readers.

Swashbuckling in a magic world—L.A. style!

Once a Princess
© *2008 Sherwood Smith*
Sasharia en Garde! Book 1.

Sasha's mother, Sun, was once swept away from a Ren Faire to another world by a prince—literally—but there was no happy ending. Sun's prince disappeared, and a wicked king took the Khanerenth throne. In the years since, Sasha and Sun have been back on Earth and on the run. Mom and daughter don't quite see eye to eye on the situation—Sasha wants to stand and fight. Sun insists her prince will return for them one day; it's safer to stay hidden.

Then Sasha is tricked into crossing the portal to Khanerenth. She's more than ready to join the resistance, kick some bad-guy butt, and fix the broken kingdom. But...is the stylish pirate Zathdar the bad guy? Or artistic, dreamy Prince Jehan?

Back on Earth, Sun is furious Sasha has been kidnapped. Sun might once have been a rotten princess, but nobody messes with Mom!

Warning: This title contains a kick-butt mother-daughter team, a wicked king, a witty pirate with an unfortunate taste for neon colors, inept resistance fighters, a dreamy prince who gallops earnestly hither and yon, and a kick-butt princess in waiting.

Available now in ebook from Samhain Publishing.

GREAT
CHEAP
FUN

Discover eBooks!

THE FASTEST WAY TO GET THE HOTTEST NAMES

Get your favorite authors on your favorite reader, long before they're
out in print! Ebooks from Samhain go wherever you go, and work with
whatever you carry—Palm, PDF, Mobi, and more.

CPSIA information can be obtained at www.ICGtesting.com
Printed in the USA
BVOW031414300512

291400BV00001B/40/P